The Shadow of the Sun

SYLVIA PELL was born and brought up in the north of England. After working in libraries and several leading bookshops, she was for a time Information Officer for the Booksellers Association. *The Shadow of the Sun*, her first novel, was inspired by a childhood visit to Versailles, a place which has always fascinated her. Her second novel, *The Sun Princess*, will be published in 1979.

Sylvia Pell lives in London with her husband and three sons and her main interests are history, travel, and exploring old buildings.

SYLVIA PELL

The Shadow of
the Sun

Collins

FONTANA BOOKS

First published in 1978 by William Collins Sons & Co Ltd
First issued in Fontana Books 1979

© Sylvia Pell 1978

Made and printed in Great Britain by
William Collins Sons & Co Ltd, Glasgow

For my mother, who enjoys a good book,
and my father, who loved 'abroad'.

This is a true story.

Prologue

1660

At the top of the wide, curving staircase of the Hôtel d'Aumont, the dark-haired girl in grey whispered her name to the footman wearing the green and gold livery of the d'Aumont family who stood on duty at the entrance to the salon. Flinging open the heavy double doors, he stepped forward and his voice boomed out her name.

'Madame Scarron!'

Nicole d'Aumont came hurrying forward to greet her guest with outstretched arms and a welcoming smile. 'Françoise! My dear, I'm delighted you were able to come after all! How is Paul today?'

'None too well, I'm afraid, but he insisted that I shouldn't miss any of the festivities . . .'

'And quite right, too. You have little enough fun. Come, everyone's out on the terrace. Hurry, it's already begun.' Nicole, linking arms with her cousin's wife, led her through the elegantly furnished salon to the long low balcony at the front of the d'Aumont town house, where several other girls were clustered together in the brilliant sunshine, the bright colours of their holiday clothes in striking contrast to the severity of the dark grey dress and plain white collar worn by Françoise Scarron. A pretty fair-haired girl of about nineteen, dressed in pale blue with a delicate lace fichu, made room for Françoise to sit beside her.

'Madame Scarron?' she said shyly, with the bob of deference to a married woman. 'The procession's already started. But you may sit here if you wish . . .'

Françoise accepted with a smile of thanks and sat down next to Louise de la Vallière, looking about her in wonder. All the city of Paris lay stretched out before her, a breathtaking sight on this hot August day in the year 1660. Every street, every house, every rooftop as far as the eye could see was jam-packed with people, a swarming, turbulent mass of humanity. With characteristic gaiety, the people of Paris had completely abandoned work in joyous anticipation of a spectacle of colour and pageantry such as had not been seen in a lifetime. All shops and places of business were closed, and had been for three days now, as Parisians prepared to celebrate. Crammed in the streets and squares, at the windows, on roofs, balconies, anywhere that could command a view, the crowds waited patiently in the heat – already stifling though it was as yet early morning. This was the day when Louis XIV of France, their beloved and handsome young King, would bring his bride home to Paris.

Louis XIV of France and his cousin, Maria Theresa, Infanta of Spain, had been married by proxy in June at Fuenterrabia, near the Spanish frontier, since it was unthinkable that a Spanish princess should leave her native soil without the nuptial ceremony having taken place. Then the Treaty of the Pyrenees had been signed, bringing a long-awaited peace between France and Spain, and next day the marriage was solemnized on French soil, at St Jean-de-Luz. Since then, the young couple, both twenty-two, had been travelling in great state through the south of France, *en route* for Paris. Now, two months later, and after they had rested for a week at the castle of Vincennes, the King was ready to make his formal entry into the city of Paris with his bride.

In the crowded streets traders were doing brisk business in oranges, cherries, and slices of melon for the crowds to quench their thirst – for the procession would take ten hours to pass. The August sun blazed down unsparingly on parade and spectators alike, and water-sellers were doing a roaring trade. Flowers, rose-petals and herbs had been strewn over the cobblestones for the horses' hooves to crush out their fragrance; bands played and church bells pealed incessantly.

There was pandemonium in various parts of the crowd as women fainted in the crush and children became separated from their parents. Street urchins and pick-pockets were having a field day. It was the easiest thing in the world, amongst such crowds, to slit the purse of a fat burgher from his belt and – passed swiftly along from one hand to another – the spoils would be shared out before the victim had even realized his loss. People whose homes lay along the route of the procession were even hiring out chairs and stools for the weary to rest their legs, a profitable enterprise, since no one wanted to sit down for long, for fear of missing any of the spectacle.

From their vantage point on the balcony of the Hôtel d'Aumont in the rue de Jouy, Nicole d'Aumont and her guests had an excellent view, not only of the passing parade, but of the house only a few yards away where sat the Queen Mother, Anne of

Austria; Cardinal Mazarin; the King's cousin, known as La Grande Mademoiselle; and other Court ladies. Not far away was the new triumphal arch of the Porte St Antoine through which the royal couple would pass and where, enthroned, they would receive the keys of the city of Paris.

'Won't you take a little refreshment, ladies, please,' pleaded Nicole d'Aumont to her guests. The little tables the servants had placed in front of them, laden with food, wine and lemonade, had gone largely ignored.

'You will have some difficulty in distracting your guests' attention from the entertainment today, Nicole,' Françoise Scarron observed, busily occupied with the needlework she had brought with her. 'Even the excellence of your chicken pasties and *tartes aux cerises* cannot compete with the attractions of the Grenadiers and the Captain of the Light Horse of the Guard in full dress uniform.'

Nicole and Françoise smiled at each other. Although rather similar in looks, both being tall, dark, slim and graceful, it was their husbands who were cousins. Philippe d'Aumont and Paul Scarron had been close companions, drinking, gambling and roistering together until Scarron, a poet by profession and a renowned wit, had been struck down by illness.

'Do put your sewing down and come over here, Françoise,' called an attractive girl with a wealth of Titian hair who, in her eagerness to see all there was to see, sat perched dangerously on the low wall at the edge of the balcony. Françoise, not for the first time envying Athenais de Rochechouart's striking beauty, thought how exceptionally lovely she was today, her green silk dress enhancing her colouring to perfection, and her finely modelled features flushed with excitement. 'How can you sit there sewing on a day like this?' Athenais demanded. 'You'll see much better from here, I assure you.'

'Thank you, Athenais, but I can see perfectly from here,' Françoise insisted. 'Won't you avail yourself of our hostess's generosity and partake of some little refreshment? I assure you that you will not miss the sight of more than perhaps twenty musketeers and half a dozen captains whilst you eat and drink.'

'You are insufferable, Françoise. May I not try to catch sight of my own brother on such a glorious day?'

'Your brother, Vivonne, saluted us as he passed by not long ago, as well you know, Athenais. *Quel beau sabreur!* You must have missed him while you were waving to the Duc de Guise,

11

whom I admit looks more impressive today in uniform than propping up a card table.'

Athenais' lovely face flushed with quick resentment. 'I should have thought that you would have far better reason to gaze at the men than I have,' she retorted, goaded into jumping down from her perch and sitting down to drink some lemonade.

The other women looked anxiously at Françoise Scarron to see what effect this reference to her invalid husband would have. But Françoise, apart from a slightly heightened colour, continued to work at her embroidery with no outward sign of emotion. An embarrassed silence fell.

'Athenais is having a last look round before she decides on the date of her wedding,' Nicole d'Aumont said, trying to make peace.

'I didn't know you were already betrothed, Athenais,' Louise de la Vallière said in surprise. The two girls, not yet twenty, were both in the Court retinue of the King's mother, Anne of Austria.

'The gentleman concerned has not yet been apprised of his good fortune,' someone cried, amidst general laughter.

Athenais' brilliant eyes flashed with anger; but she looked even more beautiful in a temper, Françoise thought, smiling over her embroidery.

'You know very well that I have been betrothed since childhood to Monsieur de Montespan,' she raged at them all.

'It doesn't prevent you from flirting with others' husbands,' Mme d'Heudicourt remarked with more than a touch of malice in her tone. Everyone laughed. Athenais de Rochechouart-Mortemart, the favourite and spoilt daughter of wealthy and aristocratic parents, could usually be relied upon to keep any gathering entertained in spite of her hasty temper.

'They say that the King will pass by very soon,' intervened Mlle de Scudéry, one of the older ladies.

'The King!' Louise de la Vallière's lips were parted. A soft blush stole over her lovely face, and she leaned forward so that her ash-blonde hair covered her face to hide her confusion. Everyone knew that Louise de la Vallière had been hopelessly in love with the King since the first time she saw him.

'You will soon see your hero, Louise,' mocked Athenais. 'But don't forget that he now has a wife – and they say that she has been well and truly bedded. I hear that he cannot keep away from her rooms. Why, we may very well have a Dauphin before Eastertide, I should not be surprised. After all,' she added, maliciously enjoying Louise's discomfiture, 'as the Infanta speaks no French, and the King very little Spanish, how else should they amuse themselves?'

'For shame, Athenais,' Mme d'Heudicourt scolded her, feeling sorry for Louise. 'The King's mother is Spanish. He is bound to understand at least some of his wife's language.'

Louise de la Vallière bit her lip and her face was downcast. 'Is the Infanta very beautiful?' she asked. 'I mean, the Queen?'

'I hear she is pretty enough,' Nicole d'Aumont said, 'but that her lack of height prevents her from looking like a truly regal Queen of France. And they say that her clothes are so old-fashioned – the Spanish dressmakers are way behind the times. Why, they are still wearing the farthingale – *guardeinfante* they call it – which has not been seen in France for fifty years.'

'She will soon learn to dress according to our ways,' Françoise said. 'Don't you agree, Athenais? You are always *le dernier cri* in fashion.'

'The Queen will hardly care for the advice of a maid-of-honour!' Louise could not hold back the acid remark, though it was alien to her usually gentle nature. There was something about Athenais' abrasive personality that seared through her normally serene disposition. It had rankled with her greatly that the vivacious Athenais, a recent arrival at Court, should have been singled out as a maid-of-honour to the Queen Mother, whereas the shy and self-effacing Louise had been a lady-in-waiting now for more than two years. 'The Queen will have her own suite, I do not doubt,' she insisted.

'Of worthy Spanish ladies, dressed in farthingales, in black from head to toe?' laughed Athenais. 'They won't improve her dress sense! They look like poles stuck into barrels.' She leaned dangerously over the edge of the balcony, waving enthusiastically to the Comte de Guiche and the Marquis de Villarceaux, riding in the procession, who were looking up at the balcony of the Hôtel d'Aumont and waving their hats as they passed. Now the cavalry regiments were going by, the Light Horse of the Guard in scarlet uniforms with white cockades, the Grenadiers in pale blue and white, the cuirassiers, breastplates glittering in the sun. The personal household of Cardinal Mazarin came next, the wily old Italian who, some said, was the lover – even, it was whispered, the secret husband – of Anne of Austria, the Queen Mother.

Whether or not there was any foundation to these rumours, it

13

was certain that Mazarin had been a most important influence in the young King's early life, for his father, Louis XIII, had died when he was barely five years old. Until her son attained his majority at the age of thirteen, Anne of Austria had held the official title of Regent; but it was common knowledge that Mazarin's had been the directing hand behind the scenes. But now, old and sick, suffering from gout and the stone, Mazarin was watching the procession at the side of the Queen Mother, on the balcony of the Hôtel de Beauvais, a fine new town house in the rue François-Miron.

The Cardinal's household, consisting of twenty-four rows of mules, richly harnessed in silver and gold plate, was followed by the gentlemen and guards in his service, escorting the Cardinal's empty carriage with drawn blinds indicating that it was unoccupied. Next came the household of the Queen Mother, followed by that of the King's younger brother Philippe, Duc d'Orléans, known as Monsieur. Then came the King's famous musketeers in their red and blue uniforms, and the faithful Swiss Guards, carrying halberds, in their splendid medieval costume, doublets with slashed sleeves and black velvet, feathered hats. It was their privilege to escort the King everywhere he went.

Suddenly a cry went up which could be clearly heard above the clatter of the horses' hooves, the rattling of the carriage wheels, and the jingling of swords and armour; even above the tumultuous cheers.

'*Le Roi s'approche! Le Roi s'approche! Vive le Roi!*'

The cry was taken up by every one of the spectators, in the streets, on the balconies, at the windows – by the whole of Paris, it seemed.

'*Vive le Roi! Vive le Roi! Vive la Reine!*'

On the balcony at the Hôtel d'Aumont the girls pressed forward in unison, jostling each other for the best view. With a fanfare of trumpets the pages of the Royal Household passed by, wearing red velvet embroidered with the gold fleur-de-lys, followed by the magnificently uniformed Marshals of France. Then, finally, came the long-awaited King himself, escorting his bride, his cousin Maria Theresa, Infanta of Spain, and now Queen of France.

Mounted on a superb Spanish bay Louis XIV, with his brother, Monsieur, and a bevy of selected noblemen, rode alongside the new Queen's carriage, drawn by eight grey horses in gold harness and covered in sumptuous golden drapings. The Queen's robe

14

was of cloth-of-gold, embroidered all over with silver and gold thread, and ornamented only with pearls so that there should be no clash with the jewels – worth a fortune – which had been Louis' wedding gift to his bride. As she gazed, Françoise Scarron was suddenly reminded of an old saying: pearls bring tears.

'It must have been made by the fairies,' Louise de la Vallière murmured at her side, looking in awe at the Queen's dress.

Small and delicate, Maria Theresa looked defencelessly young against the magnificence of her regalia. How fair her skin was; unusually white, it must have been protected from the Spanish sun since the day she was born. That pale skin, those light-coloured blue-green eyes and that silver-blonde hair were an inheritance from her Spanish Hapsburg ancestry which she shared with her aunt, now her mother-in-law, Anne of Austria, sister to the King of Spain.

But the King! After a cursory glance at his bride the women had eyes only for him.

With what grace and majesty he sat his horse, occasionally doffing his hat in deference to the tumultuous cries, gracefully acknowledging the thunderous cheers and shouts with a gesture of his hand. He wore a doublet of white satin covered with gold embroideries and precious stones that flashed in the sun. How handsome his face, his dark eyes, his noble features and sweet expression, and above all, how striking, how commanding that regal presence which was to hold in thrall all who came before him for the rest of his long life.

The girls on the balcony of the Hôtel d'Aumont waved and cheered the King and Queen with no less enthusiasm than the crowds in the street below. Louise de la Vallière gripped the rail of the balcony until her knuckles were white, her rapt gaze fixed on the King, as if her lovely violet-blue eyes willed him to look in her direction. Was he smiling at her, as the street narrowed and he looked up? It was several months now since she had last seen him, on the day when he left for Spain to claim the bride the Queen Mother and Mazarin had arranged for him. That boyish self-consciousness, which had been such a great part of his charm, had gone, she thought with regret; but in its place was a new maturity, a new ease and self-assurance in his bearing which she had not seen before.

Louis was indeed a changed man from the young King who had left Paris the previous winter. His travels through the southern regions of France had filled him with a breathless anticipation of the glory that awaited him as King of this vast and magnificent land. Through Bordeaux, Poitiers, Amboise, Chambord, Orléans, wherever he went, through the countryside and in the towns, in farming villages and cathedral cities, he had been received with an ecstatic and overwhelming welcome, fêted and honoured alike by peasants, serfs, the bourgeoisie and the great feudal seigneurs as their vision of God on this earth, their God-given King.

He had been aware from his earliest days that it was his destiny to become a great king – even as a child he had been fully convinced of his superiority to all others. His brother, Philippe, two years younger, had even been slightly encouraged in his effeminate tendencies by the Queen Mother and Mazarin, the better to provide a contrast to the vivid masculinity of the young King. Now, bringing home a Queen of France to Paris, Louis was more than ever conscious of the divine singularity of his position. The previous summer he had had a fleeting love-affair with Mazarin's niece, Marie Mancini, but, realizing that she could never become Queen of France, he had regretfully given her up. No woman could rob him of the glory he intended to enjoy as King of France. Destiny, he knew, had united him with his bride – that same destiny by which he had been created Louis le Dieu-donné, the God-given, his mother's first living child, born after twenty-three years of sterile marriage when she was forty years old. He acknowledged with pride the joy and trust of his people in their miracle Dauphin, now their King, and knew that nothing could ever deprive him of his royalty, his by divine right.

As the rue de Jouy narrowed and led into the rue François-Miron, the King reined in his horse and the entire procession came to a halt. With matchless grace, Louis removed his white-plumed hat and, in a sweeping and spontaneous gesture of deference, he bowed deeply to his mother and to Cardinal Mazarin sitting at her side on the balcony of the Hôtel de Beauvais. It was a recognition of all that they had done to protect his inheritance during those troubled days of the Fronde uprisings, the rebellions which had disturbed France during his minority. It was his way of publicly thanking them both for bringing him safely to his heritage. As the procession began to move on, the Queen Mother leaned forward with tears in her eyes to acknowledge her son's bow.

But on the balcony of the Hôtel d'Aumont, Athenais de Rochechouart's smile faded as she stared at the little Infanta, so

16

hampered by the weight and stiffness of her robes and jewels that she could hardly move. With narrowed eyes she tried in vain to estimate the value of the Queen's regalia – all that gold and silver, velvet, jewels, and priceless stones – it was impossible! Athenais put her hand to her neck, fighting back the strangling cry of jealousy that swiftly rose in her throat. It should have been me! The thought rang deafeningly in her brain. In that moment, a suffocating resentment of this dressed-up Spanish doll of a Queen, stiff as a dummy in her old-fashioned farthingale, riding in glory through the streets of Paris in a golden coach, crystallized into a deep-rooted, all-consuming hatred.

Only her royal birth, as the daughter of Spain, had given Maria Theresa the right to become the wife of a man like Louis XIV of France. One day, Athenais vowed to herself, the adulation that the new Queen was now enjoying would be hers. One day, she too would ride in splendour in an eight-horse coach, and her clothes, her jewels, her possessions would be the talk of the kingdom.

And one day, she promised herself at that moment, the King would lie in her arms. If she, Athenais de Rochechouart-Mortemart, could not be the King's wife, she would see to it that she became his mistress.

A little of her old sparkle returned as she gazed at the good-looking face of Louis, smiling up in the direction of his beloved mother, so near that she could almost have reached out and touched him.

As for Françoise Scarron, leaning forward in excitement, impressed far more deeply than she realized by the handsome young King she was seeing for the first time, she unknowingly voiced the thoughts of all three of them, herself, Louise de la Vallière and Athenais de Rochechouart, as she said dreamily to herself: 'The Queen must have gone to bed last night well satisfied with the husband of her choice.'

How could they see into the future, those three girls on the balcony in the rue de Jouy on that hot August day? How could they know that in the space of only a few short years they would be known throughout France as the past, the present and the future loves of King Louis XIV of France?

PART 1

THE RISING SUN

1661-1668

Chapter One

One fine May morning in the year 1661 a handsome coach-and-six bowled smartly along through the busy quarter of the Marais, a favourite district amongst the writers and artists of Paris.

Driving at full speed through the Place Royale, the coachman scattered a cluster of street urchins with a crack of his whip. The fruit and vegetable baskets of the market women in the far corner of the square were overturned, spilling their contents into the gutter as the coach took the corner rather too sharply, rattling along at a fine pace before turning into the narrower rue Neuve Saint-Louis. Here it was obliged to slow down before it finally came to a stop outside a small and unpretentious house where the curtains at the windows appeared to be drawn.

The steaming horses snorted, whinnied and pawed impatiently at the cobbles as a portly gentleman, no longer young, alighted and hastened up the few steps in front of the house. There, having given a couple of sharp raps on the door-knocker, he occupied himself by arranging his brocade coat over his stomach, fluffing out his lace ruffles and jabot, and settling his finely curled wig. With one hand on his sword and the other holding his plumed hat, he waited for an answer to his summons.

Although it was apparent from the elegance of his attire, and the smartness of his equipage with its accompanying footmen, that he was a person of no little importance, the serving-maid who answered his knock hesitated on the threshold, a shawl clutched hastily round her shoulders, holding the door as he made to enter.

'The widow Scarron is not at home?' he demanded with some impatience.

'Indeed, monsieur – ' The girl seemed ill at ease as she continued to bar his way. There was a laden basket at her feet.

'A pox on you! Is she or is she not at home?'

'Sir – Monsieur le Comte – ' She had recognized him now. 'She is only just returned from the funeral.'

But the Comte de Dijon was to be thwarted no longer, and he thrust his way past her into the house, stepping over the basket

21

by the door. 'Announce me!'

'Monsieur le Comte, she is wondrous grieved – '

'Announce me, I say!' With this he gave her a cuff on the ears. The girl scuttled along the passage, and a moment later returned to say, red-faced: 'Madame is in the salon, Monsieur le Comte. Please to follow me.'

He followed her up the brief flight of stairs, where she opened the door of the salon, announced 'Monsieur le Comte de Dijon', and vanished.

The room he entered was familiar to him, so that he did not cast a glance at his surroundings, only at the girl who had been standing at the window, holding back the drapes and looking out, and who now turned and came towards him.

How lovely she was! He caught his breath as if seeing her for the first time. Of a good height, slim, graceful, and fresh as the morning, the severity of the plain black gown, unrelieved by any lace or jewellery, set off perfectly her smooth skin and the expressive eloquence of her fine black eyes.

'Monsieur le Comte.'

He bent to kiss the slim white hand extended to him.

'Madame Scarron. My compliments – and my condolences. I beg you to forgive my intrusion, at a time when you perhaps have little desire for company.'

'Indeed, monsieur, delighted as I am to see you, I am just returned from my husband's funeral. Even if I were inclined to entertain visitors, I hardly think it would be seemly.'

She had approached him so that they were standing on opposite sides of the long dining-table. By accident or design? he wondered. He looked hopefully in the direction of the sofa against the tapestry-hung walls, but she did not invite him to sit down.

'And so, monsieur, perhaps you will be kind enough to excuse me.'

She is even more attractive than I remembered, he thought, and a determination for his plans to succeed prompted him to continue hastily: 'Madame, there is a matter I would like to discuss with you, if you will spare me a few minutes.' Seeing her hesitation, he rushed on: 'With the greatest delicacy, madame, and if you will permit an old friend of your husband's to mention the matter, your financial condition cannot be sound. Your husband's debts – '

'My husband's debts will all be settled, monsieur, I assure you, in good time.' Her hands were clenched on the top of a dining-chair, and a little colour had come into her pale cheeks. The black eyes hardened and an expression of wary defiance had come over her face.

'Madame Scarron, I have come here this morning specifically to discuss this matter with you, purely with the intentions of an old friend. I left my estates in the Dordogne as soon as I heard the news of Paul's death.' And not a moment too soon, he thought. Looking as she does today, all the beaux in Paris will soon be hot on my heels. He walked purposefully round to her side of the table and took her hand. 'May we sit for a moment, while I tell you of something I have in mind? Trust me, my dear; I have only your welfare at heart.'

'I would rather stand, monsieur. I have every confidence in you, I assure you. Pray continue with what you wish to say.'

How old was she? he wondered. Twenty-three, twenty-four? So assured and mature in manner, yet so lovely and virginal in appearance. He moistened his dry lips.

'My dear Madame Scarron, let us not waste time in purposeless conversation. We both know that your husband was virtually penniless and that he left numerous debts, which means that your situation is now, to say the least of it, highly insecure. Now, my dear, because I have considerable esteem for you, just as I had for your late husband, I have come to see if I can offer you some assistance.'

'Charity, monsieur!' The black eyes were blazing now, and her colour considerably heightened. 'Never while I live!'

'Come now, have I mentioned charity? My dear Françoise, you are far too sensitive. Of course, your great sorrow – so recent – such a shock – '

'Monsieur, I have had some experience of charity in my youth' – he could not help a smile at this remark from a girl of her age – 'and I do not care to repeat it. I had thought of becoming a governess – '

'Exactly so, my dear, exactly so. Now what I wanted to suggest was this . . .'

Françoise's thoughts raced ahead of his. She had met his wife, a pleasant enough woman, on several occasions. Did he not have two daughters? But surely they were past the age for a governess. Was not the elder one presented at Court last year? Perhaps he had grandchildren –

'We go to our estates in the Dordogne infrequently,' he was saying. But I would go a great deal more frequently if you were there, he thought. 'The assistant housekeeper has recently left my employ, and as soon as I heard of your bereavement and realized the situation in which you would find yourself, I immediately thought: now here is an ideal post for Mme Scarron. An excellent salary, a comfortable apartment in the chateau. I could provide you with your own carriage – '

Yes, she thought, I am sure you could. A carriage, in that God-forsaken part of the country! Where should I go, whom should I see? No one I know ever again, save when my lord and master arrived from Paris on some pretext of dealing with his affairs on his country estate.

He took her hand and kissed it, lingeringly. 'You will find me more than generous, my dear.'

She smiled at him, and he felt like a man in love for the first time. How his stock would rise when all Paris knew of his new mistress!

'I thank you most sincerely for your kind offer, Monsieur le Comte,' she was saying with a most charming smile, extending her hand once more, 'but I am not at this very moment looking for a protector. If I should be in need of one, I assure you I shall let you know.'

Villarceaux! he thought. The young dog has already made her an offer. What a swine the fellow was. Married less than a year to a lovely young wife – while he himself had been married no fewer than twenty-seven years. Surely, he had told himself often enough, he was entitled to a little dalliance here and there after all those interminable years of his wife's and daughters' endless female prattle. Paul Scarron had been happiest when surrounded by people, distracting him from his pain – he had entertained all Paris in his room, *Hôtel de L'Impécuniosité* it had been known as – and in the company of the gayest wits of Parisian society his shy young bride, Françoise d'Aubigné, had soon blossomed into a spirited, lively personality, fond of music and passionately interested in poetry and plays. He had been looking forward to having an intelligent mistress for a change, someone with whom he could actually carry on a conversation as well as merely tumble in and out of bed.

Reluctant to relinquish all hope, he said: 'You must realize, my dear, that you are still very young and inexperienced in the ways of the world, and, I believe, have no family to protect you. There will be many unscrupulous men who will not hesitate to take advantage of your situation.'

'Perhaps in not quite so underhand a manner as you have done, monsieur. And now, if you will excuse me – '

'But you cannot deny that you are in need of protection – '

'You seem to forget, monsieur, that I was married for eight years. I am not so completely lacking in experience as you seem to think. My husband – '

'Your husband was a helpless cripple, unable to turn from one side of the bed to the other! What can you know of men! You are as innocent as a maid on her wedding night!'

Her expression was chilling. He knew he had gone too far, but he no longer cared. Let her have her fling with Villarceaux, whose young wife, he knew, held the purse-strings of that marriage! Then, in a few months' time, when the money had dried up, she would soon come running to him. He knew only too well how mercenary and grasping women could be once they had acquired a taste for finery, jewels and other luxuries. Then she would be quite ready to overlook the fact that he was a man of fifty-eight, and abandon the handsome Villarceaux. So she thought she knew it all, did she? She still had a good deal to learn about the world, had young Françoise Scarron.

Françoise smiled ruefully as no one appeared in answer to the summons of the small handbell. The servants, knowing full well that they would not be paid, had lost no time in departing. Well, that was one problem less to solve.

'I regret there is no one to show you out, monsieur. I bid you good morning. Please convey my compliments to your wife.'

The door of the salon closed firmly behind her.

Standing crestfallen and somewhat nonplussed on the steps of the little house, M. le Comte was forced to realize that his plans had all come to nothing. His long journey had been in vain. But *'que voulez-vous?'* It was a beautiful May day in Paris, the sun was shining, and his wife was miles away in the country . . .

With a smile he shrugged his shoulders, climbed back into his carriage, and ordered the coachman to drive to a certain district of Paris, not far away, where he knew the lady of the house would offer him a warmer welcome.

In the house he had just left Françoise Scarron sat at her writing desk in her bedroom on the ground floor. At the sound of footsteps she started up, but the young woman who entered the room threw her arms round her, and they embraced warmly.

'Ninon! I am so glad to see you!'

'I came directly, as soon as I heard the news. We were staying in the country, near Fontainebleau, but I insisted on driving to Paris immediately to see you. Tell me, my dear, how are you feeling?'

'Oh, well enough, except that I have a severe headache. It is not surprising. I have not slept for several nights. I keep thinking I hear his stick thumping on the floor above, calling me.'

Ninon studied her friend's face anxiously. 'When does the funeral take place?' she asked, carefully feeling her way, unsure whether to commiserate with Françoise on the tragic death of her husband at the age of forty-nine, or to congratulate her on her release from a helpless cripple.

'He was buried this morning, at the church of St Gervais.' Françoise sat down at her desk and rested her head on her hands. 'I have so many problems, Ninon, I scarcely know where to begin. The most urgent of them all, as you can imagine, is money.'

Ninon sat down on the four-poster bed and, slipping off her shoes, curled up her feet underneath her. She threw off her hat and ran her fingers through her luxuriant brown hair. Ninon de l'Enclos was a much sought-after young woman of a certain age whose profession was that of a courtesan selecting her many lovers only from the highest echelons of Parisian society. People actually said that she had once taken both a certain husband and his own son as her lovers. Certainly she was a most generous, warm-hearted person who had the knack of retaining almost all her former admirers as friends once the initial heat of their ardour had cooled down. Even their wives spoke well of Ninon, knowing that she accepted only presents in the best possible taste – a country house, a coach-and-six, a diamond tiara – unlike those rapacious little tarts at the Opéra and the Comédie Française who, having once got an aristocrat in their clutches, bled the gentleman white for every last sou they could get.

'Would it help you to talk to me a little, Françoise?' Ninon asked. 'Or would you prefer it if I leave you? By the way, there was no one to let me in.'

'The servants have run away. I cannot blame them, they know I cannot pay them. Do please stay a little while, Ninon. Will you take a glass of wine after your journey?'

As they sipped their wine Ninon said: 'What are your plans now, Françoise? Will you remain in this house?'

'I cannot. Even if I wished to, I could not afford it. According to my marriage contract I am entitled to twenty-three thousand francs on Paul's death – but you know the extent of his debts. We always lived above our income. Everything I have will go to the creditors; I am surprised that they have not yet arrived. I suppose they have the decency to allow the day of his funeral to pass before making their claims. But in any case, I have no wish to live here alone. All night I have been lying awake, thinking I hear him . . .'

Ninon looked at her friend with sympathy and admiration. Tied to a middle-aged man requiring the care and patience one would give to a newborn baby, never once in Ninon's hearing had Françoise grumbled or complained of his demands during the eight long years she had been married to him.

'Would you come and live with me, Françoise? My house is small, but you are welcome to share what I have.'

'You are a good friend, Ninon, but I have decided to settle up with the creditors as best I can. They will take almost all I have, but I hope I shall be able to keep one or two pieces of furniture and a little ready money, enough to keep me going for a while until I can find a position of some kind.'

'But where will you stay?'

'I have arranged to lodge for a time at the Couvent des Hospitalières in the Place Royale.'

'A convent!' Ninon's face was incredulous. 'But it was to avoid entering a convent that you married Paul Scarron in the first place!'

'That was when I was sixteen years old. I knew that if I entered a convent then, I should end up by taking Holy orders – which I did not wish to do. It's true that my only alternative was to marry Paul, but my life with him was not such a disaster as the world seems to think. He was kind and generous with what little he had, and always good company when he was not in pain. He was good to me, and I am glad to think I was able to make his last years at least a little more comfortable. Poor man, his worst misfortune was that, when he contracted his crippling illness, his mind was not affected. His was an exceptional brain in a poor twisted body. What could be a greater tragedy? May God have mercy on his soul.'

'But you will enter a convent now?'

'Only as a temporary measure, until I can obtain a post as a governess or children's nurse. I have had some little nursing experience in the past few years, I assure you.'

'But, Françoise –' Ninon caught her friend's hands – 'you have been shackled to a sick man for years now, those years which should be the best in a woman's life. Don't you wish to enjoy yourself, and lead a gayer existence than that of a governess or a nurse now that you're free? There will be no shortage of gentlemen to escort a girl like you. Why, I know for a fact that several have admired you – from a distance of course, as a respectable married woman. But now you are your own mistress; why bury yourself in a convent, of all places? Come, live with me. We'll entertain the richest and the handsomest beaux in Paris, and you shall make your choice!'

Françoise could not help but smile at her enthusiasm. 'You are very kind, but –' She hesitated, loath to offend such a good friend as Ninon.

'But what, Françoise? At least come and stay with me for a little. Paul is dead. You are only twenty-four – twenty-five, is it? Come and stay with me, and you will see what a wonderful time a beautiful woman can have in Paris!'

'You're a good friend, Ninon. But that is not the kind of life I wish to lead.'

Ninon stared at her in amazement. 'What kind of life, then?'

'I don't really know, Ninon, what lies ahead of me. Which of us does? But I do know that I want to be of some use in the world, and not merely live for my own enjoyment. Forgive me, Ninon; you are a good woman; but above all I want to – be well thought of in the world. I want no taint of any kind, ever, to be attached to my name. That means more to me than anything else.'

'The Ursuline nuns were nothing if not thorough when they helped you to find the true faith,' Ninon observed, as she rose and began to adjust her toilette. At the age of fourteen, as her friend knew, Françoise had been forcibly taken from the Huguenot aunt who had brought her up, placed in a convent, and 'converted' to Catholicism.

'Perhaps. But you need have no fear, Ninon. I shall not take the veil. I want to be a part of this world, not live behind closed doors.'

'Do you need any money, Françoise? What of your aunt at Mursay? Will you go to her?'

'I am just now writing to her. I shall visit her, of course, but I have no wish to leave Paris permanently. I hope my friends here would miss me too much.'

'Indeed they would,' said Ninon.

'You come from Fontainebleau?' asked Françoise, as Ninon

picked up her hat and wrap and made ready to leave. 'Tell me, what is the news of the Court?'

'Oh, it is without doubt the most brilliant Court that has been known for many years. We have been lodging near by for the summer at an inn at Bois-le-Roi. Each evening we go to the entertainment at the palace. Everyone of quality may attend, so long as they are suitably dressed. Almost every evening there is a concert or a play, sometimes followed by dancing.'

'And the King?'

'The King is more handsome every day. All the ladies are dying for love of him. He likes everyone to dress as splendidly as possible, and he sets a fine example. Sometimes he himself takes part in a ballet, or dances with the ladies. He's a very fine dancer, probably because he loves music.'

'It sounds delightful. And what of the Queen? Her time must be drawing near.'

'She will be brought to bed soon, I think. The ladies are accordingly vying for the King's attention now more than ever. It is *très amusant* to see their affectations – each one wearing a lower décolletage than the next. I swear that if they did not know they would be drummed out of Court immediately, some of them would appear in the nude the better to display their charms.'

'But is the King no longer in love with his wife?'

'Who knows? But soon she will be *accouchée* – and then she will be lying-in for a month. Men do not like to remain celibate for long, and why should the King, with so many beauties willing to console him?'

Poor little Queen, thought Françoise. She has been married barely a twelvemonth. 'Who are these persons,' she asked, 'who would come between husband and wife at such a time, for the sake of riches and glory?'

'The ladies most strongly favoured to become the King's mistress very soon are his sister-in-law, the English princess, who is always in his company now that the Queen is obliged to remain for decency's sake in her rooms. And your old friend Athenais de Montespan is the second favourite.'

'Athenais! She is making her presence felt at Court, then?'

'Very much so. She has attracted a good deal of attention, for she has become more beautiful every day since her marriage to M. de Montespan. Many men have made advances to her, I believe, but she rejects them all, for it seems that she plans nothing less than to become the King's mistress. And as you know, if Athenais makes up her mind to do something, she usually succeeds!'

'What about you, Ninon?' asked Françoise. 'Why should you not become the King's mistress? You are certainly beautiful enough to lay your claim.'

'Me? Oh no, that would be far too dangerous a game for me to play.'

'But the mistress of the King would have renown, and glory, and luxuries beyond price, all the attention anyone could desire – and the King's love! She would be almost as fortunate as his wife, except that she cannot bear his rank.'

'Yes, but he who aspires to the greatest heights must also be prepared to fall the hardest,' Ninon told her. 'One slip, one fall from grace, and the lady may have to spend the rest of her life in a convent, for who can follow where the King has led? And that is not a prospect I could face with equanimity,' Ninon laughed. 'Why, I have been in love at least four times this year alone, but when I tire of *mes amants* – pouf! – it is I who dismiss them. That's the kind of arrangement I prefer.'

Laughing, the two girls embraced. 'At least you have some fine things to dispose of,' Ninon remarked, arranging her hair before the huge Venetian mirror over the fireplace. 'I know many who would like to have a mirror like this.'

'I shall not sell that. It was Paul's wedding present to me. But I will give it to you, Ninon, with the greatest pleasure, if you would like to have it, for not only will there be little room for it in the convent, but the Sisters will not approve of such objects of vanity, I think.'

'My dear, I have no need for a looking-glass. It's easy enough to see whether I am looking well or not, in the eyes of *mon ami actuel*!'

Again they embraced and said goodbye. In the doorway Ninon turned, her lovely brown eyes dancing with merriment. 'In one respect at least, Françoise, you are fortunate, I assure you.'

'And what is that?'

'I never saw anyone whom black suits so well as you!'

Françoise watched from the window as Ninon ran lightly down the steps to the waiting carriage. A young man leaped out to help her, and as he took off his hat she saw that it was Louis de Mornay, the Marquis de Villarceaux, who for several months past had been paying court to none other than herself.

Françoise could not help a rueful smile; a pang of envy struck her innermost heart. Lucky Ninon! To be so carefree, able to indulge herself so freely in her desires with never a thought for tomorrow. Whether it was another woman's husband, or a jewel that took her fancy – though destined for another man's wife – Ninon took what was her pleasure, went out to meet life and embraced all it had to offer her with open arms; whilst she, Françoise, lingered fearfully in the shadows and held it at arm's length.

What was it that had made her, Françoise wondered, so reluctant to entrust her affections to others, so wary of danger, so fearful to be hurt? The family life she had never known, or her brother's desertion of her as a lonely, imaginative child? Her father, a wastrel, had died when she was small; and when she was thirteen, her mother died, exhausted by the struggle of bringing up two children alone. There had been a happy but all too brief period with Aunt Villette at Mursay; then another aunt, appalled that her niece and nephew should be living under a Huguenot roof, had whisked them away. Françoise had been placed in a convent in order that Aunt Neuillant should reap the glory of reclaiming for the Church a good Catholic soul. Her brother had run away and never been heard of since.

Was it this disturbed and loveless childhood that had damaged her ability to trust, left her with such a deep-rooted sense of caution and made her old before her time? Or was it the anomaly of her life these past eight years – the curious existence of a married woman who yet was not a wife? At sixteen Françoise had the choice between marrying, taking Holy orders or going into domestic service. She had no vocation, and her pride in her ancestry – her grandfather, Agrippa d'Aubigné, had been a companion of Henry of Navarre – made her reluctant to humble herself in service. With no dowry, prospective suitors would be few and far between. So when Paul Scarron offered her the protection of marriage she was suitably grateful.

And it was true, as she had told Ninon, that Paul had been good to her, in a general sense. But who could tell the effects of the revulsion experienced by a sensitive young girl of sixteen forced, in the holy name of matrimony, to share the bed of a cripple?

Françoise squared her shoulders and resolved to put such dark thoughts out of her mind as from this moment. The past was over and done, and the future was just beginning. She was twenty-five years old, pretty, intelligent, talented and personable.

Ninon was a good and trusted friend, and she had many others. What could she learn from these wasted years? That even though without a dowry, she had little chance to marry, life must have something more to offer her than a future as a kept woman for that was Ninon's way of life, called by however glamorous a name.

No, that was not for her – constantly scheming how to keep one's lover, holding the creditors at bay whilst buying ever more expensive gewgaws and fripperies, and desperately trying to preserve one's looks against the ravages of time.

I want some real purpose in my life, she thought. So that, when I am old, I can look back and say, well, at least I have achieved something in my lifetime.

Nevertheless, it was not without a momentary feeling of regret that she watched Ninon and her handsome Marquis drive away.

Chapter Two

The royal palace of Fontainebleau was beautiful in the early summer of 1661. The magnificent old chateau, once a twelfth-century hunting seat, had long been a favourite residence of the French kings. In the sixteenth century François I had assembled here a group of the finest Italian artists and sculptors of the Renaissance to restore the palace, and it was now one of the royal chateaux frequently visited by the Court.

Louis enjoyed staying here, where no less than five Kings of France had been born, including his own father, Louis XIII. Because the palace was situated so beautifully in the heart of the extensive forests of Fontainebleau, abounding in game and wild life, there was ample opportunity for him to indulge himself to his heart's content in his favourite pursuits of hunting, riding and shooting. How good the air was here, away from the summer stench of Paris! It was a delight, as the early summer ripened to its full glory, to picnic in the forest in the warm light evenings. Sometimes the royal party would bathe in the river, everyone clad in long grey trailing garments, men and women alike, for modesty's sake.

Of course, there were state affairs to keep Louis occupied, holding frequent Council meetings and grappling with the financial problems he had inherited on the death of Cardinal Mazarin the previous winter. There was unemployment throughout France, and poverty was widespread. Louis spent many hours in Council with his ministers, trying to find solutions before the onset of winter, always the time when the worst miseries were experienced by the poor. But the life of the young King was not all duty. He rode, fenced, played tennis and danced away the evenings. He liked to drill his household troops, the Maison du Roi, or his musketeers, in the huge courtyard of the palace, while the ladies watched from the top of the curious horseshoe-shaped staircase leading up to the entrance, the famous l'Escalier-en-fer-le-Cheval. He was a most gracious and charming host to all who visited the Court, presenting frequent concerts, plays and ballets for their entertainment.

33

Henriette d'Angleterre, his brother's wife, whose official title was Madame though she was known to intimates as Minette, was his most frequent dancing partner, and he also liked to listen to her sing and play the spinet. Louis had arranged the recent marriage in the hope that it would turn his brother away from the undesirable influence of certain courtiers with well-known homosexual tendencies who frequented his brother's household too much for Louis' liking. Minette, though she was delicate and often unwell, even in these lovely summer months, had captivated all hearts at the French Court with her vivacity and charm – save only that of her husband. Monsieur, after an initial display of interest in his wife, had soon taken up again with his favourites, the Comte de Guiche and the Chevalier de Lorraine. To avoid the consequent wrath of his brother, he had begun to spend most of his time in Paris, at the Palais Royal.

At Fontainebleau meanwhile, the Queen, now nearing her time, was the subject of great speculation; would the forthcoming *Enfant de France* be the longed-for Dauphin or a little princess? But in private Maria Theresa began to complain to her husband that she was seeing him only at supper and in bed, where more often than not she was fast asleep when he arrived in the early hours of the morning.

Louis dismissed her complaints with a shrug. 'Why, my dear,' he protested, holding up his glass of wine to the light and admiring its ruby-red colour, 'whenever I send to you, your attendants invariably tell me that you are at Mass or praying in your oratory.'

The little Queen looked at him appealingly. 'Sire, you have only to request my presence, and I will come immediately to your side.'

The King paused, his spoon half-way to his mouth. They were taking supper together as always, alone save for the Duchess d'Elbeo, and the footmen standing respectfully to one side, waiting to serve the next course.

'Interrupt your prayers, my dear? I would not dream of such presumption.' He finished the wine in his glass in one draught and beckoned to a lackey to refill it. 'Continue to importune God for a Dauphin, *ma petite*, and let us hope that your prayers will be rewarded.'

Maria Theresa crossed herself furtively at such disrespect. She did not realize how much her piety was beginning to jar on her husband. He had needed a lively young wife who would share his boundless enthusiasm for the glorious vistas of life just opening up before him, free at last of Mazarin's restraining influence after all the years of waiting to be King. He needed someone like the high-spirited Marie Mancini at his side, or his little English sister-in-law, Minette.

He knew that Mazarin had been right to dissuade him from marrying Marie, and he had seen the wisdom of securing a peaceful Spanish frontier at the beginning of his reign. Nevertheless, he wished that his dumpy little wife was not quite so stolid and unimaginative. Even allowing for her pregnant state she was dull company, and her French was so poor that it was a constant effort to talk to her. Her accent irritated him almost as much as did the dwarfs and pet dogs with which she surrounded herself, to amuse her in the fashion of the Spanish Court. She was greedily fond of her food, even more than he was himself, being partial to stews heavily flavoured with garlic and nutmeg; and she constantly chewed bucaro, a kind of clove-scented chocolate from Mexico that her father often sent her. Yet, though he spent his days as far away from her as he could, Louis was mindful always of his duties as a husband and always slept in her bed.

As the King wiped his mouth and rose, Maria Theresa followed suit respectfully. Seven months pregnant, she was so short as to look almost square. The King gazed at her approvingly and took her hand.

'You will retire now, *ma chérie*. Your precious burden needs rest.'

'I am not tired, Sire. I rested this afternoon while you were in Council. May I not attend the play this evening, *por favor*?'

'You must not keep late hours, *ma petite*. Remember your condition. You are privileged to carry the future King of France. Now you must retire.' He beckoned firmly to the Duchess d'Elbeo, who hesitantly came forward. 'Accompany your mistress to her chamber and see that she is put to bed without delay.'

He took his wife's hand and kissed it. '*A bientôt, ma chérie*.' He made a deep and graceful bow and quitted the room.

The little Queen looked after him with tears in her eyes as he strode away. She followed him to the door of the antechamber, hoping to exchange another word with him, but he had already reached the top of the Escalier de la Reine and had begun to descend.

'The King is going to visit my aunt, his mother,' said Maria

35

Theresa, valiantly trying to fight back the tears brimming in her eyes.

The Duchess d'Elbeo, reaching her side, fussed over her and led her back into her apartments – with an inward sigh for the little Queen whom she had cared for since she was born. She deemed it more prudent not to mention that the Escalier de la Reine led, not to the Queen Mother's apartments, but to the floor below where was housed the rest of the royal suite, including Madame.

As the beautiful spring and summer of that year ripened into full maturity and began to draw towards a close, the weather became increasingly hot and oppressive. There had been no rain for weeks, and the grass and bracken in the forest of Fontainebleau were dry and brittle. For several days now there had been no sunshine, just the humid sultry heat, the sky dull and heavy with the threat of thunder. In the palace kitchens the cooks were bad-tempered. Everyone was complaining and refusing the heavy soups and stews which were the usual mainstay of the palace menus. The chefs were at their wits' end, and many a scullion and kitchen maid received an undeserved cuff. The hens would not lay, the milk turned sour on its way from the dairy, the butter was melting and rancid. There was no fish to be had, for there was no fresh water source in the vicinity, and fish could not be transported from Paris in this weather. No game or venison were available for the royal tables, the King having declined to hunt for the past week, for fear of being far from the palace when the Queen was brought to bed. In spite of the doctors' assurances that a first confinement would be prolonged, and that word would be sent to him at the first sign, his reply was always the same: 'I shall be present at the birth of my son.'

Maria Theresa, now at the end of her pregnancy, and her aunt the Queen Mother, were both victims of the heat. The little Queen, a grotesque shape, her face distorted, her legs and feet swollen and puffy, could scarcely rise from her chair to drag herself round the room a turn or two, without assistance. In vain her ladies pleaded with her to lie down and rest. She replied that she was not comfortable lying down, being unable to turn from side to side without help; and in any case, she would soon enough be confined to her bed. All her women could do for her comfort was to help her change her perspiration-soaked chemise several times a day, and sponge her brow and wrists with linen soaked in alcohol, which she found reviving. At night, the curtains of the huge four-poster bed were drawn back a little, but the windows were kept firmly closed. The night air was well known to be harmful.

Anne of Austria, paying an unexpected visit to her daughter-in-law's apartments one morning, found her seated in a comfortable chair by the windows, propped up by cushions, her feet, which did not reach the floor, resting on a stool. A pet dog lay in her lap, and a linnet was in a cage on the table by her side. In one corner an artist was occupied at his easel.

Hearing her visitor announced, the Queen tried to rise, but the older woman would not allow it.

'My dear child, do not disturb yourself, I beg you. You need not rise.' She looked at the painter in surprise. 'I did not know you were sitting for a portrait. I shall return later to see you.'

'No, my dear aunt, please do not leave. I am so happy to see you and have someone to talk with.' She clapped her hands and signalled for the painter to withdraw.

She had spoken in Spanish, and her aunt reproved her. 'You must not speak our language now, my dear. You must try hard to improve your French, since it pleases your husband.' She knew how much the Queen's heavy accent grated on her son's nerves.

She kissed her daughter-in-law and sank into the armchair which the Duchess d'Elbeo brought for her – the only woman allowed to sit in the presence of the Queen. 'How are you today, dear child? *Madre de Dios!* This heat will kill me!' She fanned herself energetically and mopped at the perspiration running down her face, wishing that she had asked her ladies not to lace her quite so tightly. 'Is it not tiring for you to pose, my dear?'

'On the contrary, aunt, it helps to pass the time. The days seem so long. What do you think of the picture?'

Anne of Austria inspected the portrait, and was pleasantly surprised. The painting on the easel well captured the lonely, rather lost look in the Queen's eyes. It was flattering, of course, for in reality her face was bloated almost out of all recognition by her condition; but it was lifelike. The artist had caught convincingly the rather blank staring expression of the Queen.

'It is an excellent likeness,' she said. 'Who is this man?'

'His name is Desève. I believe Cardinal Mazarin recommended him to the King at the time of our marriage, when my husband desired to have my portrait painted. But because it was left so late he can now only represent my head and shoulders. If the King is pleased, he will have him work on a full-length study of me with the child, when it is born.'

Inwardly she reproached herself for having mentioned the name of the late Cardinal, which she knew often brought tears to the Queen Mother's eyes. But her aunt seemed not to have noticed, for she only said as she looked at the portrait: 'It is a good likeness, nevertheless. Ask the artist to wait upon me, if you will be so kind. Perhaps I will allow him to paint me, and I shall give the portrait to the King as a present upon the birth of his son.'

She turned to her niece with a smile, but the Queen's face was expressionless. 'How are you feeling, dear child? It cannot be very long now.'

'The movements have not been so strong for the last two days. It is as if it were quietly waiting – or perhaps it is dead.'

'Theresita! Do not speak of that! The heat has upset you. You must be very uncomfortable. I shall call for a cool drink for you.'

Maria Theresa raised her hands to her face and began to cry. Anne of Austria, putting her arms round her, wisely allowed her a flow of tears before she attempted to check her. 'Do not upset yourself, *mi querida*, I beg you. These last days are hard to bear, I know. It seems as if nothing is ever going to happen. I remember well when my sons were born, for although I am so much older than you, I was over forty when Philippe was born.'

She rang for the Duchess d'Elbeo, and ordered her to bring some chicory water. Poor child, she thought, holding the girl against her, rocking her to and fro in an attempt to soothe her. How well she remembered when she, too, had had to leave Spain to marry in France, and found herself a stranger, and an unwelcome one at that – for her husband never loved her, and she was lonely and neglected in a strange land. But her niece was luckier; for she, Anne of Austria, had had to endure twenty-three years of unhappy marriage before, by some miracle, she had borne the child who was to become the joy of her existence. Anne loved her younger son, Philippe, but not with the passionate love she felt for Louis, for whom she would have laid down her life. He had been born when, at almost forty, she had given up all hope of ever bearing a child; and over the years, the rapture she had experienced, the exhilaration shared by all women who give birth to a son, had been broadened and enriched by the pride she felt as he grew into a darkly handsome young man, intelligent and thoughtful beyond his years. He was extremely attractive to women, every movement of his face and body betraying the sensuality of his Bourbon lineage. He had about him a great personal magnetism; a charm that drew one to him, and at the same time a seriousness and restraint that kept one at a distance.

The King of France was her son; he loved and respected her, never failed to visit her each morning to enquire after her health. His marriage had in no way lessened the strong bond between mother and son, for which she gave thanks to God every day.

The Duchess brought a tray with jug and glasses, and poured out drinks for the two ladies. Anne offered a glass to her niece. 'Soon you will have your baby,' she comforted her. 'Here, drink this, my child.'

Maria Theresa took the glass from her aunt and drank a little, beginning to recover her composure.

'This heat is unbearable,' her aunt complained. 'I am breaking out in a constant sweat all the time, and nothing seems to quench my thirst.' She also took a long drink and sat down in the easy chair next to her niece.

'It is not the heat, dear aunt, nor even my condition, though I am very uncomfortable. You know that I am accustomed to the Spanish sun, and heat does not upset me. But I am so very lonely here.' And the little Queen, to Anne's dismay, began to cry afresh. 'You are the only one who is kind to me, *muy querida tía*. I am shut up here in these rooms from morning till night, seeing the King only at supper, and the days are so long.'

'Is he not kind to you, my dear?'

'Oh, yes, he is good to me, but I see him so rarely. Most often I am asleep when he comes to bed, though I try very hard to stay awake. It is very lonely here in France, where everyone laughs behind my back at the way I speak.'

Anne of Austria stroked the girl's fair head affectionately, and with sympathy. 'Do not grieve so, *ma petite*,' she said, wondering how to comfort her, remembering her own friendless years in Paris. 'You are more fortunate than I was. And I pray to God your life will not be like mine, having to flee here and there in order to protect my son until he came of age, in constant fear that my enemies would have him either murdered or taken from me. I do not know which I feared the most. We were so poor, I was forced to sell my jewels, and we could keep no servants for there was no money to feed them. Those were terrible days, dear child, the days of the Fronde. How we managed to survive them I shall never know.'

'It is my good fortune that you did, so that I have *mi querida tía* and my beloved husband.'

'It is not like home here, I know, but you must try to be happy. You have a fine husband whom you love dearly, you are the Queen of France, and soon you will have your child. Let us pray to God that you will be blessed with a son.'

The expression on Maria Theresa's face was hard as she said: 'Yes, let us indeed pray that it will be a boy. A girl would have to leave her home and family to marry, as I have done.'

'Theresita! Do not speak so, I beg you.'

'For you, I will speak no more of it.'

Anne of Austria poured another glass of water and offered it to her niece. 'Do drink a little more, dear child. You are over-wrought. Try to be hopeful. In a few days it will all be over. You will be a mother, and I a grandmother – and France will have a Dauphin.'

'And the King will have his son,' said Maria Theresa as she sipped her drink.

She turned her head to look out of the window. Below, on the terrace of the sixteenth-century formal Italian Jardin de Diane, which had been laid out for the adored mistress of Henri II, Diane de Poitiers, a large number of the Court were strolling. Although Louis had indicated that he had no objection to any-one hunting in the forest these last few days as he waited for the Queen to give birth, no one would budge from his side. Every-body wanted to be near the King when the event occurred, hoping to gain his favour by being one of the first to congratulate him.

The two women watching from the window of the Queen's apartments fell silent as the group of courtiers dropped tactfully behind to keep their distance from the King and his sister-in-law, Princess Henriette. Engrossed in their conversation, the two had wandered towards the Fontaine de Diane and were watching the carp in the pond, dabbling their hands in the water like children.

At length the Queen Mother said: 'Minette is so sweet and pretty, is she not?'

In her heart she was more than a little anxious about her Louis' obvious interest and pleasure in the company of his brother's wife. Philippe's marriage, as she had foreseen, had changed nothing. He was following the example of his father, Louis XIII, who had preferred men to women. He showed no interest whatsoever in his attractive wife, and now he and his debauched friends – chiefly the Chevalier de Lorraine, whom he knew his brother did not welcome at Court – confined their activities to various well-known haunts in Paris. Anne could not help but sigh as she contrasted the Queen's lank blonde hair, the pallor of her waxen complexion, her bloated figure resembling nothing so much as a stuffed doll in a museum, with the slim, dark, vibrant vivacity of Henriette.

'Would you like to wear a little of my rouge to brighten your cheeks, dear?' she asked her niece. 'I would be happy to lend it to you. Would it cheer you a little? And after the baby is born we must have some new wigs made for you, and some new gowns in the French style. Everyone is talking about the new "transparents", made of English point lace draped over brocade so that the colour shows through. They're said to be quite daring.'

Maria Theresa stared at her. 'Thank you, aunt, but I have scarcely yet worn all the gowns in my trousseau, which cost my father thousands of crowns. Besides, I prefer the Spanish fashions. The way in which women here uncover their bosoms is nothing short of scandalous. The styles here are totally unsuitable for a Queen of France and a good Catholic.'

Anne of Austria mopped her perspiring face. Maria Theresa was certainly Philip's child. Poor Elizabeth, her mother, who had died so young; she had been a French princess, the sister of Anne's own late husband, Louis XIII, and had married Anne's sombre and austere brother, Philip of Spain, who was said to have laughed only three times in his life. When Anne had met him – for the first time in forty-six years – at the wedding the previous June, she had gone forward eagerly to kiss her brother. But Philip had kept her at arm's length, and allowed her merely to place her hands on his shoulders. Maria Theresa had inherited his dull, introverted nature.

Was Louis in fact more than a friend to his brother's wife? Anne longed to ask her niece some pertinent questions, but sympathy for the little Queen held her back. It was obvious that she suspected nothing. Why put fears into the child's head? She was unhappy enough.

'The English princess is charming, Aunt Anna. She is kind to me. She, too, is an *exilada*, away from her loved ones. She adored

41

her brother, the English King Charles, yet she had to leave him.'

'You are not away from your loved ones, dear child. Do not forget that. Louis and I both love you dearly.'

Maria Theresa made no answer. The Queen Mother fanned herself. The courtiers in the gardens were beginning to stroll back in the direction of the chateau, in order to hear Mass at twelve o'clock.

'I will leave you now, my dear. I think I shall lie down after I have heard Mass.'

Maria Theresa allowed her aunt to kiss her goodbye. She felt so hot and uncomfortable that she could scarcely move, scarcely even think what she was saying. How could women go through this experience eight, nine, ten times or even more, in their lives? she wondered. And she had not yet come to her confinement. That thought made her suddenly shiver in spite of the oppressive heat.

Tremulously she asked: 'Is it true, *mi querida tía*, that a woman so short as I am will have a difficult confinement, or perhaps give birth to a dwarf?'

'Theresita! What makes you say such things!'

'I heard the Duchess d'Elbeo and the other women talking while I was resting yesterday. They did not know that I heard.'

'My dear child, I forbid you absolutely to think of such nonsense.'

'But I dread what is in store for me, nevertheless.'

'It is the fate of all women, *querida*. But God is good. We must go through pain and fire, but we reap a fine harvest for our sufferings. What would my life have been to me without my son?'

Louis and Minette were now passing directly below the window where the two women sat, on their way into the chateau. Anne of Austria and Maria could hear their banter quite clearly. The King offered his arm to Minette to help her ascend the steps up from the garden.

There must be some way to divert his attention from her, Anne thought. There are so many pretty girls here at Court, Mlle de Pons, Louise de la Vallière, Athenais de Montespan. Surely he could be encouraged to take an interest in one of them – any-one except his brother's wife.

She kissed her niece and prepared to leave. '*Adiós, mi querida. Beso la mano*. You will send word to me immediately you have any pain? The physicians are installed downstairs, are they not?'

'Do not fear, aunt. There is a veritable regiment of doctors waiting to attend me.'

'Then put your faith in God, dear child, and pray for strength to bear your ordeal with courage. It will be less severe than you fear, I promise you.'

It is easy for you to say that, thought Maria Theresa. You are so far removed from this experience now that it is simply a haze in your memory. *Está la vida* – we come into this world, we give birth, and we die. Although we are surrounded by people, we must experience these things alone.

But she embraced her aunt warmly, knowing her to be the one person here in France who cared for her, with the exception of the King. And dull and slow though she was, she was beginning to realize that his concern was less for her than for the child she carried.

'Thank you for your visit, *muy querida tía*,' she said. '*Adiós*, I will pray to God to help me to be brave, as befits the Queen of France.'

The two women kissed each other affectionately. Both had tears in their eyes as they took leave of each other.

Chapter Three

In her room at the Couvent des Hospitalières in the Place Royale, Françoise Scarron was writing in a ledger her expenditures and accounts.

Nicole d'Aumont had offered her the use of the room she kept in the convent, so she had no rent to budget for; but when Paul Scarron's worldly goods were disposed of, she had managed to keep from the clutches of the creditors only 4,000 livres. All the furniture had gone to pay the creditors, and in addition she had borrowed 1,000 livres to pay for Scarron's funeral. That left her with 3,000 – she still owed money to the shoemaker and glove-maker, and to the tailor who had made her mourning clothes; but they would have to wait.

3,000 livres. How long would it last? It was summertime, so that she had no need for logs, and the good nuns, knowing her situation, allowed her to join their frugal table, in return for which she spent some considerable time embroidering and repairing the church vestments. Almost every night she went out to dine at the homes of her friends, who were in the top rank of Parisian society; it amused them to entertain Françoise, and to mock her piety, her sober dress and, above all, her virtue. Unwilling to be the object of their charity, she tried to repay their generosity by all kinds of small services, looking after their children on occasion, or helping them to straighten out their household accounts – for servants could never be trusted. Françoise's experience as the wife of Paul Scarron had been an invaluable lesson in the art of keeping a careful budget, and fending off any tradesmen who were too quick off the mark.

Her chief expenditure, until the winter came, would be for candles, and for the Masses she had said each week for the repose of her husband's soul. New clothes were out of the question, but shoe repairs were essential. The small sum she paid the porter of the convent, who kept her room clean, and whose wife took in her washing, accounted for the remainder of her expenses.

Though all her friends had promised to help find her a position, so far nothing had materialized. Françoise sometimes wondered if she was not a little too helpful to her friends, too ready to be a faithful unpaid standby for them to call on when they needed assistance. She reckoned that she would be able to manage until at least November, when the really cold weather set in. But she was confident that her friends would find some post for her before then. Blanche d'Heudicourt had a cousin, the Comte de Vienne, who was highly thought of at Court. Françoise had seen them talking together recently at one of Ninon's regular Friday night *soirées*. She wondered if they were trying to arrange a position for her at Court, perhaps as an assistant to the Mistress of the Robes, in view of her undoubted skill with a needle.

Yet despite all the fine promises, here she was all but destitute, and virtually starving, she thought with some bitterness. Paris was a social desert now in the heat of August, for most people had gone away to their country estates. There were none of the dinner parties to which she was usually invited, and she was forced to rely on monotonous convent fare, which hardly satisfied a young and healthy appetite. If it were not for Nicole d'Aumont's kindness, she knew, she would not even have a roof over her head.

The tap-tap-tap of the porter's wooden leg along the cobbled passageway outside her door interrupted her reverie. Françoise looked at the bundle of washing which stood in the corner, waiting to be laundered by his wife. Should she tell him she would do it herself, and save herself thirty sous? She looked down at her hands, so slim, smooth and white, of which she had always been so proud. The porter was banging on the door.

'*Voici une lettre, madame.*'

'Thank you, Gaston.' Françoise, completely mystified, examined the letter, which bore a royal seal. She took it over to the window, where the light was better.

Fontainebleau, August 1, 1661

Madame,
   I am commanded by Anne, Queen Dowager of France, to recommence payment to Françoise, widow of the late Paul Scarron, the annual pension of 2,000 livres formerly paid to the said Paul Scarron, the payment to become valid from the date of this letter.

The letter was signed by the Duc de Montausier, Financial

Controller to Anne of Austria, the Queen Mother.

A pension! A small one, it was true, but nevertheless a permanent, secure income. Françoise's joy knew no bounds. For the first time in her life she would have money of her own, to use just as she wished – with caution, for it was not a large amount, but the freedom and independence that it would provide could scarcely be measured. She sat down at once to write her thanks to Blanche d'Heudicourt who had certainly arranged this stroke of good fortune. Françoise knew that Paul Scarron had at one time received a small income in recognition of his services to literature, but it had been stopped after he wrote some insulting poems about Cardinal Mazarin, the Queen Mother's lover and, so it was rumoured, secret husband. What she did not know was that the amount of that pension had been only 500 écus; the Queen Mother, when informed of the plight of Scarron's widow by her influential friends, had been told that the sum was in fact 2,000 livres yearly . . .

Françoise's first intention with her new-found income was to provide herself with a servant, essential for a lady mixing in any kind of society, to ensure that she was well turned-out, to wait on her, clean, cook, make fires, visit the market, run errands, take messages, and generally act as a go-between. It was a wonder that she had managed to do without one for so long. Accordingly, she summoned the porter. Had there been anyone recently enquiring for work?

'A woman came yesterday seeking work, madame.'

'Where is she now, Gaston?'

'She was turned away, madame, but Soeur Gabrielle told her that she could come on Thursday morning to help with the washing.'

'If she comes tomorrow, Gaston, send her to me. I am looking for a servant.'

'*Oui, madame.*'

On Thursday afternoon Françoise was writing a letter to her aunt at Mursay when the porter brought a woman to see her. She was tall, angular, almost gaunt, barefoot and very poorly dressed, but Françoise liked the honesty of her expression. The woman looked Françoise straight in the eye and did not shift her gaze. Her lank hair was cropped short and very uneven; Françoise guessed that she had recently sold it to a wig-maker.

'Your name?'

'Nanon Balbien, madame.'

46

'You are a native of Paris?'

'I am a Gasconne, madame.' With this she unconsciously straightened her shoulders, making herself appear even taller. Françoise liked her uncompromising, even bold manner.

'And your age?'

A slight hesitation. 'Twenty-eight.' Judging by her lined and weather-beaten complexion it would have been easier to believe that she was nearer forty, but these people led such hard lives from such an early age that Françoise knew a wrinkled face was no reliable guide. The woman was obviously a peasant, used to working in the fields. Still, what did it matter so long as she was honest and did her work well?

'And your family?'

Another pause. 'I have none, madame.'

It seemed strange; but then, reflected Françoise, was she herself not in a similar position, with no close relatives? It was not hard to imagine the woman's story – some poor wretch of a husband who had either dropped dead in the fields after a lifetime of labour, or been forcibly taken for the army or the King's galleys, or had perhaps simply abandoned his wife. In any case, she thought, it is not my concern.

Aloud she said: 'What can you do, Nanon?'

'I can scrub and wash, madame. I am used to hard work.'

Poor creature, thought Françoise; that is easy to see.

'Let me see your shoulder.' Defiantly the woman bared her shoulder. There was no V for *voleuse* – thief – branded on her flesh.

'Can you cook or sew?'

There was a pause while Françoise regretted the foolishness of her question. What could a woman like this know of cookery? Such people thought themselves lucky to make porridge from the harvest gleanings. Now and then, if the husband was daring enough to risk his life poaching, they might have a hare or a chicken in some kind of stew, or sometimes a piece of salt fish might come their way, but for the greater part of the year bread and cheese, with the addition of whatever root vegetables they could find, would be their interminable diet. As for sewing, one had only to look at the woman's rough, work-worn hands to know that the question was superfluous.

Yet Françoise knew herself to be a fairly good judge of character, and there was something about the woman that she liked – the honesty of her gaze, the brevity of her answers.

Prospective servants were prone to babble on endlessly about their many accomplishments, and in particular about the financial generosity of their previous employers – so much so that one began to wonder why they had ever parted company.

'Well, Nanon, I will teach you to cook and mend. I will pay you thirty écus a month and provide for you. Will you come to me?'

'Thank you, madame.'

'Here is your bed.' Françoise pointed to the folding camp bed stored under her own curtained bed. The stone-walled room was very simply furnished, a table, two chairs, a prie-dieu, a folding stool and the writing desk Françoise had brought with her from the rue Neuve. A pair of religious tapestries on the walls completed the furnishings.

'When will you fetch your belongings?'

'I have nothing to bring, madame. You see me as I am.'

Françoise noticed that the woman's gaze lingered on the bowl of fruit on the table as she looked around the room.

'Would you like to eat something, Nanon?'

The woman seemed to swallow hard before answering. 'If madame is so kind.'

Françoise gave her some bread, a little cheese and an apple, and as an afterthought added to the plate half of the piece of salt herring she had bought that morning in the market for her dinner on Friday. Her new servant sat down, wiping her hands on her threadbare clothes and, scorning the use of the knife Françoise had given her, stared at the food for a long moment. Then, methodically breaking it all into small pieces, she began to eat, slowly at first but with ever-increasing rapidity. She has not eaten for several days, thought Françoise.

When Nanon had finished she stood up, wiping her mouth with the back of her hand.

'*Qu'est-ce que je peux faire pour vous maintenant, madame?*'

As she spoke, her face suddenly whitened and she clutched at the table for support.

'Would you like to rest a little?' asked Françoise; and Nanon stumbled to the truckle bed, pulled it out and threw herself upon it without even unfolding the blanket. In a moment she was asleep.

Françoise, sitting on her folding stool, took up her embroidery and watched her sleep soundly for several hours. As Nanon slept, with one arm over the edge of the camp bed, a cheap blackened ring which might once have been gold fell with a tinkle to the floor from her worn, bony hand. Françoise replaced it carefully on her wedding finger and returned to her sewing, looking up at the sleeping woman from time to time.

They would be together, mistress and servant, for fifty-five years.

Chapter Four

The King was bored, unutterably, inexpressibly bored. Accustomed to vigorous daily exercise in the open air, he was finding the enforced inactivity of waiting for the Queen to give birth sorely exasperating. Would the confinement never take place? The doctors had all sworn in unison that the beginning of August would be the time; it was now the third week in that month and still there was no sign of the child's imminent arrival, except for the Queen's ever-increasing languor and heaviness. Rumours were circulating the Court that the child in the Queen's womb was dead.

Louis was aware of the rumours, and although outwardly he ignored them, nevertheless he occasionally felt himself in the grip of a cold fear that there might be some truth in them. He was not a religious man, although he never failed to attend Mass, observe fast days, and give other outward signs of being a good Catholic. Yet, whenever he was with the Queen, watching that waxen, bloated face, those blank, staring eyes, and kissing that cold, flaccid hand, he found himself praying with all his soul that the child would be normal, that it would be born safely, and that it would be a son.

One morning he was sitting with his cousin Minette, his brother's wife, in her apartment, when Mme de Motteville was announced. Minette, feeling unwell, was lying on her bed propped up by pillows, pale and wan and wrapped in a shawl in spite of the heat of the day. In an effort to divert her from her discomfort, Louis had been chatting to her of the previous night's play. Through the open door the ladies-in-waiting to Madame could be glimpsed in the antechamber.

Mme de Motteville curtsied low to the King. 'Your Majesty.' Turning to Madame, she again curtsied, this time not quite so deeply. 'Madame.'

Louis smiled at his mother's companion, who had doted on him and his brother since they were born. 'What is your message, madame?'

'Sire, Her Majesty the Queen Mother asks if you will attend

her to hear Mass at twelve o'clock today.'

Louis' handsome face reddened. He knew full well why his mother had sent her companion to him with such a message. His mother was unhappy that he spent so much time in the company of his brother's wife. Well, what did she expect of him? He was temporarily restricted to the palace, for, as she well knew, he intended to be present when the Queen was confined. What did his mother wish him to do – sit with his dull wife all day whilst waiting for her to give birth? But Maria Theresa bored him to tears; and she was always bursting into tears herself, and making him feel guilty and uncomfortable because he spent so little time with her. Yet he was proud of the fact that he unfailingly awoke her, if necessary, when he came to bed – even though it had most certainly been a duty rather than a pleasure these last few nights.

Little Minette, his cousin, was so lively and cheerful, so gay and sweet. She was the only one who could divert him at the moment from his fears about the infant so slow in making its appearance. He enjoyed her inconsequential chatter about the play, the ballet, the Court in England, and her brother, the English King. Minette was lonely and neglected. Louis would never understand how his brother could prefer the company of his paramours to that of his pretty little wife.

'Inform Her Majesty my mother that I will wait upon her after I have heard Mass, and take dinner with her in her apartments.'

'Sire.' Mme de Motteville curtsied to them both and withdrew.

Louis returned to the subject of the conversation, the new play, but his previous cheerful mood was gone. Minette was quick to sense the change in his tone.

'My aunt your mother is not happy for you to spend your time with me,' she remarked sadly. As a result of the time she had spent exiled in France, her accent was a curious mixture of English and French, but not unpleasing to the ear. She had a lilting French way of speaking, unlike Maria Theresa's heavy fractured French which irritated Louis beyond endurance.

Louis knew that his mother did not suspect him of infidelity with his brother's wife. But, with the wisdom of maturity, she feared that their present closeness and their affection for one another might, in an unguarded moment, develop into something they might later regret. Her one aim was to prevent a scandal which would be harmful not only to her sons, but to Minette. Minette's mother, Henrietta Maria, was the sister of Anne's own long-dead husband, Louis XIII; Anne of Austria felt a responsibility to this little niece, only seventeen, who was being so shamefully neglected by her younger son.

Louis strongly resented his mother's interest in this affair. Did she forget that he was now twenty-three years old, a married man, and a King about to become a father? He was a most dutiful son, having only just now come from her apartments after paying his usual morning visit. Well, he was not going to jump to her every whim. He would spend a pleasant hour with Minette, and then visit her after Mass.

'My mother overlooks the fact that I am now King of France,' he said with some asperity. 'If it were not for the love I have for her, I would be inclined to answer her message more sharply, you may be sure.'

'But there is nothing improper between us, Louis, nor ever will be. You are my dear cousin, even though you insist on being King of France, and I am your brother's wife.'

At the mention of Monsieur, both fell silent. What was there to say about Philippe that would not hurt them both? Both loved him, and both felt a deep revulsion at the way in which he was beginning to spend his life. Only a week or two previously Minette had revealed that, in order to make a gift to his friend, the Chevalier de Lorraine, her husband had taken some of the jewels which were part of the dowry given to her by her brother, Charles II. Louis, seething with rage, had commanded his brother to return the jewels to his wife immediately. Monsieur, after a raging quarrel, had stormed out of his brother's presence without so much as a bow or a farewell and departed for Paris and his debauched friends, whence nothing had been heard from him for over a week. Only Louis' deep love for his wayward brother prevented him from having him clapped into the fortress of the Bastille – the certain fate of any lesser mortal who might dare to treat the King of France in such a fashion.

Minette, seeing the expression on the King's face, attempted to divert him from his thoughts. 'Do you remember, Louis, when we used to play hide-and-seek in the Tuileries gardens when I was living here with my brother?' she said, sitting upright, her large dark eyes warm with reminiscence of days long gone by. 'Do you remember the time we hunted high and low for Philippe and could not find him anywhere?'

'I remember. We eventually found him hidden underneath a baker's cart near the gates, stealing the bread rolls and eating them. What a thrashing the baker gave him!'

'I shall never forget the baker's face when he found who his culprit was!' Minette chuckled. 'Philippe was standing there, covered in sticky crumbs, crying "I am the Son of France!" How the man stared in amazement as you came along, Louis, thirteen if you were a day, drawing yourself up to your full height, and saying "That is the Duc d'Anjou, brother of the King of France. Touch him again and you will hang for it!" '

Their laughter was a tonic to them both, and Louis was grateful to Minette for relieving his black mood. What a sweet girl she was! She had the gift of being able always to perceive his moods and behave accordingly. She was ready to discuss plays and music when he felt like serious conversation, and she could always amuse him when he felt low and in need of diversion. He took her hand and kissed it affectionately. This gesture did not go unobserved by the women in the adjoining anteroom.

'I have it, Louis,' said Minette, her face resting on her knees which were drawn up to her chin in a typically unladylike attitude, her dark eyes sparkling with anticipation. 'I have conceived a marvellous plan. Since the Queen your mother is unhappy that you visit me in my rooms, you must pretend to have fallen in love with one of my young ladies. Several of them are quite pretty, so that it will be quite feasible. Then you will have a good reason to come here – to see your lady love – when in reality you come to visit me!'

'An excellent idea, Minette! Why did you not think of it earlier! But perhaps my mother will object if she thinks I am in love with anyone except my wife. She dotes on the Queen.'

'Is not the King of France entitled to take an interest in ladies other than his wife? Are you not the grandson of Henri IV?'

Henri IV, Louis' Bourbon grandfather, had been a notorious womanizer. A healthy interest in women was a trait admired and respected by the French in their King. Louis was enchanted with his cousin's plan, which not only amused him, but gave him a new sense of importance. Besides, any scheme which helped to while away these endless days of waiting appealed to him.

'The scandal-mongers who spend their time awaiting such an opportunity will soon inform my mother if I have an *amoureuse* amongst your ladies, Minette. Then she can reproach me neither by word nor look if I visit your apartments.'

'Then it remains only to select the fortunate recipient of your favours! Who shall it be?'

Louis rose and strolled across the room, glancing through the open door into the anteroom as he passed. The pageboys, under Athenais de Montespan's instructions, were about to spread a white cloth on the table and set the places for dinner. Three young ladies were clustered together, sewing, by the window, and in the far corner the Comtesse de Soissons was repairing Madame's torn riding-habit. The three girls' heads were bent intently over their work, two dark, one very fair. The remaining occupants of the room were Madame's confessor, teaching one of the pages to play backgammon, and a page polishing Madame's shoes.

'Who is the little dark girl in the red dress?' asked Louis.

'That is Mlle de Chimerault. Have you fallen in love with her already?'

'Not yet. And the one in black with a lace collar?'

'That is Mlle de Pons, my little Bretonne. She came to Court at the same time as I arrived, two months ago, and we often have a little cry for home together. But I fancy she is rather too young for such an honour as you intend to confer. She is only just turned sixteen. What about la Montespan? She is certainly beautiful enough to attract a King's attention, and she is a married woman, though she keeps her husband firmly away from Court on his Gascon estate.'

The King looked in the direction of Athenais de Montespan who, aware of his glance, began to walk about the room, turning in every direction and leaning well over the table, the better to display her charms, as she instructed the pages in their duties. Her flamboyant red-gold hair, falling loosely over her shoulders, nestled in the valley of her fine bosom.

'She is a little too overpowering, I think, for a man whose wife is about to give birth any minute, though I am not unappreciative of her charms. If I were her husband I should see that she retired to Gascony with me. I believe the winters are cold in that part of the world!'

They both laughed, thoroughly enjoying this new game.

'Then your choice must fall on Louise de la Vallière,' declared Minette. 'I am sure she is pretty enough and yet inoffensive enough to suit your taste.'

'She is the little fair one, is she not?'

'Yes, a lovely girl both in her looks and in her disposition. You will be charmed by her company on your visits here, I promise you.'

'I will see,' said Louis. '*Je verrai.*' It was his invariable answer to any suggestion. 'Now it is time for Mass, and afterwards I will dine with my mother. Perhaps I shall hint to her that I have fallen in love! *Adieu*, my dear.' He bowed low and kissed his cousin's hand.

Minette climbed off the bed to curtsy to him as he took his departure. '*Adieu*, Sire.'

At the door Louis turned back to glance in the direction of Louise de la Vallière, sitting by the window, the sunlight illuminating her ash-blonde hair and fair, delicate skin. Her colouring was similar to the Queen's, but her features far prettier than those of Maria Theresa.

'Perhaps I shall return to see my lady this evening, if she is not well enough to attend the play.'

'It will be my pleasure to welcome you, Sire. *Adieu.*'

As she lay down on her bed, Athenais de Montespan came to her. 'Will you take dinner now, Madame?'

'Thank you, no. I am feeling unwell and shall not eat today.'

The two girls regarded each other with stony resentment. Athenais was violently jealous of the English slip of a girl to whom the King paid so much attention. Minette envied not only Athenais' looks, but her freedom, in her husband's absence from Court, to indulge in any flirtation that took her fancy – while she, Minette, though tied to a man who disliked her, neglected her, and treated her badly, was unable to chat with her own cousin without censure. With a silent curtsy, Athenais withdrew.

At the dinner table Athenais ate with a hearty appetite and was full of *bonhomie*. The Comtesse de Soissons remarked upon it.

'You are full of *joie de vivre* today, Athenais. May one enquire the cause?'

'Indeed, you are mistaken, Comtesse. I am unhappy that our little Madame is indisposed.'

The Comtesse regarded her questioningly. One never knew what Athenais might be driving at. It was unlike her to show concern for anyone else. 'Madame's indisposition is no doubt due to the change of water, and possibly our food. They say the meat in England is vastly superior to ours. Madame is young, and delicate. She is probably suffering from lack of nourishment and should eat more red meat.'

Athenais chuckled, mopping up the food on her plate with a piece of bread and eating it with gusto. 'You have a family, have you not, Comtesse?'

The Comtesse looked at her with suspicion. What was Athenais getting at now? 'I have two sons, as you know, madame.'

'Then does it not strike you that Madame has now been married for two months, and that her indisposition may have a different cause?'

'She has scarcely seen her husband since her wedding day, madame!'

'He spent the wedding night with her, did he not? One night is quite sufficient for the purpose, I believe.'

The other girls at the table began to snigger. The Comtesse silenced them with a look.

'That is enough, Athenais. These girls are innocent. Pray do not refer to such unseemly topics in their hearing.'

The conversation was over. No one dared speak as they finished their meal. Athenais, however, could hardly contain her joy. The King had looked in her direction, and not without interest. Madame was very likely pregnant, and she felt sure her opportunity was likely to arise very soon. Now she would reap the rewards of discouraging other would-be contenders for her favours. She had always known that for her there would be bigger fish to fry than the Comte de Rouen and young Clermont . . . Thank God she had not allowed herself to become embroiled with them! Her reputation was still untarnished; she was a respectable married woman. Now the dreams that she had dreamed ever since she had first seen the King many years ago were about to be realized – of that she felt sure. With a light heart she drank her wine, said grace, and helped to clear away the meal.

Louise de la Vallière, engrossed in her sewing, had not even noticed the King's glance in her direction. As she took a tray of wine and water in to Madame, she could not help straightening and caressing the velvet cushions on the chair where the King had been sitting. The faintest whiff of the scent he used assailed her nostrils and filled her with joy. Then she stole quietly from the room, for Madame had fallen asleep.

During that night there was some rain, and the next day the air was so fresh and invigorating that Louis, unable to endure one more day of inactivity within the palace grounds, announced his intention of taking a short ride in the forest. The Master of the Horse was instructed to have the horses ready at eleven o'clock.

Soon after eleven the royal party rode out through the palace gates. After proceeding for a short way northward along the road to Melun, the party turned to the left, off the road into the forest itself, where they were forced to string out and ride in ones and twos owing to the narrowness of the path.

Louis, preferring as always the company of the ladies, rode alongside his cousin, Anne-Marie d'Orléans, known as Mademoiselle, or La Grande Mademoiselle. She was the daughter of his father's brother, and arch-enemy, Gaston d'Orléans, and the first lady at Court after the Queen, the Queen Mother, and Madame – who, still indisposed, was confined to her rooms this morning. Because she was one of the wealthiest women in France there had been talk in former years of marriage between Mademoiselle and the King, and later his brother Philippe, in spite of the difference in age – she was ten years older than Louis. But in the end their marriages had been arranged to bring the country political advantage. La Grande Mademoiselle's hand and her vast lands and fortune remained for the present unclaimed.

A little way behind rode the Duc de Montausier, the Duc de Montbazon, the Comte de Vardes and several others, accompanied by various ladies including Mlle de Pons and Athenais de Montespan. Grouville, the Master of the King's Horse, followed at a respectful distance.

After ten minutes or so of slow progress, walking the horses through the dense forest, they reached a clearing where the ground dropped away precipitately towards a gorge. At its bottom trickled a stream, virtually dried up after the recent drought. Pale sunlight filtered through the green and gold foliage, already preparing to assume its autumnal hue.

The King and his cousin Mademoiselle reined in their horses and watched with amusement the squirrels playing round the fallen trunks. Louis took a deep breath. How good it was to be in the open air! The damp scent of the leaves and bracken was balm to his nostrils after the close foetid atmosphere of the palace. He could not endure the stuffiness of those overheated rooms; there were no fires in this weather, of course, but thousands of candles blazed in the evenings when the rooms were overcrowded not only with members of the Court, but with people who came from afar to watch the evening entertainments, all over-perfumed, unwashed and over-dressed. The makeshift sanitary arrangements were totally inadequate for such numbers.

'How fine this air is, do you not agree, cousin?' he said to Mademoiselle.

57

'Indeed, Sire, it is a pleasure to breathe. What a pity we cannot remain longer.'

Grouville came up behind them. Removing his hat, he bowed to the King as best he could on horseback. 'There are some fine partridge in that covert over there, Sire.'

The King smiled ruefully. 'Do not put temptation in my way, Grouville. I shall return to the palace for twelve o'clock Mass, as I have arranged. Perhaps in a few days' time we shall be able to hunt once more.'

Suddenly, with a clatter of hooves, a horse passed them, covering at full gallop the dangerous rock-strewn ground which sloped sharply and dangerously towards the stream. The King stared after the rider, a young lad, in surprise. His own horse whinnied and pawed the ground impatiently.

'Who was that, Grouville?'

But before the Master of the Horse could answer him, the young rider cantered back up alongside the stream, then began galloping round and round at high speed in the lower part of the clearing. Louis saw to his amazement that the boy was riding bareback. Suddenly the boy's cap tumbled off and a cloud of long blonde hair fell to his shoulders.

'It's a woman! Who the devil is it, Grouville? She's in danger! After her, man, and help her before she's thrown!'

But the Master of the Horse, to his astonishment, did not move. 'It's Mlle de la Vallière, Sire. She is in no danger. She is the finest horsewoman I have ever seen. In fact, Sire, I would go so far as to say that I have never seen anyone ride as she can – a woman, that is,' he ended lamely, out of respect for the King, no mean horseman himself.

The three of them, Louis, Mademoiselle and Grouville, watched spellbound as the lissom young figure of Louise de la Vallière cantered round and round. The rest of the royal party had ridden on deeper into the forest. Then, to their utter astonishment, she several times stood upright on the horse's back, with only a cord in the horse's mouth for a bridle. She was clad in green breeches and a white shirt with a brown leather jerkin. Her hair was tied with a green ribbon.

Louis was transfixed. He could not take his eyes off that slim boyish figure. He could scarcely believe she was one of Madame's ladies-in-waiting, whom he usually saw so decorously employed in reading or sewing. Never in his life had he seen anyone, much less a woman, ride so superlatively, so entirely in command of both herself and her mount.

'Mlle de la Vallière is a very fine rider,' acknowledged La Grande Mademoiselle, herself an expert in the saddle.

Louise stopped her horse with a gentle touch on its neck. As it stood pawing the ground, she leapt off its back and stood patting it and trying to tie back her hair with the ribbon which had come astray, looking round for the lost cap.

Louis urged his mount forward with a slap on its rump, and he and Mademoiselle rode down the slope to her, the horses picking their way carefully over the rough stony ground.

At their approach Louise de la Vallière turned and, seeing the King, flushed scarlet to the roots of her hair. She curtsied as gracefully as was possible in breeches and boots.

The King addressed her courteously. 'We have been greatly impressed by your horsemanship, mademoiselle. Where did you learn to ride in such a fashion?'

'It is apparent that your instructor was an expert,' remarked La Grande Mademoiselle. 'Who was he?'

Louise moistened her dry lips as she answered tremulously: 'My father taught me to ride, Sire – Mademoiselle. He was a major in the cavalry and fought at La Rochelle. He taught me both to ride and to shoot.' It was the first time she had spoken to the King.

The King smiled. 'If you are as proficient a shot as you are a horsewoman, your opponent in a duel would have little chance. But a member of your fair sex has no chance to display her skill in such a fashion. 'Tis fortunate indeed. What say you, cousin? Do you not agree?'

La Grande Mademoiselle nodded her agreement. 'Do you never ride side-saddle, mademoiselle?' she asked.

'Oh certainly, Your Highness, when I must. But for preference I dress and ride in this fashion.'

Louis looked at her in undisguised admiration, striking cold fury into the heart of Athenais de Montespan who, with her companion Mlle de Pons and the rest of their party, had come up to the group in the clearing. Such a dainty, slim little thing, looking as fragile as a flower, and just as beautiful, Louis thought to himself – as if a breath of wind would blow her over. Yet how she rode a horse!

'Grouville,' the King said, 'assist mademoiselle to mount. Accompany us back to the chateau, mademoiselle, and tell us more about your father.'

Louise curtsied, but even as Grouville made to dismount she gained her horse with a flying leap and turned to follow the King and La Grande Mademoiselle. The three rode back to the palace engrossed in conversation.

Athenais de Montespan's face, as she followed behind with the remainder of the party, was hard and impassive.

Chapter Five

The entertainment at the palace that evening was to be a concert, followed by a ball. Because of the warm weather, the concert was held in the open air, on the terrace of the Cour de la Fontaine.

It was a very warm, still evening, the air a little fresher since the rain of the previous night, yet still balmy, with only the faint rustling of the leaves and the cool trickle of the fountains to be heard when the music ended. Anne of Austria, seated in the place of honour on her son's right hand, found herself conscious of vague, inner stirrings that she thought she had long forgotten. It was the perfect night for love, for satiating the desires of the flesh, a night on which all living things should come together to mate as nature had ordained. Looking down at the diamond ring on the third finger of her left hand – the priceless stone, the Rose d'Angleterre, had been Mazarin's gift to her – and listening to the music, she remembered the long, arid years of her marriage, and thought of Giulio Mazarin and the joy she had found with him.

Minette, she noticed with some disquiet, sat curled on a *tabouret* at her son's feet, listening to the music. The Queen now no longer left her rooms.

At the close of the concert it was announced, to the delight of the ladies, that a lottery was to take place before the next part of the evening's entertainment, the dancing, began. There were cries of excitement and pleasure as valuable prizes were distributed. The Comtesse de Rohan won an exquisite gold filigree scent-bottle, the Marquise de la Vrillière a carved ivory snuffbox. La Grande Mademoiselle won a dress length of valuable black English point lace. There was applause from the gathering when, having no need of it herself, she presented it to one of her ladies, Mlle de Lorges. The Comtesse de Soubise was in transports of delight over a pair of fine Spanish leather gloves. But a hush fell over the entire gathering as the King himself drew the main prize, a superb pair of matching diamond-studded bracelets.

The King looked round the assembly. In company with several others, Anne of Austria held her breath. She felt certain that he would present the bracelets to Minette.

Slowly and deliberately, the King crossed the terrace where the royal party were sitting and strolled down the steps to the courtyard, passing by both Madame and La Grande Mademoiselle. Continuing across the courtyard with his measured tread, he came to a pause where three of Madame's young ladies were seated. Mlle de Pons and Mlle de Chimerault looked on in amazement as, with a deep and graceful bow, he presented the bracelets in a most courtly manner to Louise de la Vallière.

Overcome with embarrassment at being singled out in such a fashion, conscious of the glares of the titled ladies of the Court, Louise scarcely knew what to do or say. Blushing deeply, she hung her head, and then, collecting herself with an effort, acknowledged with a curtsy the King's bow. Then, in a voice scarcely more than a whisper, she said: 'How beautiful these jewels are, Sire. I cannot accept such an exquisite gift.'

'They are in hands too fair to resign them,' murmured Louis, kissing her hand, which he could feel trembling at his touch. He fastened the bracelets on her wrists himself, unaware of the fires that leaped within her at the touch of his fingers on her flesh.

The music struck up for the dancing to begin. Louis, with a last smile for Louise de la Vallière, was about to return to the terrace when a lady was heard to remark from behind her fan: 'Is not Mlle de la Vallière duty-bound to favour His Majesty in a dance, in recognition of his generosity?' It was Athenais de Montespan.

The King turned in delight, and with another bow he extended his hand to Louise: 'Will you indeed honour me, mademoiselle?'

To his surprise he saw that the girl was overcome with confusion. Louis could not understand why the honour of his invitation should cause her distress. Such modesty was rare indeed at Court. He took her hand to lead her forward. A titter ran round the courtyard. Several of the ladies who a moment previously had been glaring at the young girl, so lovely in her white satin dress, and with her long blonde hair dressed in smooth ringlets, were now openly sniggering. Louis frowned.

Louise de la Vallière looked up at him pleadingly. 'Sire, I beg of you to excuse me.'

'I cannot, mademoiselle. I insist that you honour me with this dance.' He was mystified as to the cause of the general amusement but realized that if he retired there would only be more sniggers at Louise's expense.

There was to be no escape. Louise laid her hand on the King's arm, pale as death. He led her into the centre of the courtyard; and only then, as the music struck up the *branle* and they began to dance, did he understand the cause of Louise's embarrassment, and the reason for Athenais' suggestion.

This girl, who could ride like the wind, had an impediment in her gait. She was an ungainly dancer, and indeed executed some of the movements with considerable difficulty, her eyes lowered and her face white. Athenais de Montespan, Louis noted out of the corner of his eye, could scarcely conceal her amusement. To his fury, he now understood that, seeing his awakening interest in Louise, Athenais had deliberately subjected the girl to this ordeal. He resolved that she would be punished for it. But with his habitual imperturbable expression, he gave no sign of noticing Louise's handicap.

Mercifully, the dance soon came to an end. The King's expression was impassive as he escorted Louise to her seat and took his leave of his partner with his customary grace and charm. Did his lips linger a second or two as he kissed her hand in farewell? Anne of Austria and Madame, watching anxiously from the terrace, could not be sure. Anne was delighted at the turn things had taken. Madame, as she began to realize the fruition of the plans she herself had laid, was not so sure.

In the next few days, the sole topic of conversation at Court, replacing even that of the Queen's forthcoming confinement, was Louise de la Vallière. Was the King about to make her his mistress? Was she to be the next in the long line of beauties who had been Queens in all but name, Gabrielle d'Estrées, Anne d'Etampes, and Diane de Poitiers? Maria Theresa and her endless pregnancy were forgotten as bets were laid on the chances of the new contender – the previous odds having been laid heavily on Madame.

There was no doubt that the King was taking a growing interest in the little la Vallière. Madame, having recovered from her indisposition, watched, increasingly perturbed, as the King, in the company of her own lady-in-waiting, strolled in the gardens, feeding the carp in the Fontaine de Diane, and then began riding off into the forest with her on excursions which became daily longer and longer. Athenais watched with similar dismay; the Queen Mother with pleasure – though not without concern for her niece.

The King was determined that Athenais' vindictive spite in

deliberately exposing his sweetheart to discomfiture and ridicule should not go unremarked. Louise, with her gentle forgiving nature, had asked the King to overlook the incident, but he was adamant. Within a week Athenais was handed a letter giving her her *congé*, a royal command to absent herself from Court for a period of not less than three months.

Fontainebleau, always the home of lovers, was the perfect setting for *amour*. Henri II with his adored Diane de Poitiers, Henri IV and his mistress Gabrielle d'Estrées, had strolled in these gardens, embraced under these very trees. The gardens, with their cool fountains splashing, and their shady arbours, were a constant temptation to lovers to dally and linger, murmuring their protestations of love and desire, soon, very soon, to be fulfilled. Inside the chateau, the Renaissance galleries were profusely decorated with frescoes, paintings and sculptures portraying sensuous goddesses with high breasts and long curving limbs in voluptuous attitudes of love. These works of art, created at first under the patronage of François I and later his son Henri II, were the inspiration of the sixteenth-century Italian masters, Rosso and Primaticcio, who strove to re-create here in cold northern France the atmosphere and passions of warmer, southern climes. Even the ballets and plays, performed each stiflingly hot evening while the fountains splashed in the court-yard and the still night air was heavy with the fragrance of late summer, constantly emphasized the pleasures of love.

At last, one sultry afternoon in the last week of August, in a room lent to the lovers by the Comte d'Aignan, First Gentleman of the Bedchamber, Louise de la Vallière became the King's mistress.

Never had the act of love afforded Louis such intoxicating pleasure, such sweet satisfaction, as did the seduction and final surrender of Louise de la Vallière, this fragile girl with the angelic face and delicate features.

'*Ma petite fleur,*' he murmured in her ears, covering them with kisses as they lay naked on the camp bed in the hot, untidy little room. '*Comme tu es belle!*'

The drawn blinds and the locked door made the darkened, suffocating chamber seem like an island of their own in a sea of eternity, a world away from the State bedrooms where Louis formally bedded his Queen amidst pomp and ceremony.

Louise took his hand and kissed its palm then, overcome by

shyness, buried her head in his shoulder, hiding her face and caressing the dark hair on his chest with her fingers. '*Que je t'aime, je t'aime,*' she whispered almost inaudibly.

Her diffidence, her almost childlike innocence and above all, her chastity, appealed to the side of Louis' nature which had been influenced by his mother, who had taught him to respect and revere pure women. The coarser, Bourbon streak of sensuality was as yet untapped. Her gentleness was in striking contrast to the blatant exhibitionism of women such as Athenais de Montespan, who spent so much time and effort scheming to attract his attention. Louise alone had never tried to win his favour, for she had never dared to hope that he might return her love. She loved him wholeheartedly, entirely for himself, and coveted neither luxuries nor a high position at Court. Although he had taken her virginity, he was surprised by her passionate response. He had not realized how deeply she was in love with him, and that she had been for many months. That was a pleasure as yet not revealed to him: that she had loved him from the moment she had first seen him.

Both were totally overwhelmed by this new and intoxicating fire of their passion for each other. Louis, completely at peace, felt as though he had made love to a woman for the first time. He twined his fingers in the cloud of fair hair and caressed the whiteness of her bosom, soft as a baby's skin.

As they lay there, both reluctant to speak, to shatter the spell of the enchantment they had created for themselves that afternoon in the tiny bedroom under the eaves of the old palace, there was a sudden rap at the door. Louis frowned. No one but the Comte d'Aignan knew who was in the room.

The knocking continued. The King pulled on his breeches and shirt, and swearing under his breath, opened the door. D'Aignan stood there, red-faced, embarrassed and breathless.

'It is the Queen, Sire! The Queen is brought to bed!'

In the Queen's crowded apartment the atmosphere was so stuffy as to be almost unbearable. Louis and his mother, sitting on either side of the Queen's bed, continually mopped themselves with handkerchiefs. Sweat trickled down Maria Theresa's waxen face. She made no sound as waves of pain spasmodically washed over her and then receded, leaving her limp and passive, awaiting the next onslaught. From her earliest years she had been steeled to undergo this ordeal with courage. One of the chief purposes of her strict and pious Spanish upbringing had been to instil into her a sense of the fortune and honour that were to be hers in giving birth to the French Dauphin.

Clustered round the foot of the bed were five of the physicians to the King, one of whom claimed some knowledge of gynaecology. He had an excellent reputation, being known to have saved the lives of several ladies suffering from milk-fever in the early days following their confinement, by prescribing them violent purgatives to cleanse their systems of the harmful substances remaining in the body. Anne of Austria, who had consulted him on many occasions, had great confidence in him. Several priests were in the room, including the Queen's confessor, and also in attendance were the Duchess d'Elbeo, Doña Molina, the Queen's childhood nurse, and two other Spanish ladies to whom the Queen had promised, when she first came to France, the honour of witnessing the birth. And, besides the Council Ministers, whose presence was necessary in order to verify the birth, were as many members of the Court as were able to crowd into the room.

As the daylight started to fade, and the summer evening to grow dim, everyone present began to remark on the King's calm composure. Looking round the room, Louis took note of all who were present and was heard to say: 'Monsieur le Prince de Condé is not here. See that he is sent for immediately at Chantilly.'

Slowly the hours dragged by and evening faded into night. The Queen had felt the first pains at half past three that afternoon. Now, in the silence of the night, the clock tower by the Chapel of Ste Trinité could be heard striking four o'clock. Doña Molina leaned forward to wipe the Queen's brow with a damp sponge. The knotted towels were ready to hand her if she desired them. Louis turned to his mother, who, white with exhaustion, was beginning to slump in her chair.

'Madame, I beg you, retire to your rooms. I myself will acquaint you with the news when it is time.'

'Please do not ask me this, my son. Theresita might have need of me.'

Louis looked down at his wife's still form, her face half turned into the pillow. She had not moved, apart from seeming to flinch occasionally with pain, for some little time. Her eyes were closed and her breathing shallow.

'You can see she is not fully conscious. I insist, madame, that you retire.'

Anne hesitated. It would be a relief to let her ladies undress her, and to lie down, resting her weary limbs, to close her eyes. 'You promise that you will send if she should ask for me? I shall not be free from anxiety until I know – '

Louis rose and bowed politely to his mother. 'Good night, madame. Rest well. I myself shall come to you as soon as there is news. You have my word.'

Anne kissed her niece, looking hopefully for some sign of recognition, but the Queen's eyes were still closed, her nostrils pinched, and she seemed to be unconscious. The doctors at the foot of the bed murmured amongst themselves. Anxiously Anne made her way through the crowded room, the courtiers standing back respectfully to let her pass.

In her own apartments she stood leadenly as Mme de Motteville and her ladies helped to undress her. 'Light the tapers,' she said. She knew there was little chance that she would sleep, though she felt physically exhausted.

Obediently she lay down on the bed, to please Mme de Motteville. After the women had left her she rose, wrapped her dressing-gown round her, and stood looking out of the window, watching the first hesitant grey light of dawn lengthening the shadows over the Cour de la Fontaine. The sound of birdsong in the surrounding forest heralded the beginning of a new day. Would this day see the birth of a Dauphin? And her little niece, Maria Theresa, would she survive her confinement? Anne feared that a person of her small stature would have a difficult time. She knelt at her prie-dieu and prayed fervently for the safety of Maria Theresa, for the child to be born safely, in good health. She dared not pray that it would be a son. God's will must be welcomed with joy.

Lying on the bed once more, she tried not to think about pain, the pain that Maria Theresa was suffering, which, thank God, would be short-lived, whatever the outcome. But the pain she herself felt – had felt ever since that day some months ago when she first discovered the small tumour in her right breast, pain that she had felt only spasmodically at first, every few weeks or so – that pain was coming more and more frequently now, so that sometimes, when with her son, or in public, she had to clench her teeth and dig her nails into the palms of her hands in order not to reveal the agony that seemed to stab into her very vitals.

It would not diminish, she knew, but become worse, and there would be no relief from its grip. One of the King's former wet-nurses had died from this disease, wasting away, every day more yellow and twisted, growing weaker and weaker until both she and her son had been glad when the poor creature was relieved from her sufferings.

She dared not tell Louis of her discovery. How long, she wondered, would she be able to keep it from him? He was already noticing how tired and weary she looked. Suddenly, she had become an old woman.

She must have dozed a little while, for suddenly Mme de Motteville was shaking her shoulder, and Louis was gazing down at her. One look at his face told her all that she needed to know.

'My son! Is it over?'

'We have a prince, my mother! Your grandson is born, safe and well. A Dauphin for France!'

'*Gracias a Dios!* And Theresita?'

'She is well. I have a son, mother, I have a son!'

Mme de Motteville stole silently away, leaving mother and son to weep together in their emotion and joy.

Chapter Six

One cold wintry morning early in January 1666 Nanon, waking Françoise with a steaming cup of coffee, told her: 'The old Queen is dead, madame. They say she died in the night.'

'It is a merciful release,' said Françoise sadly. 'She had an incurable cancer, and I believe the doctors could not ease her pain. May God have mercy on her soul, for she was a good and charitable woman.'

All that day the bells of Notre Dame and most of the other churches of Paris tolled ceaselessly, and people went about their business soberly, for Anne of Austria had been popular amongst them. Had she not given them their handsome king – *le Roi Soleil* as they called him? Times had been difficult for many years now, but they bore their poverty and near-starvation, working the land and giving most of its fruits to the seigneur, with peasant stolidity, trusting in their beloved King to improve matters. He was young, his pleasantness and charm were legendary, and he had given them a Dauphin. The people of France sincerely mourned the Queen Mother, but looked hopefully to the future they trusted Louis XIV to provide.

For the last three or four years Françoise and Nanon Balbien had been living in a little house which had a modest rent in the rue des Tournelles. As time went by Françoise had found the convent life far too restricting. She realized that, with her pension providing the mainstay of her income, there was no real need for her to take up a position under someone else's roof and relinquish her treasured independence; but it was impossible to repay her friends' hospitality and entertain visitors in the convent. The Duc de Richelieu, who owned most of the property in this district of Paris, had been kind enough to let Françoise take over the tenancy of the house when the previous occupant died.

The house was small, but amply comfortable for their needs. There was a little anteroom as you came in, where guests could leave their wraps and swords, and where Françoise would often ask a waiting coachman to step inside out of the cold on a winter's day. Behind this room was the kitchen, where Nanon slept on a camp bed. On the floor above was the pleasant salon, just the right size for an intimate *soirée*, where eight people could sit down to dine, or at a pinch, ten. A small bedroom for Françoise led from the *salon intime*.

Wrapped up warmly against the cold, Françoise went to hear Mass for the Queen Mother's soul at the church of St Eustache. On her way home, a thought struck her. What would happen to her State pension now? Would it cease with the death of the Queen Mother?

Well, even so, she thought, I'm no worse off than I was five years ago. I could easily obtain a post as a governess now, I'm sure. A good deal of her time was spent teaching her friends' children their catechism, reading to them or amusing them if they were sick. All her friends agreed that Françoise had a marvellous way with children, and infinite patience.

The young widow had the *entrée* to the very best salons of Paris and was popular with everyone. Men liked her – excepting those whose advances, made behind their wives' backs, she rejected – children adored her and the women all found her quite indispensable. Not only was her skill in keeping a conversation flowing an asset to any hostess, but the discreet Madame Scarron could also be relied on occasionally to help her society friends settle their gambling debts without troubling their husbands, perhaps by disposing unobtrusively of a valuable piece of jewellery for them. Her manner, when addressed by the gentlemen, was always circumspect, as befitted a respectable widow; but what made her so invaluable in the eyes of her friends was that she appeared to have no designs on their husbands, nor even – more important – on their servants.

A curious relationship had developed between Françoise and Nanon. Although there was a class difference which could never be bridged, the two women had long since become closer than mistress and servant. Their relationship was one of friendship and affection, marked always with respect on the part of Nanon, and sincerity on that of Françoise. Perhaps their similar lack of close family ties accounted for the development of the bond between them.

Nanon had never been any more forthcoming on the subject of her family background than on the day when she entered Françoise's employ, and Françoise, surmising that the years before Nanon came to live with her held painful memories, never made any attempt to probe into her servant's private life.

Other than that she wore a wedding ring, and that she had always paid the nuns in the convent to recite Masses for the repose of the dead each year on 23rd February, Françoise knew nothing of her maid's former life. She knew her now, however, to be completely honest, and capable of any trust which Françoise might place in her, and she valued her accordingly.

For some time now they had abandoned the system of paying Nanon wages, and simply shared whatever they had. Françoise's income consisted of her State pension, a small income from the estate of her late aunt, and fluctuating and irregular payments from her friends in recompense for the many services she gave them. Nanon's contribution to the household was the money she earned by taking in washing, and by going out in the early morning to scrub the steps of elegant town houses where the well-paid servants were too lazy to do their own work. She also polished the convent silver once a month.

They lived quietly and frugally, save when guests were invited, and Françoise was careful always to pay the rent six months in advance. The market women of les Halles knew better than to try to give Madame Scarron or her maid bruised apples or a short weight of flour. Mistress and servant often went to the market late on a Saturday, when fruit and vegetables were being sold cheaply. As Françoise walked on ahead, Nanon would often stoop to pick up a cabbage or cauliflower which had rolled off a stall, and put it in her basket.

Several of her wealthy friends passed on their dresses, worn only once or twice, to Françoise, so that, after the cost of food and firewood, their chief expenditure was at the little cobbler's shop in the rue du Pas de la Mule, where Françoise had a pair of shoes made twice a year, at Easter time and Michaelmas, and a pair of sabots for Nanon. Because Nanon's feet were two sizes larger than those of her mistress, shoes could not be handed on. Once or twice a year, a hired bath was brought to the house – the copper one for Françoise cost twenty sous for the day, the wooden one, for Nanon, only ten.

Nanon, however, in addition to making all their candles, proved to have an unexpected talent for shoe-repairing, and managed to keep their shoes in use for some considerable time. She had also, under Françoise's tuition, become quite adept with a needle. The two women often chuckled over the episode of a dark blue calico dress which had been given to Françoise by one of her friends. Françoise, after wearing it for some time, gave it to Nanon who, preferring clothes a little less sober in colour, brightened it up by adding some flower-sprigged muslin at the neck and sleeves, and a deep frill round the hem to add the requisite length for her height. The dress looked so attractive when finished that Françoise took to wearing it again, having first had to shorten the frill; and the end of the story was that it was admired by Mme d'Heudicourt, who had given it to Françoise in the first place!

At the salon of Ninon de l'Enclos in the Place Royale that January evening, however, the talk was all of the death of the old Queen and the King's grief.

'The King has gone to Versailles to mourn, and will return to Paris for the interment in Saint Denis in February,' the Duc de Coislin told Françoise in Ninon's famous Yellow Room, where everyone in chic Parisian society met from time to time on Friday evenings. 'It seems that he is completely stricken by his mother's death, although it was well known that the doctors had long since given up all hope.'

'Nevertheless, to lose a much loved mother, who has always been so close to him, must be a shattering experience,' Françoise said. 'Even when it has been expected, the finality of death still comes as a shock.' She was remembering how much she had missed her husband when he died, far more than she had expected.

Although as fond as ever of her friend Ninon, she was an infrequent visitor to Ninon's salon, not caring to have her name closely linked with that of the most famous courtesan in Paris. She preferred to entertain Ninon in her own home, where the two friends often spent a pleasant afternoon drinking chocolate à deux.

'Our beloved King must be sorely grieved over the loss of his mother,' Mme de Beauvais was saying. 'Of course, his father is only a memory. His dear mother was everything to him.'

Everyone listened to the plump, rosy-cheeked Mme de Beauvais with close attention, for it was supposedly she, a former lady-in-waiting to Anne of Austria, who, acting on the late Queen's instructions, had been instrumental in helping Louis to part with his virginity at the age of fifteen. Now the wife of a rich banker, she lived in a mansion in the rue François-Miron.

Out of respect for the late Queen, Ninon had cancelled the musicians who were to have entertained her guests that evening, and, now that supper was over, the visitors sat talking quietly in little groups.

'The King will derive some consolation from the Duc d'Orléans, will he not?' Françoise asked. 'I believe he is much attached to his brother.'

'It is not always easy to understand the King,' replied Mme de Beauvais. 'Perhaps because he became conscious of his strong reliance on his mother at an early age, he is most at his ease in the company of women; although it is true to say that he loves his brother dearly. Yet he keeps Monsieur at a distance.'

'It would seem that they proceed in opposite directions most of the time,' Blanche d'Heudicourt remarked maliciously, for it was true that Louis was always surrounded by the ladies – his wife, his mother, his sister-in-law, Madame, and his mistress, Louise de la Vallière – whereas his brother's marked propensity for the company of young men only seemed to increase with the years.

'Do you know,' continued Mme de Beauvais, 'that every morning his old wet-nurse, Perette Dufour, has the *entrée* to his apartment, to kiss him good morning. Our dear King never forgets those to whom he owes an obligation.'

'In that case he must be possessed of an astonishing memory,' remarked Françoise, at which everyone burst out laughing.

'The question now being discussed feverishly at Court,' said the Duchesse de Coislin, who with her husband had brought Françoise to the Place Royale in their coach, 'is whether or not the King will officially recognize his mistress la Vallière, now that his mother is dead.'

'But it is common knowledge that Louise de la Vallière has been his mistress for nearly five years,' said Françoise.

'And during that time she has borne the King at least two children – or is it three?' asked Mme d'Heudicourt.

'And what has become of these children? Are they living at Court?' Françoise asked.

'Of course not,' someone answered. 'What a scandal that would cause! They are being looked after by Mme Colbert, but I believe – '

'But they both died,' said Mme de Beauvais, 'the first little one in its first winter, and the baby only a few weeks ago, poor thing. Fortunately they had both been baptized.'

'How sad,' said Françoise, remembering her own childhood, when she had been bandied about like a parcel from one aunt to another, and scarcely knew her mother. Very many babies die soon after birth, I know, she thought, but these poor little ones did not even have the loving attention of a mother or father during their short sojourn on this earth. But Mme Colbert, the wife of the King's financial controller, was an excellent woman; they would not have been neglected.

'But out of respect for his dear mother the King has never yet given his mistress official recognition as *maîtresse en titre*, and the children were illegitimate,' Mme de Beauvais continued.

'But can la Vallière continue to hold her position?' said Mlle de Scudéry. 'I hear that there is another contestant gazing at that most glorious pinnacle with starry eyes.'

Mlle de Scudéry, a tall thin person in her late fifties, with scraped-back, greying hair, her pince-nez perched on the end of her nose, looked nothing like what she actually was, Françoise thought with some amusement – a successful authoress whose books were in great demand by everyone in society.

'You are beginning to sound like one of your own novels, Mlle de Scudéry,' remarked the Duc de Coislin. 'I must beg to be excused from the rest of this conversation.' And he went off to join another group, leaving the ladies to their gossip.

'It's true that the King's visits to the Hôtel de Brion are not now so frequent,' observed Gisèle d'Albret. The Hôtel de Brion was a little house in the grounds of the Palais Royal in which Louis had established his mistress.

'In that case, Mlle de la Vallière must have had the assistance of divine intervention,' said Ninon de l'Enclos, joining their group, 'for I have it on very good authority that she is pregnant again.'

'There is someone – I shall call her Quanto – who will not be pleased to hear that,' said Madame d'Albret.

Everyone smiled at this reference to Athenais de Montespan, an incorrigible and reckless gambler. *Quanto va?* was a phrase used in the game of *hoca*, at which she was known to have regularly staked large sums of money.

'On the contrary, Quanto may well be pleased to hear that her rival is incapacitated for a time. It may give her the advantage she needs to strike home,' Mme de Beauvais pointed out.

'Come, ladies, you've had enough time for gossip,' the Maréchal d'Albret remonstrated, beckoning to a lackey to bring his wife's furs. Amidst general laughter the group reluctantly broke up. Françoise, standing beside the Duchesse de Coislin as they waited for the servants to bring their wraps, said as she looked around: 'I don't see Madame de Sévigné here this evening.'

'My dear Françoise! Can you be serious? She has never set foot in the salon of Mlle de l'Enclos, and never will, if I am not mistaken.'

'For what reason?'

'You really don't know? I suppose you are too young to remember, my dear. Mme de Sévigné's husband was killed in an *affaire d'honneur* which was fought over Mlle de l'Enclos. Our friend was a widow at the age of twenty-six. And to cap it all I hear it said' – she leaned closer to Françoise and lowered her voice – 'that the son is going the same way as his father. But do not repeat this, I beg you.'

'Ninon is ageless,' said Françoise, as she watched her friend, beautiful as ever, bidding her guests goodnight.

Chapter Seven

Almost exactly twelve months later, late in the month of January 1667, the woman who had been referred to as Quanto was to be found pacing the apartments of the Palais Royal, the Paris residence of Monsieur and Madame, in a state of some agitation.

Athenais de Rochechouart-Mortemart, since her marriage Mme de Montespan, was walking up and down the length of the elegant salon hung with exquisite paintings and works of art. She seemed, however, totally uninterested in her surroundings, and went constantly to the window, drawing aside the heavy blue gold-corded curtains to watch visitors coming and going in the snow-covered courtyard outside.

Suddenly she started up as the door opened, but instead of the person she awaited, a young maid entered the room.

'Will you take dinner with Mme de Brancas and Mme d'Heudicourt, madame? They are awaiting you in the antechamber.'

'No. Tell them to dine without me. If a visitor asks for me, Lison, see that he is sent up here directly.'

'*Oui, madame.*'

Athenais sat down in front of the fire to warm her stiff hands, for the room was icy in spite of the brisk blaze. As the gold carriage-clock struck two there was a sound of boots and Louis Victor, Comte de Mortemart, Duc de Vivonne was announced.

A tall, handsome man in his early thirties, with a soldier's bearing, wearing a sword and a fur-lined cloak, strode into the room. Though his wavy chestnut hair was darker than that of Athenais, there was nevertheless a marked resemblance between brother and sister.

'Vivonne!' Athenais sprang to her feet and embraced her brother warmly. After giving her a perfunctory kiss, he flung off his cloak and advanced towards the fire.

'*Nom de Dieu!* Have you ever known such weather! Yesterday, on the way in to Paris, we could get no food at any of the inns where we stopped. We went from seven in the morning until eight at night with only a drink to sustain us. I was afraid my horse would drop dead under me with hunger and exhaustion.'

'I left a message for you to come to me immediately. Did you go straight to bed?'

'What – in Paris! Certainly not! What do you take me for! You have become very sober now that you are a wife and mother. I was out carousing until three this morning. That's why I have only just got out of bed. Is there any food to be had here, Athenais?'

'I will order something for you in a moment, Vivonne. But first I want to talk to you.'

'I'll talk much better on a full stomach, I promise you. Here' – he passed her a handbell which stood on a small table – 'allow me something to eat, and I'll be in a much better mood for talking.'

Forced to acknowledge the truth of this, Athenais rang the bell and ordered Lison to bring food and wine. Then she turned to her brother who, with his long legs outstretched and his head flung back against his chair, looked ready to fall asleep.

'You are looking in fine fettle, Athenais,' he remarked, admiring the heavy green velvet dress which so admirably suited her auburn-haired beauty. 'And where is my good brother-in-law today? And my nephew d'Antin?'

'They are in the country. Montespan took d'Antin to see his grandmother for Christmas and the New Year. Monsieur and Madame are gone to St Cloud.'

'And you stayed here, alone, over the festive season? You are up to some little game – what is it? No, no,' he held up his hand as she started to interrupt, 'come now, Athenais, I know you! What is it? You can confide in your brother. A little dalliance you don't want Montespan to know of? Well, no great harm in that. But you will remember that your sister is now the Abbess of Thianges, will you not? We don't want any disgrace in the family!' And he laughed heartily. To his even greater amusement Athenais, prevented by the arrival of the maid from answering, could only glower at him. Lifting the folds of her heavy velvet gown, she swished round to the window where she stood looking out until the maid, having put the food and wine down on a tray, had gone. Then she turned on him with a flushed face.

'You are insufferable! Why do you jump to such conclusions? Have I said anything about a lover?'

'Then why the need to see me so urgently?'

'I wrote to you before Christmas. Did you not receive my letter?'

'Oh – something about paying gambling debts, was it not?' He took out his purse. 'Don't allow that to worry you, my dear Athenais. I'm happy to give you a Christmas present. How much do you need? One thousand louis?'

Athenais clenched her hands with rage but, controlling her temper, spoke clearly and evenly. 'I wrote to you bidding you ask my father to advance me fifteen thousand louis to pay my debts, which I will repay him over a period of five years from the rents on my dower estates, so that I need have no recourse to Montespan.'

'But why should Montespan not have the privilege of paying his wife's debts?'

Athenais poked the fire, wondering whether to take him into her confidence, but decided against it. 'Because the last time he paid my debts he restricted me to a limit of five thousand louis on any one occasion, which I have considerably exceeded.'

'But why not write to father yourself? An agreement of this nature must, in any case, be put in writing.'

Athenais smiled up at her brother as he came to stand beside her, munching a drumstick. 'You have so much more influence with him than I, Vivonne. I must beg him for a favour on my knees, whereas he would be loath to refuse you, his heir.'

'Nonsense, Athenais. You have always been able to twist men round your little finger, and father was the victim on whom you first practised when you were scarcely out of the cradle. Now, let us start again. Why do you really need this money? Are you with child?'

Athenais jumped to her feet. 'You forget yourself! Have I not already told you that I do not have a lover?'

'There is, of course, your husband,' her brother said, meditatively chewing at his chicken leg and spitting the skin into the fire. 'I suppose it would not be beyond the bounds of possibility for you to be respectably *enceinte*.'

'That is not the case, I assure you.'

'Very well. Then why do you need this money?'

Watching her silent face carefully, he said: 'Tell me, what news is there of the King and the Court these days? I hear that la Vallière is pregnant again.'

Her face told him all he needed to know. 'Where did you hear that?' It was almost a shriek.

78

Trying to control his amusement, he replied as he handed her a glass of wine: 'Why, 'tis the talk of Paris, or at least, it's all I heard talked of in the taverns we visited last night. *A votre santé!* Your good health, my dear sister.'

'It's not true! The King is tired of her!'

'You think so? It would seem otherwise to me, but then I do not live at Court, for which God be praised.'

'Vivonne! You must obtain that money for me!'

Disengaging her arms, he said quietly: 'Only if I know what is its purpose.'

'The King is tiring of la Vallière! The simpering, crippled, pockmarked ninny! How she has held him for five years I shall never know. But she will not keep him through another pregnancy, that I know!'

'But was it not la Vallière who returned to the ball fully dressed, when the Court was at St Germain last October, having given birth to her daughter that very afternoon? The delicate features of Mlle de la Vallière would seem to conceal an iron constitution.'

'A pox on her!' Athenais raged. 'Her fourth pregnancy in five years! The Queen has also carried four children in the last few years. She is only just got up from her lying-in. The King must be heartily sick of pregnant women. He will start to look in other directions –'

'And you think the rays of the Sun King will fall upon you, Athenais?'

'And why not? I have waited so long for the King. Ever since I first saw him, before his marriage, I have thought of no one else.'

'Not even your husband?'

'Not even my husband.'

'Nor your son?'

'Certainly not my son. He is nearly three years old, and will soon be sent to a tutor.'

'Perhaps he would prefer to see his mother more often?'

But Athenais was not listening. She held out her hands to the fire, and staring fixedly into its blaze said, as if to herself: 'I have only one dream – to have the King as my lover. Why else do you think I stay here, at Madame's beck and call, dependent on her every whim when I could be mistress on my own estates, ordering others to and fro?'

'And how do you intend to achieve this, Athenais? For I

know you better than to imagine you will allow things to take their own course. You have some scheme well planned, I doubt not. You can confide in your own brother. Come, tell me.'

'I have a plan, I don't deny it. For six years I have waited, to no avail. Now I intend to help things along a little.'

'And just how do you propose to do this?'

'The King is not insensible to my looks, I know,' said Athenais. She stood up, and turning this way and that in front of the gilt carved mirror which hung above the fire, noted approvingly her shapely outline, svelte and graceful, the body of a young matron, the breasts full and round, having fulfilled their purpose but unspoiled as yet by constant childbearing. 'I have often seen him looking at me when he comes to visit Madame.'

'But does he come to see Madame or her ladies-in-waiting? I wonder how it is that Madame is not afraid to have two such beautiful flowers in her garden. I suppose it is because she has no fears of Monsieur being affected by their beauty. I am happy I need not fear for my sister's virtue.'

'Pray do not concern yourself with my virtue. I shall be the custodian of that. Procure the money for me, I beg you, Vivonne, and I guarantee, within six months I shall be the King's mistress and you will be well recompensed for your trouble.'

'And our father?'

'He shall have his money three times over.'

'But you still have not revealed your plans to me.'

'And I have no intention of doing so. I simply repeat, within six months I shall be by the King's side.'

Her brother walked over to the window and stared out at the snowy courtyard where his horse was being walked up and down by a lackey. Coachmen warmed their hands at braziers and horses stamped their feet and whinnied, their breath forming little white clouds in the cold air.

'You must allow me to question your confidence, Athenais. You have been in the household of Madame, first as lady-in-waiting, then as maid-of-honour for – what is it now – five years?'

'Six.'

'And in the course of this period you have often been seen by the King?'

'Of course.'

'And does he speak with you?'

'Twelve months ago, when our mother died soon after the old

Queen, he expressed his condolences to me. And he enquired after my health when I had the measles, shortly after that: but la Vallière, a pox on her, told him that as I was not looking my best covered in blotches, I had no desire to see anyone.'

'Then what reason have you to think that after all this time he will suddenly single you out?'

'Because, my dear brother, I have already told you, la Vallière is a fool, nothing but a simpering fool. Men must eventually tire of those big blue eyes and breathless endearments. Now that she is pregnant again, three months after her last confinement, the King will start to look around him.'

Louis Victor, Duc de Vivonne returned to the fireside, threw himself down in the armchair and crossed his long legs, staring meditatively into the fire. 'Have you considered that he might rediscover the charms of his wife?'

'What! The King settle down to a life of devotion and prayer with that dowdy Spanish nun he's married? It is not in his nature, I assure you. No, the King will seek a replacement for la Vallière, and I intend to fill the gap. I know that he finds me attractive, but my face has become too familiar. I intend to employ some bold tactics to bring myself anew to his attention.'

'And what is this master-stroke to be?'

'Can you allow a woman no secrets? Confine your attentions to my success, in which you will richly share, I promise you.'

He laughed, rose, throwing his cloak over his arm, and bent to kiss her goodbye.

'I will do what I can for you, Athenais, since it would appear to be to our mutual advantage. Let us both hope your confidence is not unfounded. *Adieu.*'

'As soon as possible, Vivonne! Promise me! Monsieur and Madame return from St Cloud at the end of February.'

'And your husband?'

'The Devil take him!'

'May God preserve me from women,' her brother said as he took his departure. At the door he turned. 'You know that the name I bear, Rochechouart-Mortemart, is one of the oldest and most honoured in France. Have I your assurance that you intend to do nothing which will cast a slur on that name?'

'Unless you consider that your sister being *la maîtresse en titre* to the King casts a slur on your honour, I give you my word.'

Satisfied, he saluted her and left. Athenais listened to his footsteps as they went and then watched him ride away from the window.

The little maid, Lison, appeared in response to her summons.

'*Oui, madame?*'

'A carriage, immediately. And bring my fur cloak and muff. Quick! *Dépêche-toi!*'

Warmly wrapped in her cloak, the hood framing her hair and a mask held to her face, Athenais hurried out to the waiting coach and ordered the coachman to drive to the well-known beauty shop in the rue St Denis, *A la Perle des Mouches*.

Hardly had the carriage left the grounds of the Palais Royal, however, when Mme de Montespan, apparently changing her mind, ordered the coachman to take her instead to the establishment of a certain Mme Voisin, a charlatan, in the rue St Antoine.

Chapter Eight

Two or three weeks later, towards the end of February, the snow on the ground had gone but it was still bitterly cold. Few people were about to watch the arrival of the King's guests at the Palace of the Louvre, although it was only nine o'clock in the evening. Well wrapped in furs, the visitors were loath to part with their wraps on entering the palace, where even the blazing fires in the State rooms and the thousands of candles in their silver candelabra could not warm the chill corridors, and the smoky draughts from the old fireplaces made the air sharp and unpleasant. Freezing gusts of air blew from the wide staircases and through the open doors, for the King liked his guests to wander freely through the State rooms at these *soirées – Jours d'Appartements*, the entertainments were called.

Tonight there was to be a violin concert; sometimes there was a ballet performance in which the King, an excellent and graceful dancer, might take part. Until supper was served and the entertainment began, visitors could stroll through the apartments chatting, mingling freely and gossiping apace, admiring the paintings and works of art, playing billiards if they so desired, or gambling. Tables were laden with every kind of cold meat, crystallized fruits cleverly arranged in pyramids, nuts, sweetmeats, all beautifully laid out on silver dishes, and the guests were encouraged to help themselves. The vast silver containers holding wine, lemonade, tea, coffee or chocolate, were constantly being refilled. Footmen strolled throughout the crowded gaming-room bearing trays of glasses of wine so that those seated at the tables need not leave the play to refresh themselves. The atmosphere here was stuffy and oppressive, the fireplaces smoked badly, and the low ceilings were not conducive to good ventilation.

Athenais de Montespan, sitting near the gaming-tables, fanning herself as she looked round the room, nodding and smiling occasionally to a passing acquaintance, noticed neither the stuffiness nor the cold, though many of the ladies found an excuse to linger near the fire. She was conscious only of the knowledge that this was the occasion for which she had waited so long, for which she had so long planned and dreamed that she felt that she knew its outcome before it even took place. An electric thrill seemed to permeate her whole body; the knowledge that tonight she was going to risk everything she possessed in an all-out bid to capture the King.

There could be no going back, she knew. The financial outcome of the evening meant little to her – but to throw herself at the King for his attention, that was a manoeuvre that, if it failed, could not be repeated. Well, she told herself, a bold move in battle often wins the day. Not for her to spend every waking hour praying at her prie-dieu, attending Mass five times a day, as many women did, in the hope that the King's glance might fall upon her. Some women even pretended to faint to attract his attention! No – but she was prepared to risk everything she had in terms of money and reputation to attract the King.

It must succeed! It will, it will, she repeated to herself as she continued to smile and glance pleasantly around the room. Beads of sweat began to gather under the little curls on her forehead. With a dainty hand she patted them away with her perfumed lace handkerchief. Fools, she thought, acknowledging the salutes of some of the Court gallants on the other side of the room; before the year is out they will be bowing and scraping to me. With a resolute gesture she rose and began to make her way a little nearer to the gambling-tables.

Everything was in her favour. Monsieur and Madame were still at St Cloud. Because the King had been interested in the pretty and vivacious Henriette d'Angleterre in the early days of his marriage, Madame was inclined to regard him with a slightly proprietorial air. Madame would be quick off the mark to prevent Louis taking any interest in another of her ladies-in-waiting. Then Athenais' maid, Lison, well paid to find out these things, had reported to her that the Queen had such a heavy cold she could not put down her handkerchief; also that it was her time of the month, the first since giving birth recently. The King's cousin, La Grande Mademoiselle, whose racy conversation and anecdotes the King was known to enjoy, was confined to her rooms having taken the purge that morning. That left only one contender for the King's attentions this evening – for Louis, having once dismissed his councillors, preferred to enjoy the company of the ladies for the remainder of his day.

Earlier that evening, during the extra-long ritual of being scented, rubbed down with perfume, dressed, powdered, beribboned, jewelled and costumed, Athenais had called casually to Lison as she came scurrying with a selection of shoes for her mistress's consideration: 'Were those flowers delivered to the Hôtel de Brion as I ordered?'

'*Oui, madame.* Gaston the lackey told me that he handed them directly to the *femme de chambre* of Mlle de la Vallière. Where is that knave of a hairdresser . . ?'

It was now almost ten o'clock. Athenais moved still nearer to the tables and began to pretend an interest in the game in progress.

'How well you are looking this evening, Madame de Montespan.'

'Thank you, Madame d'Evray. May I return the compliment?'

Mme d'Evray turned to her husband. 'Do you not agree that Mme de Montespan is looking particularly charming this evening?'

M. d'Evray's gaze swept over the lady. Athenais had dressed with meticulous care, discarding one gown after another to the despair of her maid, her auburn hair curled up in ringlets hanging on either side of her face, with tiny tendrils escaping on to her forehead, softening her rather hard expression. The cut of her Court dress of cinnamon-coloured Genoese velvet revealed almost fully her perfect breasts, nestling in a foam of silver and gold lace, while velvet ribbons, embroidered to match her gown, decorated the curls on top of her head. The delicate sheen of pearl ear-rings emphasized the translucency of her fine complexion. But while the ladies admired the elegance and good taste of her dress and the effect of her ensemble, it was her expression and smile which seemed to have the most effect on M. d'Evray; an expression which so clearly conveyed its meaning that he could not help but blush.

'Indeed, my dear, I must agree with you . . . she is looking not merely charming but ravishing this evening.'

'And where is your friend, Mlle de la Vallière?' asked Mme d'Evray, looking around.

Athenais looked about her in some surprise. 'She has not yet arrived? No doubt she will be here soon.'

'Mlle de la Vallière is unwell,' reported Mme de Chevreuse, standing near-by and hearing their conversation. 'Some beautiful flowers sent by an admirer proved to have rather too strong a scent for her, and she is suffering from a migraine.'

Athenais was all concern. '*Quel dommage!* Let us hope she will be fully recovered after a good night's sleep. In her delicate condition she must be particularly careful.'

The three, who had obviously not been acquainted with the news of Mlle de la Vallière's condition, were left open-mouthed as Athenais concentrated all her interest on the game in progress. The clock struck ten. Her palms and the soles of her feet were moist, but her lips and her throat felt dry. She longed to take a glass of wine but dared not move from her place by the table. People were pressing and jostling behind her, trying to watch the game. A minute or two more ticked by endlessly. She went up to the valet in blue livery at the gaming-table and purchased a number of counters from him. At last came the sound she had been waiting for.

'The King – make way for the King!'

Silence fell throughout the State apartments; everyone moved to one side or other of each room, leaving a wide passageway for the King and his retinue. Only in the gaming-room did activity continue undisturbed – the King had expressly forbidden the gambling to stop in his presence – but the loud chatter was subdued to a respectful hush. Athenais' fingers tightened on the handle of her fan. '*Quanto?*' the croupier called. '*Quanto va?*'

The slow, rhythmic tap of the King's cane on the polished floor came nearer and nearer with measured precision as, followed by the Captain of the Guard, he proceeded slowly and majestically through the apartments. As the royal party reached the doors of the gaming-room, there was a flutter of confusion around the table nearest to the fireplace. People drew their breath in surprise and little ripples of whispered conversation ran round the room. Something appeared to have taken place which had eclipsed even the arrival of the Sun King in the doorway.

The King turned to the Marquis de Dangeau. 'What is it, Dangeau?'

'I will investigate, Sire.'

The King and the Captain of the Guard approached the tables. Dangeau, fluttering with excitement, had been informed of the cause of the commotion. 'It seems that Madame de Montespan has just staked one hundred and fifty thousand pistoles on a game of *hoca*, Sire.'

'Indeed.' The King's face was inscrutable, displaying neither surprise nor interest.

The King and his retinue were standing by the table, directly at the back of Mme de Montespan who, having positioned herself with the greatest care so that the King and his party would approach her from behind, turned as if in surprise at his approach and sank into a low and graceful curtsy, affording him at one and the same time the full impact of her beauty, and a good view of her white bosom and décolletage as she remained on the floor. Several seconds passed before the King, in an instinctive gesture of good manners, put out his hand to assist her to rise.

She rose slowly and gracefully for the maximum effect, looking up at him languorously, her blue eyes soft and full of expression, the heady perfume she always wore assailing his nostrils as she reached her full height. She had taken care to select a pair of shoes with heels which were not too high; the King, not more than five foot six, was sensitive about his height, and always wore shoes with high heels to give him added stature. Louis' eyes swept over her exquisite figure, moulded to perfection by the tight cut of the brown velvet, swelling out over the full breasts yet hugging tightly her neat waist and the slender curves of her hips before flaring into soft folds. Louis, as much a connoisseur of women as of horses and dogs, was prepared to guess she would have the slim shapely legs that went with a full-bosomed figure. She had the perfect creamy skin of all true red-heads, unmarked by small-pox, and to emphasize it Lison had spent hours delicately outlining the veins on the inside of the wrists with a blue pencil, and carefully fixing the *mouches* on Madame's face – *la passionnée* at the corner of her eye, and one near her lips, *la baiseuse*, meaning 'kiss me'. A thin layer of wax was painted on her lips to make them gleam. The effect was perfection. Louis looked at her, surprised at the feelings she aroused in him.

Her ploy in making him take her hand had been a successful one – the touch was effective in the extreme. A sensation he had not experienced for a long time overcame him. For six years he had been sleeping with the same two women every day and every night, his wife and his mistress. Both were timid, placid souls whose only desire and interest was to please him, and who trembled at his every word. He began to wonder what it would be like to possess this woman, who looked at him with such a mocking, provocative expression in those alluring eyes.

'You gamble for high stakes this evening, madame.'

'Your Majesty is displeased?'

'I should be sorry to see you lose so much money.'

'I am a woman who likes to take a chance, Sire.' The expression in the lovely blue eyes was challenging. Louis fully understood her message. He raised his hand for the game to continue. The Duchesse de Chevreuse picked up her card. The King, disdaining to show any more interest in the affair, strolled on with his party into the next room.

The bystanders watched, holding their breath, as the Duchesse de Chevreuse turned over her card. One look at her face was enough to make the outcome clear. *Quelle chance!* She threw up her cards in the air. She had won 300,000 pistoles!

Everyone turned to Mme de Montespan with expressions of sympathy. Affecting distress, she retired to the other side of the room, her lace handkerchief covering her face, where everyone left her alone to recover her composure. In reality she had never felt such exhilaration. She was fully aware of the effect she had succeeded in making on the King. She had no doubt that, though she might be the loser of 150,000 pistoles, the outcome of the evening, as far as she was concerned, would be successful.

About ten minutes later, the King's party was making the return journey through the apartments before the King retired to take supper with the Queen in her rooms. Athenais, by dint of looking in the tiny hand-mirror she carried, had made sure that her curls were in place, her rouge unsmudged, and the *mouches* undisturbed. She fanned herself daintily and affected a subdued expression.

The King, re-entering the gaming-room, strolled over to her. Again she curtsied, at shorter length this time. One cannot employ even a winning strategy twice, she thought.

'You have lost your money, madame,' said the King gravely, after one look at her face.

'*Cela ne fait rien, Sire.* True, I have lost my money, but I have been honoured with Your Majesty's conversation. Tomorrow evening, perhaps I shall win it all back. If not, *c'est la vie.*'

Louis could not help admiring her *sang-froid.* 'Your husband is prepared to accommodate a wife who plays for such high stakes?' he asked.

'I'm afraid I don't allow my husband too much of a say in my affairs, Sire.'

'And your husband does not assert himself?' asked the King, greatly amused.

'He has little choice, Sire. If he wishes to spend the Paris social season chasing stags in the country and disporting himself with serving-girls, I consider that I am entitled to amuse myself as I like. Don't you consider it a fair arrangement?'

The King laughed at the new experience of such talk from a woman. Madame, his sister-in-law, and La Grande Mademoiselle, his cousin, were the only women who ever made him laugh. But he had no desire to sleep with either of them. This thought made him realize how much he wanted to know whether Athenais would prove to be as stimulating a companion in bed as she was provocative in her dress and conversation. There was little doubt in his mind that she would. God, how bored he was with his Queen, and la Vallière, both of them always pregnant, and the Queen always on her knees praying, praying for her soul, for the King's soul; praying first to conceive, then that she should be safely delivered, then in gratitude that she had been . . . She had become very plump, she had constant toothache, and the winters in France gave her continuous colds. Without the Spanish sunshine she drooped and withered. He was heartily sick of her. La Vallière, too, was becoming something of a millstone round his neck. She had kept her figure better than the Queen, but he was beginning to find her constant protestations of love embarrassing. At the slightest impatience from him, her big blue eyes welled up with tears which made him very uncomfortable.

Now almost thirty, Louis' sexual life had not really begun until he married at the age of twenty-two. With the Queen, it had been a simple matter of begetting children, although since the birth of the Dauphin, two more babies had died, both little girls. Their fourth child, Marie Thérèse, born the previous winter, was now just over a year old. But she was a delicate little thing. Thank God the Dauphin, a sturdy boy of six and a half, was growing up. The fact that he had an heir meant that he need never sleep with the Queen again unless he wished. Yet he flattered himself that he was punctilious in carrying out what he considered to be his marital duties – he invariably paid his nightly visit to her bed, no matter what time of night he quitted that of his mistress. That was why the physicians had gently reprimanded him on the subject of the Queen's many miscarriages, still-born babies and sickly children; 'You are giving her the dregs of the bottle, Sire'.

La Vallière was not the woman with whom to explore the avenues of sex. He had fallen in love with her when he first became disenchanted with his wife, a year after his marriage. It had been a pastoral idyll, his love-affair with Louise which began that summer at Fontainebleau, an enchantment of the senses, of youth and love in the full bloom of summer. They had spent the long golden days of August and September that year riding, picnicking, making love and dreaming in the forest's leafy glades. She had been the faery princess, the sweet beauty of a young man's dreams, a plaything with a passive disposition and the looks of an angel. It was a period of his life which he would remember always with delight.

Now, at thirty, his sexual appetite was becoming keener with every year that passed. Louise's sensitivity was, he knew, beginning to shrink from some of the new forms of love-making he tried to introduce. She never protested, but he felt her body tense and knew that her submission was born only of her deep love for him; she derived no pleasure from it. He was beginning to long for a partner who would respond with abandon to his advances, who would sometimes take the initiative, caress him, arouse him to a frenzy, and satiate to the full the smouldering passions, the Bourbon sensuality, that were an underlying part of his nature.

As he looked into the lovely eyes of Athenais de Montespan, languorous, heavy with the promise of delight as yet untasted, their provocative message was clear and created in him the desired effect. What heights of passion, he wondered, could be reached in the arms of a woman like this? She was no virgin, as both the Queen and la Vallière had been. Their virginity had been his to claim. Athenais de Montespan was an experienced woman. She had been married several years, and had a little son, d'Antin, though it was common knowledge that she took no interest in her husband who was rarely seen at Court. He liked to think that it was not merely in the interest of self-advancement that he, Louis, was the sole object of this beautiful woman's attentions. He remembered how furious he had been with her that summer evening at Fontainebleau when she had so spitefully exposed Louise to ridicule before the Court. It all seemed long ago now. He felt flattered that there seemed to be no limits to which this woman would not go in order to attract him. She had, he well knew, pursued this objective with single-minded devotion for more than six years. Well, perhaps now was the time to take her at her word and sample what was so willingly offered him. His eyes flickered lazily over her. The lady had been waiting for him all this time, hoping he would come to her. Why keep her waiting any longer?

'I trust that you will be more fortunate tomorrow evening, madame,' said Louis, and with a slight inclination of his head he withdrew, continuing his stately progress through the apartments, his retinue following behind.

Athenais, walking over to the windows, stared out unseeingly for some little time at the dark figures of the coachmen, barely discernible as they huddled over the glowing braziers provided for them in the courtyard of the palace. She knew that she had succeeded in arousing the King's interest. It had been only too apparent in his face. Now she wondered what the next step would be. It could not come from her, that she knew. The next move must be the King's. But that he would make that move, she now had no doubt.

Deep in her thoughts, she scarcely noticed a footman approach, handing her a note. Startled, she opened it hastily and read: *The King requests the pleasure of the company of Mme de Montespan at* Medianoche *this evening, in his private apartment.*

Medianoche, the midnight supper that followed a fast day. But – she tried to collect her thoughts – today was no fast day. The King was at this moment taking supper with the Queen as usual.

At the realization that then came to her, a brilliant smile lit up her lovely face. Crumpling the note and throwing it into the fire, she made her way as quickly as she could without attracting attention through the crowded rooms and thronged galleries to the staircase which led down to the entrance.

'My coach!' she demanded of the footmen on duty there. 'Send Madame's coach to the entrance immediately!' Monsieur and Madame being at St Cloud she had, by means of a handsome *pourboire*, appropriated the use of Madame's carriage for the evening.

A footman ran down the staircase to summon the coach, whilst a tiring-woman helped her to don her wraps. The coach was waiting at the entrance when she descended the stairs.

'The Palais Royal! Make good speed!'

The coach jolted out of the cobbled courtyard and through the gates of the Louvre, but Athenais, huddling in her wraps in the corner of the coach against the bitter cold, hardly noticed the rattling and the discomfort. She could scarcely believe that the moment for which she had so long schemed and planned had come. Her mind raced as she alternately summoned up and rejected a thousand different ploys and phrases with which to fascinate the King. She knew that she was at a crossroads in her life. One false step, she thought, and my career at Court will be over. Yet she also knew that if she played her cards with skill she would soon be the uncrowned Queen of France, and a determination hardened in her brain to succeed in that, just as she had finally succeeded in all her other plans. The day of that ninny la Vallière was over at last. She would soon have her packed off to a convent.

Arriving at her apartments at the Palais Royal, she cursed vehemently at finding her room cold and in darkness. The little maid, not anticipating the return of her mistress before the early hours, had just dozed off to sleep on her camp bed.

'Lison,' she called. 'Lison! *Dépêche-toi!* Bring tapers! Make a fire immediately!'

She gave the girl a resounding slap across the face to wake her. 'Lison! You lazy slut!' She shook her violently. The girl sat up and blinked drowsily. 'You little good-for-nothing! Rouse yourself this minute, or I'll turn you out into the street!'

Hastily collecting her wits, the girl ran to light the tapers and make up the fire from the embers which smouldered in the grate. Athenais, seating herself at her commode, looked in the mirror and, opening her box of beauty aids, frantically selected powders, rouges, and patches. The little maid scuttled hither and thither as Athenais called out directions over her shoulder to the girl to heat the curling tongs, and to bring her first a seductive transparent lace-edged chemise, then a gown made of pure silk, smooth, soft and sensuous to the touch, then different jewellery, shoes, laces and ribbons.

Lison, her fingers blue with cold, painstakingly re-dressed her mistress's hair and brought creams and perfumes for her body, the two of them occupied in using every feminine trick and device they knew to make Athenais inviting and enticing for her rendezvous – which, she knew, would be the most important of her life.

PART II

THE SUN
AT MORNING

1668-1669

Chapter Nine

The city of Paris was stiflingly hot that summer of 1668, and as always, the Marais district, built on marshland, was swept with fever because of the foetid air. In the centre of the Marais many fine new town houses had been built, but in the outlying parts of the district there was much suffering amongst the poor living in their shack-like dwellings and unable to obtain supplies of fresh water. By the end of July most of the aristocracy were preparing to leave Paris for the healthier air of the country.

In the little house in the rue des Tournelles, Nanon complained that the clean linen she had hung outside in the tiny yard to dry, was stolen the moment her back was turned.

'I am sorry that your work was to no account,' said Françoise, 'but very likely the linen is in the hands of people who need it even more than we do.'

Nanon grumbled behind her mistress's back, disgruntled at her excessive, and in Nanon's view, misplaced, generosity. Although the two women lived very frugally themselves, Françoise insisted on doing all that she could to relieve the distress of the poor, visiting them frequently with her basket over her arm – the basket containing, Nanon suspected, bread, cheese and eggs from their own small store.

Nanon tried to dissuade her mistress from these visits, pointing out that she was exposing herself to the infection which was rife throughout the district – but to no avail. Françoise continued to do what little she could for the poor, even if it was only sending for the priest to hear a last confession or give the last rites of the Church. The nuns in the convent in the Place Royale entrusted her with funds from the poorbox, with which she purchased bread and simple medicaments from the apothecary in the rue Barbette and distributed them to the needy; also some cheap wine, safer to drink than the water.

Françoise had been due to leave Paris at the end of July with her friend Mme de Montchevreuil, who had invited her to spend the month of August at her estate in the Auvergne. A week before they were due to leave, however, Mme de Montchevreuil fell ill of the fever, and so the trip had had to be temporarily postponed.

As Françoise arrived home late one hot afternoon, tired and dusty, carrying a heavy basket of washing which she asked Nanon to launder without delay in order to return it the next morning to some poor soul who had no change of linen, Nanon gave her a letter which had been delivered that morning.

Françoise examined it with curiosity. It was stamped with a heavy seal and addressed in bold, flowing handwriting. To her surprise, the letter proved to be an invitation from Athenais de Montespan for Françoise to drive with her in her carriage that evening in the Cour de la Reine. It had been sent from the palace of St Germain – a step up from the Palais Royal, Françoise thought wryly.

Nevertheless she was delighted at the prospect of a drive in the cool of the evening. The Cour de la Reine, a wide thorough-fare bordering the Seine, had been laid out by Catherine de Medici in the previous century and was a well-known society rendezvous. It was pleasant to stroll or drive along the tree-lined avenue by the river on a summer evening, to see and be seen.

The letter informed Françoise that Mme de Montespan would send the carriage for her at seven. Accordingly she gratefully drank the cup of sage tea that Nanon brought her, ate a light supper and went upstairs to change her clothes and refresh her hands and face with orange-flower water.

Promptly at seven she was ready and waiting, but instead of the expected carriage clattering down the street, two linkmen with a sedan-chair knocked loudly at the door, demanding to know if Mme Scarron were there, their orders being to convey her to where Mme de Montespan awaited her in her carriage in the Cour de la Reine.

Nanon looked anxiously at her mistress. 'It's all right,' Françoise told Nanon – she had taken great care in warning Nanon always to be extremely careful about where she went, and with whom, for life in Paris was far more hazardous than it was in the country. 'I recognize their livery – it is of the King's Household.'

'But I understood you were to drive out with a lady,' Nanon remarked, puzzled, watching anxiously as her mistress was borne away by the two footmen, who shouldered their burden with no apparent difficulty.

Although the velvet-lined sedan-chair was not uncomfortable, the method of conveyance was somewhat bumpy, and Françoise was not sorry when her chair was put down at the side of a magnificent coach-and-six with the royal coat of arms emblazoned on the doors, standing a little to one side of the entrance to the Cour de la Reine, amongst the trees.

The footmen opened the door for her, and assisted her to climb out of the sedan and into the coach, no easy feat for the step was rather high. Inside the coach sat Athenais de Montespan, wrapped in a hooded cloak in spite of the warm evening. Françoise, who had not encountered Athenais for some little time, was surprised to find no one else present – she had imagined that one or two mutual friends, such as Mme d'Albret and Mme d'Aumont, would be of the party.

'*Vous allez bien*, Françoise?' asked Athenais, holding out her hand in greeting. Françoise took it warmly, for although the two women tended to indulge in friendly arguments, they had known each other for quite a long time. When Françoise was first introduced to Paris society by her late husband, Paul Scarron, Athenais de Montespan, or Mortemart as she was then, had been one of the first people she had met.

'I am very well, thank you, Athenais,' answered Françoise. 'And you?'

'Will you not sit?'

Françoise sat down, looking round her with awe at the luxury of the blue-velvet-lined coach with its padded back, blue velvet cushions corded in gold with gold fringes, and even two small footstools upholstered to match. She could not resist tapping her fingernail on the window, which proved to be of real glass.

Athenais smiled, her rather downcast face illuminated with some of its old sparkle.

'You are certainly living in grand style, Athenais. I am surprised you still care to converse with your old friends.' – Now that you are living in royal circles, she had been about to add; but managed to stop herself in time.

Athenais' eyes flashed imperiously. 'And why should I no longer acknowledge my friends?' she demanded.

Françoise was contrite. 'I'm sorry, Athenais, it was unfair of me to say that. Please forgive me.'

Athenais' smile was brilliant as ever. The lovely red-gold curls framed her face, rather pale under the black hood of her cloak, and her blue eyes were dazzling. There were diamonds at her throat and tiny pearl ear-rings fastened in her ears. After a brief silence, Françoise began to wonder why Athenais had invited her here. She did not seem to be in a mood for conversation; yet there must be some reason why Athenais, now so exalted in the royal favour, had chosen to renew acquaintance with her old friend.

'May we drive along a little?' Françoise asked. 'This coach is sheer luxury.' She looked forward to waving nonchalantly to people of her acquaintance through those novel glass windows.

'Certainly.' Athenais tapped on the window with her fan. The footmen, standing to attention, opened the door.

'Drive on,' Athenais commanded. The footmen leaped on to the back of the coach, the coachman cracked his whip and the great coach lumbered slowly forward along the Cour de la Reine. Torches and lanterns hanging in the trees gave a fairy-like illumination to the avenue. Françoise noted with satisfaction how people turned to admire the luxurious carriage and wonder at its occupants.

'Have you ever visited Versailles?' Athenais said, after a few minutes.

'The royal hunting lodge? No, I have not. It is being rebuilt, is it not?'

'Versailles is to be completely redesigned,' Athenais told her. 'The architects wanted the King to pull down his father's old hunting lodge, but the King would not allow it. He insisted on retaining the original building, and adding to it. Versailles is to be remodelled in the style of Vaux-le-Vicomte.'

'Won't that cost a great deal of money?' wondered Françoise, thinking of the sufferings of the poor she visited each day. Vaux-le-Vicomte was the palatial chateau built by Fouquet, the former Minister of Finance, which had impressed the King so much that it had led to an investigation of his financial activities, and to his banishment to a fortress for life.

'In a few weeks' time,' continued Athenais, 'the King is to give an entertainment at Versailles, a *divertissement*, before the workmen begin to build.'

Françoise wondered what this had to do with her.

'Would you like to attend the entertainments, Françoise?'

'Indeed, I would most assuredly, but – '

'But what?'

'If I were invited – and if I had something suitable to wear.'

'The invitation I can guarantee for you – and you need not

98

worry about clothes. I have many dresses worn once only that I should be happy to lend you. We are of a size, I think.'

'You are very kind, Athenais. But – ' Françoise bit her lip, wishing that she did not have to cajole favours from all her friends.

'What problem have you thought of now?'

'Shall anyone else I know be invited, do you think, Athenais?' Athenais stared at her. 'Why do you ask?'

Françoise was forthright. 'I have no means of getting to Versailles. It is a good eighteen kilometres, is it not?'

Athenais threw back her head and laughed. '*Nom de Dieu!* What problems you create, Françoise! There will be many people of your acquaintance travelling to Versailles – but do not concern yourself; in the unlikely event of your having no means of transport, I will send this very coach for you. The King has placed it entirely at my disposal.'

But Françoise was eagerly anticipating the *divertissement*, for the King's entertainments were famous. 'Will there be a play, Athenais? Or a firework display?'

Athenais, after seven years of watching Court entertainments, had become somewhat blasé. '*Comme vous êtes ingénue*, Françoise. But I think I can promise you a play. Molière is writing something new for the King, I believe.'

'You are very kind, Athenais.'

Athenais yawned. Françoise wondered why she seemed so flat, so lacking in her old zest for life, now that she had at last attained her desired object, the glorious position of the King's mistress. She seemed reticent in discussing Court life, and Françoise was reluctant to press her. So for a little while they chattered inconsequentially of old acquaintances and of Françoise's doings, though she could see that Athenais was bored. Yet Athenais made no move to broach any more serious matter of her own. Once or twice she stopped the coach in order to exchange a word or two with an acquaintance. As it became dusk, Françoise said: 'I should be returning home soon, Athenais. My servant always waits up for me, though I tell her to retire.'

Athenais laughed incredulously. 'What an old maid you are becoming, Françoise! 'Tis scarce past nine o'clock. At St Germain the evening entertainment has not even begun. However, if you wish, I will see that you do not keep your maid from her bed.' Chuckling with amusement, she gave orders to the coachman to drive to the rue des Tournelles. As Françoise alighted, thanking her profusely, she added as an afterthought: 'Mme d'Heudicourt will be driving out to St Germain to see me on Thursday week – if you accompany her, you may choose your dress for the *divertissement*.'

With many thanks, Françoise bade her goodnight and hastened into the little house, where Nanon was preparing hot milk for her in the kitchen. She realized, as she sipped the warming drink, that she was faintly puzzled. It had been pleasant to see Athenais again, and to revive their friendship; yet Athenais, she thought with some amusement, was not the sort of person to make disinterested gestures. There must be some reason why she had gone to the trouble of renewing their acquaintance. She wondered idly what it could be as she and Nanon snuffed the candles and prepared for bed.

Chapter Ten

The road to St Germain lay westward from Paris through the sleepy villages of St Cloud and Louveciennes. It was a road wide enough to accommodate two carriages, and was kept in good repair, for the Court travelled frequently between Paris and St Germain-en-Laye, where the King had been born and lived as a child. The Court spent most of the summer there, and at Fontaine-bleau, and was in residence at the Louvre during the winter, for Paris was neither pleasant nor healthy during the hot summer months.

Françoise and Mme d'Heudicourt greatly enjoyed the journey. It was delightful to breathe the country air, although Mme d'Heudicourt's carriage was in no way comparable to the one in which Françoise had driven with Athenais in the Cour de la Reine. But she was enjoying the novelty of a day out, and after a couple of hours on the road they ate the bread rolls and cheese Mme d'Heudicourt had brought in a large basket, and drank wine with some biscuits Nanon had baked that very morning.

At last, after passing through the hamlet of Marly, the road began to climb, and Mme d'Heudicourt, looking out of the window at the high ground before them, announced: 'We are almost there, Françoise! Now the road goes up to the castle.'

The road did indeed begin to climb, twisting and turning through the wooded country which thickened into the forest of Laye. Now and then a party of riders from the castle would rejoin the road from the forest paths and the carriage was obliged to let them pass.

'Athenais must really be living in fine style,' Françoise exclaimed – for the hundredth time that morning, Blanche thought with irritation. 'To have her own apartments at St Germain . . . Wasn't it kind of her to think of us, and invite us for the day?'

Françoise was like an excited child, Blanche thought, taking a little mirror from her reticule and patting her blonde hair into place, careful to arrange it so that it covered the dark roots. She put a little scent on to her handkerchief and began to dab her forehead. The day had become very warm. She wished she had not allowed her maid to lace her quite so tightly, but she had been so anxious to look elegant for the outing to St Germain.

'Of course she is living in luxury, you goose,' she remonstrated. 'What else do you expect of a king's mistress?' Really, Françoise was so unsophisticated. She sniffed as she eyed disparagingly her friend's well-worn shoes and neatly-darned stockings. What a little fool the girl was! It was common knowledge that more than one influential aristocrat had offered her the honour of becoming his kept mistress – all of which offers she had declined.

Françoise has rather too good an opinion of herself, Blanche thought, fanning herself, for a woman without any means. Why, she must be thirty if she was a day, and with no dowry what marriage could she hope for? She could hardly be expecting, now, to catch a rich husband. Certainly, she had the *entrée* to all the best houses. But that would not provide her with a fire at her feet and a roof over her head when she lost her youthful attraction. Blanche marvelled that Françoise always appeared so serene, so pleasant and smiling, as if life held no problems for her. And she certainly had kept her looks; why, there was not a grey hair to be seen in that smooth dark head. One would not take her for a day over twenty-five.

'What has happened to poor Louise de la Vallière, now that Athenais has usurped her place?' Françoise was asking. 'Has she been sent away from Court?'

'I believe that she has asked to join the order of the Carmelites,' Blanche replied, 'but the King will not allow it.'

'Why not?'

'It would look strange for a heavily pregnant woman to enter a convent, wouldn't it? Perhaps after her baby is born in the autumn . . .'

'It must be sad to lose a man's love after bearing him four children,' Françoise mused.

Blanche shrugged her shoulders. 'The King has made her a duchess and she may drive a coach-and-eight. Look, Françoise!'

The huge grey castle at the top of the hill was visible through the trees – a few minutes more, and their carriage was clattering through the gates. Grooms appeared to conduct the carriage to the stables, and the lodge-keeper ordered a lackey to escort the ladies to the apartments of Mme de Montespan, which were on the ground floor, directly below the Queen's wing – the apartments which had once been occupied by Diane de Poitiers, the mistress of Henri II. The King believed in following tradition.

On arrival at the apartments of Mme de Montespan a maid conducted them to the boudoir. There they found her lying on her bed, fully dressed, her hair curled and her face painted.

After the initial greetings Mme d'Heudicourt asked: 'Are you feeling unwell, Athenais?'

Athenais flushed. 'No, certainly not. I am taking a rest before the King comes to visit me at two.'

The two women looked at each other uncertainly. Did this mean their presence was unwelcome?

Athenais laughed. 'You need not look like that, my friends. The King enjoys the company of pretty women. I will present you to him.'

Both Françoise and Mme d'Heudicourt were alarmed. 'Oh no, Athenais. We are dusty from our journey, and not looking our best.'

Athenais had already regretted her spontaneous offer. Despite their protestations, both women had taken great care with their appearance and were elegantly attired. Françoise, in a fresh green cotton dress with a white collar and lace fichu, looked particularly attractive, her dark hair dressed a little more fashionably than was her usual severe style. The light colour, Athenais thought, suited her dark good looks infinitely more than the dark colours she usually wore.

'Well,' Athenais hesitated, 'what is the time?' The maid knocked at the door. 'It is one o'clock, madame. Will you take dinner now?'

'Will you dine with me, ladies?'

'We had something to eat in the carriage,' said Françoise, 'so we are not hungry.' She went over to the floor-length windows and looked out. 'How beautiful it is here, Athenais, after the heat of Paris. May we stroll in the grounds a little?'

'Of course. Well, if you are not hungry, let us choose your dress, Françoise, and then you may explore the gardens while I play cards with the King.' She had the grace to blush at this. 'Return here at four, when the King goes to his Council meeting, and we will drink chocolate together before you return.'

The maid brought out several dresses for Françoise to choose from and the three spent some time picking and choosing an ensemble for Françoise to wear for the *divertissement*.

'What exquisite material!' said Françoise, stroking the soft folds of the brown velvet dress, embroidered with gold and silver, which Athenais had worn the night at the Louvre when she had first captivated the King.

Athenais smiled mockingly. 'Indeed, that has been a lucky dress for me. You may wear it if you wish – and I hope it will prove to be as fortunate for you.'

'But the evening may be warm for velvet,' suggested Mme d'Heudicourt, 'for it will be the last week in August. You might be very uncomfortable.'

Françoise acknowledged the truth of this, and her next choice fell upon a black lace edged with purple ribbons, and with a stomacher of purple brocade. 'No, no, those are the colours of mourning,' chided Athenais; 'I had to wear it for a year when the old Queen died. Wear something a little brighter, for the love of God. Look, this silk is very pretty, and would suit you to perfection.'

The dress that Athenais held up was of pale green watered silk, the tiny seed-pearls which decorated the stomacher continuing along the low neckline to the shoulders. The voluminous sleeves were edged with Valenciennes lace.

'It is lovely,' Françoise admitted, 'but is not the neckline too low?'

'Oh, don't be such a prude, Françoise,' scolded Athenais.

'Try it on,' suggested Mme d'Heudicourt.

'May I? Athenais?'

'Of a surety you may, you goose. Lison, bring the mirror.'

Françoise undressed and slipped on the dress, Lison fastened it up the back and they were all fascinated by the effect. The colour suited Françoise's dark hair and eyes admirably. Françoise was dubious about the décolletage – her own dresses were always firmly done up at the neck – but her friends were adamant.

'You look truly lovely, Françoise,' said Mme d'Heudicourt. 'I have never seen you look so well.'

'You do not think the cut of the neck immodest?'

'Françoise! You are an unmarried lady – do you want to remain so for ever?'

Françoise looked again in the cheval-mirror Lison had brought and placed in front of the dressing-table. There was no doubt that she looked most attractive.

'I will lend you my wedding lace fichu to wear over your shoulders, if it will make you feel more comfortable,' offered Mme d'Heudicourt, but Athenais would not hear of it.

'There is to be no further discussion,' she said. 'Lison, bring a fan to go with the gown. Now, no more talk of fichus and covering your shoulders, Françoise. You will come to the *divertissement* looking as stunningly attractive as you do now, and at the very least you will capture a duke or a marquis to marry, since I know that you spurn all other liaisons.'

Suddenly there was a knocking at the door, and the door opened to reveal a flustered Lison, the ivory fan in her hand, curtsying low and deeply as in walked a handsome man of thirty or so, dressed in coat and breeches of blue moire fastened with gold braid inlaid with diamonds. His luxuriant dark hair was tied with gold and blue ribbons, and he carried a plumed hat under his arm, his other hand resting on his sword-belt, which was secured by two gold lilies each set with a large diamond. The calfskin shoes which matched his snuff-coloured stockings were buckled in gold. His dark eyes rested on the two visitors with lively curiosity, as with one movement the three women sank into a deep curtsy.

The King! thought Françoise, hardly daring to raise her eyes.

Athenais, momentarily nonplussed, decided to make the best of the situation.

'Your Majesty,' she murmured, rising to her full height.

'I see you have visitors today. I shall return when you are not engaged.'

'Your Majesty, may I present my friends?'

'That will be my pleasure.'

'Your Majesty, Mme d'Heudicourt, and Mme Scarron.'

At the mention of the name Scarron, the King seemed to show some recognition. Probably he had heard of Paul Scarron the poet, thought Françoise, as she and Mme d'Heudicourt again curtsied deeply. The King came forward, and with singular charm took the ladies' hands in turn and allowed them to kiss his own.

'And where do you keep these charming ladies hidden?' he asked Athenais. 'I have not seen them at Court before.'

'We are visiting the Court from Paris,' Mme d'Heudicourt told him, 'at Mme de Montespan's kind invitation. We return this evening.'

'In that case, will you allow me to show you some of the beauties of the gardens myself? I was born here in this palace, and I flatter myself that no one knows the place as I do.'

Hardly able to believe their good fortune, the ladies gratefully accepted, and the King gave his arm to Athenais, which mollified her slightly, for she was inwardly seething with rage. The little party strolled along the formal terrace, admiring the superb view it afforded of the Seine valley. A bodyguard of two Swiss Guards followed at a little distance.

'You see the lower woods down there,' the King was saying, as they stood by the wrought-iron railing that bordered the esplanade. 'I used to play there with my brother when we were children. I had this terrace deliberately constructed so that I could continue to admire the view without expending so much energy. My brother and I used to climb up here in the old days. Now I am afraid I have reached an age where I prefer to stroll in the company of the ladies.'

'It is truly beautiful here, Sire,' said Françoise. The air was very heady and invigorating high above the forest; the lush green slopes of the hanging gardens stretched away almost as far as the eye could see. Far below in the valley the thin white ribbon of the Seine glittered in the sun.

'This terrace measures more than two kilometres,' said the King. 'Do you feel capable of strolling its full length, ladies? The view from the far end over Mont Valerian is without equal in Europe.'

Athenais was about to decline, but Françoise accepted joyfully. 'Oh indeed, Sire. It is delightful here. What pleasure it would be to picnic here, and admire this view for a whole day.'

'In that case, you must pay another visit to St Germain. We shall arrange an al fresco meal and I shall try to join you,' said Louis, rather taken by this attractive girl in green with the dark sparkling eyes and the air of infectious gaiety. She reminded him very much of his sister-in-law, Minette, whose company he so much enjoyed. Could this really be the same Françoise Scarron whom Athenais had portrayed as dull, sober and pious? Surely not. She was far too attractive to lead the kind of life Athenais had described to him.

They walked on, Athenais hot and tired and feeling unwell, longing to return to the castle but afraid to suggest it in case the King decided to continue the walk in the company of Françoise Scarron. At last, to her considerable relief, he took out his watch and consulted it.

'Three-thirty! The Council meets at four. I must return to the castle.'

The women curtsied as he made them a low bow.

'I will say *au revoir* to you, ladies, for I hope to have the pleasure of meeting you again soon. My sincere regrets that I must abandon your charming company for that of my councillors.'

'We have been invited to the *divertissement*,' said Mme d'Heudicourt.

'Excellent! In that case, I look forward to seeing you again in three weeks' time. I have great plans for the gardens at Versailles. Perhaps I shall show you whilst you are there, Madame Scarron, for I can see you enjoy being outdoors.'

He took his leave, and they watched in undisguised admiration as the stately figure disappeared into the distance, escorted by the Swiss Guards.

As the three women strolled slowly back in the direction of the castle, Athenais turned to Blanche d'Heudicourt.

'Had you not better instruct the Master of the Horse to have your carriage ready, and the horses fed and watered?' she asked. 'You will want to leave fairly soon in order to arrive in Paris before nightfall.'

'Indeed we shall. I will walk on briskly and give the instructions, whilst you follow at your leisure.'

'Have them ready to leave at five,' Athenais suggested. 'That will give you ample time for your journey. Await us, then, in my apartments, and we will take a collation together before you leave.'

Blanche hurried on whilst Françoise and Athenais followed at a slower pace. Other people were strolling on the terrace in twos and threes admiring the view, and presently a small *calèche* passed them by. In it was a small plump lady, very fair – Françoise realized that it was the Queen. Beside her sat a small boy, also very fair, staring straight ahead, looking neither to right nor left, as the courtiers bowed and curtsied at their passage. Athenais made a low curtsy and Françoise did the same. The Queen gave a slight nod in Athenais' direction.

'That is the Queen and the Dauphin,' Athenais informed Françoise.

'The Dauphin does not look like his father, does he?'

'In no way does he resemble him. They say he has everything of his mother, which I gather means that he is none too bright.'

They were nearing the castle rapidly now, and Athenais determined to broach the subject she had been trying to bring to the surface for some little time.

'Françoise,' she began, 'do you have any concern about the future?'

Françoise looked at her in surprise. Was this the gay, irrepressible Athenais talking so soberly? It was completely out of

107

character. 'Not particularly,' she said. 'Do you think I should?'

'Well, your situation in life is – how shall I put it? – insecure, to say the least. If you do not marry again – '

'I doubt very much if I shall marry again,' Françoise chuckled, 'but I have been living quite comfortably now for seven years since my husband died, and there is no reason why I should not continue to do so. All you married women are the same – you want nothing but to marry me off! I suppose you have some rich old grey-beard in mind . . .'

'As if I would insult you in such a way. You are still very attractive, Françoise, and your looks belie your age.'

Françoise could not help but laugh. 'I am all of thirty-one years old, Athenais. Even so, I do not feel that I am yet in my dotage. It is possible to be quite happy without a husband. I consider that I lead a good and useful life, helping others, and I am well satisfied with my way of living. I may well never marry again.'

'But what of financial security? You have a small pension, haven't you? Suppose that source of income were to – '

'The King was generous enough to continue my pension when his mother died, and Nanon and I supplement our income by means of our earnings.'

'Come, come, Françoise, be realistic. You live in a tiny rented house. Do you not aspire to some improvement in your way of life, such as, for instance, your own home?'

'But I have my own home.'

'I mean your own property, Françoise, so that the threats of landlords and raised rents mean nothing to you.'

Françoise was silent for a few moments before she answered. 'Even if I were to hope for such a thing, I have no hope of realizing it.'

'You are wrong, Françoise. I mean to ask you to render me a service, for which you would be very well remunerated.'

Françoise looked at her in surprise. What service could she perform for Athenais, who lived at the Court of France in the lap of luxury?

'Ask what you wish, Athenais. I shall be happy to help you in any way I can, but I look for no remuneration.'

They were almost within reach of the chateau, where Mme d'Heudicourt would be awaiting them. Athenais drew her friend down upon a seat, and for a few moments she toyed nervously with her parasol and fingered the silk-covered brim of her cartwheel straw hat. Françoise was puzzled by her apparent agitation.

'Françoise,' she said at last, 'I am with child.'

For the thousandth time she cursed her misfortune in becoming *enceinte* just at this juncture, just when everything was going so well. The King was enchanted with his new mistress and could hardly stay away from her bed. It was the talk of the Court that he was visiting her two and three times a day. People were beginning to talk of a new Diane de Poitiers, which delighted Athenais, for the charms of Diane had enslaved her royal lover, Henri II, all his life, in spite of the fact that she was many years his senior.

But now she was with child, and soon, all too soon, the beautiful body in which the King took such delight would become distorted and grotesque, her graceful movements heavy and gross. Remembering how the Queen looked when she was carrying, Athenais shuddered. At least, she consoled herself, she had kept her looks when she had borne her son, d'Antin. But that had been over four years ago. Now she was nearing thirty. Would she be able to regain her figure so easily this time?

And the King – could she continue to hold his interest through the last half of her pregnancy? There were several newcomers at Court, pretty and younger than herself . . . To keep up her spirits she repeatedly reminded herself that la Vallière had successfully kept her hold on the King throughout her previous three pregnancies, and what that ninny could accomplish, surely so could she.

Françoise, meanwhile, was staring at her friend in astonishment, realizing at last why Athenais looked so pale and lifeless in spite of the turn her fortunes had taken, why she was so lacking in her old zest and energy. It was no wonder that she needed to rest before receiving the King. And Louis' reaction? Françoise, with her usual innate caution, felt her way carefully.

'That is good news, Athenais,' she said hesitantly, 'd'Antin will like to have a brother.' There was, of course, just the possibility that the child could be legitimate.

'It is not Montespan's child,' Athenais said, fanning herself with vigour. 'You know who is the father.'

Inwardly she cursed Mme Voisin, to whom she had gone for help the moment she suspected that she might be pregnant. She had tried everything la Voisin could suggest to try to rid herself of the life forming in her womb, swallowing pills and potions by the score, even having a Black Mass said over her body and muttering incantations to the Devil – but all to no avail. More than two full moons had passed, and she knew now for a certainty, by the absence of her normally excellent appetite, her continual queasiness and a general feeling of malaise, that her fate was sealed.

Françoise was wondering what part she was to play in all this. Seeing that Athenais was not forthcoming, she asked: 'And what assistance can I render you, Athenais? I shall be glad to help in whatever way I can.'

Athenais looked her full in the face. 'If I do not miscarry' – if only that could be, she thought – 'I want you to make arrangements to take the baby when it is born and have it put out to nurse.'

Françoise was speechless. Trying to overcome her astonishment at such a proposal, she answered: 'What you ask is quite impossible.'

'Why, pray?'

'I could not possibly take on such a responsibility.'

'Why not? You will be well paid for it.'

'That is not the point. I have had no children of my own and I know nothing whatsoever of young babies. I would not be a fit person to take charge of a newborn infant.'

'You require to know nothing. You would arrange for a suitable nurse.'

'Do you seriously suggest that I take a child into my home, and endanger my good name for the sake of financial benefit? How little you know me, Athenais. My reputation means more to me than that.'

'It is not necessary to have the child looked after in your home. You would contrive to rent a house, or rooms, and install there a nurse and a couple of women. Don't let the expense concern you. And once the arrangements are completed, you need never show your face there again. All I ask is that you be discreet. No one must know anything; it is to be done in the utmost secrecy.'

'I repeat, it is completely out of the question, Athenais. I refuse to take the responsibility of caring for the King's child.'

'You have not been asked to care for it. You have been asked only to make the necessary arrangements, a small service to perform, I think, for such handsome rewards.'

'But how can I arrange to farm out a child like a bundle of washing, with no further concern for its welfare? Do you know how many babies die who are put out to nurse? Even the best cared-for children have a delicate hold on life. You know that the Queen has already lost two baby girls, who had the most constant care – and yet the attentions of the best doctors in France could not save them. No, Athenais, what you ask is quite impossible, and I consider it highly unfair of you to make such a demand.'

There was complete silence for several minutes as each of the two women sat lost in her own thoughts. Nothing could be heard save the crickets chirping in the long grass, and the cry of the curlews wheeling overhead. Françoise felt hot and tired and ready to cry. Athenais had no right to ask such a thing of her. She had been only too willing to help her if she was in any trouble, but to ask such a thing – no, she could not even consider it.

Meanwhile Athenais was asking herself yet again why, oh why, this had had to happen now, just as she was about to achieve all that she had planned and schemed for for so long. La Vallière would give birth to her brat in the autumn, and she felt sure that then she would be able to prevail upon Louis to let his former mistress enter a convent and rid himself of her for good. Then Athenais would be openly acknowledged as the King's *maîtresse déclarée* instead of merely *la maîtresse peu délicate*, as she was now.

'Have you considered,' Athenais said at last, 'that your Royal Bounty might one day come to an end?'

Françoise looked at her in incredulity, reminded of a snake poised with its venom, ready to strike. Was Athenais really capable of stooping to such means to achieve her ends? Well, she would have to take the risk. Under no circumstances did she mean to become involved. Her cautious nature and intuitive common sense told her that she should steer well clear of Athenais de Montespan and her schemes.

'When la Vallière's babies were born . . .' she began.

'Madame Colbert took them in and had them nursed. Louise is also carrying, and will be delivered in October. But her case was different. I am a married woman, as you know. No one must know that I am pregnant by the King. It would cause a dreadful scandal, and embarrass the King to such an extent that he might send me away.' At this prospect her blue eyes filled with tears. Even Françoise found it difficult to remain unmoved at the sight of Athenais sobbing, for it was so completely out of character that one could imagine the inner torment she was going through. 'Françoise,' she pleaded, 'you must help me. There is no one else who can. Everything depends on it. My future is in your hands.'

'What does the King say to all this?' asked Françoise. 'Have you informed him?'

In fact Louis had guessed her secret himself, only a few days ago, when teasing Athenais over her pallor and her lack of appetite. He had charged her with it laughingly, and she, seeing that his mood was playful, had admitted the truth. To her inexpressible relief, his reaction was not what she had feared. She had been half afraid that he might send her back to her husband in Gascony.

'The King is pleased,' she told Françoise. 'He loves children, yet of the six that have been born to him, only three have survived. The princess is a sickly little thing. She will not live to grow up.' She thought it unnecessary to tell Françoise that the King's real fear was that her husband, Montespan, might claim the child as his own. What business was it of hers?

If only it were not for the King's well-known affection for his children, and his grief when they died, she thought, it would be easy enough to take steps to deal with the child as soon as it was born. A few louis d'or pressed into the midwife's hand would easily ensure that the newborn infant never saw the light of day. Or there were the services of the notorious *meneurs*, the people trafficking in unwanted babies for the sake of a few sous. Carts full of these abandoned unfortunates, born to parents who already had too many mouths to feed, or to harlots, or born illegitimately to women whose husbands were away in the army, left Paris daily for 'homes in the country'.

But the King had made it quite clear that the child must be properly cared for – in that respect he had as much concern for his by-blows as for his legitimate children – and she dared not take such a risk.

'And what was his suggestion?' Françoise asked.

'Exactly as I have described – that some suitable, discreet and trustworthy person should be selected, to take the baby away when it is born, without fuss, and arrange to have it cared for. I suggested you as being the most tactful person I knew' (she did not add 'the most impoverished'). 'The King was well pleased with the idea, and now that he has met you, no doubt is even more satisfied. It was obvious that you made an excellent impression today.'

112

Françoise was speechless. Athenais had already put her name forward to the King without even consulting her on the subject. She was now in a situation where to refuse would be actively to risk the King's displeasure.

Athenais knew that she held the winning cards. She did not want to force Françoise's hand, but the next few months were a crucial time for her. Nothing must be allowed to sour her relationship with Louis, not now, when he could so easily turn to someone else – even, God forbid, return to la Vallière; it was not impossible. She shuddered at the thought. Everything must be done to make the next few months pass smoothly and swiftly until the time when she would once again be the svelte and desirable plaything he coveted. She had not spent the best years of her youth waiting, saving herself for the King, when she could easily have made other advantageous alliances, in order to be cast aside after only a few months.

Louis had already bestowed on her some fine jewellery, including a valuable diamond parure; but she aimed much higher than that. Her ambition was to acquire estates, lands, property, as well as jewels, and a few reliable sources of income for her retiring years, such as the duty payable by all the butchers' shops in Paris, which the King had already made over to her. As for titles? Pah! When the time came for her to give way to a successor, she did not intend to leave the Court as la Vallière would, with the title of Duchess and very little else to show for her years as the King's *maîtresse en titre*, other than the infants she had borne him, and a few paltry baubles. La Vallière, fool that she was, had never been interested in tangible proofs of the King's affection. She had fancied herself in love. *Quelle stupide!* As if a man's love would keep you warm in your old age! She, Athenais de Montespan, intended to place her trust in better security than that.

'Reflect on the matter for a while,' Athenais suggested. 'You can give me your answer when we meet at Versailles.' She knew, as did Françoise, that there could only be one answer.

Athenais rose and folded her sunshade. 'Come, Françoise, Blanche will be waiting for us.' Together they walked back to the castle, where Mme d'Heudicourt was waiting in Athenais' rooms.

On the journey back to Paris Blanche d'Heudicourt was puzzled by her friend's uncommunicative silence.

'I trust you enjoyed the day, Françoise,' she said anxiously.

113

Françoise smiled at her. 'Oh, greatly, Blanche. You need have no fear of that.'

Mme d'Heudicourt continued to enthuse over the King's gracious and friendly manner. 'But, Françoise,' she continued, 'did you notice that Athenais ate nothing at all this afternoon, and how pale she looks! There are shadows under her eyes – I could swear that she is unwell. I hope that it is merely her time of the month, and that she is not about to succumb to the fever.'

'Oh, I doubt it. Probably she is suffering from a surfeit of late nights. Life at Court must be most exhausting, so many entertainments, ceremonies, and changes of clothes. The King keeps late hours, and no one may retire before he does.'

At the mention of the King's name, Mme d'Heudicourt fell to discussing him once more, and declaring for the hundredth time how she looked forward to seeing the envious faces of their friends when they heard about their promenade with the King. Françoise was grateful for her friend's volubility, which enabled her to remain silent for the greater part of the journey, the needlework she had brought with her lying idle in her lap as the afternoon's conversation went through her mind over and over again.

At last, to her relief, the lights and the gates of the city of Paris lay before them. Soon they would reach home. Home, she thought with a touch of disquiet, to that shabby little rented house.

Not until Athenais had broached the subject had she realized how much she did indeed yearn for a real home of her own.

Chapter Eleven

The next few days passed for Françoise in a state of mental turmoil. Try as she would, she could not put the problem of Athenais de Montespan out of her mind. There was no ignoring the fact that, like it or not, she was directly involved in this impossible situation. Without first consulting her, Athenais had already suggested her name to the King, and he had approved the suggestion. To decline her assistance, therefore, at this stage, would be deliberately to court the King's displeasure.

Françoise felt deeply concerned, however, at the idea of putting a newborn baby out to nurse with no further concern for its welfare. Though at night she tossed and turned, sleepless, she could come to no conclusion as to what course of action she should take. Athenais' insistence on absolute secrecy meant that there was no one to whom she could confide her problem. Nanon, watching her mistress becoming paler, thinner and more harassed each day, picking at her food and irritable over the slightest thing, wondered what had brought about this change in her mistress's usually calm demeanour.

Ninon de l'Enclos was speechless when Françoise told her that she had been invited to the *divertissement* at Versailles, for she herself had been unable to secure an invitation. The forthcoming *divertissement* was the chief current topic of conversation in the salons of Paris. Everyone was grumbling about the distance, the journey, and the inconvenience involved, for there were only two inns in the village of Versailles, and many would have either to sleep in their carriages or travel back late at night. No one, however, who could possibly lay hands on an invitation would dream of missing the event.

'Tell me,' Ninon said to Françoise one afternoon as they sat by the open window in the salon of the little house in the rue des Tournelles, the sun streaming in on to the brightly polished table where a pot of flowers stood on a little crocheted mat. 'How on earth does my shy friend *la veuve* Scarron manage to secure an invitation to the *divertissement*, whilst the notorious Mlle de l'Enclos has been unsuccessful?'

115

Françoise, never unoccupied, looked up from her needlework. 'It is quite simple,' she answered. 'I was invited by Athenais de Montespan.'

'Our mutual friend Quanto, as Mme de Sévigné always calls her?'

'The very same.'

'But now that she is in high favour at Court, with a certain gentleman who must remain nameless, we rarely see her.'

'Nevertheless, I have seen her recently, and she has invited me. We are old friends.'

'And what shall you wear for this auspicious occasion?' Ninon asked with more than a touch of acidity in her tone, knowing full well that Françoise did not possess a suitable gown.

'I have managed to borrow a dress,' Françoise admitted. How she wished that she did not resent so much having to wear borrowed or cast-off finery. Would the day ever come when the necessity did not arise?

Nanon entered the room with a carafe of wine, a jug of water, and some freshly baked biscuits which she placed before her mistress.

'What a regular tartar your servant is!' Ninon said, after the door closed on Nanon. She munched a biscuit with appreciation. 'What an excellent lieutenant she would make in one of the King's regiments. I must inform the Comte de la Feuillère; he is looking for new recruits!'

'Do not mock her, Ninon. She has a rather forbidding exterior, I admit, but she is kind, and honest as the day is long.'

'Does she ever smile?'

'I cannot say I have ever noticed it. Poor soul, she never speaks of her past, but I think it could not have been happy.'

'But you are also reticent about your own early days, Françoise. I understand that they, too, were not very happy?'

But Françoise rarely chose to talk about her past, even to such a good friend as Ninon, so she only said: 'If I have been unlucky in my family, I have been truly fortunate in my friends.' She put down her needlework, and poured out wine and water. 'I do hope this lovely weather continues until next week,' she said, 'for the excursion to Versailles. I am so sorry you can't be present, Ninon.'

'I share your sentiments completely. But I must say, for a young lady about to be entertained by royalty, you do not look very happy, Françoise. Living with your gloomy servant has a bad effect on you. Where is your smile? I have not seen it today.'

Françoise was quiet as she busily plied her needle. Ninon guessed by her friend's silence that her words had struck home. After a few minutes she said: 'Something is worrying you, Françoise? Won't you confide in me?'

'I cannot, Ninon. It is true that I am preoccupied, but I cannot discuss the matter.'

'If I can help you in any way, you have only to ask.'

'In this case, even a kind friend can be of no assistance. It involves a decision which only I can make.'

Ninon looked at her friend anxiously. 'It concerns your friend Athenais de Montespan, does it not?'

'How did you – ?'

Ninon smiled. 'I was right. Come, Françoise, I know that you have not seen her for an age. Now, suddenly, you are the best of friends, and she is lending you clothes for a fête at Versailles. And what does she claim from you in exchange for these favours? Do not compromise yourself, I beg you, Françoise. You are surprisingly innocent in the ways of the world, my young friend.'

'Not as innocent as you think,' Françoise maintained. Secretly she was glad that by bringing the subject out into the open Ninon had made it possible for her to discuss her problem without a complete breach of Athenais' confidence – though she was not a little surprised at her friend's perspicacity in arriving so quickly at the heart of the matter.

'If I ask you for your opinion, Ninon, will you give me your solemn word that the subject will remain confidential?'

'My dear child, all my lovers confide their secrets to me, and I treat them with the solemnity of the confessional. I never reveal anything I have been told in confidence. You may unburden yourself without qualms, I promise you.'

'Quanto is *enceinte*!' Françoise told Ninon, the words tumbling out in a rush, so great was the relief of being able to talk of it. 'And the father is not her husband. It is – who you think it is.'

'And so there is the problem of the little one?' Ninon nodded her head wisely.

'Yes.'

'And you have been asked to arrange the matter, no doubt, relieving Quanto of such inconvenient details?'

'*C'est ça.*'

'And for this service you will no doubt be well remunerated?'

'So I am told.'

117

'Then why so downcast, *ma petite*? You are tailor-made for such an exercise, so reliable, so discreet. If ever I find myself in the same predicament, I shall also call on your services.' And Ninon threw back her head and laughed heartily.

'How can I make you understand?' said Françoise, throwing back her head in an uncharacteristic display of temper, and beginning to pace up and down the room in an agitated manner. 'It is a child's life we are discussing, not a bundle of washing to be disposed of.'

'What a strange creature you are, Françoise. You have been asked to perform a duty which will cause you but little exertion, and for which you will be handsomely paid – and that, for a person of your means, should be the end of the matter.'

'But Ninon, consider. You know what kind of women will take in an extra child to nurse – drunken sots with too many children of their own. What possible chance of survival do you think the baby has? If the husband doesn't throw it against the wall one night in a drunken rage, or if it doesn't eat dirt off the floor, a cat will try to suck milk from its lips and smother it. A newborn baby needs the most devoted care.'

'But tell me,' said Ninon, 'if the prospective mother is not concerned with such matters, are you not taking rather too much upon yourself? If the child has been placed in your charge by the mother and father, whoever they may be, then theirs must be the ultimate responsibility. You would merely be carrying out their orders, in the same way as the nurse, or whoever you select to take charge of it. If anything unfortunate did happen to the child, you could never be blamed.'

'I can't regard the situation in that light, Ninon, however hard I try. Were I to accept the care of the child, even indirectly, then in my own mind that child would be my charge. And I positively refuse to accept the responsibility of looking after the King's child! It is unfair of them to make such a demand!'

Ninon, seeing that her friend was dangerously near to tears, was silent for a moment. Then she said quietly: 'You are too conscientious by far, Françoise. You cannot take the troubles of the world upon your shoulders, you know.'

'Those are my feelings, nevertheless.'

'Your sentiments do you credit, my friend, but you will not take it amiss, I hope, if I point out to you that there are rich pickings to be had at Court by those who manage to insinuate themselves into the good graces of the King. This business will give you an excellent chance to ingratiate yourself with our friend, Quanto, who will soon be a force to be reckoned with, I am sure. They say the King is firmly in her grip. Why, if there is one person whose favour I should wish to enjoy at this moment, that person would be Athenais de Montespan. She may well be able to find you some well-paid sinecure of a position at Court. I would not let such a chance pass me by if I were you.'

'But I have no desire to live at Court, Ninon, to be restricted, confined to a certain pattern of life, albeit one of luxury and grandeur. I much prefer to be mistress of my own small domain, free to come and go as I please.'

'In other words, you prefer to be a big fish in a little pond, rather than a small fish in a bigger pond.'

'Yes, perhaps that is true. How well you know me, Ninon! Perhaps better than I know myself.'

'Do you think perhaps you place too much emphasis on your independence?' Ninon asked, taking out a tiny patch-box and looking at her reflection in the mirrored lid. 'Although I must admit, I have no wish to be subject to the whims of any master, even though he were my husband. That's why I have never married, though I have had what many women would call excellent offers.'

'If you had been obliged to live as I did with Paul Scarron,' said Françoise, stroking the fur of the marmalade kitten which had jumped up on her lap, 'for eight years at someone's constant beck and call, scarcely knowing a moment's peace, never free from his demands on my time and patience, you would appreciate, Ninon, why I never wish to be placed in that situation again, but to remain my own mistress, answerable to no one.'

'But you were fond of Paul, Françoise. You had some happy times together. If it were not for his illness – '

'Paul was kind to me,' Françoise admitted. 'He married me when I was penniless – took me in and gave me a good home, treated me always with respect. But he was helpless and needed someone to care for him. We both kept our side of the bargain. At the time I did not resent his demands. I was younger then, of course. I was only sixteen when I married. But when Paul died, and I had a taste of freedom for the first time in my life – then I vowed that I would not surrender that freedom lightly a second time. It is for that reason I doubt very much if I shall marry again, though my friends refuse to be convinced. But I know you understand me, Ninon. We are kindred spirits, you and I.'

119

Ninon drew on her silk mittens and rose to leave, her parasol over her arm. Linking arms, the two girls walked slowly down the stairs to the front door, where Ninon's sedan stood waiting.

'The world was not made for women like us,' Ninon said with laughing resignation. 'Women like Athénais de Montespan, and Louise de la Vallière, who can subjugate the men and make them dance to their tune – they are the lucky ones, they are the ones who rule.'

'You are the mistress of your own little world, Ninon. There are many men who would be happy to live under your rule.'

'Ah, but such men don't interest me! There is the paradox of woman! At heart we still want to be dominated by our men, though we pretend to put up a struggle.'

'Perhaps the world will change one day, and women will be free to lead their own lives,' said Françoise, as they embraced each other, and Ninon climbed into her sedan and was borne away.

A few days later Françoise and Nanon were returning from a shopping expedition to the Pont Neuf. The old bridge was a positive hive of people swarming to and fro, traders crying their wares, preachers ranting, song-sellers in top voice waving their song sheets, pedlars strolling up and down, children weaving their way in and out of the crowds, helping themselves to an apple or a bunch of grapes from the stalls as they passed. Quacks of all nationalities were selling their medicaments and remedies with assurances of their certain powers of healing, country folk displayed their baskets of fruit and vegetables beside children selling bunches of watercress and dairy girls with buckets of fresh milk suspended from yokes over their slim shoulders. Carts arrived all the time with fresh supplies of newly baked bread and rolls from the village of Gonesse just outside Paris, where the best bread was made with the finest flour, far better quality than the rough black bread sold at Les Halles.

There were shoemakers with their samples tied to a frame, drapers with tempting rolls of linen and lace, brocade and satin, glovemakers, pedlars with packets of needles, thread, and ribbons of every kind. Most of the traders on the Pont Neuf sold their wares from boxes placed on the wide parapet of the bridge, which could be collected up quickly in case of rain. Some had stalls, but only those tradesmen with assistants who could keep a careful watch for thieves, for such tempting displays of goods were an open invitation to the underworld of Paris. Every few yards one came upon a beggar, apparently blind or crippled, but these people did not perturb Françoise, for she knew that with the onset of nightfall many of them would disappear into the Cour des Miracles, the thieves' den of Paris, where their blindness or other handicaps would miraculously disappear for the night – until they took up their crutches or eye-bandages again in the morning, for the next day's business.

Françoise's basket, which Nanon carried, was full of fripperies she had purchased for the outing to the *divertissement*, a new ribbon for her hair, a pair of silk stockings, and a remnant of green velvet which she intended to embroider herself with bugle-beads and gold thread before giving it to the shoemaker to have made into a pair of high-heeled shoes. She looked longingly at the black velvet tippets edged with white fur, the newest fashion, but her budget would not run to such expense. So she contented herself with two yards of black lace with which to edge her last year's tippet and, as a final extravagance, bought some fine ruffles with which to edge her petticoat.

On the way home, in spite of her new purchases and the forthcoming outing to Versailles, her heart was heavy. They walked slowly along the Quai des Celestins, avoiding the Place de Grève, where pitch was being burnt, the fumes being thought to prevent the spread of the infections and fevers which were rife in the city of Paris during the summer months. Try as she would, Françoise could not ease her mind of her anxiety and uncertainty over the subject of Athenais de Montespan and her coming baby.

As they entered the Place St Gervais, on a sudden impulse, Françoise turned to Nanon.

'Continue home, Nanon,' she said. 'I will follow you later.'

Nanon looked at her mistress with puzzlement, but no explanations were forthcoming. A huge elm tree, rumoured to date from Roman times, stood in the centre of the small square, and mothers sat gossiping in its shade while the children played around their feet.

'Do not be anxious, Nanon. I shall soon be home.'

Nanon looked wonderingly at Françoise's face, so pale and drawn, at the lines which were beginning to show in the fine skin near her dull, listless eyes. 'Are you quite well, madame?'

'Please do as I ask, Nanon.'

'*Oui, madame*.' Nanon curtsied and went on. At the corner of the rue François-Miron she looked back. Françoise was standing motionless, watching the children laughing at their play.

Once Nanon was out of sight, Françoise crossed the cobbled street and went into the old church of St Gervais. Inside, after the noise and brightness of the square, the cool dim atmosphere and the faint smell of incense which floated from the altar seemed to act as an immediate panacea. The spacious silence of the church with its lofty ceiling soothed her nerves. She knelt and crossed herself. The sunbeams on the stained-glass windows of the nave made multicoloured patterns on the cool tiled floor. She bent her head, and rested her forehead on the seat in front of her. For some time she remained there, not in prayer, but simply allowing her thoughts to wander freely, and finding repose in the peace and silence.

At the sound of footsteps she raised her head. Père Gobelin, her confessor, was standing by her side, surprised to find her in the empty church in mid-afternoon. The stout, black-robed figure, a heavy gold cross gleaming on his broad chest, looked anxiously at her.

'Good day to you, Madame Scarron!'

'Good day, Father.'

'You pray alone today, madame.'

'Yes, Father.' Her lips trembled.

'Something is troubling you, my child?'

Françoise hesitated. 'Yes, Father.'

'Will you allow me to give you God's guidance?'

A longer pause. Ninon had spoken of the silence of the confessional. Yet Athenais had enjoined her to secrecy, a promise she had already broken by taking Ninon into her confidence. But I never asked for this burden to be placed on my shoulders, Françoise thought rebelliously. Am I then wrong to ask for help?

Père Gobelin sat down beside her. 'Will you not confide in me, dear lady?'

Haltingly, Françoise told him that she had been asked in confidence to take and care for the child of a high-born lady, whom circumstances prevented from bringing up the child herself.

The priest was silent for a moment.

'And the lady in question is married, and therefore cannot keep the child?'

'Yes.'

'And what of the father?'

'He is – already married.'

122

'And therefore this child is the fruit of a double adultery?'

There was a silence for a few moments before she answered: 'That is so, *mon Père.*'

The priest considered for a little while, and then asked: 'And yet, by means of this service to your friend, you can be of help and assistance both to this lady, whomsoever she may be, and to the as yet unborn child?'

'That is correct.'

'Then it is your bounden duty in the eyes of God to accept the charge. From what I know of your character, dear lady, I know that it is not in your nature to shirk your duty.'

'But, Father, I am hesitant to accept such a serious responsibility. I remember too well my own childhood – bandied about from pillar to post without a settled home. It is my considered opinion that a young child needs a secure environment and the constant care of a loving mother.'

'We cannot go through life without taking on duties of a serious nature, my child. You have no husband, and have not been blessed with children of your own, therefore you are not encumbered with personal responsibilities. God has seen fit to lead you to this task. You must not refuse.'

'Father Gobelin, I have not borne a child of my own. How then am I fitted for this responsibility?'

'God did not place us on this earth to lead a frivolous and meaningless existence, dear child. If He has ordained this task for you, you must grasp it with both hands, gladly showing Him that you are His instrument on earth, desirous of carrying out His will.'

'Yes, Father.'

Françoise bent her head obediently. Père Gobelin, making the sign of the cross over her, recited a Benediction.

'Let us pray together, my child.'

Together they knelt and prayed in the dim silence of the lofty church. When Françoise emerged once more into the hot dusty square and the brilliant sunlight, she felt cool and refreshed in body and in mind. The mothers had gone and the square was quiet without the sound of their children's laughter. With renewed vigour and with a sense of purpose, she walked quickly and energetically along the rue St Antoine in the direction of the rue des Tournelles.

Chapter Twelve

The morning of the long-awaited excursion to Versailles dawned fresh, sunny and bright. Françoise was up earlier than usual, and had long since been dressed, ready and waiting, when the carriage of Baron and Mme d'Heudicourt came rattling down the street.

Nanon had insisted on packing a basket of food for the journey, although Françoise pointed out that Versailles lay nearer to Paris than St Germain, and that the journey of almost ten leagues should take no more than two hours on such a fine summer day. Nevertheless, the basket, covered with a clean linen cloth, was taken aboard the coach and stowed away safely under a seat. Françoise bade Nanon adieu, and gratefully accepted Baron d'Heudicourt's assistance in climbing up into the coach.

She was delighted to find that Mme d'Albret and Mlle de Scudéry were to be their companions for the journey. Mme de Sévigné and Mme de Coulanges were travelling with the Aumonts in their carriage. Bets had already been placed on which party would arrive first at Versailles.

When Françoise's appearance had been duly admired, and the ensembles of the other ladies discussed, the party settled themselves as comfortably as possible, though the voluminous skirts of the ladies meant that the accommodation was somewhat cramped. Baron d'Heudicourt congratulated himself on his good fortune in having four such delightful travelling companions.

'All Paris seems to be on the road to Versailles today,' Françoise remarked, drawing back the leathern curtain – for the d'Heudicourt carriage boasted no windows – to watch the long lines of coaches filing slowly through the city gate, the Porte de St Cloud.

'Everyone who was able to beg, borrow or steal an invitation for today has certainly done so,' agreed Mme d'Heudicourt.

'But why such interest in Versailles?' asked Gisèle d'Albret. 'It is only a hunting lodge, not a palace like Fontainebleau, and certainly not so pleasantly situated as St Germain.'

'The King probably finds it convenient to have a country

estate within easy reach of Paris,' suggested Mlle de Scudéry.

'Certainly, at the pace we are travelling today that would be an advantage,' answered Baron d'Heudicourt, with a certain amount of impatience, for the congestion on the road was such that after travelling for more than an hour the party had barely left the city.

'We must resign ourselves to a long journey,' said Françoise.

In order to pass the time Nanon's basket was brought out and found to contain sausages, bread rolls, cheese, hard-boiled eggs, fruit and wine. The party fell to with gusto, for they had all been up early that morning, and the next hour passed pleasantly enough as they shared the food. By the time they had finished it was almost noon, and the coach was about to cross the Seine by the Sèvres bridge.

'Do you see the Chateau of St Cloud over there on the right?' the Baron said. 'Soon we shall be passing through the woods of Meudon, and then another half-hour or so will bring us to Versailles.' And true enough, it was little more than two o'clock when their carriage began the descent down the long, sloping, leafy approach to Versailles. Having heard so much of the magnificence of the Court of Louis XIV, the ladies were not a little disappointed when they saw the hunting lodge itself.

'The chateau is certainly not very large,' Mme d'Heudicourt said with regret in her voice, as the long line of coaches queued to pass through the gates. 'How will there be room to accommodate all these people?'

'The gardens are very extensive,' her husband reminded her. 'No doubt the greater part of the entertainment is to take place outdoors.'

'Then it is fortunate that the weather is so fine,' said Mme d'Albret.

It was true that the old red-brick hunting lodge, built by the King's father, Louis XIII, would not be able to hold such numbers of people as were now descending from their carriages in the oval courtyard. The carriages and horses were led away by the ostlers and lackeys, as the visitors, glad to abandon their cramped quarters, strolled in company with the crowd who were making their way across the inner courtyard. Here, on either side, stood the buildings originally intended to accommodate the members of the King's suite when they accompanied him on his visits to Versailles. Unlike his son, the chief aim of Louis XIII had always been to escape from the company of ladies.

Passing underneath a handsome portico, the company now found themselves in a smaller marble-paved courtyard where tables had been set up and the visitors were offered cool drinks and refreshments – which were gratefully accepted. They were then invited by the ushers to pass through the ground floor of the chateau and inspect the gardens at their leisure.

On being informed that a performance of a new play by Molière was to commence at four o'clock, Françoise and Mlle de Scudéry were overjoyed. Baron and Mme d'Heudicourt excused themselves and went off to converse with friends who hailed them.

'Shall we try to find Mme de Sévigné and Mme de Coulanges?' Françoise suggested.

'An excellent idea,' agreed Mlle de Scudéry, 'though how we shall ever find them in this crush, I do not know.' The two strolled through Le Nôtre's formal gardens. At the end, steps led down to a terrace bordering a lake where swans glided. Avenues of trees had been planted on each side of the gardens, which seemed to stretch as far as the eye could see. Françoise, much to her annoyance, found herself glancing round the throng, ostensibly looking for their friends but realizing that, in truth, she was wondering whether amongst such a crowd she would ever see the commanding figure of the King.

Near the Rondeau des Cygnes they found Mme de Sévigné and Mme de Coulanges, and together they began to stroll back in the direction of the chateau, for Françoise was anxious to have a good seat for the play.

'How exquisite these gardens are,' enthused Mme de Coulanges as they stopped to admire the sweet-smelling stock, tuberoses and jasmine, and orange trees in tubs. 'I have never seen anything to compare with them.'

'Look, there are the seats for the performance,' Françoise exclaimed, pointing to where the footmen and lackeys were arranging the chairs. The terrace, it seemed, was to take the place of a conventional stage. The ladies changed the direction of their walk accordingly. Françoise searched the faces of the people passing them by in vain.

'The King does not walk out today?' she ventured to ask Mme de Sévigné at last. Mme de Sévigné regarded her young, eager face with considerable amusement.

'The King is working with his ministers,' said Mme de Coulanges – and she and Mme de Sévigné roared with laughter. At last they took pity on her. 'It is at this time of day that the King usually visits his mistress,' explained Mme de Sévigné, seeing Françoise's bewilderment.

Françoise felt herself flush, and was angry with herself. Why should the King's activities be any concern of hers? She was furious at her own *gaucherie*.

As they neared the chateau, the people on either side of them began to part, making a path for a *calèche* to drive by. Sitting under one of the two sunshades fixed to the back of the conveyance, Françoise recognized the Queen, in company with two other ladies. As the equipage passed, Françoise turned to her friends, her lips framing a question. Mme de Sévigné laughed.

'Yes, the Queen is once more with child. Poor lady, I fear that she suffers in vain. She does not bring healthy children into the world.'

As the Queen's *calèche* drew up at the entrance to the chateau, a group approached from the other direction. Françoise immediately recognized with a thrill the handsome figure of the King. Athenais de Montespan, dressed in white and gold, walked beside him. Behind followed several ladies and gentlemen unknown to Françoise, save for the Duc de la Rochefoucauld escorting Louise de la Vallière, the new Duchess of Vaujours, looking as beautiful as ever. The black gown she wore, open at the front and loosely fastened with black velvet bands and rosettes over an underskirt of white embroidered with silver, masked but could not conceal the fact that she was seven months pregnant.

'I see that the air here is highly beneficial to the ladies,' murmured the Baron d'Heudicourt, coming up behind Françoise and her friends. 'They are all brimful of good health – do you not agree?' Mme d'Albret and Mme de Sévigné shouted with laughter. Françoise, however, remembering Athenais' pregnancy, as yet a secret to the others, was preoccupied with her own thoughts.

An usher came forward to assist the Queen to descend from her *calèche*, her ungainly short figure, heavily pregnant, making it no easy feat to reach the ground in safety. The King, Athenais and their party arrived at the steps at the same moment as she prepared to enter the chateau. The King bowed low to his wife, and with a courtly gesture offered her his arm to negotiate the steps; but Françoise was amazed to see that Athenais, instead of falling back to let them pass, merely acknowledged the Queen with an inclination of the head and sailed up the steps ahead of her, the King appearing not to notice this insult to the Queen.

'Athenais treats the Queen with scant respect,' Françoise said wonderingly, turning to Mlle de Scudéry, who merely shrugged her shoulders.

'They say the King is besotted by her, and for the moment, certainly, she can do nothing wrong,' she answered. 'Perhaps she, too, will end by becoming a duchess.'

But now the ushers were ringing handbells and asking the visitors to take their seats for the play.

The play, the first performance of Molière's *George Dandin*, was over at about half past six. With tears in their eyes from so much laughter, Françoise and her friends discussed the performance.

'I don't think I have ever laughed so much in my life,' said Françoise, her black eyes sparkling with pleasure.

'It will certainly be another triumph for M. Molière,' agreed Mlle de Scudéry.

'Come, come,' interrupted Mme de Coulanges, 'supper is about to be served.' A small army of footmen and lackeys were setting up trestle tables, laying them with white cloths and setting them with cutlery, plates and every variety of supper dishes. Françoise realized how hungry she was. Mlle de Scudéry smiled as she saw her eyeing the food.

'No one may dine until the King arrives,' she said. 'Let us hope that we shall not have long to wait.'

Fortunately they had not, for only a few minutes later a fanfare announced the arrival of the royal party to dine. The King, with the Queen on one side and the Duchess of Vaujours on the other, sat at the chief table. When the royal party were seated, the company were invited to take their places. To Françoise's amazement, Athenais de Montespan strolled over to join them, and sat down beside Gisèle d'Albret.

'Athenais does not sit with the King?' Françoise murmured questioningly to Mlle de Scudéry, who could not help smiling at her young friend's innocence.

'Discretion is the order of the day,' she replied. 'La Vallière is still supposedly the King's official mistress.'

'But he has hardly exchanged a word with her! Is it not general knowledge that Athenais – ?'

'Because, my young innocent, their *affaire de coeur* is a double adultery. Don't forget that Athenais has a husband. The King does not care to risk losing his high reputation in the eyes of the

128

world by allowing his Court to acquire the standards of the virtual brothel it became in the time of his grandfather, Henri IV.'

'But does not this place la Vallière in an invidious position?'

Mlle de Scudéry lowered her voice to a whisper as she leaned close to Françoise. 'And since when has our King begun to concern himself unduly with the feelings of other people? Probably he will allow her to retire to a convent when she has borne her child.'

Françoise began to eat in thoughtful silence. Now and then she stole a glance at the table where the royal party sat, each with a cadena, a gold fork and spoon in an individual case, in front of him. The centrepiece of the table was an eagle carved out of a solid block of ice. Françoise marvelled at the skill necessary to produce such a work of art in such a short time – it was already starting to melt. Suddenly she became aware that Athenais, seated on the other side of Mme d'Albret, was addressing her.

'I was just remarking, Françoise, how very handsome you look today,' Athenais was saying. 'May I enquire the name of your dressmaker?'

Françoise flushed with embarrassment as everyone near-by turned to look at her in Athenais' borrowed Court dress, which Nanon had skilfully adapted to her trim figure, less voluptuous than that of Athenais, so that it now fitted her to perfection. Françoise, who was so often forced to wear discarded finery, had over the years acquired the knack of adding her own personal stamp to an ensemble which had not originally been made for her. She had added a dainty pearl necklace and tiny pearl ear-rings to match the seed-pearls embroidered on the bodice of the green silk dress, and Ninon de l'Enclos had shown her how to dress her hair in a new style, parted in the middle and looped up at the sides with a black ribbon. The effect was one of quiet sophistication. She had excellent taste, though she preferred to dress rather more quietly than Athenais.

Françoise was determined to let nothing spoil the pleasures of the day, not even Athenais' waspish humour. 'Please allow me to return your compliments,' she said. 'I am happy to see you looking so much improved since we last met.'

Athenais had never looked lovelier. The first three months of her pregnancy and its attendant discomforts having passed, she seemed completely transformed from the pale, listless woman she had been that day at St Germain. Then, in addition to feeling queasy most of the time, she had been stricken with cold fear lest she should lose the interest of the King during her pregnancy. Now, since Louis had continued to express only vast amusement at her secret, she was feeling her old self again; the King seemed to regard it as a tribute to his manhood to have three women *enceinte* at the same time.

No wonder she was looking well, now that she basked securely in his admiration. Her face and bosom had filled out but her waist as yet remained slim, whilst her lovely eyes glowed with well-being. The pearly sheen of her gold-embroidered white satin dress enhanced the clarity of her superb skin, and the diaphanous white gauze of her draperies, edged with gold ruffles, set off the magnificent colour of her hair to perfection. It was easy to see why the King found her so entrancing.

'That's a devilishly attractive woman,' Baron d'Heudicourt murmured with admiration to Françoise. And indeed there was a new glow, an inner radiance about Athenais which her friends had not seen before. Was it because of the new life she carried within her? Or was it the physical satisfaction of her affair with the King, known to be a virile and ardent lover?

Whatever the reason, Françoise reflected with an inner pang, she herself had never had any reason to look so exuberantly happy, so brimming with *joie de vivre*. Until now she had been completely satisfied with her existence. Now, for the first time since Paul Scarron had died, she began to wonder whether indeed she had chosen the right way of life. She, too, could have had lovers and been kept in luxury. Beside the dazzling Athenais de Montespan, Françoise, only two or three years her senior, felt old, careworn and dull.

'We must look around for a cavalier for you, Françoise,' Athenais was saying, while Françoise blushed with embarrassment at being made so conspicuous. 'There are many fine *galants* here today – who will be your choice? Name him, and he shall dance one long attendance on you, I promise you!' Françoise tried to remind herself that Athenais had good intentions.

In fact, Athenais' motives in deciding to match her friend with a cavalier were completely selfish. She had sized up Françoise's impressive appearance today with more than slight consternation, and had decided to find a husband for her without delay, though her lack of a dowry would make this far from easy. But the influence of the King's favourite counted for a great deal – a word in the right quarters could work wonders. The memory of the attention the King had shown to Françoise at St Germain still rankled in Athenais' mind. That incident must not be allowed to repeat itself. Athenais wondered if she had been right in asking Françoise to become involved in her affairs; at the time she had seemed so eminently suitable . . .

'That young lady is the widow Scarron of whom you have spoken?' the King had asked her, the day after Françoise's visit to St Germain. 'But she is *charmante*.'

The cold fear that gripped Athenais' heart like a steel manacle whenever the King showed even a passing interest in a woman had suddenly possessed her. 'She is deeply religious, Sire, and leads a life of dull respectability. That is why I thought that she would prove suitable for our purpose.'

'Pious she may be, but I did not find her dull,' answered the King. 'On the contrary, I found her manner pleasant, her conversation lively, and her looks most attractive. You say that she is of gentle blood? Then we must find a husband for her here at Court. It is unnatural for an attractive young woman to remain celibate, unless she has a vocation.'

From that moment, Athenais had resolved to see Françoise safely married, though not at Court where she would be within the King's orbit. Still, once the arrangements for the coming child were made, they would keep her safely out of the way in Paris most of the time.

With this comforting thought in mind, Athenais began to eat the lavish meal with her usual hearty appetite. Françoise, thoroughly enjoying herself, inwardly reproached herself for her childish habit of blushing at her mature age. With her usual good spirits she joined in the animated conversation which ensued as the meal progressed. The subject of discussion was the play they had seen that afternoon, a rare treat for Françoise, for of her wide circle of friends only M. and Mme de Montchevreuil enjoyed the theatre, and only very occasionally did they invite her to join them in a visit.

The King, sitting with the Queen on one side of him, dull, and intent only on her food, and Louise de la Vallière on the other, sullen and melancholy, was seen to glance several times at the table where Athenais de Montespan and her friend Mme Scarron were keeping everyone in gales of laughter with their merriment.

As the meal drew to an end, Françoise was amazed to see Athenais suddenly freeze into immobility in the act of lifting a sweetmeat to her lips. Turning to discover the cause of her consternation, she saw only a slightly-built young man of thirty or so, soberly dressed in black, mounting the steps to the terrace where the guests were seated. He appeared to be in mourning, for long bands of violet crêpe fell from his hat and were draped from his shoulders. She had the feeling that she had seen him before, but could not remember under what circumstances. A hush fell over the gathering at his approach, and the laughter and chatter suddenly ceased.

'*C'est M. de Montespan!*' said Mlle de Scudéry, clutching at Françoise's arm.

'Athenais' husband?'

'The very same! He means to cause trouble, I'll be bound!'

'*Holà*, Montespan!' called out the Comte de Vaudreuil. 'What brings you to Versailles?' People began to titter, knowing full well the reason that had brought M. de Montespan hot-foot from his Gascon estates.

'What brings me to Versailles?' asked Montespan in a menacing manner, approaching the table where Athenais and Françoise sat, and halting half-way between it and the royal table where the King watched with interest, only a faint glimmer of a smile playing round his lips.

'Yes, what brings you to Versailles at this time of night, and why are you dressed like an undertaker?'

Athenais was like a statue, completely transfixed. She seemed unable to draw a breath, and her face was deathly pale. Was her husband bent on causing a disturbance? Was he intent on creating a scandal in the hope that the King would have her sent away? Was this to be the end of everything, of all her plans, her schemes, her ambitions? She longed to cry out, to tell him to go before the King noticed him, but it was too late.

'I'll tell you why I dress in this fashion,' roared M. de Montespan to the onlookers, leering at his wife and looking round the company in general. 'Because I am in mourning for my wife!'

The complete silence that fell upon the company was unnerving to Françoise. She looked around the gathering. No one moved or spoke, awaiting the King's reaction in order to follow his lead. Several moments ticked by. Athenais' throat was dry, and she dared not lift her eyes to meet those of the King.

The King threw back his head and laughed, chuckling until the tears almost ran down his cheeks, and the entire gathering followed suit until the peaceful garden was in an uproar. Everyone rose from the tables and soon the place was in complete confusion, all the company laughing and joking over the buffoonery of M. de

132

Montespan, who, meanwhile, approached his wife and took her arm.

'Come, Françoise,' said Mme de Sévigné. 'We are to see fireworks and illuminations now.' The royal party had already left their table.

'But Athenais?'

'Athenais is more than capable of protecting herself, I assure you.'

Doubtfully, Françoise allowed herself to be led along by her friends. The company wended its way down the terraced gardens in the gathering dusk to where some quaintly-shaped boats were moored upon the canal.

'They come from Venice, and are called gondolas,' Mlle de Scudéry explained.

The visitors were rowed along by the Venetian boatmen, the only ones with the necessary skill to ply the craft. One or two were occupied by musicians, and for some little time the only sounds were the strains of the violins as the gondolas floated along the water, glimmering in the twilight.

When they were at some little distance from the chateau, the boatmen laid down their oars, and as they looked back at the building, the fireworks began to explode with loud bursts of sound and flashes of light. The final display was of fireworks that exploded in sunbursts and interlaced L's, a tribute to the Sun King who had provided the entertainment.

Françoise, dabbling her hand in the cool water in the August darkness of that perfect night, knowing that she would never forget her first visit to Versailles, wondered if she would ever come here again. The one disappointment of this perfect day was that no opportunity had arisen of speaking with the King.

It was only on the journey home, her head banging rhythmically against the upholstery of the coach as she recalled the pleasures of the *divertissement* and tried hard not to fall asleep, that she remembered there had been no chance to discuss the arrangements that would have to be made with Athenais.

Chapter Thirteen

It seemed as if there was hardly any autumn that year, the golden warmth of summer gradually dwindling towards the end of September until October began, blustery and cold, and the chill wind dispersed the leaves in their heaps along the city streets. November arrived. Fog hung like a curtain over the river, and morning and evening a fine mist could be seen clinging damply to the huge dark outline of the palace of the Louvre.

Françoise and Nanon were fully occupied. The fevers of summertime had given way to the misery and distress of winter amongst the poor, the cold that they must endure in their threadbare clothes and freezing garrets, suffering from the usual winter ills with insufficient food to warm them.

With the money entrusted to her by the nuns at the Convent of the Petite Charité, Françoise bought flour, and she and Nanon would rise early to make a dough which they took to the baker in the rue Birague. Later, they would call back to collect the freshly baked loaves and then set out to distribute them to the needy. They made it their business, however, always to be home by four o'clock at the latest, for thieves and vagabonds abounded in Paris after nightfall and made the streets unsafe for all, particularly women.

In the evening, unless Françoise was dining with friends, the door of the little house in the rue des Tournelles was safely bolted as early as five, and after they had supped early, Françoise would often retire to bed where it was easiest to keep warm without using precious fuel. Nanon would sit rocking herself in the little kitchen, staring into the dying fire until it went out, when she too went to bed.

So the months quickly passed, and people were already beginning to talk of Christmas and the New Year. Françoise was anticipating a quiet Christmas, for the Heudicourts, with whom she usually dined on Christmas Day, would be out of town visiting relatives, and the Montchevreuils were spending the winter at their estate in the south of France. Gisèle d'Albret was expecting a child early in January, and consequently would not be entertaining over the festive season.

At the Louvre, where the Court was in residence until the New Year, the usual dazzling sequence of entertainments continued for the winter season, with Athenais de Montespan their star, Queen in all but name, radiantly beautiful and setting a new fashion with the loose, flowing gowns she had begun to wear. The King provided an endless round of concerts, plays, and balls for the amusement of his Court, but those who composed the audiences at these functions attended chiefly from a sense of duty, for their only real enthusiasm was for gambling.

Every night in the gaming-rooms of the Louvre, richly dressed ladies in their satins, brocades, velvets and gold lace, demurely concealing their painted faces behind exquisite fans, risked beatings from their husbands by playing for outrageously high stakes. And there were many unscrupulous gentlemen – the splendour of their beribboned and frilled ensembles, their flowing periwigs and high, tapping heels, more than matching the ladies' – who lost no opportunity, despite their gallant manner, of taking advantage of a lady's lack of skill at play. Working in groups of two or three, the professional gamblers would arrange it so that a couple of them flirted with the lady to distract her full attention from the game, whilst the other pressed home his advantage. Others played hoping merely to raise some ready cash, or simply for the thrill of the game; but, whatever the reason, the lure of the gaming-tables seemed irresistible to all. Every night fortunes changed hands on the throw of the dice.

Athenais de Montespan, now that she was able to rely on the King's credit, was the most inveterate and reckless gambler of them all, and was to be seen playing cards, winning and losing back colossal sums of money, from morning till night. Even the Queen had succumbed to the craze, and played constantly in the company of the Comtesse de Soubise, at a discreet distance from the table where Athenais de Montespan held court.

'Our friend Quanto seems to be higher in the King's favour than ever, despite her condition,' Mme de Sévigné remarked knowledgeably one evening when Françoise dined with her and her sister-in-law, Mme de Coulanges. 'Last night at the Louvre, she leaned her head on his arm in a most familiar manner as he stood beside her at the card tables, which everyone took as warning to other hopefuls that she has him still firmly in her toils.'

'It seems that pregnancy agrees with her, unlike the poor

Queen,' said Mme de Coulanges. 'I saw her a few days ago, leaving René's perfume shop on the Pont St Michel, and I must say, I have never seen her look lovelier.'

'When will she be confined, do you estimate?' asked Mme de Sévigné. 'Early in the New Year?'

'Oh, no, not before Eastertide, I imagine,' answered Mme de Coulanges. 'She cannot be more than five months, I am sure.'

'You think so? I would say six or seven, myself. But then, you have carried nine children. As the mother of only two, I must allow you superior knowledge of the subject.'

'Is it general knowledge then, that Athenais is soon to bear the King's child?' Françoise asked. It was a relief to know that the secret she had been tormented by for so long was now out in the open.

'It is what might be called an open secret, my dear. No one dares openly mention la Montespan's condition at Court, yet it is perfectly apparent to any woman with eyes in her head that she is carrying.'

Françoise, suddenly noticing the lateness of the hour, went to find a servant to bring her wrap. Despite their protests that it was yet early, she insisted on saying goodnight, after profuse thanks for her friends' hospitality. Athenais, her pregnancy and her forthcoming confinement were not subjects she was anxious to discuss.

The day before Christmas a note arrived for Françoise, inviting her, if she was not otherwise engaged, to visit Ninon de l'Enclos on Christmas Day. Françoise, wrapping herself up warmly for the day was bitterly cold, bright but not sunny, first went to hear Mass at the church of St Paul des Champs. Then, after buying a small posy of flowers in the rue Birague, she made her way to the Place Royale. To her surprise she found Ninon in bed, suffering from a bad cold.

Ninon welcomed her warmly, for they had not seen each other since October. 'My dear Françoise! How happy I am to see you! Will you permit me to receive you in this fashion? As you see, I am indisposed, and did not feel like the effort of dressing myself.'

'Do not disturb yourself on my account,' said Françoise, kissing her warmly.

'Will you allow me to entertain you *à la ruelle*?'

'With pleasure,' answered Françoise. The *ruelle*, the space between the bed and the wall, was furnished with a comfortable *fauteuil* and a footstool. She seated herself in the easy-chair, and smiled at her friend. 'It is cosier here than it would be in the salon, since we are *tête à tête*.'

'I have invited no one else. I have not seen you for an age, and thought we could spend a quiet day together.'

'Nothing could delight me more, Ninon, except that I am sorry to find you unwell.'

Ninon rang for the maid. 'It is nothing more than a cold in the head, *chérie*, do not concern yourself. Besides, this is the only way to keep warm in this weather. Put these flowers in water, Paulette,' she instructed the serving-girl who appeared. 'Will you take some hot chocolate, Françoise, or a little wine?'

'The chocolate would be warming – but it is a festive day today, Ninon. Let's drink to the future and what the New Year may bring.'

'How right you are. Bring some wine, Paulette, and a rug for madame's knees. It is bitterly cold in here. Make up the fire, will you?'

'Well, Ninon,' asked Françoise, violently blowing her nose, 'what have you to tell me after this long time?'

'Very little, my dear, except that I am madly in love.'

'What, again? For the fourth time this year?'

'Yes, madly, hopelessly in love.'

'Why hopelessly? I thought you held all your admirers in thrall! Does this one resist?'

'Yes, a little. That is what makes the drama of the affair. There is no spice in instant capitulation!'

'How long has this been going on?'

'Oh, for a few weeks. He is a cousin of the Marquis de Villarceaux. His name is Jean-Jacques de Renville. His cousin brought him to my salon for one of my Friday night *soirées*. As soon as I saw him I fell madly in love. Charles is broken-hearted, but I have no doubt he will recover.'

'Not Charles de Sévigné?'

'The very same. You are friendly with his mother, I think? She will be happy to hear that I no longer have designs on her son. She has not yet forgiven me for the death of his father who, as you may know, died in an *affaire d'honneur* – though she was well rid of that rake. He had had every woman of quality in Paris – and some who were not of quality, besides – when he married her. On his death she became a rich widow, as free as the wind. I consider she has a good deal to thank me for!'

Paulette brought the wine and poured out glasses for the two ladies.

'Well, Françoise? What shall the toast be?'

'To your good health and fortune, Ninon.'

'And to yours. *Santé!*'

Sipping the wine, Françoise presently began to feel a little warmer. 'You may take my cloak and gloves, Paulette.' The little maid made up the fire and went out, Ninon instructing her to bring dinner sharp at two.

'I do not intend to let my indisposition affect my appetite,' she joked. 'And how is your sergeant-major, Nanon?'

'Oh, as well as ever. She has a tough constitution and never seems to suffer from colds or bad headaches as I do.'

'The peasantry acquire immunity to these things early in life, my dear. They have to be strong to survive their early days. She is a country-woman, isn't she, and used to working on the land?'

'Indeed, I have no idea. As I told you, she has never said anything to me of her life before she came to me.'

'And how has life been treating you of late, Françoise? Your friend Athenais de Montespan is in high favour, I hear, even though she is nearing her time. The royal nurseries will soon be choc-a-bloc, since the Queen and la Vallière were both recently delivered.' Ninon laughed delightedly, her arms round her knees. 'The King is nothing if not generous with his favours!'

'They say he is very much in love with Athenais. I am glad to hear it.' Against her will, Françoise thought of the summer day when she had strolled on the terrace in the sunshine at St Germain with the King, so handsome and smiling, at her side.

'Tell me,' Ninon said, 'when is your little charge due to arrive in this world?'

'Early in April, it seems.'

'Then you have ample time to make your plans.'

'Athenais has sent me a sum of money for the purpose, and I intend to take some rooms for the nurse and child. They will need servants, too, of course.'

'And where shall you establish your nursery?'

'There is a house in the rue d'Alexandre, I believe, where there are rooms to let. It is a quiet street, near enough for me to visit frequently. When Christmas is over I shall make it my business to see if it is suitable.'

'How thorough you are in everything you do, Françoise. I do

138

hope if ever I am in such a delicate situation you will come to my assistance.'

Paulette, entering with their dinner on a large tray, brought up a little table for Françoise and Ninon placed the tray across her knees.

The dinner was excellent, lavish – two kinds of *potage*, roast partridge, beans and lentils. Afterwards Paulette brought the ladies a bowl of scented water in which to freshen their hands, and another tray of nuts, fruit and sweetmeats.

'Shall we have a game of *tric-trac*?' Ninon suggested when they could eat no more.

About four, when Paulette came to draw the curtains and light the *torchères*, Françoise looked out at the darkening street and said: 'It is time for me to go. I do not care to be abroad alone after dark.'

'Oh, please don't leave, Françoise. I shall order my sedan for you when you wish to go, and the footmen will escort you.'

Françoise hesitated.

'Please, Françoise. I assure you that you will be carried home in safety when you want to leave. Stay and take supper with Bragelonne and Vivonne.'

'Athenais' brother?'

'Yes. He is a frequent visitor here when he is in Paris.'

'But what of your lover, Jean-Jacques? Where is he tonight?'

'Oh, his wife insisted that he accompany her to the country over Christmas. What a nuisance these wives can be! No wonder the men get so bored with them. Paulette!' The girl appeared at the door. 'Is the fire lit in the *petit salon*?'

'*Oui, Madame.*'

'Then bring me my dressing gown, and send Janine to help me arrange my hair. Hurry!'

'Do you suppose the men will object to my *déshabillé*?' she asked Françoise as she sat down at the dressing-table and Janine came to brush her hair.

In her heart of hearts Françoise did indeed feel that it was most unseemly to appear so, but, she told herself, Ninon's way of life was not hers. 'Your friends will love you, no matter how you dress,' she told Ninon loyally. 'But I fear that you risk a fever in that thin gown.' Ninon wore a dressing-gown made of Indian cotton imported from the East, the latest fashion.

'Oh, I prefer not to wrestle with my lacings tonight. I am far more comfortable like this.' Ninon swivelled round to face the

139

maid as Janine carefully powdered her mistress's face and tied a ribbon in her hair.

'Would you like to borrow some powder or rouge, Françoise? Oh, come now, *chérie*!' She laughed at Françoise's horrified expression. 'It's Christmas Day. Let's give you a patch or two, just for fun.'

Françoise refused to succumb to Ninon's blandishments. Powder and paint were not for her. Admiring Janine's adept handiwork, however, she allowed her to rearrange her hair. Just as the girl was putting the finishing touches to her coiffure, there was the sound of horses clattering below.

'The visitors are here. Janine, tell Paulette to bring mulled wine to the *salon intime*, and ask Gaston to set up the card tables. Come, Françoise.'

The two women crossed the landing and entered the *petit salon*, more cosy and less intimidating than Ninon's famous Yellow Room where she held her Friday night *soirées*. After a few minutes, while the men divested themselves of their cloaks and gloves outside, Paulette announced: 'The Vicomte de Bragelonne and the Duc de Vivonne.'

Two men entered the room. Ninon introduced them to her friend, and the necessary salutations were made.

'Mme Scarron and I have met before,' Vivonne said, smiling down at her from his height of six feet. 'Allow me to present my friend, the Vicomte de Bragelonne.'

'*Enchantée, monsieur*.'

'The pleasure is mine, madame.'

Bragelonne, much shorter than Vivonne, was nevertheless a highly presentable young man of thirty or so, elegantly dressed and with a pleasant manner which Françoise immediately liked. As they sat chatting over the mulled wine, Vivonne told Ninon how glad he was to find her at home. 'Everyone seems to be either out of Paris over Christmas, or else staying in bed to keep warm.'

'In truth, that is what I have been doing all day. Is that not so, Françoise? You may flatter yourself that it was only the prospect of your visit that induced me to forsake the comfort of my bed. How long is your leave?'

'Only four days. I have to return to winter quarters on Friday. However, in that short time I intend to wine and dine enough to fortify myself for the privations of the winter in Flanders, in addition to satisfying my other needs.' Ninon had the grace to blush at this, while Françoise pretended to be admiring the pattern of her crystal wineglass. 'Bragelonne, the lucky fellow, has a whole fortnight in which to divert himself with the ladies.'

'Yours is the penalty of being a Marshal of France,' Bragelonne told him. 'The services of a mere Captain of the Guard can be dispensed with more easily.'

'What shall we play, gentlemen?' Ninon asked as Gaston set up the card tables. '*Quadrille, lansquenet* – What is your choice'

'Upon my soul, I know not,' said Bragelonne. 'If you ladies are going to rob us of our pay tonight, perhaps we should not allow you to decide. What say you, Vivonne?'

'What is your preference, Madame Scarron?'

Françoise, reluctant to admit that she was not acquainted with the game of *lansquenet*, plumped for *ombre*, and they settled down to play. She was uncomfortable at the prospect of gambling, for she felt that it was wrong to play with money which could feed the poor who suffered so much in the winter; but Ninon, suspecting her friends reluctance, tactfully insisted that the stakes were kept to a minimum. After an hour or so, Françoise was astonished to find that she had won twenty livres, but quietened her pangs of conscience by resolving to donate it to the nuns. At the end of the first game, Françoise went to call a lackey to take a message to Nanon, who was expecting her home for supper, to let her know that she would not be home till late.

'Where have you been hiding your charming friend? Bragelonne asked Ninon as he dealt the cards. 'I am sure I should have remembered if I had met her before.'

'Françoise often visits,' Ninon replied. 'It is pure coincidence that you have not previously met.'

'She is a widow, I think you said?'

'Yes, she lives very quietly with only one servant, and does not often go out in mixed company. She has her own circle of friends with whom she dines *en famille*.'

Bragelonne pricked up his ears. So the attractive Mme Scarron has an ideal love-nest, with no servants to spread gossip. This sounded as if it would reward further investigation. Vivonne, guessing the nature of his thoughts, nearly burst out laughing. Bragelonne, he knew, was barking up the wrong tree. How many times had Athenais told him what a virtuous old prude Françoise Scarron had become!

Gazing at her as she entered the room, however, he was forced to admit that she looked very far from being the dried-up, respectable old virgin-widow – the picture Athenais maliciously painted of her. True, she was dressed in black as became a widow, but it seemed to accentuate her air of quiet elegance, as did the sophisticated way in which her hair was dressed, drawn back from her oval face. With her beautifully expressive dark eyes and slightly sallow complexion, she had the classic good looks of an Italian madonna. She reminded him of the portraits of the Medici women in the Louvre. Yes, there was something extremely attractive about Françoise Scarron, something in the graceful way she moved and carried herself. She was certainly not the type he usually bedded – but, given a little encourage-ment . . . In contrast to Françoise's quiet black dress with its high neck, its severity relieved only by the whiteness of her collar of Valenciennes lace pinned by a fine cameo brooch, Ninon, painted and uncorseted, looked raddled and blowzy. Her face was beginning to reflect her way of life. Françoise seemed al-most young enough to be her daughter.

After they had supped on the remains of the partridge, with pastries and salads and wine in plenty, the two women sat back in their chairs while the men regaled them with lurid tales of their adventures with the army. Vivonne, a seasoned drinker, downed the contents of several bottles of burgundy apparently without any effect. Bragelonne, on the other hand, was flushed, for the small room with its strong fire had become very warm, and his speech, previously so clipped and precise, was now slurred. Nevertheless, Françoise was enjoying herself, revelling in the men's obvious admiration; Bragelonne was openly flirting with her.

'I declare,' Ninon whispered to her as the two men argued about the next game of cards, 'you spend so much time in the company of women, Françoise, that you have forgotten how to enjoy yourself with men.'

Françoise nodded smilingly, forced to admit the truth of Ninon's statement. She did indeed spend the greater part of her time in the company of her women friends and their children. Bragelonne's outrageous flirting made her feel feminine, attrac-tive and young again. It was certainly a contrast to the role of unpaid housekeeper-cum-governess she usually adopted in the homes of her wealthy friends, who, although they entertained her generously, nevertheless made sure that they received payment in kind.

As the church clock of St Paul des Champs struck ten, the

men announced their intention of going to a gaming-house to play *hoca*. 'The stakes here are too small to suit us, Ninon,' Vivonne complained. 'Why, I've been playing like a fox all night, and I have succeeded only in losing ten livres to Mme Scarron.'

'You could scarcely have a more charming partner to whom to surrender your money,' murmured Bragelonne lazily, stretched out in his easy-chair, his head lolling against a cushion, his hand holding out his empty glass.

'Then you should be glad you were playing for small stakes,' Ninon said. 'No, Bragelonne, I shan't send down for any more wine – you'll drink me out of house and home. Go and win your drinking money elsewhere.'

'Come, Bragelonne.' Vivonne hauled his protesting friend out of his chair. Bragelonne yawned, reluctantly straightened his periwig and adjusted his cravat.

'I shall have Gaston order the sedan to be made ready,' Ninon told Françoise, who was looking a little anxious. But the men were aghast at this suggestion.

'Mme Scarron to travel alone at this time of night? Under no circumstances,' Bragelonne protested.

'The footmen shall accompany her, and Gaston, too, if necessary,' Ninon said. 'Or should you like to spend the night here, Françoise?'

'It is only a short distance to the rue des Tournelles,' Françoise protested. 'If it were daylight I should be able to walk home in five minutes.'

'Well, it is not daylight, and you shall not travel unaccompanied,' Bragelonne assured her.

The two women said goodnight at the top of the stairs, Françoise insisting that Ninon should not expose herself to the cold by the open door in her thin dressing-gown. Then, having donned their cloaks, Françoise and her two escorts went out into the street where the sedan was waiting. Bragelonne handed her in and then, to her amazement, got in beside her. The chair, meant to provide accommodation for only one person, albeit allowing plenty of room for their clothes, was cramped for two. Before Françoise could remonstrate, the footmen picked up the chair and moved off. Vivonne rode behind with the two horses; Françoise could hear the clop, clop of their hooves on the cobbles as they turned the corner of the Place Royale into the rue des Francs Bourgeois.

'I trust you are not incommoded by my company?' Bragelonne murmured, slipping his arm round Françoise's shoulders. His face was flushed, his eyes bloodshot. She could smell the drink on his breath as he leaned close to her, and she shrank away as far as she could in the confined space. She knocked on the window of the sedan to hurry the footmen but, struggling with the weight of two persons instead of the usual one, they could go no faster.

'Come, is my company so repellent to you?' Bragelonne said as she tried to push him away, his arms now round her waist. He began to grope under her thick cloak but she held it close.

'You are insolent, sir! Don't you dare touch me!'

He held both her arms so that she could not move, and with his weight pressed her back against the velvet upholstery, trying in vain to kiss her while she moved her head frantically from side to side.

'You're hurting me! Please let me go! Vivonne! Vivonne!' she shrieked – but knew that he could not hear her, and wondered whether, even if he could, he would come to her aid. Perhaps the whole thing had been arranged between the two of them.

'You're hurting yourself! Keep still and you won't be hurt. Come now, *chérie*, just a little kiss – ' His lips were wet and utterly repugnant. She could not move as he pressed his caresses upon her. All she could do was pray that in a moment the footmen would set her down. They could not be far from her home now, and they knew exactly where it was, having carried Ninon there so many times.

Bragelonne was infuriated by her resistance. 'Damn you, you bitch,' he panted, as she dug her fingernails into the back of his neck. 'You're a widow, aren't you? No innocent virgin! What's one more slice off a cut loaf?'

For answer, as he disengaged one of her arms to drag her fingers from the back of his neck, she put her hand up to her head and, swiftly drawing out one of the silver, pearl-topped bodkins that held up her hair, she jabbed it into his neck as hard as she could – praying that it would not kill him, but knowing it would be useless to stick it into the lower part of his body where it could have no effect through the thickness of his clothes.

Bragelonne let out a scream and pressed his hand to his neck. Blood was trickling through his fingers. Françoise forced open the door just as the footmen were setting down the chair outside her house, and ran to her front door, banging on it frantically as Nanon made sleepy haste to open it.

Bragelonne staggered out of the chair and lurched unsteadily to Vivonne who looked down at him in surprise from the back of his horse.

'*Nom de Dieu!* The vixen! She's cut me, and damned near killed me!' The handkerchief he took from his neck was dark with blood. He pressed it back to stop the bleeding.

Vivonne threw back his head and roared with laughter. The door of the little house was firmly closed by now, lights appeared at the windows and inside Nanon was lighting torches to see what help she could give Françoise, who was sitting crying on the bottom stair.

'So you let her win all that money for no result!' Vivonne cried, convulsed with laughter. 'That was an expensive ride, my friend!'

Cursing profusely, Bragelonne managed to mount his horse. The footmen had turned the chair round and were disappearing in the direction of the Place Royale.

'I could have told you that you would achieve nothing with Mme Scarron,' Vivonne told his friend, still laughing. 'How often has my sister warned me not to waste my time with her!'

Bragelonne, regarding his blood-soaked handkerchief, was not amused. 'She's a widow, damn her, isn't she? What virtue has she to protect, I'd like to know!'

'Widow she may be,' Vivonne chuckled as he turned his horse, 'but she's that rare thing in this city, a woman of virtue. No, I'm afraid you backed the wrong filly tonight, Bragelonne.'

'Where are you going?'

'Back to see Ninon, to divert her with your adventures. I wager she'll be vastly amused. Good night!'

Vivonne spurred his horse and rode off in the direction of the Place Royale. Bragelonne, seething with rage, went off alone to a bawdy house where he won 200 livres at a game of backgammon and found a plump young girl fresh to the profession from the country – a combination of events which helped to console him for his lack of success with Mme Scarron.

Meanwhile Françoise, having sent Nanon to bed, bathed and then lay sleepless on her bed, its curtains drawn. She had scented her face and arms with all the Carmelite water she could find in an effort to blot out the memory of Bragelonne's grip, the smell of his breath and the aroma of male sweat as he had pressed his body close to hers, forced his lips on hers.

She wondered why she was unlike other women, who openly

145

encouraged such advances – for she had a strong suspicion that even women like Gisèle d'Albret, married to a Marshal of France, and Blanche d'Heudicourt, married only a few years, took lovers on occasion. Why then did she cling to this celibate existence, when she enjoyed the flattery and admiration of men?

A wry smile touched her lips as she began to think about the men who had figured in her life until now. Her father, from whom she had known nothing but curses and kicks; her brother, to whom she had been greatly attached, and who had run away when their frail little mother gave up the struggle for existence and died. Her husband, Paul Scarron –

At the thought of Paul Scarron and her life with him she buried her head in the coolness of the pillow. How everyone had sympathized with her when he died and she was left a widow at the age of twenty-five. Yet she knew that most of her friends were glad for her sake that she was free of a helpless cripple. If only they knew! They had pitied her, those well-meaning friends; for, knowing Scarron's condition, they had imagined her to be a virgin after eight years of marriage. And indeed she was, in the sense that her virginity remained intact.

But if the defences of her body had not been assaulted, her mind told a different story; of a young girl forced to undergo unspeakable intimacies – married to a man who, while he could not reach a glass of water standing beside his bed, would nevertheless delight in fondling the soft, young flesh of the wife lying beside him. And eventually, much against her will, those strokings and fumblings had aroused in her maturing body desires and passions that could not be satiated, and she would lie there caught up in a welter of uncontrollable emotions, tormenting her soul and her conscience, while he, drugged with opiates for his pain, slept like a baby.

As the years passed, she had been forced to conquer her natural longings and desires. She wondered despairingly if she would ever now be able to give herself wholeheartedly to a man. Was she condemned to spend the rest of her life afraid to come out from the shadows?

Burying her face in the pillow she wept softly, so that Nanon would not hear, until the cold light of dawn, entering the uncurtained window, found her asleep.

Chapter Fourteen

The morning of January 6th, 1669 was damp and cold. A pale, watery sun was struggling to shine through the early morning mist as Françoise and Nanon left the rue des Tournelles just before eight, walking briskly in the direction of the quartier des Halles. There was a great deal of shopping to be done as Françoise had insisted that this year she should have the pleasure of entertaining her friends to dinner on Twelfth Night.

Taking the shortest route along the rue du Roi de Sicile and the rue des Lombards, they crossed the rue Quincampoix and arrived at the street markets of les Halles. The streets were crowded even so early in the morning, for the winter days were short. They soon found themselves surrounded by the market people calling their wares, servants shopping for the *hôtels* of the rue St Honoré, housewives, traders, thieves and beggars of all descriptions. Keeping a firm hold of her purse, Françoise held up her skirts as best she could to prevent them trailing in the mud and refuse which littered the streets, while Nanon, who wore sabots, held the baskets.

Their first purchase was the extra candles which would be needed to light the salon, and then they spent some time selecting the best vegetables they could find to make the soup, brown, swelling onions, thick orange carrots and fat white leeks. They bought an ox tongue, a pair of larded pigeons, artichokes, garlic and sorrel for seasoning, apples for a fruit pastry, and sugared almonds to offer the guests with their dessert. Because these last proved so expensive, Françoise reluctantly had to forgo the preserved cherries and *bonbons d'anis* which looked so tempting, for there was still the wine to purchase, and extra firewood to have sent in.

When they had finished their shopping, they went to hear Mass at St Eustache, and by twelve noon they were home again. While Françoise unpacked their purchases, Nanon rolled up her sleeves, put on her apron and prepared to make the soup, which would take many hours. The pigeons could be dealt with later. Françoise left her in the kitchen – for under her tuition

147

Nanon had become an able cook – and went to choose two of her best linen tablecloths from the linen cupboard. One alone would not be large enough to cover the dining-table.

There was a knock at the back door and Fleurette arrived, the daughter of the carpenter who lived round the corner in the rue Barbette. Françoise had asked her to come in to help for the day and wait at table, which she was happy to do for 30 sous. Françoise put her to polishing the wall-sconces in the salon and the little girl, barely more than thirteen, set to with a will.

By five o'clock everything was in readiness. A cheerful fire burned brightly in the fireplace in the salon and the *torchères* were all lit. The warm but gentle glow of fire and candlelight did not reveal the shabbiness of the threadbare Persian carpet, which had seen better days. The few pieces of silver Françoise possessed, an elegant candelabrum, a large epergne and a prettily engraved sugar-dish, stood in the centre of the table, which Françoise had laid with great care, even following the old custom of providing for her guests a bowl of rosewater to refresh their hands in between courses – although most people now used a fork as well as a knife. On a small side table, covered with a crocheted lace cloth, stood the pewter coffee pot, tiny coffee cups, and the small silver bon-bon dishes filled with the sugared almonds and comfits. Françoise was pleased with the effect. It was a pity there were no flowers available at this time of the year, to make a centrepiece for the table. She put the carafe of red wine on the table, and noticed that she had forgotten the napkins. When she had arranged them on the table, she closed the heavy brocade curtains, for it was quite dark outside, and went to change. As she was dressing and arranging her hair she realized she had forgotten to order juniper wood from the fire-wood merchant, to keep the air fragrant and prevent the salon from becoming too stuffy. Well, it was too late now.

Promptly at half past six the guests began to arrive, first Mlle de Scudéry, and then Nicole d'Aumont, each in her sedan. Françoise had barely greeted them and helped them to divest themselves of their furs when, with a rattle of wheels, the Sévigné coach arrived, and the lackeys were opening the doors and helping the ladies to descend: Mme de Sévigné, her daughter, whom Françoise had not previously met, and Mme de Coulanges.

After they had exchanged kisses and compliments and New Year greetings – for they had not met since before Christmas – Mme de Sévigné turned to the elegant, willowy young lady of twenty-three or so, dressed in the height of fashion, who stood beside her.

'Well, what do you think of my daughter, Françoise? Is she not truly the prettiest girl in France? Allow me to present to you the future Madame la Comtesse!' Mlle de Sévigné was soon to be married to the Comte de Grignan, and the fond mother was bursting with pride at the fine match she had arranged for her daughter. No need to mention that the gentleman in question was nearly forty and had already buried two wives.

Françoise curtsied politely, but the prospective Comtesse languidly extended a cool white hand which she soon withdrew, looking round the small anteroom where they stood with every appearance of surprise. As Françoise led the way upstairs to the salon, she expressed some astonishment to her mother at finding herself in such humble surroundings.

Mme de Sévigné lifted her skirts and took her daughter's arm to mount the staircase. 'Oh, but you will enjoy yourself tonight, I promise you, my dearest,' she assured her. 'The company of Mme Scarron is *délicieuse*.'

The future Comtesse de Grignan appeared unconvinced, and glanced with disdain around the small salon where Mlle de Scudéry and Nicole d'Aumont were already seated at the table, leaving the two easy-chairs vacant for the guests of honour, Mme de Sévigné and her daughter.

Mme de Coulanges had not visited Françoise's home before. 'What a delightful salon you have, Françoise,' she said.

'I am afraid it is somewhat cramped – '

'Well, it is not large, but it makes a charming *salon intime*. Very pleasant, my dear, very pleasant.'

Marguerite de Sévigné, sitting stiffly in her armchair, stared at the shabby carpet and old-fashioned curtains. Her lip curled slightly in distaste.

'May I offer you an aperitif, ladies?' Françoise suggested.

Mme de Sévigné shook her head. 'Not for me, my dear, but my dearest Marguerite is partial to a drop of cherry brandy before her meal.'

Françoise hastened to pour out a liqueur for Mlle de Sévigné, and to offer some to the other ladies. They had barely finished drinking and wishing each other a happy New Year when Fleurette tapped at the door.

'Shall we serve the dinner now, madame?'

Françoise smiled. Fleurette was neatly dressed and had remembered to tidy her hair, but her hands looked none too clean.

'Go and wash your hands,' she whispered, 'and then tell Nanon to serve the *potage*.'

When Fleurette reappeared, staggering under the weight of the huge tureen of soup, the guests were all seated at the dinner table.

'*Ma foi!*' Mlle de Sévigné remarked, wrinkling her nose delicately as, the soup finished, Françoise neatly dissected the pigeons on their serving-dish. 'I declare, the birds here in Paris smell like a dung heap compared to those of Aix.'

Françoise looked at her in some surprise. Though their tiny kitchen boasted no oven, Nanon had perfected the art of cooking a roast before a roaring fire, by means of a twisted string. The pigeons were done to a turn.

'My dearest Marguerite is just returned from a visit to the south of France,' Mme de Sévigné hastened to explain, 'where the birds feed on thyme and marjoram, and the fragrance of the herbs penetrates their flesh. What a pleasure it is to dine in Provence! They have quails and turtle-doves which are so tender that they fall apart at the touch of a knife. Her future husband, you know, is to be Lieutenant-Governor of Provence.' Everyone congratulated the future Governor's wife most warmly.

The dinner was praised by all. Fleurette managed to break only one plate, and that on its way back to the kitchen. Françoise was well pleased.

After dinner, the traditional Epiphany cake was cut, *la Galette des Rois*, and, amidst excited laughter, Mme de Coulanges was found to have the bean in her portion.

'How shall we honour you?' asked Mlle de Scudéry, once the excitement had died down. It was a tradition that the finder of the bean should be the queen of the evening.

'I know!' Nicole d'Aumont said. 'Everyone must make you a New Year's gift.'

This idea was seized upon, and Mme de Sévigné, opening her purse, immediately offered a louis d'or as her contribution, followed by another as the gift of her daughter. Françoise hurriedly went into her bedroom and came back with a pretty scent-bottle of Hungary water which Ninon had given to her on New Year's Day. Nicole d'Aumont gave Mme de Coulanges the exquisite painted fan she carried. Mlle de Scudéry could only promise to dedicate her new novel to Mme de Coulanges, at which that lady, beaming with pleasure, was more than delighted.

Nanon and Fleurette, who had been watching the cake-cutting ceremony from the door, brought the coffee pot and brandy to Mme de Coulanges to pour, as befitting the mistress of ceremonies. They offered her their congratulations, having nothing else to give.

Over their coffee, brandy and sweetmeats, Françoise asked Mlle de Sévigné when her wedding was to take place. The young lady yawned, raising a delicate white hand laden with rings, the nails long and polished, to her mouth before she answered.

'Oh, early in the spring, but the date must wait until M. le Comte de Grignan receives confirmation of his appointment.'

'So inconvenient, when there are so many arrangements to be made,' fussed Mme de Sévigné.

'You will miss her sorely, won't you,' Françoise sympathized, trying to quieten the sense of deprivation she always felt at the thought of such close family relationships. She often wondered why it was her destiny to be so completely alone in the world, knowing that with the exception of Nanon, who was after all only a servant, there was no one who really cared whether she lived or died. Oh, she had many friends, to be sure, but Françoise had already seen enough of the world to know that blood was thicker than water. Friends, even husbands and wives, quarrelled, had differences, and went their separate ways; but the bond between mother and daughter, sister and brother, could never be broken. Sometimes she wondered if her brother were still alive. It was not likely, as he had been only eleven years old when he ran away, too young to be able to support himself. If he were living, he would be over thirty now. Probably he would be married. Strange to think that she might have nieces and nephews somewhere in the world.

Mme de Sévigné's rather downcast face brightened somewhat. 'I shall be distraught to part with her,' she confessed, 'but I have something to tell you, Françoise. Mme de Coulanges and I have decided to cheer ourselves up by taking a short trip once the wedding is over. We shall take the waters at Vichy, put this wretched winter weather behind us, and tone ourselves up for the spring. Won't you accompany us, Françoise? You will be put to no expense,' she took care to add, seeing Françoise about to shake her head, 'for I shall take a suite of rooms, and we shall travel in my coach.'

'How kind you are, madame. But I am afraid I cannot join you.'

'But why, Françoise? There is nothing to keep you here.'

Inwardly, Françoise was bitterly disappointed. How she would have enjoyed a week or two's holiday. But Athenais was due to give birth about the end of March. She dared not risk being away from Paris when the baby was born, for although, according to Athenais, she might not be needed when the child had grown a little, it was just after the birth that she would be required to take charge. She bit her lip and looked down at the nutshells on her plate. Was she always to be prevented from doing what she herself wished to do in life? When would she ever be free to follow her own inclinations? Frantically she searched her mind for some plausible reason which would prevent her from accompanying her friend.

'I am sorry, madame. It is out of the question. Nanon and I spring-clean the house at that time, just before Easter.'

'Oh fie,' interrupted Mme de Coulanges. 'You are too conscientious, Françoise. We shall be back before Easter, and if you do not manage to do the spring-cleaning in time there is nothing to prevent you doing it a week afterwards. No one will hold it against you.'

'Why, you live alone, Françoise,' pleaded Mme de Sévigné, 'and have no ties – '

'It is precisely for that reason. I could not leave Nanon alone in the house – '

'Why the woman is only a servant. But in any case, we shall need serving-women to attend the three of us, so she may accompany us if you wish.'

'Perhaps Françoise has her reasons for not wishing to make the journey,' Nicole d'Aumont suggested, as Françoise racked her brain for some other objection. 'Perhaps she can find gayer company in Paris than the gout-stricken generals and elderly rheumatics of Vichy.'

'But such an opportunity – ' began Mme de Sévigné.

'Opportunity for what? Come now, ladies. Surely you are not still hoping to marry me off? I thought you had given up that futile occupation years ago!' To put an end to the subject, Françoise made an excuse to go down to the kitchen for a few minutes.

'I declare Françoise becomes more of an old maid every day,' Mme de Sévigné sighed, as Marguerite and Nicole d'Aumont excused themselves from the table and went to sit closer to the fire.

152

'Perhaps it is the effect of our company,' suggested Mlle de Scudéry anxiously. 'We must encourage her to mix with younger friends than ourselves.'

'I'm afraid our friend Françoise is too talented for her own good,' Mme de Coulanges answered. 'She is one of these ultra-capable people who excel in everything they do. Men prefer a little more helpless femininity in a woman, don't you think?'

'How right you are,' Mme de Sévigné agreed fervently. 'Sometimes I congratulate myself on being a widow. One is entirely free to be one's own mistress. However, I fear Françoise has chosen a lonely road through life.'

Fleurette began to clear the table, and Françoise, reappearing, invited her guests to join her in a game of *brélan*. Everyone took part with zest – with the exception of Mlle Marguerite, who sat with ill-concealed boredom staring gloomily into the fire. Françoise decided that she greatly preferred the company of Mme de Sévigné, who now sat laughing and joking with Mlle de Scudéry, to that of her daughter.

When the guests were ready to leave, Mme de Sévigné hugged her young friend warmly. 'Well, my dear, it will be some little time before we meet again.'

'I wish you God speed on your travels, madame. Return to us safely, won't you?'

'Indeed I will. *Bonne nuit, ma chérie.*'

Marguerite de Sévigné gave a slight nod of her head, and Mme de Coulanges kissed Françoise before the Sévigné family was borne away in their huge coach.

Nicole d'Aumont and Françoise embraced each other. 'Good night! *Bonne année!*'

Mlle de Scudéry also bade Françoise goodnight, and climbed into her sedan. '*Adieu*, Françoise! *A bientôt!*'

Françoise stood on the doorstep watching the coach and the two sedan-chairs disappear into the frosty night, and then, shivering, she bolted the door and went inside to compliment Nanon on her cuisine.

The week after the dinner party, Gisèle d'Albret was brought to bed of her third daughter, and Françoise was obliged to spend some little time at the Hôtel d'Albret, alternately consoling her friend for the fact that she had not produced a son, and occupying and amusing the two girls who were not allowed to visit their mother during her lying-in. It was almost two weeks before the

Maréchal d'Albret received word of the birth at the army's winter quarters, and sent a message that he was on the way back to Paris. Consequently, it was not until the last week in January that Françoise found herself free to look over the rooms available in the rue d'Alexandre, which she was thinking of renting for Athenais' coming baby and its nurse.

It was a dark and dreary morning when she set out from the rue des Tournelles. She noted that it took her little more than a quarter of an hour, along the rue des Francs Bourgeois and the rue St Denis, to reach the street she was looking for. The rue d'Alexandre, a small turning off the rue St Denis, was quiet, away from the busy main street, and narrow, the houses clustered together in a jumble of steps, doorways and gateways. A few women stood gossiping at doors, huddled in their shawls, and one or two children played ball in the road. Here and there a beggar shambled along, sunken into his rags for protection against the cold. There was little traffic, for the street was not wide enough for coaches.

Number 9, the house she was looking for, looked as if it was unoccupied, for the paper window-panes were torn and dirty, and no one arrived in answer to the bell. At last Françoise approached one of the women near-by, who was eyeing her with some curiosity.

'Does the widow Landin live at number 9?'

'Aye, madame, she does.'

'Then why does no one answer?'

The women threw back their heads and laughed uproariously at this, and then one, younger than the rest, detached herself from the group. 'She's dead drunk most times, madame. Come, I'll take you to her.'

She led the way, and Françoise followed as she pushed open the door and went up the few stone steps which led to a half-landing. 'Wait here. I'll go upstairs,' she said to Françoise.

Françoise waited, looking round her at the stone walls, the unswept steps and their ramshackle railing. The place could not possibly be suitable, she decided. She was about to make her escape when the young woman came down the stairs, accompanied by a dirty slattern huddling in a black shawl, a cap awry on her unkempt grey hair. Françoise looked at her with distaste.

'You have rooms to let, I believe?' she said, wondering why she did not walk out. This place could never be made suitable, whatever the rooms were like.

The old woman did not answer, but opened the door on the half-landing and motioned for Françoise to go in. She passed through, bending her head to avoid the low doorway.

To her considerable surprise she found that the rooms inside were pleasant, or rather, could be made so. There was one large room with a high window and a good stone fireplace, and behind, a smaller room, also with a fireplace and good windows which overlooked a small yard with one or two trees. A closet for brooms and chamber-pots completed the accommodation. Françoise was pleased. Even on such a dreary winter morning the rooms were quite light. In spring and summer, with trees blossoming in the yard, they would be quite pleasant. There were a few pieces of rickety furniture, a table, stools, a pallet bed.

'What is the rent?'

'Twenty livres the month, madame.' It was little enough.

'With firewood, and cleaning?'

'My son can bring the wood, I do the cleaning.'

This promise did not hold out much hope, but, thought Françoise, I can always pay one of the women near-by to keep the place clean.

'I will take it for twelve months, beginning the first of February, and I will give you two hundred and fifty livres.'

The old woman's face lit up. '*Merci mille fois, madame!*'

'But only on condition that the place is kept clean. You understand?'

'*Mais certainement! Merci, madame!*'

'I will come on the last day of January, and if the place is in good order I will move my furniture in on February 1st. You understand?'

'*Tout à fait. Merci, madame!*'

At the door, Françoise turned. 'You can get rid of all this furniture. I shall bring my own.' The old woman was in transports of delight. A dealer would give her at least ten livres for it, enough for several bottles of brandy.

On the way home Françoise thought over the arrangements to be made. The little room next to the kitchen would be suitable for the baby and the nurse to share. The larger room would have to serve for a cook and serving-girl to eat and sleep in; it was quite large enough to hold a table and two camp beds. A dresser would be needed for the crockery and so on, and a cupboard or two – how would she go about getting those windows repaired?

These thoughts occupied her all the way back to the rue des Tournelles.

On January 31st, Françoise paid another visit to the rue d'Alexandre and was pleased to find the rooms and the stairs thoroughly swept and dusted, and the fireplaces washed. She duly paid the first month's rent, and then occupied herself with the business of purchasing the furniture.

It was ironic to go about freely spending money on furniture and curtains and things such as she could never have afforded herself, with scarcely a thought for their cost. Still, she thought ruefully, I am unlikely ever to have use for a cradle. The carpenter in the rue Barbette made a cradle for her, and a dresser, and told her where she would be able to purchase the table and chairs she needed, and the beds. She bought the material for the curtains on the Pont Neuf, and had it made up by a sewing-woman Nanon knew of who lived in the rue du Pas de la Mule. There was still the problem of having the curtains hung and the windows mended. In the end she solved it by borrowing a ladder from the old woman's son when he repaired the window for her, and hanging the curtains herself.

Busy with all these occupations, and the buying of the crockery and cutlery, sheets, linen for the baby, the month of February quickly passed. Nanon wondered what was keeping her mistress so occupied, but Françoise did not explain.

By the first week in March, everything was ready. Françoise had engaged a woman to come in every day to cook and generally look after the place. She had yet to find a girl to do the marketing and washing, and be on the premises at night – and of course, at least one wet-nurse, possibly two.

On a Friday evening the week before Easter, Françoise was returning from one of Ninon's *soirées* with Baron and Mme d'Heudicourt. They set her down at her front door, the Baron, after a cautious glance round for cut-purses and vagabonds, helping her to alight and escorting her to her front door. 'Good night!' called the d'Heudicourts as she opened the door with her key, and their coach rolled away. Françoise was just fastening the latch when there was the sound of a horse galloping along the quiet street. A moment later there came a loud knocking.

Françoise, keeping the chain on the door, opened it a crack. Outside, beside a panting, sweating horse, stood a rider dressed in the livery of the King's Household. Immediately she knew why he had come. But so soon? Athenais had said the end of

March. What was it today – the sixteenth?

'Madame Scarron?'

'Yes.'

'A letter for you, madame.' He hesitated, not knowing whether there would be a reply. Françoise opened the letter, which had the seal of the Royal Household.

A friend would like to see you at St Germain-en-Laye was all it said.

Françoise's heart sank. At this time of night? It was nearly midnight. Must she travel to St Germain at night? Obviously, Athenais had been brought to bed – the journey would take more than two hours, and she had not arranged for a coach. Should she travel now or wait till morning?

The messenger became impatient. 'Is there an answer, madame?'

Françoise knew she had no choice in the matter. 'Go to the Palais de Luxembourg and send a hire-coach here to me immediately. Tell the driver it is a matter of urgency. You understand?'

'*Oui, madame.*' With a bow, he mounted his horse and rode away.

Inside the little house, Françoise stood in a state of confusion. The moment she had been awaiting so long had finally come, leaving her completely nonplussed. For some reason, she had never imagined the summons to St Germain arriving at this time of night. She knew this for foolishness; babies were prone to arrive at all hours. She went upstairs to look for her warmest travelling clothes and warm boots. Should she wake Nanon, to tell her where she was going? The woman would be frantic with worry if she found her bed unoccupied in the morning. Perhaps she would be back by then. She could not leave a note, for Nanon could not read.

Nanon, however, a light sleeper, could hear Françoise bustling about and came out of the kitchen, blinking with sleep, a shawl over her nightdress.

'What's amiss, madame?'

'It is nothing, Nanon. I have to go on a journey.'

'At this time of night?'

'It is important, Nanon. I have had a summons and must go – there is no danger, I assure you.'

'To travel alone at night, madame! Let me go with you!'

'No, Nanon. I must go alone.'

'Please, madame. It is not safe – '

157

Françoise heard the coach rattling along the street. 'Do not fear, Nanon. I will be home in the morning.'

Nanon was in the kitchen, frantically filling a basket with anything she could lay her hands on, some cheese, an apple, half a loaf, a bottle of wine.

'At least take some sustenance, madame, for your journey. Here, and a rug for your knees.'

Smilingly, for there had been a lavish supper at Ninon's that evening, Françoise thanked her. 'Do not fear for me, Nanon. There is nothing wrong.'

The coach-driver was aghast when she told him her destination.

'St Germain-en-Laye! At this time of night!'

'What is the price?'

The man scratched his head. He had only once before driven such a distance, and could not remember how far it was, save that it was a long way. He hesitated.

'I'll give you thirty livres for the journey there and back. It will be worth your while.' She opened her purse to show it contained only two or three louis d'or and a few coins. She had no wish to have her throat cut for money she did not carry. 'I'll pay you on my safe return.'

The man hesitated. His wife had died a few months ago, and he had a new wife, a young girl, plump as a partridge, waiting for him at home. A fine time to keep a man from his bed! But thirty livres – it was more than he could earn in a month. He shrugged his shoulders in resignation.

'I'll take you, madame.'

With a sigh and a crack of his whip he turned the carriage round in the direction of the Porte Maillot.

Chapter Fifteen

Near a side entrance to the chateau of St Germain the coach
stood waiting, as it had been waiting for several hours. In the
distance a church clock struck – was it five or six? Françoise
strained her ears to hear, for she had no watch. In spite of Nanon's
rug her legs were so cold that her feet felt quite numb, and she
could not feel her toes at all. How long had they been waiting?
She tried to think. It must have been about three in the morning
when they arrived at the chateau, and surely she had been sitting
in this coach for at least another two hours.

The coach was standing near the apartments of Athenais de
Montespan – Françoise remembered, from her visit, where they
were situated. In the distance she could just see the beginning of
the terrace where she and Mme d'Heudicourt had strolled with
the King and Athenais on that hot August afternoon last summer.
Only a few short months ago, yet it seemed as if it had never
happened. But this baby was to be reality.

At the thought of the baby Françoise began to worry afresh.
Perhaps it had been still-born. Yet would they not have got a
message to her, knowing that she had been sent for? The
messengers might have passed them on the road. Should she
have herself announced? She was at a loss to know what to do.
—Athenais had sent a secret message, probably it was best just
to wait.

Stamping his feet and thwacking his hands on his sides, the
driver came to the door of the coach. She adjusted her mask and
drew back the curtain for him to speak to her.

'How much longer, madame? *Nom de Dieu!* 'Tis cold. Will
the sun never come up to warm our bones?'

As Françoise was about to answer, a woman in hood and
shawl emerged from the near-by entrance. She hastened up to
the coach, and curtsied. Françoise recognized her as Lison,
Athenais' maid.

'Will you come this way, madame?'

Françoise accompanied her into the chateau. Lison asked her
to wait in the anteroom, and she tried to warm her hands, which

were stiff with cold in spite of her gloves, at the small fire in the grate. Through the open door into the next room she could see two women sitting at a table. A maid was serving them with bread and cheese and ale, and the two women ate heartily.

'*Nom de Dieu!*' one of the women was saying, tackling her food and drinking with gusto. 'What a time that took! I never thought we'd see the end of it.'

Suddenly Françoise shrank back, recognizing her. She was Mme Robinet, the midwife who had attended Gisèle d'Albret recently, and who must have seen Françoise several times at the Hôtel d'Albret during Mme d'Albret's lying-in.

'But the first is always slow,' the other woman said to her companion.

'First! Who said anything about a first? She has a boy over five years old.'

'Ah, that explains it. The muscles harden after a long gap, and it's like a first all over again. You're better off to have 'em all one after the other – like I did, sixteen children I've had, all in thirteen years.' She slapped her huge stomach with both hands. 'And do I look any the worse for it? I'm not thirty 'til after Michaelmas!'

'Then you'd better watch yourself, or you'll have time for sixteen more,' the other woman told her.

'No fear of that! They took 'im for a soldier just before the last one was born. Was I glad to see the back of 'im! With any luck he'll not come back from Flanders! They say once these Dutchmen get hold of a pack of Frenchies . . . I can earn my living better than he ever could.'

Françoise rose from crouching over the fire as Lison entered the room, holding in her arms a bundle wrapped in several blankets, and round all, a thick rug. Diffidently, Françoise approached. Drawing aside the voluminous wrappings, she could see that somewhere in the middle of them was a dark head. She looked at Lison who, seeing her nervousness, said: 'Shall I help you out to the coach, madame?'

Gratefully, Françoise agreed. Lison handed the bundle up to her as she climbed into the coach.

The driver groaned inwardly and spat with disgust as he saw the carefully wrapped bundle. All this fuss and bother, and driving out here through the forest to this God-forsaken place in the middle of a winter night, just for the sake of one brat born on the wrong side of the blanket. Keeping a man from his bed and his wife, all because some fancy lady had pupped a by-blow she didn't want her husband to know about! The ways of the quality were strange indeed, he reflected. Well, the sooner he got his passenger back to Paris with her fancy bastard, the sooner he'd get his money.

After all, he fell to thinking, as the horses began the long descent through the forest to Le Pecq, there was no necessity for his wife to know anything about thirty livres. Ten would be ample to keep her happy. That would leave him more than enough to get roaring drunk at the tavern tonight, and maybe take to bed a different wench. You got bored with the same woman every night, he thought, cracking the whip over the horses' heads, especially when they were always carrying their brats and being brought to bed. And by the time they had finished with all that, they were blowzy and shapeless, and no good to any man in his right mind. The first few months of marriage were the only ones a man could really enjoy.

Well, thank the Lord the journey back was in daylight. That had been a fearful ride last night, up this winding road on the side of the hill in black darkness. He had to admit that his passenger had some spirit. Not many women would have been induced to make such a journey alone at night.

Inside the coach, Françoise shifted her position, for her feet ached with cold. Her hands were a little better, after warming at the fire. She wished she had asked if she might use a closet before she left. The bundle in her arms was perfectly still. Peering into its depths she saw the tiny head and part of the baby's face. It seemed to have plentiful dark hair, and the long dark eyelashes lay on the minuscule cheek. Its eyes seemed closed. Was it a boy or a girl? She had not thought to ask. How long would it sleep? Suppose it woke before they reached Paris, and needed feeding? Having left in such a hurry, she had not thought to send a message for the wet-nurse. She prayed that the baby would not wake before they reached the city, and tried to keep as still as she could, though the coach rattled and jolted along at a fine pace, the driver pressing his horses forward to their limit, anxious to reach home.

At the chateau bridge there was a slight delay, and not much farther on the coach stopped at a poor-looking inn. The driver came to her side. 'I'll have to water the horses, my lady. Them's just about done.'

'All right. Here,' she opened her purse and took out a few

coins. 'Buy yourself some ale to keep out the cold.'

The driver touched his hat. '*Merci, madame.* Shall I ask the landlord to bring something for you?'

Françoise looked at the inn, a mean place if ever there was one, a couple of mangy goats tethered outside, and poorly-dressed women going in and out collecting jugs of ale. 'No, thank you.' All she longed for was to relieve the needs of nature.

In a moment the innkeeper hastened out, the driver having told him there was a lady of quality outside.

'At your service, madame! What can I obtain for you? Tell me your wishes, please. Some ale, a meal – ?'

'Is there a privy fit for a lady to use?'

The innkeeper hesitated. 'There is, madame, but – it is in the yard. If you would care to use my wife's closet – '

'Thank you.' Suddenly she remembered that she could not leave the baby unattended. How would she carry it with her? The driver intervened, seeing her hesitation. 'I'll attend the little 'un, madame.'

As she was about to protest, he picked up the bundle and held it to his chest with undoubted expertise. 'I've fourteen of 'em at home, madame. I know how to dandle a baby, never you fear.'

Gratefully she followed the innkeeper inside the building.

It was noon when at last they reached the Porte Maillot, and there they had to wait as the Customs officers inspected the coaches entering the city. The baby was beginning to stir, it was making funny little clucking sounds and its tiny hands poked their way out of its wrappings and clawed at the air.

Françoise called to one of the boys loitering near the coaches, hoping to hold the horses for a few sous.

'Do you know the rue St Fiacre, near the rue St Denis, in the quartier des Halles?'

'I know the rue St Denis, madame.'

She took out the remaining coins from her purse. 'Run quickly to the *épicerie* in the rue St Fiacre, and ask for Jeannette Granot. Tell her to come immediately to the rue d'Alexandre. Do you understand?'

'*Oui, madame.*' He snatched the coins and ran off.

'Make haste!' Françoise called after him. She wondered if he would even take the message.

The streets of Paris were busy, for it was a fine day, still cold but with the pale sunshine of early spring. At last they drew up at the corner of St Denis, the rue d'Alexandre being too narrow for a coach. The driver helped Françoise to alight and then carried the bundle for her to the house where she had rented the lodgings. At the door Françoise took it from him and thanked him.

'I shall have to spend about an hour here,' she said. 'You can either wait for me, or come to my house in the rue des Tournelles at six, when I will give you your money.'

'I'm going for my dinner, now, my lady. My stomach feels as if my throat's been cut. I'll come at six.'

Françoise went into the house, where everything was in order: the baby's linen, neatly folded blankets for the servants' beds, tablecloths and towels. There was crockery and cutlery, pewter plates, even chamber-pots stood in the closet. She would have to send out for some food for the servants when they arrived.

There was a knock at the door and the wet-nurse arrived, breathless. She was the wife of the grocer who kept a little shop in the rue St Fiacre, and had had seven children, the last only a month ago, so Françoise had felt sure she would have the requisite experience.

'The baby's here, Jeannette. I think it's hungry – '

'The little darling,' breathed the woman, taking the bundle from Françoise's arms. She looked round her. The room was very cold. 'We'd better not unwrap the blankets until there's a fire. Shall I make it for you?'

'Would you, Jeannette? I must send word to the servants to come. I did not expect it so soon. You won't have to make fires once they're here.'

'I know that, madame. But we must get the place warm for the little one.' She stacked the firewood with expert hands and looked round for a flint and tinderbox. 'Is it a boy or a girl, madame?'

Françoise had to admit that she did not know. Once the fire was going and the chill of the room began to subside somewhat, Jeannette started to unwrap the blankets.

'Oh, the pretty little darling! It must be a girl, with that dainty little face – although my eldest looked like an angel when he was born, and he's a proper little ruffian now.'

The baby, divested of its wrappings, did indeed prove to be a little girl. Françoise started up in alarm at the blood on the baby's stomach, and the blood-stained sheet.

'It's nothing, madame,' Jeannette reassured her. 'It's only the cord, which will drop off in a day or two, you'll see.'

Françoise did not know what she was talking about, and was unusually flustered. 'Shall I go for the servants, Jeannette?' she asked. 'Can you stay here until they come?'

'Yes, indeed, madame. They's all had their dinner at home, and the big ones can look after the baby, bless him. They love him dearly, the big ones do. Don't you want to see her feed?'

She had wrapped the baby in the clean linen Françoise had brought and, sitting down, unbuttoned her dress and put the baby to the breast. The baby, its tiny face at first searching from side to side, found the nipple at last and began to suck. Françoise was overcome by the tiny, starlike hands which were almost transparent – the blue veins could be clearly seen. She felt a strange fascination; she wanted, and did not want, to watch – both at the same time.

After a few minutes the woman gently disengaged the baby's mouth. 'We'd better dress and swaddle her now, madame.'

'Has she had enough, Jeannette? She didn't suck for very long.'

'They hardly take anything the first day or two, madame. Seems they need a rest after their journey! By the third day she'll be feeding like a hungry man, you'll see.'

Françoise watched fascinated as, taking the linen from the cradle, Jeannette first put a little nightgown on the baby and then deftly wrapped the tiny limbs round and round with the white swaddling bands, which held the arms close to the body. She finished by putting one of the little caps Françoise had provided on its head. Françoise marvelled at the fact that she, who prided herself on her efficiency in everything she did, could only stand and watch helplessly whilst a woman who could neither read nor write dealt so expertly with the baby.

'Are there no napkins for her, madame?' asked Jeannette.

Françoise rebuked herself furiously for having overlooked something so obvious. 'I did not think – '

'We could tear a towel in two – or tomorrow I could bring some – '

'I will buy some today,' Françoise told her. 'Is there anything else you need?'

'She should have a cosy shawl, madame. If you buy the wool I would crochet it for you. I can finish it by Monday.'

'That's very kind of you, Jeannette.'

Jeannette carefully laid the baby, fast asleep, in the cradle, and gently rocked it to and fro.

'Do the swaddling bands not impede the movements of the child, Jeannette?' Françoise asked, as both women stood gazing at the sleeping child, still little more than six hours old.

'It is for that reason we use them, madame, so that the limbs will grow straight.'

Françoise turned to go. 'I shall send the servants here as soon as I can, Jeannette.'

'Shall I stay here tonight, madame?'

'No, Jeannette, your family need you. Will she need feeding in the night, do you think?'

'She may, madame.'

'There is another wet-nurse in the rue St Denis – I was given the name. I will see if she can stay the nights. If you can spend the day here it will be sufficient.'

'*Merci, madame.*'

'*Au revoir*, Jeannette.' As she left, she turned to look again at the sleeping child and tried to see a resemblance in her to her mother or father, but the tiny sleeping face, screwed up in a scowl, seemed to have an expression all of its own. A feeling of deep compassion overwhelmed Françoise as she quietly tiptoed out of that shabby, run-down house in a poor and crowded street, leaving a child of royal blood asleep in the arms of a stranger.

Chapter Sixteen

Françoise soon found herself looking forward to her visits to the rue d'Alexandre. She liked to arrive there early in the morning, if possible, when Jeannette was feeding the baby, to watch her suck – as Jeannette had promised, she fed hungrily. Then when Agnès, the maid, brought a basin of water, Jeannette would wash her carefully, sitting on a low stool, a towel over her lap. Françoise marvelled that the tiny body, slippery and wet, did not slip through her hands.

'Don't you fear, madame,' Jeannette laughed one morning, seeing her face. 'I've washed too many babies in my time to let one fall on the floor.'

Then they would change her clothes and wrap her in the shawl Jeannette had crocheted for her, so warm and soft. When she was four weeks, Jeannette pronounced that the swaddling bands could be discarded.

Françoise began to spend nearly all her time at home, knitting and crocheting tiny jackets for the baby, and making little frocks for her. She wondered about the baby's christening. Athenais had written her a letter thanking her for taking the baby and enclosing a note for 500 livres, but since then she had heard nothing. She wondered why Athenais did not come to see the child. She had written to her many times, telling her how lovely the baby was and how well she was thriving. She decided that she would have to arrange for the baby's baptism herself.

The ceremony took place at St Gervais on a beautiful day early in June. Nanon, who had had to be let in on the secret, had insisted on making the baby's gown herself. She and Françoise spent many days when the gown was finished, painstakingly decorating it and the tiny matching coif with dainty lace. They made a bearing-cloth in which to carry the child to the altar, of scarlet flannel edged with gold ribbon. Ninon de l'Enclos gave the baby a piece of coral on a gold chain, thought to bring luck, and which would later serve as a teething-ring. Jeannette had asked if she might be present, and burst into tears as Françoise held the baby over the font and the Abbé Gobelin pronounced the Benediction. Françoise had notified Athenais that the christening was to take place, but again had had no reply.

'What keeps you so busy these days?' Mme de Sévigné asked Françoise one evening late in June, when Françoise was dining at the home of Mme de Coulanges. 'We scarcely see you.'

Françoise blushed and searched for an answer. She was spending most of her days at the rue d'Alexandre, and recently had begun to turn down evening invitations in her anxiety to complete all the sewing of the baby's clothes before the christening ceremony.

'Fie, Marie,' Mme de Coulanges scolded her sister-in-law. 'What Françoise cares to do is no concern of ours. Perhaps she has *un bel ami*. It would be surprising if she had not. How well you are looking, Françoise!'

Françoise was indeed glowing with health and good spirits. In some strange way, since the arrival of the baby she had felt a more serene contentment than she had known for many years. It was all-absorbing to watch the baby developing, each day becoming more of a little person in her own right. Lately she had begun to look around the little house in the rue des Tournelles, wondering if she should take the baby to live there with her and Nanon. Jeannette had promised that she would still attend her daily if she decided to move the baby, but there would be no room for other servants – and there was always a great deal of washing to be done.

Mme de Sévigné interrupted her train of thought. 'I do declare, Françoise, you haven't even heard us. You must be in love, there's no doubt of it.'

'What did you say, madame? Forgive me, please. I was thinking of something else.'

Mme de Sévigné and Mme de Coulanges exchanged conspiratorial glances, both overjoyed at the prospect of Françoise being in love.

'Won't you tell us his name?' Mme de Sévigné pleaded.

'Whose name, madame?'

'Your *bel ami*, of course.'

'I have *no lover*; you are quite mistaken, I assure you.'

But they refused to be convinced, and at last Françoise, despairing, attempted to change the subject. 'Is it true that the Court has gone to Fontainebleau for the summer?'

'So I hear,' replied Mme de Sévigné. 'The Duc d'Anjou is a

sickly child, and it was thought the air at St Germain might not agree with him.'

'The royal children do not thrive,' said Mme de Coulanges. 'Fortunately, the Dauphin grows apace. It is said that he has the stature of his father, though he resembles his mother.'

'You mean that his tutors despair of him,' replied Mme de Sévigné. 'The Queen, his mother, has lived in France now for nearly ten years, and still can hardly speak a word of French.'

'What of Louise de la Vallière?' asked Françoise. 'Is she still living at Court?'

The two women laughed. 'Very much so,' answered Mme de Sévigné at length.

'I thought she wished to retire in order to enter a religious order.'

'That is her desire, but the King, for reasons which are not clear, keeps her at Court against her will.'

Françoise was puzzled. 'If Athenais is openly acknowledged to be the King's mistress, what possible reason can the King have for keeping Louise at Court when she does not wish it?'

'You seem to forget, my dear Françoise, that our friend Quanto is a married woman.'

'Has her husband been creating more scandal? Do you remember that day at Versailles?'

'Indeed I do. Oh, my dear, he does all manner of mad things, driving around in a carriage with a pair of horns fixed to the roof, breaking into Athenais' bedroom at St Cloud in the middle of the night and beating her – '

'Beating her! Under the King's roof! Is he mad?'

'And now he has held a mock funeral for her, telling everyone of the premature death of his wife from an advanced case of ambition!'

'The King will have him sent off to Pignerol, or to the Bastille if he is not careful,' remarked Mme de Coulanges.

'Nevertheless, he is her legal husband,' said Françoise, 'and must have some rights – '

'Rights! What rights does a woman have whose husband deserts her? Now it is a man's turn for a change . . .'

Françoise left them still arguing as she put on her tippet and gloves and prepared to leave for home.

One morning in July Françoise walked briskly towards the rue d'Alexandre, her basket over her arm. It was a beautiful day, the sun shone brightly in a cloudless sky and the streets were thronged with people taking the air. Street-sellers stood on every corner crying their wares. Françoise hesitated as she passed a girl with a tray round her neck selling fresh white bread rolls; she felt sure that the baby would like to taste a little piece of that delicious soft bread. She had asked Jeannette a few days before when the baby would be ready to eat some real food, but Jeannette, knowing that once the baby was weaned her days at the rue d'Alexandre would be numbered, had put her off.

'Oh, not for some time yet, madame. Why, she's scarce four months old – my boys never took a bite of food till they were over a year, and you should see them now.'

'But surely, a little piece of soft white bread could do no harm. She seems to have a good appetite – '

'Oh, that she has, madame.'

'White bread's no good to her,' mumbled the old woman sitting by the fire, the widow Lamart, who lived near-by and came in to cook each day.

'What did you say?' asked Françoise.

'I said white bread's no good to her, madame. *Pain de Gonesse* – pah! Soft white bread for the fancy rich!' She spat contemptuously into the fire. 'Black bread, that's the stuff! Good for your bowels – not that white muck that clogs them up.'

Françoise, looking at the old woman's bright eyes and rosy cheeks – she was well over seventy – wondered if she might not be right. All her rich friends were chronic sufferers from constipation.

'When she's a bit older,' Jeannette offered, 'we can make it into pap with a little milk, madame. But not yet.'

Françoise, prepared to bow to Jeannette's superior knowledge of infant feeding, accepted her opinion. Nevertheless, it was an almost overwhelming temptation to buy those rolls and pop a little piece into the baby's mouth. She hurried on.

There were other matters to occupy her. She had almost made up her mind to take the baby to live with her and Nanon. She missed her too much when she was away from her, and there was always the fear that some harm might befall a child looked after exclusively by servants.

'I wouldn't trust that Marie Potier, if I were you,' Jeannette had said to her a day or two before. Marie was the wet-nurse who came at six when Jeannette went home.

'Why not, Jeannette?' Françoise knew that Jeannette resented

169

anyone else performing what she considered to be her exclusive function, that of feeding the baby.

'I just don't trust her, madame. She's slovenly and careless.'

'But the baby doesn't wake at night now, Jeannette. Marie doesn't feed her any more, as you know. It's simply a question of someone being here. Surely you can understand that.'

'There's old Lamart.' The old woman often slept on the premises if her son were not at home, in order to avoid burning her own firewood. Françoise did not object – it was safer for two people to be with the baby.

'She doesn't sleep here every night. Besides, she's an old woman and a bit deaf. If a fire started, or an intruder got in, she might not hear anything. And as for running for help – No, there must be someone with the baby at night. But I'll look around for someone else to replace Marie.' She wondered whether to tell Jeannette that she was thinking of taking the baby to the rue des Tournelles. Better wait until she made up her mind one way or the other.

'Well, I still wouldn't trust Marie Potier,' Jeannette grumbled. 'How many times have I told her not to put the candles on the mantelpiece where they could fall on to the crib! But no, she likes to sit close up to the fire at night, with a bottle in one hand, rocking the crib with the other so that the baby doesn't wake up! One of these nights she'll fall into the fire herself, she's been that drunk!'

This worried Françoise considerably, and as she hastened along the rue Rambuteau, the shortest route to the rue d'Alexandre, she racked her brains once again as to how she could close down the little establishment and take the baby to the rue des Tournelles. Her sophisticated friends would insist upon some explanation, and might easily jump to the wrong conclusions. And why should she jeopardize her own reputation for Athenais' benefit? Yet, thinking of the baby's bright black eyes and curly hair, and the way she smiled and crowed with glee when Françoise entered the room, she felt her resolution wavering. Compared to the joy of being with the child, the preservation of her good name became less and less important.

As she hurried along the rue St Denis she thought with a glow of anticipation of the way the baby would laugh when she gave her the rattle she had in her basket, which the carpenter in the rue Barbette had made for her. Fleurette had told her father that Mme Scarron was looking after a baby, and he had made the rattle for her out of odds and ends of wood, rounded, polished, and painted in red and blue. Françoise could hardly wait to see the baby's face when she gave it to her. She wondered if the child would be able to hold it in her plump little fingers.

Now that she was four months old there was no doubt that with her dark, curly hair and olive, almost sallow skin, she strongly resembled the King. Her nose, strangely prominent for such a young child, was her father's exactly, an inheritance from his Moorish ancestors. Françoise worried about whether it would spoil her looks when she grew up – features which were imposing in a man could be unfeminine and unattractive in a woman.

There were other matters, too, which occupied her mind. The day before, she had received a letter from Athenais. It had been sent from the chateau of Chantilly, where the Court had gone on a visit for a few weeks. The note, of only a few lines, thanked Françoise for all that she was doing, enclosed some money, and ended: *On July 23rd I shall pay a visit to Paris. I shall make it my business to visit the friend you mention in the rue d'Alexandre, whom I am happy to hear is in good health. A very important person will be with me.*

This news had thrown Françoise into a complete tizzy, for the important person, she knew, could be none other than the King. She had lain awake for most of the night making plans – giving no thought to her own ensemble but resolving to sew a completely new outfit for the baby for the occasion. This morning she intended to recruit one or two of the neighbouring women to take down and wash all the curtains, and give the place a thorough spring-cleaning the day before the intended visit.

Deeply engrossed in her thoughts, she turned into the rue d'Alexandre. Reaching the house, she entered quickly without noticing that the door was ajar, mounted the steps to the half-landing and went into the main room. It was empty. There was no fire, but the day being so warm the old lady had probably thought it unnecessary to make one, and gone to do the marketing. She pushed open the door to the baby's bedroom, wondering at the quiet in the house, and blinked in disbelief at what she saw.

The curtains at the windows were drawn, although it was nearly ten o'clock. Candles were burning on either side of the cradle, as well as on the mantelpiece. The cradle stood in its usual place by the fire, but the sheet was drawn up and she could not see the baby's face. Instead of Jeannette, a priest dressed in black sat in the corner, his hands folded in prayer. Françoise recognized him as the parish priest whom she had often seen in the rue St Denis, and going in and out of the neighbouring houses.

She clutched at the door-jamb as he rose and approached her, making the sign of the cross. She wanted to put out her hands, to prevent him coming towards her, but try as she would she could not move. She tried to cry out, to stop him from uttering the words framing on his lips, but she could make no sound. Slowly and inexorably, he came towards her. There was a look of deep compassion on his face as he gently took her hands.

'Madame Scarron, isn't it?'

Her throat made a sound she scarcely recognized. She wanted to scream. How could she stop him from telling her what she already knew?

'The little one is dead, madame. May Jesus Christ have mercy on her soul.'

The ground seemed to come up to meet her, and he caught her in his arms as she swayed and fell.

Chapter Seventeen

The dying rays of the sun slanted eastward over the Val d'Oise, and the interior of the coach-and-six travelling at full speed across the plain of Fontenay was hot and dusty. The coach-driver licked his dry lips and urged the horses forward. Soon they would be approaching Beaumont-sur-Oise, where both horses and driver could refresh themselves. The worst part of this long journey would be over, for the rest of their way lay along the banks of the river Oise, through the forest of Chantilly to where the vast chateau stood on the far side.

The two women passengers in the coach, both dressed in black, sat silent and still as they had done for the past three hours. The countryside through which they were travelling was beautiful, with its rolling hills and fields. The country people were working to bring in the harvest while the weather still held. Now and then, as they drove through a small hamlet, geese and hens scattered in every direction before the coach, and villagers turned to look after it.

Neither Françoise nor Nanon, each lost in her own thoughts, was aware of the countryside. Nanon watched her mistress anxiously. Françoise sat stiffly upright in the corner of the coach. Her black eyes seemed darker than ever and her face was deathly pale by contrast. She seemed to have aged considerably in the course of one day. She had made no move, nor spoken, since they left Paris more than three hours ago, save to remove her white lace collar and put it away; now the unrelieved black of her dress showed up her unnatural pallor. Nanon wished that she would cry, scream, fling herself into Nanon's arms, do anything but sit there like stone, unable to move. She knew that that was the worst kind of grief – those who could weep, and scream and tear their hair were able to relieve their anguish, but those who hugged their agony to themselves, as Françoise was doing, suffered the most.

Françoise, for her part, felt as if she was in a dream. A mental picture of the little room in the rue d'Alexandre seemed to float before her eyes. She tried to ignore it, to look out of the window and concentrate on what she saw, but the wooded hills and coverts they were passing – for they were heading towards the river now – seemed hardly to exist, and the only reality was the dim room with the candles burning, and the tall black-robed priest standing before her. She closed her eyes to try and shut him out of her mind.

'Are you well, mistress?' Nanon asked with concern.

Françoise opened her eyes and saw the lined, anxious face of Nanon leaning towards her. She nodded, not trusting herself to speak. Her thoughts revolved around the events of the morning, over and over again, trying to find some conclusion, some reason for it; but there was none. She had tried to speak, to ask the priest what had happened, but still no words would come.

'The baby was found to be dead this morning, madame,' he had told her. 'The servants ran away in fright, but Jeannette Granot came to call me here. Where shall I find the parents of this child, who I believe was in your care?'

Then Jeannette herself had burst into the room, her clothes and her hair untidy. She flung herself at Françoise's feet and burst into tears.

'I had to see you, madame. Oh, Lord have mercy upon us! The little darling!'

Françoise's lips framed the words: 'Marie Potier.'

'Oh, no, madame, it wasn't her fault,' Jeannette insisted. 'The poor girl's half crazy with grief and fear – I've just left her.'

'Tell us carefully what happened,' said the priest.

'When I came in here,' sobbed Jeannette, 'Potier was lying dead drunk as usual. I shook her and banged her to wake her up, but she was dead to the world. Then I wondered why the baby wasn't making any sound, as when she sees me she knows it's time for her feed. She lay quite still, and I could see by her eyes – oh, madame – ' Jeannette burst into fresh floods of tears. Still Françoise could not move or speak. It was as if these things were happening to someone else, and not herself.

'I managed to rouse the girl, and when she saw the baby she half fainted. Lamart came in, and she took one look at the baby and ran away. Potier ran out in a terrible state – I was afraid she'd kill herself. I went home with her, and on the way I knocked up the good Father. Then I went to tell my family. Oh, madame, madame!' Wordlessly she took Françoise's lifeless hand and held it, her tears flowing uncontrollably.

'Potier told me that the baby was as happy as a lark last night,' she said. 'She woke for a little while at midnight, and they played with her, and then they put her back to sleep. And then to find her like that this morning, oh, it's more than anyone can endure – '

'It's true,' asserted the old woman, who had now entered the room. 'The child was perfectly well. And then – '

A crowd of onlookers had gathered at the door, several of the neighbouring women, even the old slattern Landin from upstairs. 'There was a baby died like that in the rue St Denis last winter,' one woman said. 'Put to bed happy one night, and stiff as a board next morning . . .'

Françoise looked despairingly at the priest, who read her unspoken words. 'Come along, come along,' he said, shooing them all out of the room. 'Please leave – yes, you too, Jeannette.'

'Can I do anything for you, madame? Anything at all! Shall I go home with you?'

Françoise managed to find her voice. 'Go to the rue des Tournelles,' she said, 'and tell Nanon to come here.' Suddenly she needed Nanon's strength, her arms around her. Nanon Balbien would know what to do.

'The parents,' the priest was saying to her. 'We must apprise them of this melancholy news.' It's obvious that she's the mother, he thought, although she pretends not to be. For he had seen people confronted with such things many times, and Mme Scarron was deeply affected. She did not weep, but her hands were clenched tightly in her lap, her eyes dark and staring. A widow, wasn't she? The child was plainly her own, the result of some little escapade which must remain concealed. Jeannette had told him that Mme Scarron was supposedly looking after the baby for a lady of quality, but that she was sure that it was her own, for no one ever came to see the baby, and what mother would neglect such a lovely child?

'The child wasn't ill,' Françoise said pleadingly to the priest. 'She was in perfect health – I saw her yesterday – '

'It happens, dear lady. I have seen such cases as this before. It is inexplicable.'

Why should she be taken like this – an innocent, tiny child? She covered her face with her hands. He hoped that she would weep now, and release some of her grief in that way, but she could not cry. He took her hand.

'Let us pray, madame. Those whom God loves most, die young. Come, let us seek solace in our Lord.' Together they

175

knelt and prayed, Françoise reciting the words automatically, as if in a dream.

Nanon arrived, flushed and breathless. 'Oh my lady, my lady.' She helped Françoise to rise, and the two women stood looking at each other, wondering what could have happened to wreck their world. Nanon put her arm round her mistress.

'Come, let's go home.'

Obediently, like a child, Françoise turned to go. Then the thought struck her. Athenais! And the King! They must be informed, without delay.

'If you would be so kind as to acquaint me with the address of the parents,' the priest was saying. 'There are arrangements to be made.' Arrangements. Yes, she supposed there were. Interment had to take place within twenty-four hours, that was the law, to prevent the spread of disease; and in the summer the law was enforced more stringently than ever, for the benefit of public health.

'No arrangements can be made yet,' she heard herself saying. Chantilly! It was nearly four hours away. To travel there and back – the funeral would have to take place in the morning. What would Athenais' wishes be on the subject? Should the child be buried as an ordinary resident of the parish, or in the chapel of the Mortemarts, on their estate? Or in the royal vaults at the basilica of St Denis? She was, after all, the daughter of a King of France.

'It is the law, Madame Scarron.'

Suddenly she seemed to snap back into some vitality. 'Then the law will have to wait!' she told the priest. 'Call me a hire-coach immediately. I must leave on a journey. I will communicate with you as soon as I can, probably tomorrow morning.'

'You'll take me with you, madame?' pleaded Nanon.

'All right, Nanon. Who will stay here – with – ?' She turned in the direction of the silent cradle.

'I can send someone to sit here,' offered the priest. 'For a small payment.'

Françoise opened her purse and took out several louis d'or. 'For your good offices, Father. And if you will arrange for someone to come – '

'Immediately, madame.' There was something about her authoritative air that made him wonder after all if the fictitious parents really did exist – and if so, who they were. Only persons of some importance would be ready to flout the law.

176

'You will convey to me your wishes?'

'Where can I find you?'

'At the vestry of St Eustache. *Adieu, madame.*' He bowed respectfully and left.

At the door she hesitated, looking back at the crib, and then left the room, leaning heavily on Nanon's arm.

As they reached the castle of Beaumont-sur-Oise, high above the river, the driver slowed down the horses. The town was built on tiers of rich, fertile land sloping down to the valley of the Oise. Carefully the driver coaxed and negotiated the horses safely round the steep twists and turns of the old town's cobbled streets until they reached the riverside, where an inn stood on one side of the main square. Drawing up outside, he came to the door of the coach, wiping the sweat from his forehead, his hat in his hand.

'I'm stopping for water, my lady.'

Françoise gave him some coins from her purse. 'Take some refreshment yourself, but be quick about it.'

'Thank you, madame.'

'How long now till we reach Chantilly?'

'Not long now, my lady. It's along the river from now on, fresh and cool.'

'Thank you. Make haste *s'il vous plaît.*'

'*Oui, madame.*' He touched his forehead respectfully and hastened to see to the horses.

'Do you wish to pray, mistress?' asked Nanon, seeing Françoise gaze across the square in the direction of the small church of St Justin, where the bells were pealing for evensong.

'There is no time, Nanon. We must reach Chantilly without delay. Do you need to descend here?'

'I shall manage for another hour, if that is how long it will take.'

'Good. We shall be on our way directly.'

'Do you not crave a drink, my lady?'

'There is no time to waste – '

'Wait one moment, madame.' Nanon descended and went into the inn, returning in a few moments with a *pinte* of wine, a little water and two mugs.

'Thank you, Nanon. How much does that cost?'

'Fifty sous, madame.'

Françoise gave her the money, and she hurried back with it to the inn. In a few moments they were on their way again, Nanon pouring out their drinks with difficulty in the jolting coach.

About seven o'clock in the evening, as they neared Chantilly, they found themselves driving along by the edge of a lake, for the chateau itself, in a mirror-like setting, was surrounded on three sides by water. The only sounds were those of the birds of the forest and the gentle lapping of the water from the lake and from the stream of the Nonette behind them – for the river Oise now flowed away towards Pontoise. The cool air was sweet with the scent of the pines, and the dark trees stood out against the dim sky.

'How beautiful this place is, madame,' Nanon remarked. But Françoise, who normally in such surroundings would be in transports of delight, seemed, after her temporary animation when they had enjoyed the cool drink, to have sunk again into a torpor, and was staring silently out of the window. Nanon, who had never known who the baby's parents were, could not know that she felt sick and nervous at the prospect before her, that of telling a mother that she had lost her child.

At the entrance to the Petit Château, the porter came out of his lodge to enquire their business.

'My business is with the Marquise de Montespan,' said Françoise. Athenais had succeeded in achieving at least one of her many ambitions; since the birth of the baby she had become Mme la Marquise.

The porter directed them to the Grand Château, where the royal suite was housed, and they drove on. At the entrance, the ostlers came forward to take the horses and the driver, having been told to await instructions, went off to the stables with the grooms and lackeys. Françoise and Nanon, smoothing down their creased and crumpled clothes and trying ineffectually to tidy themselves, entered the chateau, where they looked about them in awe at the magnificence of their surroundings.

Chantilly, originally the home of the Montmorency family, and more of a palace than a chateau, had been given to the Prince de Condé, known as the Grand Condé, in 1643, as a reward for his magnificent victory over the Dutch at Rocroi. Only a palace such as this would be able to offer both accommodation and entertainment to the Sun King and his Court. Françoise and Nanon walked along the corridors, marvelling at the elaborate gold lacquer everywhere, the superb paintings and the silk-panelled walls. Françoise stopped a passing girl and enquired the

178

whereabouts of the apartments of Mme la Marquise de Montespan.

Following the girl's instructions they turned along a small passageway which led to a suite of rooms overlooking the Cour d'Honneur. Françoise's throat was dry, and there was a feeling of nausea in the pit of her stomach as she knocked at the door. What would Athenais' reaction be when she heard the news?

The door was opened by a lady dressed in evening attire, the Comtesse de Nevers, one of the ladies in the suite of the new Marquise. She looked askance at the two women, shabbily dressed in black, who stood before her dusty from their long journey.

'What is your business here?' she enquired sharply.

'My business is with Mme la Marquise de Montespan,' Françoise told her.

The Comtesse looked the two women up and down from behind her painted fan. Who could such women be, calling at such a time in the evening? They could not be hairdressers or dressmakers, to judge by their clothes. Could they have come calling at this time to render a more personal service – abortionists, perhaps?

'You may confide your message in me,' she said.

'I regret, madame,' Françoise said coolly, 'that it is a personal matter I may confide only in Mme la Marquise herself.'

The Comtesse regarded the dishevelled visitors with un-disguised malice. 'In that case,' she replied, 'I am afraid you have wasted your journey.'

'How so, madame?'

'Mme la Marquise is not here.'

'Not here! It's not true! I received a letter from her at Chantilly only two days ago.'

'Nevertheless, madame' – she pronounced the word with a sneer – 'Mme la Marquise is not here. She left yesterday to take the cure at Bourbon.' She made to close the door in their faces, but Nanon put out her foot to prevent her.

'How dare you!' breathed the Comtesse, aghast at the temerity of the creature. 'I'll call a lackey to have you put out – '

Françoise was trying to keep calm. Bourbon! It was several days' journey away. 'When will she return?' The funeral arrangements must be made tomorrow.

'She does not return to Chantilly. Next week the Court returns to Fontainebleau for the remainder of the summer.'

There was no help for it. 'In that case,' asked Françoise, 'be so kind as to direct me to the royal suite.'

The Comtesse regarded her in open-mouthed incredulity.

'The apartments of the King, if you please.'

'The King!' The Comtesse burst out laughing. 'What makes you think he would grant you an audience?'

'That is none of your business,' Françoise told her. 'Now, if you will be so kind – '

The Comtesse laughed until the tears ran down her cheeks at the idea of visitors such as these entering the presence of the King. 'The King is not at Chantilly!' she roared. 'Now take yourselves back to the slums of Paris where you belong!' This time she succeeded in closing the door in their faces.

Françoise and Nanon sat in a corner of the Grand Vestibule, which, at first deserted, began to fill as the Court and the guests of M. le Prince de Condé gathered for the evening's entertainment. A little distance away they could hear violins playing in the ballroom. Opulently dressed in silks and satins, the women strolled to and fro, eyeing the men from behind their fans, modestly, or boldly, depending on their whim, tossing their powdered ringlets, displaying their décolletages to the best advantage. It became very warm as the rooms and corridors filled with people who, having spent several hours dressing for the evening, now began to appear. Dandies in long periwigs and silk stockings flirted with the ladies. As the hall grew crowded, people drifted out on to the wide terrace overlooking the still water of the lake where boats were waiting to glide silently around the chateau on the mirror-like surface of the water. The night was still, silent, with little moonlight; couples began to descend into the boats for a secluded rendezvous on the lake before the grand ball began.

Françoise was in a state of complete confusion. Since leaving the rue d'Alexandre that morning there had been only one thought in her head, to seek out Athenais, break to her the news of the baby's death and carry out her wishes concerning the funeral arrangements. Now that Athenais was out of her reach, she knew that she must see the King. It was just as she had feared from the start of this business – she would have to assume total responsibility for a child which was not her own. Athenais, although she had sent her money for the child, had washed her hands of it completely.

People were tittering at the two dowdy women dressed in black sitting in the corner. Françoise noticed their malicious smirks and their jokes at her expense. In a few moments, she knew, the steward of M. le Prince de Condé would be bound to enquire what they were doing in such exalted company, so poorly dressed, and would politely ask them to leave. The shame of such an exit did not concern her in the least – the only thought in her mind was how she could contact Athenais, or the King, so that she might return to Paris and carry out their instructions. Her head ached, and all she longed for was sleep – to sleep, and to forget that the events of the day had ever happened.

As she looked round the crowded vestibule, trying to summon the courage to approach one of the superior, elegantly liveried footmen who strolled amongst the crowd bearing trays of cool drinks, and to ask whether or not the King was in residence at Chantilly, a tall man wearing a sword came up to her with a questioning look on his face.

'Françoise, isn't it?'

'Vivonne!' Never in her life had she been so glad to see anyone. 'I need your help desperately.'

'What on earth are you doing here?'

'I came to see your sister – '

'So did I, but they tell me she is not here. Never mind' – his eyes followed a pretty young girl, mincing along in high-heeled shoes, laughing and flirting with the young fops who surrounded her – 'I am sure I shall be able to console myself for my wasted journey.'

'Vivonne, I need your help. Is the King staying here?'

'The King? Why do you ask?'

'I need to see the King on a matter of some importance. Please tell me, is he in residence here or not?'

'What makes you think the King would see you?' he asked, fishing for information. What on earth could her business be with the King? Such titbits were always useful; if not to himself, there would be others more than willing to pay for interesting pieces of information.

'Please do not press me, Vivonne. Believe me when I say that my business concerns your sister, and that I must see the King without delay. Now, will you please – '

Vivonne held up his hand in warning at her raised voice. 'Quietly, now! There are eyes and ears everywhere. Are you quite well?' Her face was white and her dark eyes seemed to burn with fury. For the first time he noticed how dishevelled and dusty her clothes were.

'As you see, we have just arrived from Paris, solely with the intention of seeing Athenais. As she is not here, I must speak to the King immediately.'

'Then you are doubly unfortunate. The King is with the army, supervising military manoeuvres. I am on my way to him when I leave here, to take up my new orders.'

Her face, which had first clouded with disappointment, brightened again. 'You go to the King? Then please, allow me to accompany you. Forgive me – I had forgotten to congratulate you on your new appointment.' Athenais had recently obtained for her brother the post of Commander-General in the Navy.

'I regret, it is out of the question, I ride at first light to Compiègne, to take up my command, and then I leave for Brest.'

'I insist on accompanying you, Vivonne. Will you believe me when I say that I intend to see the King? I have already travelled this distance, and I shall go with you to Compiègne.'

'It's impossible, I'm afraid. We ride at daybreak, as I told you.'

'I was brought up in the country. You think I cannot ride bareback? You will not outdistance me, I promise you.'

Vivonne sighed. Françoise, he was beginning to see, was made of the same mettle as his sister. Once they had made up their minds, these women, it was like leading a horse to the water – it would drink only if it chose. Still, Athenais' schemes had certainly proved to be as advantageous as she had always promised him. Perhaps there would be some advantage to be gained from allowing Françoise to ride along with them.

He turned to Nanon, standing silently alongside. 'What of your servant? She will have to remain.'

'She can await me here. Can you please arrange for us to lodge here tonight? We should be most grateful. We are tired and dusty from our journey, as you can see.'

He hesitated. 'I can ask the steward, but etiquette demands that I present you to our hostess, the Princess.'

'Look how shabby we are! Vivonne take pity on us!'

He escorted them to the stairway. 'As you wish. But amongst these people one must behave in a certain way. I consider it would be a lack of courtesy to lodge under this roof uninvited, even though amongst such numbers you will be unnoticed.'

'You are right, Vivonne,' agreed Françoise. 'What must be, must be. At least give us a chance to tidy ourselves, I beg you.'

Vivonne summoned a passing footman. 'Take these ladies to a room where they can refresh themselves after their journey.' He bowed to them. 'I will request a few minutes with the Princess in half an hour's time.'

Françoise took Vivonne's hand. 'You will never know how grateful I am to you, Vivonne. Please accept my thanks.'

He disengaged his hand. She was beginning to look a little more like herself, now that she was smiling and a little colour had come into her cheeks. 'Have you eaten since you left Paris?' he asked.

'No, not since this morning.'

'Hurry, then, and soon we'll see that you have something to eat.'

Obediently the two women hurried away. Sighing, Vivonne accepted a glass of wine from a passing footman and downed it in one gulp. These women! He looked forward to taking up his naval command and escaping from them for a while.

In a short time Françoise and Nanon reappeared, having combed their hair, washed their hands, tidied their clothes as best they could. Nevertheless, they were conspicuous in their unrelieved black amongst the bright hues of the other guests of the chateau.

Mme la Princesse de Condé, who was having her hair dressed for the evening, was at first disconcerted when the Duc de Vivonne was announced before her toilette was completed. However, remembering that the said Duke was none other than the brother of Athenais de Montespan, she decided to allow him the privilege of an interview. La Montespan was riding high in the King's favour.

'Madame la Princesse.' He bowed low and kissed her hand.

'Monsieur le Duc. We are pleased to have you with us. How long is your stay?'

'I regret that I must leave in the morning. I came to see my sister, only to find her gone.'

'Yes, she left yesterday for Bourbon. Then you must leave tomorrow? *Quel dommage.*' She glanced over his tall, athletic figure with undisguised appreciation. M. le Prince, the famed warrior who took Rocroi at the age of twenty-two, was now nearly fifty, and she, at forty-two, was beginning to take more than a passing interest in younger men. Suddenly her inviting expression changed as she noticed a tall, shabbily dressed woman in black standing behind him. At first she took her to be some sort of servant, but to her astonishment Vivonne turned, took her arm and brought her forward.

'May I present to you Mme Scarron, of Paris?'

Françoise curtsied respectfully. The Princess gave a slight nod in her direction and turned again to Vivonne.

'Can we not persuade you to remain with us a little longer?' she asked. She moved towards him, snapping open her fan, turning this way and that the better to display her figure. A cloud of perfume emanated from the yards of material in the pearly grey satin of her gown which, caught up with roses, billowed as she walked. A long veil of silver lace fell down her back, and her silver-blonde hair was dressed with rosebuds. Tiny rose-pink slippers peeped from underneath her dress. Françoise had never felt so out of place and uncomfortable in her travelling clothes, her hair and her shoes thick with dust.

'I'm sorry, madame. My orders are to leave at first light.'

'Oh, you military men!' she chided him. 'I declare you're as bad as my husband. Don't you ever turn your attention to such matters as dancing and enjoying yourselves? It's nothing but muskets and army manoeuvres all the time when you get together.'

'In that case, Madame la Princesse, I am happy to inform you that I have recently been given the command of Commander-General to His Majesty's Navy.'

The Princess laughed, a light tinkling laugh that reminded Françoise of the bells that hung from the baby's cradle. The baby! She clenched her hands so that the nails bit into her flesh. Would this woman never stop mincing and prancing round the room in her efforts to attract a man nearly ten years her junior?

'However,' Vivonne was saying, 'I have come to ask you if we may trespass on your hospitality and find a room for Mme Scarron and her servant, who are unable to travel back to Paris until the morning. As Mme Scarron is my sister's friend, and came here especially to see her, I have taken upon myself the liberty of asking you.'

The Princess scarcely glanced at Françoise. She called over her shoulder and a footman hastened forward.

'Find suitable accommodation for this person and her maid.' She extended her hand to Vivonne. There was no doubt he was the most attractive man at present staying at the chateau. 'This is on condition that you escort me in to supper.'

Vivonne glanced over his shoulder in resignation at Françoise as she led him from the room.

Chapter Eighteen

The way to Compiègne lay through the Forêt d'Halatte and along the banks of the river Oise. Françoise had risen at the first light of dawn, refreshed after a good night's sleep in a comfortable bed. The serving-girl who had been assigned to them brought her a large bowl of Chantilly porcelain, a jug of warm water and, unbelievable luxury, Marseilles soap. Nanon was still fast asleep on her camp bed at the foot of the large bed when Françoise, after drinking the sage tea the girl brought her, slipped quietly out of the room.

'Tell my servant that I shall return by nightfall,' she told the girl, giving her a few coins. Then Vivonne was tapping impatiently at the door of the antechamber, calling quietly so as not to rouse the people sleeping near-by. 'Françoise! If you ride with us, we're leaving!'

They were a party of six riding through the forest, the Comte d'Epernon and the Vicomte de Tours, two of Vivonne's soldier companions to whom he was shortly to say farewell, herself and Vivonne, and two grooms whom Vivonne had brought along in order to escort Françoise back to Chantilly. Françoise was glad that the Vicomte de Bragelonne was not of the party. Fortunately for her, Vivonne, recovering from the excesses of the previous night and suffering from a sore head, set a pace which was not too fast; it was many years since Françoise had sat a horse, and she was unsuitably dressed.

At the hamlet of Villers-Saint-Paul they stopped to buy bread rolls from a baker just opening his shop, and munched them as they rode along.

'Did you take any supper last night?' Vivonne asked Françoise apologetically, remembering that he had promised to take her in to supper. He yawned. If only that damned Condé woman hadn't been so demanding! God, she was enough to reduce a man to shreds, especially when he had to ride the next day. He had not even enjoyed his adventure, having been in mortal fear that M. le Prince, in attendance on the King in Compiègne, might suddenly return. He did not relish his chances in a duel with the Grand Condé.

'Yes, we were served supper in our room,' answered Françoise, remembering Nanon's pleasure at the meal brought by a handsome, superior footman in silk stockings, green satin breeches and green and gold coat, who had bowed low to Françoise – and to Nanon, much to her delight. Cold meats, a selection of salads, fresh white rolls, pastries, sweetmeats and lemonade, all served with silver cutlery and dainty damask napkins. She herself had had little appetite after the long journey and the shock and sorrow of the day, but had tasted a little to please Nanon, who made a good meal. The girl had made up their beds for them, and by ten o'clock they were both sound asleep. Françoise, who had not thought that she would be able to sleep, had been surprised when she was awakened by the sounds of the herons on the water outside their window at dawn. She smiled to herself a little ruefully. At least Nanon was enjoying their expedition. For herself, she longed for nothing more than to receive the King's instructions, return to Paris and try to take up the threads of normal life again. Never again, she promised herself, would she ever allow herself to become involved in such a situation.

At the thought of the baby, and of Father Dangerre awaiting her instructions at St Eustache, a cold chill stole over her heart and she shivered a little, although the day was by now very warm. She looked round at the greenery of the forest, the squirrels leaping along in their wake, the bright dappling of the water of the river a few yards away. How beautiful the world was! How could God allow such things to happen on a summer day?

'You know that I shall be riding on to Brest from Compiègne,' Vivonne was saying to her. 'The grooms will accompany you back to Chantilly.'

'Yes, I know,' Françoise answered. 'I told you that it is a matter of the utmost urgency on which I must see the King.'

Vivonne looked at her, a faint smile playing round his lips. He wondered what her chances were of seeing the King. Even if Louis were in the mood for a pretty woman, dressed as she was –

'Let us hope your journey will not be in vain,' he remarked.

Françoise heard him, but set her lips tightly and ignored him. In a concentrated effort not to think of the events of yesterday, she fixed her mind determinedly on the future. For some time now Gisèle d'Albret had been asking her to come to the Hôtel d'Albret as governess to her daughters. She decided that she could not accept a living-in post, which would mean dismissing

Nanon, but perhaps she would make some arrangements on a daily basis which would allow her to keep the little house on the rue des Tournelles.

It was nearing two o'clock when, the Forêt d'Halatte having given way to the magnificent forest of Compiègne, they rode past the forbidding grey twelfth-century *donjon* of Beauregard where Joan of Arc had been captured two hundred years before. Ahead of them they could see the ancient castle of Compiègne, home of the French kings since Carolingian times.

'If the King is out supervising the army exercises you will have little chance of seeing him today,' Vivonne warned Françoise as they rode into the castle yard.

'We shall see,' replied Françoise, as Vivonne and a groom helped her to dismount. Lackeys walked the horses away. The Comte d'Epernon and the Vicomte de Tours bade farewell to Françoise and went off to find their headquarters. Vivonne and Françoise mounted the steps of the castle entrance, where Vivonne enquired the whereabouts of the King.

'The King goes to hunt at three,' replied the steward. 'The Master of the Hunt was told to have the dogs and horses in readiness, it being such a fine day. The manoeuvres have been postponed until tomorrow.'

Three o'clock! It must be half past two now. Françoise looked imploringly at Vivonne, who asked the steward to direct them to the royal suite. A sentry was detailed to show them the way. At the door of the King's apartments, Vivonne bowed to Françoise, and excused himself.

'Well, I wish you *bonne chance*, Françoise. I must leave you now – my appointment with the King is at six, when he is officially to hand over my orders, and I have many other things to attend to before then.'

He kissed her hand and bowed. Françoise took his hand in hers. Her eyes filled with tears. 'How can I thank you, Vivonne? Even if I am not successful in seeing the King, be assured of my gratitude for what you have done for me. I hope one day to be in a position to render you some assistance.'

He laughed, his eyes sliding impudently over her figure. Her clothes, shabby the day before, were now in a state of complete disrepair after being slept and ridden in. Long branches in the forest had made tears in her skirt, and her hair was coming down at one side. Yet her face was flushed with the exertion of the journey and her lovely eyes shone with the nervous thrill she felt at – as she hoped – being about to see the King. She could not have presented a greater contrast to the Princesse de Condé, dressed, perfumed and powdered within an inch of her life. Yet he knew which of the two he would prefer to bed. One day, he thought, I'll have our young widow Scarron, and see if she's as cold in bed as she likes to pretend.

'At your service, madame. One day I'll hold you to your promise.' With another bow he walked away, the sound of his boots echoing in the distance along the stone corridor.

A footman opened the door of the royal apartments in answer to her knock. The two sentries on either side of the door looked askance at Françoise, for the King's visit to Compiègne was purely on military exercises; there were no women in the party. The footman too looked down his nose at Françoise, who asked if the King might grant a brief interview to someone who had travelled from Paris to consult him on a matter of the greatest urgency.

'Your name, please, and the nature of your business?'

Françoise wrote down her name on the piece of paper he gave her.

'Your business, if you please.'

She added to her name, *friend of Mme la Marquise de Montespan.* The footman sniffed, and closed the door in her face.

Louis was amazed when the Prince de Condé handed him the piece of paper. Scarron – wasn't that Athenais' friend who was looking after the baby for her? Quite a pretty girl, as he remembered. What on earth was she doing here at Compiègne? Well, it would make a change to see a pretty woman after the past fortnight's surfeit of dogs, horses and soldiers. 'Show her in, Condé.'

Françoise was led through the antechamber and the dining-room to a pleasant room overlooking the castle ramparts. In the yard below there was a great deal of noise. The horses and dogs were being assembled for the King's hunt. The King sat in an easy-chair by the window, engaged in his usual after-dinner occupation of feeding titbits to his pet dogs, Bonne, Ponne and Nonne, who were leaping up to his knees for them. He wore a jerkin of Spanish leather over a plain white shirt, and a valet knelt at his feet removing His Majesty's shoes and putting on his riding boots. His dark hair was simply tied in a queue at the back. The large airy room was cool, with its stone floor and stone walls, and in the huge open fireplace stood pots of the King's favourite strongly-scented flowers, jasmine and tuberoses.

'*Bonjour*, Madame Scarron. What brings you all this way to see us?' The King's greeting was cordial enough, but he was shocked at the change in Françoise's appearance. What had happened to the lovely, laughing girl dressed in green he had admired that day at St Germain last summer? She was dressed like a ragbag, and how thin she was. Her great dark eyes burned like coals in her white face as the enormity of the news she had to impart to him overcame her with faintness.

Suddenly Louis realized that something was wrong, terribly wrong. 'Are you ill, madame?' he asked with concern.

Françoise made no answer, but simply looked at the Prince de Condé who had ushered her into the royal presence. With a motion of his hand the King dismissed him. The valet had already left the room, taking the King's shoes with him. Louis brushed the dogs away and rose, taking Françoise by the hands.

'Something is wrong, madame.' He gestured to a stool. 'Please seat yourself. Do not be afraid.'

Still she stood motionless, those great dark eyes regarding him silently. Louis became impatient.

'For God's sake, madame! What is your message!'

The words of the little speech she had prepared fled from her brain. 'It is the child, Sire.'

'Athenais' baby? The little girl? Is she ill?'

'She is dead, Sire.'

The pleasant expression on the King's handsome face hardened. Without a word he turned and walked over to the window. For several minutes he stood looking out at the bustle and confusion in the yard below. The scent of the flowers rose in an overpowering cloud, and Françoise clutched at the edge of a table for support. She was afraid that any minute she might collapse as the relief of having informed at least one of the baby's parents of its death overcame her.

There was a knock on the door which the King ignored. At last he turned to Françoise. His brown eyes glistened as he gently motioned to her to sit. Françoise sat down on the stool and covered her face with her hands. At last, at long last, she could weep. The pent-up emotion she had hugged to herself for more than twenty-four hours, the fear she had had of telling Athenais or the King the news, at last released itself and she was able to indulge in the healthy relief of tears. The King said nothing, leaning his arm on the mantelshelf above the fireplace, his head resting on his arm.

When she had slightly recovered herself, he asked: 'Please tell me everything.' Françoise told him, as briefly as possible, exactly what had happened. Louis was satisfied with her explanation.

'I have now lost five of my children,' he said. 'In this respect, Fortune treats me no more kindly than the humblest of my subjects. The Queen's first little girl died in exactly the same way.'

'It was such a shock, Sire. I have not yet recovered, as you see.'

He looked at her tear-stained face and dusty clothes. He was impressed by her genuine grief and her single-minded sense of duty in coming straight to see him. It was obvious that she had not changed her clothes nor rested. Most women under such circumstances would have invented some tale, sent some message. Not her. The truth, and the duty of reporting it, she had taken upon her own slim shoulders. He wondered how old she was. She did not look more than thirty, yet she had the moral fibre of someone much more mature. He realized that she was the first woman for whom he had felt – not attraction, but admiration, since his mother died.

'She was such a beautiful, happy child,' Françoise continued. 'A joy to us all, Sire. You should have seen her on the day she was christened!'

Her face clouded as she remembered the instructions she must ask of him. 'Your instructions, Sire. I have come for them. Arrangements have to be made – '

'Ah, yes,' said the King. He rang a handbell. The Prince de Condé returned.

'Sire?'

'Cancel the hunt, Condé. I shall not hunt today.'

'*Mais certainement.*' He cast a look of disdain at Françoise. Who was this upstart, forcing her way in here, and what message could she have brought which he had not been fit to hear?

'Are there any women here,' asked the King, 'who can attend to this lady? She has travelled far, and is in need of tiring-women.'

'There is only Mme de Beauclerc, the head linen-keeper, Sire.' And quite good enough for this nonentity, he thought.

'Have her prepare a room for this lady, and see that she attends to her needs.' Françoise tried to speak, but he waved his hand. The Prince de Condé bowed and left the room. They heard him in the next room giving a lackey his instructions, deeming it

191

below his dignity to carry them out himself.

'Now tell me how you travelled here,' asked the King.

'We journeyed by coach to Chantilly,' replied Françoise, 'where I hoped to find Athenais – the Marquise. From there, the Duc de Vivonne allowed me to ride with him.'

'You rode from Chantilly?' No wonder she looked as she did, after travelling from Paris the day before.

'Yes. My waiting-woman awaits me there.'

'Allow me to place at your disposal a carriage to convey you back to Paris.'

'You are most kind, Sire.'

A lackey knocked and the King beckoned him to enter. 'Madame de Beauclerc is here, Sire.'

'Tell her to come forward.'

A portly lady of sixty or so, her white hair neatly dressed in a bun, entered blushing and covered with confusion at finding herself in such an exalted presence.

'Be so kind as to attend this lady and afford her every comfort,' the King said to her. 'I shall give you the instructions I desire carried out before you leave,' he told Françoise.

'Thank you, Sire.'

Within a short time, refreshed, washed, her hair combed, her hands and face scented and her clothes brushed and pressed, she was again shown into the presence of the King. Louis sat writing at a desk. He handed her a letter with the royal seal, noting with approval the change in her appearance.

'I am pleased to see you looking more like yourself,' he told her. Françoise blushed modestly. 'See, the coach awaits you.' Françoise looked out of his window and saw a coach with the royal fleur-de-lys waiting at the gates, the ostlers harnessing the horses. 'You will at least travel back in more comfort than you came.'

'You are too kind, Sire.' She curtsied, taking the envelope he handed her. He took her hands in his.

'May I compliment you, Madame Scarron, on the exemplary way in which you have carried out the trust reposed in you?'

'Sire, may I ask only if you will communicate with Athenais – la Marquise?'

He promised that he would spare her that melancholy duty. Then as she turned to go, he remarked with a smile: 'We may shortly be in need of your assistance once more, madame.'

She turned, incredulity in her eyes and a question on her lips.

'In February, I believe, madame, la Marquise de Montespan may again have need of your services.'

She could not believe it. All she wished was to wash her hands for ever of Athenais and her baby. Surely he could not seriously be suggesting that she start all over again?

There was a twinkle in his eyes, as he remarked: 'Let us hope that your experience will stand you in good stead for the next occasion, madame.'

She saw all her careful plans for the future collapse at the prospect of preparing for another secret baby. Yet she knew, looking at the King's handsome sun-tanned face, a little thinner and more lined than the open, boyish countenance she had admired so much on the day of his arrival in Paris with the Queen, that she could refuse nothing this man might ask of her. There was a kind of magnetism about him. He had a charm that drew one inexorably towards him, yet at the same time a regality that kept one at one's distance. What was it the Duc de Richelieu had said of him one evening at Ninon de l'Enclos' salon? 'Whatever the circumstances of his birth, the world, upon seeing him, would have recognized him for its master.' How true that was.

At the door, her hand on the knob, a thought suddenly struck her and she turned back. He was smiling at her now, a smile that made her long to fling away her black robes of widowhood and don the gay colours of the ladies by whom he was surrounded. She resolved at that moment that when the mourning period prescribed for the baby was over, she would never wear black again. One did not need to wear sombre colours for those one had loved. She knew that she would carry the memory of the baby's face in her heart until the day she died.

'Sire – the cure at Bourbon.' Mme de Sévigné had told her blood-curdling tales of the ordeals one had to undergo there – standing naked with hot water sprayed on you, drinking the vile waters. If Athenais was pregnant when she went there, there was more than a good chance that she would not be when she returned. Suddenly she realized why Athenais had wanted to make the journey.

'Sire, was it safe for la Marquise to travel and undergo the cure, in her condition? It might cause some harm to the baby – '

The King's face clouded. He too realized, now that Françoise had pointed it out, why Athenais had been so anxious to spend the time while he was with the army visiting Bourbon. To lose weight and improve her frequent headaches – so she had said.

He loved children and could not have too many of them. Athenais, however, lived in constant fear that he would be attracted to someone else whilst she was heavy and cumbersome. His lips tightened. If she came back safely he would see to it that she did not travel again until the baby was born. It might be a son this time. He did not, however, intend to discuss such intimate matters with Mme Scarron. He bowed his dismissal.

Françoise, glancing up as she climbed into the carriage, saw the outline of the King standing watching from the window as she was driven out of the castle yard and away through the forest to Chantilly.

PART III

THE NOONDAY SUN

1670-1673

Chapter Nineteen

Late in the afternoon of a wet, dreary day in February 1670, a hackney coach stood outside the chateau of St Germain-en-Laye, quite near to where Françoise Scarron had waited when Athenais de Montespan's previous baby had been born almost a year before. A light but persistent downpour of rain dripped steadily from the trees and sloshed along the gutters, soaking the horses and saturating the driver to the skin.

Although it was little more than four o'clock the dull greyness of the day was fast fading to a sullen twilight, which meant that it would be nightfall within the hour. Hundreds of feet below the hilltop where the chateau perched on the crags, a fine impenetrable mist hung over the valley of the Seine, the river itself blotted out by low cloud and rain. No sound could be heard save the crunch of the coach-driver's feet on the gravel as he paced up and down, the pouring rain and the horses whinnying and pawing at the ground.

Inside the coach, Françoise, huddled up in her thick cloak, allowed herself for the first time in many months the luxury of dwelling on thoughts of the little baby girl for whom she had waited here in this very spot just a year ago, and who had come to mean so much to her. For some considerable time now she had, with her usual sheer strength of will, refused to indulge such thoughts. After the traumatic shock of the baby's sudden death she had flung herself into a positive frenzy of activity, managing to reach her bed in the evening in such a state of exhaustion that she fell asleep the moment her head touched the pillow, so that the memories that were too painful to be borne could not touch her.

She had never thought, when she was summoned here to St Germain in the middle of that wild March night a year ago, what an effect the baby would have on her orderly, well-planned way of life. As far as she was concerned, she had been asked to perform a duty, one that she did not wish for but could not avoid. She had taken away that child to care for it in much the same spirit as she would if she had been asked to look after a Persian

197

carpet, or a rather valuable piece of furniture whilst its owner was away. Never in her wildest dreams had she imagined the place that the baby would assume in her life – that she would become so much a part of her that she would miss her more and more with every day that passed, see the little face with its bright black eyes and dark curly hair in her sleep, and each day wake with an emptiness in her heart because the child was no longer there.

How could it happen, she thought, that in such a short span of time a child could assume such power over another person – and a stranger, not a relative, at that. The baby had lived for only four months. Four months; usually, such a short time was enough only to scrape the barest acquaintance with another person – for it took Françoise, with her reserved nature, years, not months, in which to make a friend. Ninon de l'Enclos she had known now for more than twelve years, Mme de Sévigné and Mlle de Scudéry for almost as long. She felt as close to Nanon Balbien, her servant, as anyone could be, after living under the same roof for almost ten years. Yet within the space of a few brief weeks – she closed her eyes, re-living for a moment the joy that the baby had brought to the house in the rue d'Alexandre – a baby's plump fingers could twist themselves round your heart.

The driver of the coach was knocking at the door. Françoise, shivering with cold in spite of her thick cloak and the lap mantle over her knees, adjusted her vizard and opened the door a crack.

'How much longer, madame?' the man demanded. Rain dripped from his hair, his hat and his clothes were wringing wet, his face grey and pinched. The cold, damp air seeping into the coach from the open door served to clear a little of the smoke rising from the miniature brazier of warm coals under Françoise's feet.

'I don't know. Soon, I should think.'

'I'll be down with the ague tomorrow if we stay here much longer, madame. This weather's fit for neither man nor beast.'

'You will be well paid, never fear.'

Still grumbling, he shut the door with a bang and began to pace up and down again to keep warm, cursing audibly his folly in having accepted such a fare.

Françoise, coughing a little from the damp air and the smokiness of the carriage, fell to thinking about the arrangements she had made for the new baby. She had taken a small house in the rue Birague this time, conveniently near to the rue des Tournelles, where she had installed a whole troupe of servants, a cook, a housekeeper, a washerwoman, two serving-girls, even an old man to act as concierge, and no less than four wet-nurses, two for daytime and two for the night. She had even hired a young girl to come in daily for the sole purpose of rocking the baby's cradle. Though no blame for the other baby's death could be laid at anyone's door, for her own peace of mind she intended that this baby should always be in the care of more than one person, both by day and at night.

After her initial shock when the King had informed her that day at Compiègne last summer that there would soon be another baby for her attentions, she had tried to overcome her immediate reaction of inner frustration – that the plans she had begun to formulate in her mind for the future were to be thwarted once again. And gradually, she had found herself awaiting the arrival of this baby with almost as much anticipation as if it were her own. Every week, every month ticked off on the calendar in the kitchen of the little house in the rue des Tournelles, meant that time was drawing a little nearer to the day when she would hold a baby in her arms again. She wondered if this time it would be a boy or a girl. Would it be as dark and plump as the little girl who had died so soon, or would this new baby inherit its mother's looks and colouring? One thing was certain: a child born of two such handsome parents could not be lacking in personal charm.

What was it like to give birth? she wondered, her hand stealing involuntarily underneath her cloak to touch her flat stomach. To wait, patiently and stoically day after day, month after month, watching one's body become bigger and more ungainly, a grotesque travesty of a woman's shape, and then, finally, to be brought to bed, there to endure, unrelieved by opiates, the agonies and indignities of childbirth. To be delivered of a red-faced, squalling infant that might live no more than a few hours and put one's own life at risk. The mother who survived the perils of childbed had still to face the danger of milk fever or the flux during her lying-in.

Whenever her married friends found themselves *enceinte*, Françoise, although congratulating them with feigned enthusiasm, had in reality regarded them as objects of pity. Now, remembering those short-lived days of happiness last summer, and the baby who had brought so much joy into her life, she wondered if she would ever give birth to a child herself. It was unlikely, for a widow who had now passed thirty-five. She would, she knew, have to content herself with a child at second-hand. Yet she was beginning to realize that more than anything on earth she longed passionately, with every fibre of her being, to hold a child once again, to be the focal point of another human being's existence, and to lavish on that child all the reserves of love and affection which, with no one to bestow them on, she had kept repressed for so long. She thought of the little dark-haired baby, laughing and chuckling as she had seen her for the last time. She would not be reunited with that little soul in this world, but soon, very soon now, there would be the new baby to take in her arms.

The driver was banging on the door again, and she opened it as little as she could. Behind him loomed the great mass of the castle, stark and grey. Lights were beginning to show at the windows, reflected in the puddles of the alleyways. There were pools full of dead leaves and twigs along the Grande Terrasse, stretching away into the distance. Françoise could not help but smile wryly as she thought of Athenais' fury at being cooped up here in the country all these months. The King, true to his word, had seen to it that when she returned from her fruitless visit to Bourbon, having failed there in ridding herself of her unwelcome pregnancy, she remained safely here at St Germain to await the birth of the child. Poor Athenais! How she must be straining at the leash, longing to return to the glittering delights of the winter season at the Louvre, and to the glories of her position as the King's mistress. But probably the King had visited her here often enough, for the King had never taken the fact of pregnancy in a woman as justification for denying her proof of his love – though such details remained beyond even Mme de Sévigné's powers of discovery. No doubt the lovers would soon be enjoying a rapturous reunion; and the expression on Françoise's face behind her velvet mask became sober once again.

'I'll wait here no longer, to catch my death of cold!' the driver was shouting, pointing to his saturated garments. 'I'm for Paris, and some dry clothes.'

'I can't leave yet!' she answered. 'I must wait a little while longer.'

'You can return with me, or stay here; just as you please, my lady. But I'll wait no longer here for you or anyone.'

There was a sound of footsteps on the gravel path behind him and two people appeared out of the gloom. A well-aimed cuff from a young man elegantly dressed in the height of fashion sent the driver sprawling to the ground, where he lay in the mud nursing his ear, making no attempt to get up.

Françoise looked in surprise at the slightly-built young man who had laid him out so easily. With a graceful gesture the nobleman swept off his hat and, in spite of the rain, pouring harder than ever, made a most courtly bow.

'Madame Scarron?'

'Yes.'

'The Duc de Lauzun, at your service, madame.'

Lauzun! A rumour had been current in Paris for some time that Athenais de Montespan and the Duc de Lauzun were indulging in a love-affair. Françoise had guessed correctly that this was a false rumour spread to lay the responsibility for Athenais' pregnancy at the wrong door. Any impecunious young courtier would be happy to oblige the King in this way.

Lauzun beckoned to the footman who accompanied him, and the man stepped forward. Françoise perceived that he held in his arms a large bundle of blankets. The baby – exposed to this terrible weather! She held out her arms. 'Please give that to me!'

Oblivious of the precious contents of the bundle he carried, the footman handed it up to her. Lauzun delivered a kick in the direction of the driver, now struggling to get up.

'How dare you threaten your betters in such a fashion! Get up there and convey madame swiftly and safely to Paris, or you'll answer for it with your hide.'

The driver, needing no second bidding, leapt up to his box and began to whip up the horses and turn the carriage. Lauzun handed Françoise a letter with the King's seal. 'His Majesty, who was present, commends the child to your care,' he told her, 'and these are his instructions.'

The King was here at St Germain, only a few yards away, and she had not known!

'Madame la Marquise – is she in good health?'

'Perfect, madame, God be praised; sitting up and calling for brandy.'

Françoise laughed. It was easy to imagine Athenais doing that. As the carriage began to draw away she called to him: 'The child! Is it a boy or girl?'

The expression of cheerful confidence on Lauzun's face faded in a trice. '*Ma foi*, madame! I never thought to ask!'

The horses' hooves grated on the gravel as they gathered speed and the coach rattled and jolted through the gateway and began to draw away from the castle along the road for Paris. Françoise looked back for a moment through the small aperture at the back of the coach. The two men had already disappeared from sight, and the huge grey building was almost obscured by a curtain of mist and rain. Ahead of the coach, the road twisted down through the forest of Laye to the bridge at Chatou and then across the flat valley of the Seine to the vast bustling city of Paris – where every day hundreds of thousands of people rose, ate, slept, made love, quarrelled, gave birth, and died. Here in her arms lay a child suspended between those two worlds – the Royal Court of France into which it had been born, and the everyday life of bourgeois Paris in which it would be brought up. A tremendous upsurge of emotion and protective love overwhelmed her, compassion for this baby emerging from the womb to be carried away and passed from hand to hand by strangers.

The King loved his children, she knew, but he had many other concerns to occupy him, not the least of which were the quarrels between his wife and his past and present mistresses, Athenais de Montespan and Louise de la Vallière. Poor little mite, whose only fault was to be born out of wedlock. Françoise doubted that Athenais would take very much interest in the child, judging by the marked lack of attention she had shown its sister.

She looked down at the tiny warm body in the blankets on her lap, and discarding the saturated outer blanket, gently lifted it to her, holding it close to her body for warmth. How light it was, this delicate little creature – it seemed to weigh almost nothing by comparison with the plump, chubby body of the baby which had died. There was only a little fine down on its head, quite light in colour, and the tiny face was pale, but not sallow as its sister's had been; the lashes were not black but brown.

As she gazed down at the miniature face with mixed feelings of awe and rapture, the child opened its eyes. Blue-grey eyes stared at her for a moment, unwavering, unblinking, as if mutely questioning 'Who am I?' For a minute or two the young woman dressed in black and the newborn infant regarded each other in silence, as if each was taking the other's measure. Then, satisfied, the baby closed its eyes and seemed to sleep.

Instinctively, Françoise tightened her grasp around the tiny body lying so trustingly asleep in her arms. This child was not going to die in infancy if it lay within her power to prevent it. With God's help, she intended to raise this child and watch it grow to maturity. Here, she knew, lying peacefully against her breast, was her own child – as surely as if she herself had given it birth.

Never since the childhood of Louis XIV himself had any child been so adored, so spoilt and doted on and fussed over, as the baby in the house in the rue Birague.

The King had decreed in his letter of instructions that his son's name was to be Louis-Auguste, an amalgam of his own name and that of the illustrious Roman emperor. The child was to be baptized at the age of four weeks, at St Eustache, and he would send his own chaplain to officiate on the occasion. The King's chief musician, Lully, would arrange the music – St Eustache was famous for its music – and a representative of the King would also attend. A considerable sum of money, he wrote, had been lodged with the Italian bankers in the rue des Lombards, and Françoise had authority to draw on it as and when she saw fit. He added in conclusion that he intended to visit his son when a suitable occasion arose.

This, Françoise knew, meant when he had the opportunity to arrive incognito. It was not easy for the highly popular King to leave the Louvre, or visit Paris for the day from St Germain, without a considerable amount of attendant publicity. It was virtually impossible for him to slip away from Court unnoticed, for he spent his whole life in the public gaze, from the *levée* at eight in the morning when no less than twenty-odd people had the right of entry to his chamber to assist His Majesty with his toilette, until the official *coucher* at eleven at night, a similar procedure. His time spent in privacy with Athenais had to be squeezed in somewhere between his hearing Mass, which he did every day of his life, his hunting, and his official working sessions, not to mention his long consultations with the architects working on the renovated palace of Versailles, his visits to the royal nursery, the time spent with his wife, and his attendance at all the many Court entertainments. Perhaps the limited amount of time the lovers were able to spend together contributed in some way to the success of their love-affair, now entering its third year.

From Athenais herself, Françoise heard nothing. Mme de Sévigné reported that, released from the penance of all those weary, waiting months at St Germain, she had thrown herself with gusto into the social life of Court once more, beautiful as ever, and apparently even higher in the King's favour than before. Haughty, capricious, avaricious, Athenais de Montespan seemed to have discovered the secret of keeping the Sun King entranced by her charms. Her clothes and jewels were reported to outshine those of the Queen herself.

'The King is having a magnificent house built for la Montespan at Clagny,' Mlle de Scudéry reported one evening at supper at the Hôtel d'Albret.

Mme d'Albret raised her eyebrows. 'Athenais seems to be assured of a long run in the King's favour,' she remarked. 'He would hardly go to the trouble and expense of building her a house if he had any thoughts of parting with her.'

'Why should he?' asked Françoise. 'She is very lovely, and her company is gay and diverting. I have no doubt she keeps him amused after the monotony of long sessions with his Council.'

Mme de Sévigné sniffed. 'If only my darling Marguerite had not been snatched away to Provence, our friend Quanto would not have found it so easy to lure the King away from la Vallière. You have seen her, have you not, Françoise? Is she not lovely?'

Françoise had to admit that she was, but did not contribute her opinion of the Comtesse de Grignan's personality, which she found as stimulating as that of a slab of wet fish.

'If my darling Marguerite were at Court, where her nobility of birth would have placed her had she stayed in Paris, she would have given Quanto a run for her money, I assure you.'

The company in general did not agree with these sentiments voiced by the fond mother, but were too polite to say so.

'The King hears Mass with the regularity of a God-fearing man,' remarked Mme de Coulanges, 'yet it would be a better show of piety were he to confine his attentions to his wife.'

'Oh, come,' protested even Mme de Sévigné. 'After ten years in this country the Queen can still hardly speak French. She has no interests other than her dwarfs. She spends half her time on her knees. The King is a sophisticated man, and seeks more worldly pleasures.'

'And as a consequence, our friend la Montespan spends most of her time on her back,' put in the Maréchal d'Albret from his place by the fire, as the ladies sat gossiping and sewing under the chandelier where the light was better. His wife gave him a look of remonstrance and put her fingers to her lips – her two older daughters had been allowed to stay up for supper as there was company.

'My dear,' Gisèle d'Albret said to Françoise, as she helped

204

the younger of the girls with her tapestry work, 'will you not reconsider your decision not to become our governess? The girls would like it dearly.'

'Oh, yes,' the two girls clamoured. 'Dear Aunt Scarron, won't you come to live with us?'

Françoise blushed to the roots of her hair. She spent all her days and as many evenings as she could at the rue Birague, declining as many invitations as she could, without offending her friends. When she did accept an invitation to supper, her behaviour was so out of character as to puzzle her friends completely, and her conversation seemed devoid of its usual vivacity and gaiety, for she seemed preoccupied and vague. Her absent-mindedness was concern as to whether, in her absence, the baby was being properly cared for, whether the nursery at the rue Birague was being kept too hot or too cold, and whether the nurses were paying the child their full attention, or drinking and gossiping and leaving him unattended. And she, for her part, was beginning to find her friends' endless gossip and chatter boring and inconsequential. She was concerned with far more important matters – little Louis-Auguste would cut his first tooth any day. When he laughed and gurgled a little lump could be clearly seen in the pink gum. Perhaps it would come through tomorrow.

'I'm sorry, my dear Anne-Marie,' she said to the younger girl, slipping an arm round her shoulders. 'You know I love you dearly – but I can't come to live with you.'

'Don't you want to be our governess, Tante Scarron?' asked the older girl, Marie-Blanche.

'It isn't that, my dear. I'll always come to see you, and help you in whatever way I can, but I seem to have too many demands on my time to be here all the time.'

Mme d'Albret looked at her curiously. It was true, Françoise seemed always to be busy these days. She wondered what it was that kept her so fully occupied, for she seemed to have no time for anything; she never mentioned books she had read – and she had formerly spent a good deal of her time reading the latest books and plays. Blanche d'Heudicourt had often told her that Françoise was constantly declining her invitations. It had been some considerable time since Françoise had even come in during the day to see the new d'Albret baby, whom she had doted on when she was born. And although Françoise had only a small royal pension, she was beginning to dress better than she ever had done – always very soberly in dark colours, it was true, but her dresses were made of good-quality materials, she wore immaculate collars and cuffs of Valenciennes lace, and her shoes and gloves were of finest Spanish leather. As governess to the daughters of a Marshal of France in the d'Albret household, she would receive a handsome salary; yet she could afford to turn it down. Had it been anyone but Françoise Scarron, Mme d'Albret would have sworn that the erstwhile respectable widow had at last seen the rewards to be gained from a life of pleasure.

A few days later Gisèle d'Albret and Blanche d'Heudicourt, discussing Françoise *tête à tête*, found that they were beginning to worry over the change in their friend. She had always been the first one to call on them if anyone in the family were unwell, or some little trouble had put them out of countenance; now they had to plead with her to spare them an evening visit. They could not agree, however, on whether they should ask her to confide in them.

Françoise is perfectly capable of taking care of her own life, thought Blanche d'Heudicourt; but Gisèle d'Albret was of a different opinion.

'If she is in any kind of dilemma, would it not be of help to her to talk it over with a close friend who has her interests deeply at heart?'

'I think not. Knowing Françoise as I do, I feel that if she wanted to discuss anything, the approach would have to come from her. Were we to attempt to probe into her affairs, she would shut up like a clam.'

Mme d'Albret had to admit the truth of this statement, and they began to talk of other matters.

At four o'clock promptly, Blanche excused herself on the grounds that she had to call at the dressmaker's on her way home. Gisèle d'Albret, however, watching from the window of the Hôtel d'Albret, noticed that her sedan was borne away along the rue des Francs Bourgeois and turned, not in the direction of the dressmaker, Mme Vinert, in the rue de Turenne, but straight along the rue Rambuteau in the opposite direction.

So it was true that, as had been secretly rumoured for some time, Mme d'Heudicourt, married only a few years, was having an affair with the Marquis de Béthune. Gisèle d'Albret sighed. Was there no such thing as marital fidelity nowadays? With a despondent expression on her face, she went up to the nursery, to supervise the children's supper.

Chapter Twenty

In thinking that there might be some cause for concern in Françoise's life, her friends could not have been more wrong. Not since the days of the previous summer, with the baby in the rue d'Alexandre, had she been so happy and contented. There seemed to be some special *rapport* between her and this new baby, Louis-Auguste. He was not a contented child as his sister had been, but inclined to be fretful, whether over his feed, or cutting his teeth. His digestion was temperamental. When he was upset and tearful, whatever the cause might be, Françoise was the only one who could soothe him. His fair skin was delicate; these winter days, his lips and chin were often chapped. If he was not cleaned with the greatest care when he soiled himself, an angry red rash would break out all over his bottom, causing him to scream with anger when he was being changed.

But in Françoise's arms he would quieten down, and she would rock him to and fro, holding him close to her body, murmuring words of comfort which he seemed to listen to and understand. When she laid him down in his crib he would scream if she attempted to tip-toe from the room, but if she continued to rock the crib and talk to him, he would remain peaceful, sucking noisily at his thumb for comfort. In short, he was a tyrant of the first order, and for the first few months of his life held Françoise in complete subjection to his whims and fancies. He was the master and she his willing slave.

Nothing was too much trouble for her, no sacrifice of her own time, or rest – however tired she might be – too much for the sake of this darling child. Nanon reproached her when, with a house full of servants, she herself changed his napkin or coaxed him to sleep. 'I believe she would feed him, too, if she were able to,' she muttered to herself, but dared not say so to her mistress.

One day, sorting out cupboards at the rue des Tournelles, Nanon found, carefully wrapped in a clean piece of white linen, the stick of coral and the red and blue rattle which had belonged to the other baby. Françoise had already left, as she did each morning the moment she was dressed and ready, taking her breakfast at the rue Birague in order not to miss a moment of the baby's day.

Later in the day, when Nanon arrived to see if her mistress had anything she wanted her to purchase at the Pont Neuf, she took the toys out of her basket. Before Françoise could stop her she held them up before the baby, who was lying in his crib, just awake after his morning sleep.

'Look, mistress,' she said. 'You must have forgotten about these. Are they not splendid for the baby?'

Little Louis-Auguste, attracted by the bright colours, immediately held up his hands, ineffectually trying to reach them. Françoise's face darkened with anger.

'What right have you to take those things from my cupboard?' she demanded. She snatched them from Nanon's hands and clasped them tight. Nanon, who had never heard a cross word from her mistress in more than ten years, looked at her in amazement.

'I only thought the baby would like them – '

'Then you had no right to think!' Françoise hesitated. The baby, accustomed to having his own way in everything, was beginning to howl with frustration at not being given the pretty bright-coloured toys. Esmé, the nurse, sitting on the low stool unbuttoning her dress in readiness to feed the baby, looked at her open-mouthed. Mme Scarron was usually the most gentle, the kindest of employers.

Françoise approached the cradle and stood looking at the child. She had not wanted to give these toys to Louis-Auguste for two reasons – partly because she wanted to keep them as something to remind her of his sister, but mainly because she feared that they had brought bad luck. As a good Catholic, however, she told herself that she was being foolish, and her ideas were pagan; God would surely protect this child she loved so dearly. How could a stick of coral and a rattle harm him? She handed them over. Louis-Auguste examined them with joy and began to try and cram them into his mouth.

The nurse gently took them from him, and seating herself on the stool, pushed the nipple into his mouth as he opened it to protest. For the next few minutes there was silence as he contentedly sucked the breast. Françoise, sitting on the opposite side of the fire, watched with a strange feeling, almost of resentment that an ignorant woman who could not write her own name should perform such an intimate service for the baby – a service that she herself was not capable of. It made her feel excluded.

When the baby began to turn his face away and play, she dismissed the nurse. Nanon had gone out in a huff, jealous of the lavish attention her mistress paid to the baby. Putting on her white apron to protect her clothes, for the baby had a habit of bringing up most of his feed all over her, Françoise lifted him from the cradle where the nurse had placed him and sat down, taking him on her lap. This was the time of day she loved best; the servants were in the kitchen having their dinner, and Nanon had gone out. She was free to play with the baby to her heart's content, without their disapproving looks. She held him against her and lavished kisses on his little face and neck, blew into the palms of his hands to make him laugh, and danced him up and down, realizing with pleasure that he was becoming too heavy for such games. In spite of her fears that he was not taking enough nourishment, because he brought back so much of his feed, he was obviously thriving.

Sitting him up, she played a game with him, tickling his chest and singing a nursery rhyme he knew well. It was November and the day was bitterly cold. The room where she sat, however, caught all the pale winter sunshine, and with a bright fire burning it was almost warm. Outside people were going about their day-to-day business in the streets of Paris. She wondered what interest they could find in shopping, visiting dressmakers, the markets of Les Halles, going to chat and gossip with friends – all the pleasures which until quite recently she herself had enjoyed. Now the world had narrowed down to this one room and the child she dandled on her lap. Louis-Auguste had become the centre of her existence.

The sound of a carriage drawing up outside caught her attention, and she glanced out of the window. A coach-and-eight stood there, the horses pawing the ground and snorting as if they had just made a long journey. The coach, though very fine, bore no crest or armorial bearings on its doors, nor were there monograms on the harness; but instantly she knew who it was. A well dressed man of about thirty-five, elegant but restrained in brown velvet, and wearing a sword, was being helped to descend by a lackey.

Françoise looked round in flustered confusion – the King! Thank goodness the room was fairly tidy. She kicked a basket of clean linen, waiting to be put away when the girl had finished her dinner, under the chaise-longue which stood by the window, and put the baby down in the cradle, hastily taking off his short embroidered bib. There was not time to remove the full-length bib. She set his lace-edged cap on straight, and began to remove her apron, praying that the child had not mussed up her hair.

Before she could divest herself of her apron the door opened and in walked the King. Behind him she could see the lame old concierge stammering out protests. A gentleman in a military uniform she did not recognize handed him a coin or two, and with an apologetic look at Françoise, who nodded her recognition of the visitor, he limped away. Thank goodness the other servants were at their dinner.

She sank into a deep curtsy, but he put his fingers to his lips in a warning gesture. She realized what he meant. Not until the door had closed and the King's escort stood with his back to it, did she whisper: 'Your Majesty.'

The King smiled at her, enjoying her all-too-evident confusion. He was surrounded by so much falseness, so much servile flattery, that he liked to see people as they really were. 'Good day, Madame Scarron.' He walked over to the cradle. 'I trust my son is well?'

'He is in excellent health, Sire, I am happy to say.'

Louis looked down at the child, who gazed back at him with an unblinking stare from those blue-grey eyes. 'See how fearlessly he regards me,' wondered the King. 'A complete stranger.'

As he spoke, the child began to cry, suddenly frightened by the visitor with the loud masculine voice. 'Your hat, Sire,' Françoise suggested. The King removed his hat, decorated with a large ostrich feather. Louis-Auguste stopped crying and continued to stare at him in wonder.

'He is not used to a man's voice, Sire,' said Françoise apologetically. 'Shall I remove his bib?' She prayed that his dress underneath would not be soiled. His clothes were fresh each morning, but dribbles of regurgitated milk somehow found their way on to the front in spite of the bibs he wore.

'No, do not disturb him,' Louis said. He extended his finger and Louis-Auguste, instantly attracted by the emerald and diamond ring the King wore, grasped it firmly.

'He may put your finger in his mouth, Sire,' Françoise said in alarm. Louis-Auguste, she knew, was capable of biting anything that took his fancy with his new teeth – two each, top and bottom – even his father's finger. After all, the child was not to know that the finger belonged to a King of France.

Louis laughed. 'He will not hurt me,' he said, looking in wonderment at the baby, his third living son. If only his legitimate children looked as fit and healthy as this one did! Louise de la Vallière's baby boy had died recently, and his second son, the Duc d'Anjou, was a delicate child. He was two and a half now, but remained tiny and thin no matter how much they tried to fatten him up. Little Louis-Auguste's face was full and round, his eyes bright and curious as he regarded his father. Now he looked at Françoise for reassurance, and as she smiled down at him his face broke into an answering smile. Françoise overcame her longing to snatch him up and cuddle him to her breast. That would have to wait until the King concluded his visit.

'He does not resemble me in the slightest,' the King remarked with a little disappointment in his voice. On the other hand, he did not look like Athenais either, he thought, except perhaps for his fair skin. Françoise, who had had more opportunity than anyone to study his face and his expression, privately thought that he had more than a look of Anne of Austria.

'Do you not think he resembles your late mother, Sire? May heaven bless her name.' Françoise would never forget how Anne of Austria had rescued her from penury in the first days of her widowhood.

The King stared down at the child, hoping to see some resemblance in his features that would remind him of his beloved mother. 'I fear I cannot see it,' he remarked at last, 'save for the eyes, perhaps. That was the colour of her eyes exactly.'

'Perhaps it will become more marked as he grows older, Sire.'

He turned to her and held out his hand for her to kiss. 'I am in your debt, madame, for the excellent care you are taking of my son.'

She flushed, and made a modest curtsy. 'It is nothing, Sire. I derive much pleasure from his company.'

'Nevertheless, you spend a good deal of your time confined here, I do not doubt. A pretty young woman would be better employed in gracing the Court, claiming the attention which is her due.' Indeed, he thought. How charming she looked today, her face flushed with the warmth of the fire and the excitement of his unexpected visit. Dressed, beneath the snowy white apron, in a high-necked gown of soft grey wool, a cameo brooch fastened demurely at her throat, she could not have presented a greater contrast to the ladies by whom he was perpetually surrounded – stiff as ramrods in their iron corsets under their tight-fitting gowns, hardly able to bend, and bursting out of their daring décolletages – each one cut lower than the next. He was beginning to feel that he had almost had a surfeit of bosoms and bare shoulders. Almost, but not quite.

In her homely dress and apron, Françoise had the indefinable look of motherhood about her. Here in the humble rue Birague she had managed to create the essential atmosphere of a home that he, brought up in palaces, had been denied. A delicious smell of cooking floated from the direction of the kitchen. One could never smell food cooking at St Germain or the Louvre; the kitchens were miles away from the King's apartments, he could never enjoy this delicious sense of mouthwatering anticipation. The man who was beginning to make all Europe tremble looked round the cosy room, with its unmistakable trappings of childhood, its piles of clean linen, its scattered toys, the blankets warming by the fire, and realized that he had been deprived of his own childhood. It had been spent in trying to remain one step ahead of his enemies, and in learning to be a King.

'We must pay you a salary, madame,' he said

'It is unnecessary, Sire. I already have a pension.'

'Nonsense! It is a widow's pension, is it not?' He wondered what kind of man her husband had been. An invalid, that he knew. He could imagine her taking care of him. If ever I am ill, he found himself thinking, I should like to have her nurse me. But that was nonsense. He was never ill.

'You will be paid a salary in keeping with your position as governess to my son. You will teach him his letters and his catechism later on?'

'Of course, Sire.'

'Then your salary shall consist of twenty thousand livres annually, dating from the month you took up your position. Last February, was it not?'

'Yes, Sire.' She was incapable of speaking. It was more money than she had ever had in her life.

'I shall instruct Colbert to carry out the necessary arrangements. You already use the Italian bankers, do you not?'

'Yes, Sire.'

'Good. You may draw on it from tomorrow. Good day, madame.' He extended his hand and she bent to kiss it. 'I shall pay you another visit before long.'

She went forward to open the door for him. Suddenly she bethought herself. 'Sire – the Marquise? Is she quite well?'

'In excellent health, as ever.'

'She could not come – to see her son?'

'She was having a dress fitted for the ball of St Hubert, I believe. Good day, madame.'

'Your servant, Sire.'

She watched from the window as the two men, the King escorted by his Captain of the Guard, went down the steps. The King climbed into the waiting coach and the Captain went to instruct the driver to proceed. In a few moments the coach was out of sight. She went over to the baby, to see what impression his father had made on him, but he had fallen fast asleep.

For the first time in her life, Françoise was faced with the happy dilemma of wondering how to use her new-found affluence to best advantage.

It had been in her mind for some time to buy a house, larger than the small establishment in the rue des Tournelles. Now, however, she knew that the only house in which she would be happy would be one she shared with Louis-Auguste. There was no point in her and Nanon exchanging one house for another. Their home in the rue des Tournelles was quite large enough for their needs.

She decided, therefore, to ask the King on his next visit whether, in the event of her buying a larger house, he would allow her to take Louis-Auguste to live with her. In the meantime, with her customary caution, she decided to continue her way of life exactly as she had always done. She bought a fur-lined cloak and a beaver muff for herself, some new clothes and shoes for Nanon, and some much needed kitchen utensils which Nanon had been asking for for some considerable time. She gave some thought to the buying of a coach or a sedan-chair, but postponed the plan until the question of the house should be decided, for there was no yard in which to house a coach at the rue des Tournelles, nor was there accommodation for lackeys and footmen. There seemed to be little point in spending money on new furniture or carpets for her home as she spent so little of her time there. All her days were spent at the rue Birague, from early morning until nine or ten at night; unless she had an invitation she could not refuse without giving offence, when she would reluctantly leave at six o'clock to go home and change her clothes.

One evening late in December she was invited to supper at the Hôtel Richelieu. She was unhappy about leaving Louis-Auguste, for he had been fretful all day. His nose was running and his forehead hot. At noon he took his feed reluctantly and then immediately brought it all up again. Before she left the rue Birague to go home, where Mme d'Albret was to call for her in her coach at seven, she left all instructions with the serving-girl. The night nurse, who had just arrived, was in the kitchen having supper.

'Keep the cradle well away from the window, where there are draughts, but not too close to the fire or you will make him over-heated.'

'*Oui, madame.*'

Such a fuss, the girl thought rebelliously, over some noble-man's fancy by-blow. She herself was one of twelve children who had been orphaned and left to grow up as best they might.

'You won't forget, will you, Gabrielle?' Françoise was fond of the girl, who was cheerful, high-spirited, and sang as she went about her work. Jeannette Granot had recommended her to Françoise when she had gone to see if Jeannette could work for her in the rue Birague. Jeannette's husband had died, leaving her with the *épicerie* to run and seven children to care for, so that she was unable to go out to work; but she had recommended Gabrielle, a country girl recently come to Paris, living two doors away. Françoise had immediately taken a liking to the fresh-faced, rosy-cheeked girl, and employed her as a serving-maid. She had taught her a great deal and thought she might one day take the place of the housekeeper, who suffered from arthritis.

'Remember, Gabrielle, if his face seems hot, sponge him with a little warm water, just his face and hands.'

'*Oui, madame,*' the girl answered obediently. Would Mme Scarron never go home? Joseph, the young footman from the neighbouring Hôtel Sully, was coming to see her tonight.

Françoise took a final glance in the cradle before she left.

'Gabrielle!' The girl was just leaving the room. 'How many times have I told you not to settle him for the night still wearing his bib?'

'I thought, madame, in case he should posset himself.'

'How many times must I tell you it is not safe for him to sleep with a bib tied round his neck? The string might become tight as he moves! If he makes a mess, his clothes must be changed. You have plenty of spare linen. Do you understand?'

'*Oui, madame!*' Grumpily the girl went to take off the offending bib. The others had gone for their supper. There would be no meat left by the time she got there, that much was certain. What a fusspot the woman was! Let *her* change a nightgown covered in vomit by candlelight.

Françoise went home and changed, still with a feeling of intense irritation. Gabrielle was a bright, intelligent girl, but as stubborn as an ox. The more Françoise tried to help her learn, and the more she gave her instructions, the more determined the girl seemed to go her own way.

Supper at the Hôtel de Richelieu did not improve her mood, in spite of the excellence of the meal and the pleasant company. Her friends were beginning to bore her. The endless chit-chat and exchange of Court gossip was tedious and repetitious – she had a constant feeling of *déjà vu*.

'I declare,' Mme de Sévigné was proclaiming, 'Paris is becoming so fiendishly expensive I shall be forced to retreat to Les Rochers for Christmas and the New Year.'

'You find the country less ruinous to your purse, madame?' someone asked.

'Well, at least on my own estates I can eat my own chickens, my own rabbits and my own milk, butter and cheese, even though my tenants don't pay me my rents.'

A discussion on the reluctance in general of tenants to pay their rents and taxes followed, which bored Françoise even more than had the Court gossip. She was beginning to find it very difficult to look non-committal when the King and Athenais were mentioned in discussion at the supper table. She took refuge in a game of backgammon with Mlle de Scudéry, who decided to leave early with a migraine, and Françoise seized the opportunity to ask if there were room for her in her sedan.

'Of course,' answered Mlle de Scudéry. 'You are as thin as a herring. Now, if it had been Madame de Sévigné . . .'

Françoise hushed her, and they made polite remarks to their host and hostess and left together.

It was a frosty night, and Françoise was glad of her new fur-lined cloak. At the rue des Tournelles Mlle de Scudéry's footmen put down the chair and helped Françoise to climb out. Keeping an eye out for vagrants or cut-purses who might be lurking in the shadow, they escorted her to her door.

As she put the key in the lock and the sedan turned the corner into the rue St Antoine, a sudden impulse overcame her. Replacing the key in her velvet purse, she started to run. Her thin shoes were uncomfortable on the frosty ground and she was hampered by her heavy cloak, but she soon arrived at the rue Birague. She ran up the steps of the house and in a moment unlocked the door.

The house seemed to be in complete darkness save for a light coming from under the kitchen door. She went straight to the nursery. It was completely dark. The fire had gone out and the room was icy cold. She felt on the mantelpiece for the match and tinderbox, struck a light and lit a candle. There were two chairs before the empty fireplace, and the baby's cradle stood under the window. Gabrielle and the nurse must have sat before the fire gossiping until it went out, and then adjourned to the kitchen. She went to look at the baby. He was sleeping, but his face was pale and cold, his lips and fingers a little blue. He had kicked off his covers in his sleep, and his little legs were bare and icy cold to the touch.

She covered him up as warmly as she could and went straight to the kitchen. At the sound of the door being thrust open the two youngsters kissing and cuddling in a dim corner started up guiltily. Jacques, the old man, was sound asleep in front of the fire. In the other chair the cook was snoozing, but woke up at the sound of the commotion that ensued. The young footman from the Hôtel Sully, seeing the expression on Mme Scarron's face, slipped quietly out of the back door.

Françoise advanced towards Gabrielle, who was cowering in the corner, and slapped her hard across the face.

'Go and make a fire in the nursery, and then get out of here! Don't let me see your face again!'

The girl screamed and began to cry. The cook followed the footman's example and slipped out of the door. Agnès, the nurse, came into the kitchen. 'Mercy me! Whatever's going on here? Mistress, at this time of night!'

'Yes, at this time of night, when you don't expect to see me! How dare you let the fire in the nursery go out!'

'It seemed wasteful to make it up, mistress, when there was a good fire in here – '

'Wasteful! How many times did I tell you before I left, Gabrielle, to keep the baby warm? You know he has a cold.'

Gabrielle threw herself at Françoise's feet. 'Please don't turn me out, mistress. I've nowhere to go, and nothing – '

Françoise's face was as hard as stone. 'Make up the fire in the nursery and then leave the house. Don't let me see your face again. Agnès, warm blankets here by the fire and then cover the

216

baby with them. How long is it since he was fed?'

'Not since half past seven, mistress.'

'Did he feed well?'

'No, madame, only one side.'

'Then when you've warmed the blankets I'll wake him and you can feed him again.'

'Wake him, mistress?' She knew only too well how difficult it could be to get Louis-Auguste to sleep again once his sleep was broken.

'Do as I tell you, Agnès, or you'll be the next to leave.'

'*Oui, madame.*'

Gabrielle scuttled in, her hands dirty from the fire. 'The fire's burning, madame. Oh, madame.' Her tear-stained face was covered with smuts. 'Please forgive me. Please don't send me away.'

Françoise's face was expressionless. 'Take your things, if you have any, and leave the house this moment.' The girl threw herself on the floor and cried brokenly. Agnès, returning with the blankets to warm them by the kitchen fire, spoke up for her.

'She's nowhere to go, mistress, and it's bitter outside. She's neither cloak nor shoes – '

'Give her a blanket to put round her shoulders.'

Gabrielle, realizing her fate was sealed, sat silently as Agnès put the thickest, warmest blanket round her. Agnès wondered whether to offer the girl her own shoes to borrow for a day or two, for the girl had only a thin pair of house-slippers, but decided against it. Who knew whether she would ever get them back? Who would ever have thought Mme Scarron capable of turning a girl out in the street on a night like this? It must be true what the servants had long ago decided: that the baby was her own, and all this pretence of looking after him for someone else was just a show. The quality could make mistakes just like everyone else, but they could get away with it, she thought bitterly, as Gabrielle, holding the blanket tightly round her, went towards the door.

'You may go to the convent of the Petite Charité in the Place Royale,' Mme Scarron was saying to the girl, 'and bid them, for the love they have for me, to take you in for a few days until you can find work.'

Gabrielle gave no sign of having heard these last instructions. Drawing the blanket closely round her, she went out. In a moment she had disappeared into the darkness. The cook and the concierge stared at each other, afraid to speak, but Françoise ignored them and went back into the nursery where the fire was now burning brightly.

Agnès had lit the tapers and was suckling the child on the low stool by the fire. Françoise waited patiently until Louis-Auguste turned his head away. Then, taking him gently from the nurse's arms, she kissed him, cooed over him, buried her face in the softness of his little neck, and finally laid him in the crib, tucking him in closely with the warmed blankets. He had lost that deathly paleness and regained his normal colour. Warm and contented, he was soon asleep. She put the stick of coral, which he liked to chew in the mornings, into his hand. Françoise, gently rocking the cradle and looking down at him as he slept, had already forgotten Gabrielle. Life had so far denied her the love of a mother, a father, a brother, a husband, and a child of her own. But what did any of it matter, so long as she had Louis-Auguste?

Chapter Twenty-one

In the spring of the year 1671 there were other matters to occupy the King's attention, besides the child growing up in the rue Birague.

'How long is it since you have seen your brother Charles?' Louis asked Minette quite casually one pleasant spring day as they strolled together along the terrace at St Germain. Minette looked very pretty in a gown of flowered Indian cotton, with dainty silk mittens and a fashionable cartwheel hat to protect her hair and complexion from the sun. So thin as to be almost bony, she wore a light gauze wrap around her shoulders, preferring to keep her bosom and shoulders covered, unlike most of the Court ladies.

'It is almost ten years to the day since I left England,' Minette answered him.

Ten years! It seemed almost a lifetime since the day she had bidden farewell to her mother and her brothers, all weeping broken-heartedly. What sorrows and ordeals her mother, Henrietta Maria, had had to endure! Her husband, Charles I, had been murdered in cold blood by the English, and she had lost several of her eleven children. Then James, Charles II's heir, had been foolish enough to marry one of his sister's ladies whom he had got with child; and Minette, her youngest daughter, had had to sail from England for ever, destined for the Court of France and a disastrously unhappy marriage.

'How would you like to see your brother again?' Louis was asking her, anticipating with pleasure the effect his question would have. He needed the help of Charles II, or rather that of the English Navy, to back him up in a war he proposed to wage on the unsuspecting Dutch; and who would succeed better in enlisting Charles' help than his own dearly loved sister?

'Do you mean it, Sire?' Minette stopped and turned to face him, her lips parted eagerly, her dark eyes, of late so dull and lacking in their usual lustre, bright and shining. How thin she was! Charles would think they had been starving her here at the Court of France. But she was not a strong person.

'Yes, I mean it.'

Minette could scarcely contain her delight. Her black eyes danced. She looked, Louis thought with a pang, as she had not looked in nearly ten years, happy and gay, the carefree youngster she had been when she first came to France. Poor child! Her life with his brother had been a disaster. After dutifully giving her two children, Monsieur had returned to the arms of his favourites and shamefully neglected his pretty wife.

Minette was excitedly making plans. 'How long shall I be able to stay in London, Sire?' she asked. 'And how many shall there be in my suite?' How wonderful it would be to arrive in style at Whitehall, her ladies dressed in the very latest Paris fashions! The English ladies would soon be rushing post-haste to their dressmakers to have them copied. And she would be able to relax a little the dignity demanded of her as second lady at the Court of France, and go riding and hawking with her brothers, Charles and James, at Richmond and Windsor. It would be just the three of them again, as in the old days. Now, who were those ladies so talked of at the English Court – Lady Castlemaine and Nelly Gwynne . . . ?

'I'll wager they are no more beautiful than the Marquise de Montespan,' she said, thinking aloud.

Louis looked down at her in quizzical amusement. One of the reasons he felt so much at ease in her company was her petite stature. He was ultra-conscious of his height which, about average, he felt to be a disadvantage to his exalted position in life. He would have liked to tower above the rest of the world in physique as well as in authority. Skilful arrangements and clever use of chairs and footstools always contrived to show him as the tallest figure in a group portrait. 'You will outshine all the English ladies, *ma petite*,' he assured her.

Minette left St Germain on a lovely day in June. Louis came out to her carriage to bid her farewell. Monsieur was in Paris, sulking because he had not been consulted over the visit.

'Try to enjoy yourself, Minette,' Louis advised her. 'Have no fear for your children. I will protect them as my own until your return. You have the papers for your brother securely locked away?'

Minette assured him that she had. Her travelling companion, Louise de Keroualle, nodded confirmation.

'Do not stay away too long,' Louis murmured, his eyes on Louise de Keroualle, who fanned herself modestly, eyes lowered, enjoying his glance. 'Our Court is losing two of its most beautiful flowers.' Louise was dark and vivacious like her mistress, but much more curvaceous, Louis noted. Her bosom pouted prettily under the revealing folds of gauze draped over the dress of hare-bell blue that exactly matched the colour of her eyes. He decided that on their return he would make it his business to become better acquainted with Louise de Keroualle.

Athenais, standing beside the King, noticed his glance, and her mouth set in a tight line. So that was the way the wind was blowing! She decided there and then to make it her business to see that la Keroualle did not return from her journey. That would teach her to bestow sidelong glances on the King. That was *her* prerogative, and hers alone.

'Then do not forget to assure the King of our love,' Louis said. He kissed Minette's hand. Minette's eyes filled with tears.

'*Adieu, Sire. A bientôt.*'

'*Adieu, chère Minette.* May God go with you on your journey.'

At a nod from the King the long line of carriages and baggage wagons rolled forward and out of the gates of St Germain.

St Germain was dull without the company of Minette. The King's second son, the little Duc d'Anjou, had died recently, just before his third birthday. The Queen grieved and prayed constantly in her rooms that she might bear another healthy child; of her many pregnancies and confinements, only the Dauphin was left to her. Athenais de Montespan and Louise de la Vallière bickered and quarrelled endlessly. Athenais was not self-effacing, as Louise had been during her term of triumph; revelling in her unchallenged position as the King's mistress, she spent fortunes on her clothes, flaunted herself before the Queen in jewels given to her by Louis, and sneered openly at Louise.

'Here, Fifi will keep you company for a while,' she said one day to Louise de la Vallière, throwing her a little pet dog as she and the King strolled past in the direction of Athenais' apartments to take their afternoon siesta.

Louise spent many hours on her knees in bitter tears, praying to God to sustain her in her ordeal – for she was rapidly becoming the laughing-stock of the Court. The King was adamant in his refusal to allow her to enter a convent, his view being that her presence at Court covered his double adultery with Athenais. And so poor Louise was forced to live in close conjunction with

Athenais, who spared her nothing. She it was who helped to curl Athenais' hair, who carried her prayer book when they went to Mass, and walked behind the King and Athenais when they strolled in the gardens, holding the leash of Athenais' pet dogs. There was only one person who suffered from Athenais more than Louise, and that was the Queen herself.

'That slut will kill me one day,' Maria Theresa said to the Duchess d'Elbeo, as Athenais, sitting at a card table only a few yards away, laughed and flirted openly with the King.

'Do not let her see that she is able to distress you, child.'

'How can I do otherwise?'

'By ignoring her, Your Majesty. Once she sees that she is unable to hurt you, she will cease to flaunt herself.'

'She will never do that,' said Maria Theresa. 'She is the type of woman who takes pleasure in the discomfiture of others. I cannot understand the King's affection for a woman so unkind, and so uninterested in her children. I believe they are being looked after somewhere in Paris, and that she hardly ever goes to see them.'

Poor child, thought the Duchess d'Elbeo, looking from the plump homely face of dumpy Maria Theresa to the sparkling, vivacious Athenais de Montespan, flirting outrageously with all the men in sight, but reserving her most wanton glances for the King who was even now leaning over her to see the cards she held. How could the Queen be so ignorant of the ways of men – and of her own husband?

However, even Athenais' high spirits were somewhat quenched when, in July of that year, she discovered that she was pregnant again. For some days she sulked in her rooms. As a result, the King was almost totally deprived of congenial female company. His cousin, La Grande Mademoiselle, had retired to her country estates in a fit of pique when Louis had refused her permission to marry the Duc de Lauzun, an upstart who coveted her rich lands and huge fortune. On impulse, the King decided to remove the Court to Fontainebleau, where he would be able to spend days on end hunting, and forget all these quarrelsome women. Athenais, being a poor horsewoman, would not allow Louise de la Vallière to ride with him as in days gone by; Louis was glad of it, for her reproachful looks disturbed his conscience.

Soon the entire Court of more than five thousand people was on the move to Fontainebleau. The baggage wagons had gone on ahead in order for the chateau to be made ready for them. The King travelled in a coach, accompanied as always by Athenais and Louise, and this time also by Mlle de Thianges, Athenais' niece, whom she had recently brought to Court. The Queen was in a coach a mile or two ahead of them, accompanied by her Spanish suite. She had lately given up the effort of trying to speak French, and surrounded herself with ladies who could speak her own tongue.

In order to divert himself a little, the King had decided that on the way through Paris to Fontainebleau he would visit his son Louis-Auguste in the rue Birague, and give the child's mother her first opportunity of seeing her son. He had thought of sending word on ahead, to acquaint Mme Scarron of his proposed visit, but on reflection decided against it. He liked to see people as they were when they were not expecting him.

Athenais was none too pleased when he told her of his intention. She had been hoping to arrive at Fontainebleau at about the same time as the Queen and obtain for herself some of the apartments in the royal suite. She had already sent ahead an equerry to grease the palm of the steward there. Had the King not been accompanying them she would even have tried to claim the Queen's bedchamber, knowing that Maria Theresa was incapable of putting up a fight. Now this tiresome visit to the brat and Françoise Scarron meant they would arrive so much later, that her plans were likely to be thwarted. Maria Theresa would already have installed her suite in the royal apartments by the time they got there.

Furious inwardly, Athenais put on a bright face and did her best to entertain the King with her usual flow of spirited chatter. Louise, the Duchess of Vaujours, sat in silence, clasping her little girl of five, Marie-Anne, on her lap. The King was glum, unusual for him. Charles II, in his joy at seeing his sister, had sent urgent messages to Monsieur requesting him to allow her to extend her stay. The King, knowing it was vital to the success of Minette's mission to secure Charles' signature to the proposed treaty, had been forced to overcome Monsieur's objections and send permission for her to remain ten days at Dover, where the English Court had travelled in its entirety to meet her.

Athenais, who had been hoping that the King might have forgotten his intention of visiting his son, was, however, disappointed when the coach drew up at the rue Birague, and the King instructed the Duchesse de Vaujours to await them in the coach.

Françoise and Louis-Auguste were in the nursery, building a tower made of coloured bricks, when visitors were announced. Françoise anxiously smoothed down her plain holland dress and put her hand to her hair, which this morning was not dressed, simply hanging down her back tied with a ribbon. Thank goodness Louis-Auguste was neatly attired in a dress she herself had made for him; he had just taken his weekly bath in the copper bath-tub standing near the fire, and a clean handkerchief hung from his waist. Although the day was warm, Françoise took no chances where he was concerned. He was not a robust child. She drew him forward proudly by his leading-strings as Athenais swept forward and lifted him up in her arms, covering him with kisses.

'My darling little one!' She gave a convincing exhibition of maternal affection. Louis-Auguste, his face scratched by the jewelled clasps on her dress, fought and kicked. He hated the overpowering smell of the strong perfume she wore.

'He is unsure of strangers,' Françoise said apologetically as the child turned to her, holding out his arms for her to take him from this strange woman clutching him so tightly, smothering him with kisses.

'Strangers! Do you forget I am his own mother?' Athenais looked daggers at her former friend. She knew about Françoise's handsome salary. Who had been responsible for putting her in the way of such affluence? Françoise had good reason to be grateful to her.

'Let me see the child,' the King intervened, taking Louis-Auguste's hand and drawing him forward. These women! Were they not capable of five minutes' conversation without drawn swords? He put his hands on Louis-Auguste's arms and looked him full in the face. The child stood quite still, regarding the handsome stranger, so finely dressed, with curiosity, for he rarely saw any male visitors.

'Can he say anything?' enquired the King.

'Only his name,' answered Françoise.

'Tell me your name, *mon petit*.'

Louis-Auguste stared at his father with great concentration. Then 'Louis-Auguste' he pronounced quite clearly, drawing out the difficult name in his childish tones.

The King laughed, rumpling the little boy's light brown curls with affection. 'Well done!' he approved. 'How old is he now, madame?'

'Eighteen months, Sire.'

'He is a fine child, is he not, Athenais?'

'Of course, Sire. Has he not extremely handsome parents?'

They laughed, and the look of affection which passed between them, excluding Françoise, was the look of all parents with pride in their child – only in the case of Athenais the expression was affected. The King, on the other hand, was truly impressed by his son.

'He is a pretty child,' said Françoise, and Louis-Auguste turned to her, burying his face in her lap, suddenly overcome by shyness. 'And he shows signs of considerable intelligence. He understands all that I say, although as yet he speaks but little.'

Athenais took a louis d'or from her purse and handed it to the child, who regarded it with wonder and, before Françoise could stop him, popped it into his mouth. Françoise jumped up in terror and forced his mouth open to remove it before he could swallow it. Louis-Auguste began to cry with anger.

'How dare you make my son cry!' demanded Athenais, in a fine temper. 'Why do you force your hands into his mouth?'

'It is dangerous,' Françoise told her. 'He might swallow it. May I put it away until he is a little older?' she said, retrieving the coin.

'Nonsense. You would take away a gift to a child from his own mother?'

To keep the peace Louis produced a sweetmeat from his pocket, a sugared almond biscuit. He held it up to the child temptingly.

'Shall he have this instead?' Louis-Auguste approached him and looked up at it eagerly.

Françoise hesitated. 'He has only just finished his dinner, Sire. He has a delicate digestion – '

Athenais was beginning strongly to resent Françoise's dictatorial attitude. How dare she patronize the child's own parents in this fashion? 'Come here, my little darling,' she said, taking the biscuit from the King and offering it to the child. 'See what a lovely biscuit Mama has for you.'

Louis-Auguste, needing no second bidding, took the biscuit from her and crammed it into his mouth. As Françoise prayed that the King would not decide to joggle him up and down on his lap, Athenais drew him close to her once more, deciding on a last display of maternal devotion before the visit drew to a close.

'*Mon petit chou*,' she said, embracing the child tightly. Louis-Auguste, struggling to free himself, was sick all over her dress.

Athenais screamed, and thrust the child away with such a push he all but fell into the fire. Françoise, hardly able to keep herself from laughing, put Louis-Auguste into his rocking chair to keep him safe from the fire before she went to the door to call a servant.

The maid brought towels and a bowl of water and began to sponge Athenais' dress. Françoise saw that the King was scarcely able to contain his amusement. Athenais brought out a small vial of perfume from the velvet purse she carried and began to dab it daintily behind her ears, but even her strong perfume did little to disguise the unpleasant odour. Françoise went to open the window, noticing in surprise as she did so that the Duchess of Vaujours was waiting patiently in the carriage outside. Athenais was protesting that she could not travel on to Fontainebleau in a badly stained dress.

'Perhaps I can lend you a gown,' offered Françoise. After all, it was not so long ago that she had borrowed one belonging to Athenais. Athenais, however, looked furious at her suggestion. Françoise was forgetting the difference in their stations. As if she, the King's favourite, would deign to wear a cast-off from a nursemaid to the King's children!

'It will not be necessary,' she answered, in icy tones. 'The Duchess of Vaujours and I are of a size.'

'Perhaps she has a wrap to lend you,' observed the King. 'Although the day is warm – '

A message was sent out to the Duchesse de Vaujours, waiting in the coach. Poor Louise had no option but to enter the house, remove her dress in another room and lend it to Athenais, she herself being forced to continue the journey wrapped in a travelling cloak, though it was indeed a very warm day. Françoise, unaware of her friend's pregnancy, was amused to notice the considerable struggle Athenais had to fasten up the dress, even with the help of the maid. She would spend the rest of the journey in some discomfort. When the two ladies went out, having exchanged clothes, Françoise returned to the nursery where she found the King singing and rocking his son gently in the rocking chair.

'I had the carpenter make it for his birthday, Sire,' she said – then instantly regretted the mention of his birthday. She had thought the King might send him something on that day, but it had obviously slipped his mind.

'Ah! My apologies!' He took some louis d'or from his pocket. 'What would be a suitable gift for him, do you think?' He thought of the magnificent horse on rockers in the royal nursery, such a contrast to this crude little chair. 'Would a high-chair be useful, for him to take his meals in? Or a gold *cadena*?'

Françoise hesitated.

'What can you suggest, madame?'

One thing Louis-Auguste adored was music; he was always toddling to the window as fast as his little legs would carry him if a street musician was outside.

'He is fond of music, Sire – '

'Ah! In that he takes after me, as you may know, madame. Music is one of the great joys of this life, and one in which our pleasure does not diminish as the years pass. A guitar or a lute perhaps – '

'He is too young for that as yet, Sire.'

'I have it! A drum and sticks.'

'He would love that, Sire. An ideal choice.'

'Then so shall it be.' He handed her the money. 'I leave it in your hands. And I look forward to hearing him play the drum like a sergeant-major on my next visit.' He rose and ruffled the child's curls as he rocked to and fro in his little chair.

'The ladies await you outside, Sire.'

'Yes, so I see.' He looked out of the window to where the two women sat in the coach. Another two hours' journey lay ahead of them. A curious desire to stay here in this pleasant room with Mme Scarron and his little son overcame him. He extended his hand for her to kiss. She curtsied and picked up the child, and together they went to the front door to watch the visitors drive away in their fine coach with the magnificent horses and liveried footmen.

Athenais was seething as Louis finally took his place beside her in the coach. What could he have found to talk about to Françoise all that time?

As the coachman whipped up the horses Louis looked back at the woman and child standing on the steps. A tiny kitten, frightened by the horses, darted from under their hooves and up the steps. Louis-Auguste laughed with pleasure and Françoise scooped it up in her hands to show him. The Most Christian King of France, looking back at them, was somewhat disconcerted to see that in their interest over the black and white kitten, the two bent heads, one dark and one fair, did not even lift to acknowledge his departure.

Minette and Louise de Keroualle were never to return to St Germain. Charles II, an even greater womanizer than his cousin, Louis XIV, was immediately impressed by the dainty charms of his sister's lady-in-waiting, and when Minette – her stay in England ending all too soon – sailed for France from Dover, Louise de Keroualle waved her goodbyes from Charles' side. Athenais was spared the trouble of finding her a situation well away from Louis; she never saw France again, and bore Charles several children before eventually becoming Duchess of Portsmouth.

Minette, on her arrival in France, was told that the Court had removed to Fontainebleau where the King eagerly awaited the result of her mission in England. She despatched letters to the King, giving him the news he desired: that her brother had signed the secret Treaty of London, and that she would proceed to Fontainebleau to discuss it with him in detail as soon as she had seen her children, who had been taken to St Cloud with their nurse upon the departure of the Court from St Germain. She arrived at St Cloud on the Saturday night, to a joyful reunion with them.

Two days later, Louis was awakened very early in the morning to be told that there was a messenger from St Cloud. The news was broken to him that Madame was dead.

Louis could not believe it. He went to the Queen's apartments, where they sobbed together for some time, for the Queen had been fond of Minette. At last the truth was pieced together. Madame, after a happy day at St Cloud with her children, had been taken ill during the night, felt unwell the next day, and finally died during the following night. The cause of her death was not known.

The news of Madame's sudden and unexpected death caused a furore. Charles II, who had parted with his sister not a week before, then apparently in the best of health, insisted on a full report being made to him. There were strong rumours that Madame had been poisoned, and suspicion not unnaturally fell upon Monsieur's favourites, the Comte de Lorraine and the Marquis d'Effiat; it would have been to their advantage to rid themselves of Madame, for their sole purpose in life was to obtain favours from Monsieur in the form of money, perquisites, jewels, benefices – in fact anything they could lay their hands on. Minette had tried to warn her husband of their avarice on several occasions, but he would hear nothing against them.

Louis had no choice but to have an autopsy performed on the body. Greatly to his relief it was found that Minette's death was from natural causes. No trace of poison was discovered in the body.

The Court was forced to move to the Louvre, where mourning could be properly observed for Madame. There 'the three Queens', as people were beginning to call them, were forced to spend the winter, each with her own private penance – the Queen, still mourning the death of her son and of a beloved sister-in-law, one of the few people in France who had treated her with love and respect; la Vallière obliged in spite of her title to submit to the jibes of Athenais, and to witness her rival's complete dominion over the man she still loved; and Athenais de Montespan forced with resignation to await the birth of her next baby.

Louis, surrounded on all sides by bickering ill-tempered women, and grieving deeply for the loss of his beloved Minette, was consoled during the long dreary winter only by the thoughts of the war he intended to wage against the Dutch in the following year.

Chapter Twenty-two

The following spring there was a new baby for Françoise to care for in the rue Birague.

Françoise, however, had decided that there was no longer sufficient accommodation in the rue Birague for the new little Louis-César and all the necessary wet-nurses, in addition to the regular staff of servants who waited upon Louis-Auguste. In May of that year she finally gave up the house in the rue des Tournelles, and she and Nanon, the two children and the staff of almost thirty servants, moved into a house on the outskirts of the city, right at the end of the Faubourg St Germain, almost in the village of Vaugirard.

There Françoise was happier than she had ever been in her life. The house was spacious, with fine large rooms, and there was a delightful garden for the children. Françoise herself had a room overlooking the garden, furnished with tapestries and the Venetian mirror she brought with her from the rue des Tournelles. She had a large, comfortable bed made of polished walnut, with damask hangings in green and gold – for she was prone to suffer from headaches and neuralgia in the winter and liked to sleep with the curtains drawn, making a cosy nest for herself in the big bed. For this reason, too, she had shutters affixed to her windows. While the workmen were doing this she had them put bars across the windows of the nursery, a large sunny room separated from her own only by a small chamber where Nanon, housekeeper to the establishment, now slept. Louis-Auguste was full of curiosity, and was apt to run and climb dangerously wherever the fancy took him. She could take no chances with his safety. Also with safety in mind she had the garden wall built higher. In winter, when there were food shortages, there were often skirmishes and riots amongst the poor. There could be danger if rumour should spread that these were the King's children playing in the garden at Vaugirard.

But there were no signs of danger that lovely summer of 1672, and Françoise spent the long hot days in the garden with the children, never tired of watching them at their play.

The new baby, Louis-César, was an amiable, sweet-tempered little thing who gave her none of the trouble she had had with Louis-Auguste; but adorable as he was, the deep bond between herself and Louis-Auguste remained unbroken. They were mother and son in everything but fact.

'He could scarcely be a prettier child if he were a little girl,' Françoise remarked with doting pride one morning to Agnès as they sat sewing in the garden, her eyes following Louis-Auguste as he chased the black and white kitten round the flower beds, now and then stumbling over his long frock and apron. Gabriel, a village lad employed as his *gentilhomme de la manche*, ran after him round the garden, to catch hold of him before he fell by the hanging sleeves of his dress, which, at the age of two and a half, had now replaced the leading-strings.

'You would not admire him nearly so much if he were, madame,' replied Agnès, intent on her sewing. No longer a wet-nurse, her daughter being the same age as Louis-Auguste, she was employed simply as a servant, and her little girl slept in her room and was sometimes allowed to play with the royal infants. Françoise did not know if she had ever had a husband, but she was a good and reliable servant. The episode of Gabrielle had been an invaluable lesson to her. Fully occupied with her duties as housekeeper, Nanon took little interest in the children.

'Why do you say that?' asked Françoise, carefully embroidering Louis-Auguste's monogram on a linen handkerchief.

'Because it is the ambition of all women to give birth to boys, madame.' She stopped, in sudden realization that she had said the wrong thing. It was so easy to forget that Mme Scarron was not supposed to be the child's real mother.

Françoise was interested, however, in her theory. 'But why, Agnès? Your little Yvette is adorable.'

'Because women are worth nothing in this world, madame. Only men can succeed to property, and exercise authority over their wives.'

'It is true that women have no rights,' Françoise agreed, 'but a girl can take better care of her parents in their old age – '

Agnès smiled cynically. 'What care can she take, madame, if she has nothing? A boy can always marry into money, even if he has none.'

Françoise had to agree that this was true. But in the case of her own relationship with Louis-Auguste these theories were irrelevant. She was not his real mother, and could look for nothing from him in her old age. In fact, it was not a thought that ever crossed her mind. She was content to enjoy him just as he was now. Sometimes she wished that he would never grow older, but remain the baby that he still was, in spite of his two and a half years. But then, remembering his sister – the little sister who had died – she reproached herself for the wickedness of her thoughts.

In September of that year the King returned from the Dutch campaign. Having invaded the provinces of Holland in April, the French army of 120,000 men had advanced virtually without opposition, and in June had crossed the Rhine, the frontier of Roman Gaul. After that it had seemed that nothing could stop the French in their march to Amsterdam and Utrecht, and victory. Then, at the very last moment, triumph was snatched from Louis' grasp. The Dutch, in a final effort to save their country from a French invasion, and annihilation, had pierced the walls and dyke which protected their low-lying country from the North Sea, and flooded it completely.

Louis was shattered by the news. For more than two years he had been preparing for this ultimate victory over the Dutch, and now, at the final moment, his plans lay around him in ruins. It was high summer; soon autumn would be here, and a winter campaign would be impossible. He had no choice but to leave an army in occupation of the frontier and return to Paris to await the spring.

That was a long, bitter winter for Louis. In June, while he had been away at the war, Maria Theresa had given birth to her sixth child, a little boy, Louis-François. In November of that year, after Louis had been at the Louvre a little more than four weeks, the baby died. The Dauphin, aged eleven, was now the sole representative of Maria Theresa's numerous pregnancies, miscarriages, and six live births. Even Louis hesitated to subject her to any more. For the first time since they had been married he began to sleep in his own bed.

By December, Athenais was pregnant again, a state which did nothing to improve her temper. She and Louise de la Vallière bickered and quarrelled continually. Louise was constantly in tears. Louis began seriously to consider allowing her to carry out her dearest wish – to enter the Carmelite convent. La Grande Mademoiselle, his cousin, was still sulking at her country estates over his refusal to allow her to marry the Duc de Lauzun, and would not return to Paris.

It was a dull Christmas at Court that year and the usual festivities took place in a subdued atmosphere. But in the New Year stimulation was provided by a new arrival at Court.

'They say that Monsieur and Madame will be present at Mass today,' Lison reported to Athenais de Montespan on New Year's morning, 1673, as she came in early to make the fire.

Athenais waved her away from the fireplace impatiently. 'Summon a lackey to do that,' she commanded. 'Here, help me to dress.' Shivering with cold, she boxed the girl's ears to make her hurry, and the two of them retired behind a Chinese screen as the lackey made the fire.

One dress after another was discarded as being too tight, not tight enough, or not sufficiently elegant to impress the newcomer to the Court, the Princess Palatine, the German princess whom Monsieur had unwillingly been pressured into taking as his second wife for his brother's political advantage.

'They arrived from St Cloud this morning,' Lison informed her mistress, 'and will take dinner with the King today.' Athenais glared at her as her cold hands fumbled with the fastenings of the gown they had finally selected. What a butter-fingers the girl was – but she was a dab hand at gleaning useful information. She tossed her a gold coin as a New Year's token. The girl went out stammering her thanks.

Athenais surveyed her reflection in the long mirror, well pleased with herself. She had finally chosen a dark blue velvet gown, trimmed with gold lace, sufficiently low-cut to reveal her smooth shoulders and creamy bosom to advantage, yet not so low as to allow her to freeze to death in the stone-floored chapel on a winter's morning. With it she wore the diamond parure which had been one of Louis' first gifts to her, in the early raptures of his love, and one which she knew the Queen hated to see her wear. Tiny diamond drops sparkled in her ears. She turned this way and that before the mirror, noting with satisfaction that her waist showed as yet no sign of her condition to the casual observer.

Remembering the affection that had existed, albeit purely on a platonic level, between Louis and Minette, she was determined to put the newcomer in her place right from the beginning. There should be no such attachment between the King and his new sister-in-law; she would soon show this German woman, Lotte, or whatever her name was, who was the second lady at Court after the Queen.

Lison returned carrying her velvet cloak, lined with sable, and her matching sable bracelets. Gloves and muffs could not be worn for Mass, but the bracelets would keep her hands from turning blue with cold.

'The hairdresser is here, madame.'

Armand, the most fashionable coiffeur in Paris, bustled in, a little man, plump and greasy, with long dark curly hair, a shiny face, and perfumed and bejewelled like a woman. Many of his clients, unable to lay their hands on ready cash, paid their fees with a discarded bracelet or ring.

'Hurry, Armand, it's almost nine-thirty.' Even Athenais, notoriously unpunctual, dared not be late for chapel. The King, whose daily activities were planned by the clock, was capable of giving her one of his coldest looks were she to arrive after the service had begun. Louis took his church-going very seriously, possibly because of his levity in other directions.

Armand was enthusing over his newest style, which he had created only a day or two earlier – with Athenais in mind, he swore.

'*C'est le style hurluberlu, madame.*'

'Whatever's that, Armand?'

'*Oh, c'est magnifique, c'est merveilleux, madame.*' He began to describe the style to her, with a great deal of gesticulation, but she cut him short.

'All right, Armand, I have every confidence in you. But make it speedy! I must be in chapel by ten.'

Armand applied himself to his work with the enthusiasm of a true artist, and Lison clapped her hands with admiration as Athenais turned to her for approval.

'Oh, how fine you look, madame. None of the other ladies can compare with you, madame.'

'*Vous êtes exquise, madame,*' echoed the hairdresser.

Athenais stood up and handed the coiffeur a velvet purse full of gold louis. 'You've excelled yourself, Armand. Take that for the New Year, and come back tonight at six, as usual.'

'*Merci bien, madame.* And for the New Year, *tous mes voeux!*'

'Never mind that now. I'll see you this evening.' She closed the door on his protestations of gratitude.

Lison draped the cloak round Athenais' shoulders, still full of compliments. '*Que vous êtes élégante, madame!*' The hair-style

234

consisted of close curls massed all over the head, with one or two stray ringlets falling down on the back of the neck, as if in careless disarray. Carefully they arranged the veil of gold lace, compulsory for chapel attendance, so as to display the new style.

Even Louise de la Vallière, arriving to escort Athenais to chapel and carry her prayer book, looked at the woman she loathed in admiration. She herself was dressed in black, her blonde hair straying here and there from under her mantilla.

'How beautiful you look this morning, madame,' she told her. They had long ceased to call each other by their first names.

Athenais, looking at Louise's lifeless demeanour, pale finely chiselled features, the blue eyes, once so beautiful as to win a king's heart, now cold as stone, could not but feel a little sorry for her. Secure in her hold on the King, she could afford to be a little more generous to Louise. She decided to make a New Year's resolution to be kinder to her former friend.

'Come, we'll be late,' she said. As a first step in her new resolution she invited Louise's little girl, Marie-Anne, to accompany them to Mass. With the child holding her train, she would make quite a dramatic entrance.

However, when Monsieur, looking somewhat sheepish, appeared in chapel with his bride, it was all Athenais and the other Court ladies could do not to burst out laughing. Liselotte, the Princess Palatine and the new Madame, could not possibly have afforded a greater contrast to the delicate, sprightly girl who had been her husband's first wife. Almost as wide as she was tall, with crinkly hair unfashionably dressed, she had a peasant's weather-beaten complexion and typically heavy, stolid German features. Her clothes were impossibly dowdy and out of date, and she wore no powder, paint or patches, but sensible heavy shoes and an old-fashioned fur tippet hanging down over her shoulders.

Athenais was almost delirious with joy to realize that the King's new sister-in-law would never give her occasion for concern. The King, though he might occasionally dally with a maid or lady-in-waiting, invariably picked out the prettiest girls for the honour of his favours. The idea of his casting a glance in the direction of this heavy German *frau* was ludicrous.

At dinner that day, as the King entertained his brother and his new sister-in-law in his own apartments, the talk of all was how on earth Monsieur, with his dislike of women in general, had been able to bring himself to sleep with his wife. She was peasant-like not only in her looks but, according to French ideas, in her manners – even though she was the daughter of the Elector of the Palatinate.

Yet in spite of her lack of feminine charm, Liselotte and the King soon became firm friends. The German princess, used to spending long hours in the open air, roaming the hills of the Palatinate on horseback, was more than happy to go stag-hunting with the King in the forests of Versailles. Louis enjoyed her company, for her conversation was lively and uninhibited. Unlike the Court ladies, she cared nothing for her looks or her clothes, and seemed positively to enjoy an exhausting day in the saddle, arriving back at the palace with dishevelled hair, an aching back and her riding habit torn and dirty. In fact she soon adopted only two forms of dress, Court dress and a riding habit, and was never seen in anything else. Louis forgave her many of her frequent lapses of Court etiquette and her gaucherie – which he would not have overlooked in others – because she amused him so much. It was strange, he thought, how much better he got on with his brother's wives than with his own. Maria Theresa and he seemed to have little to say to each other as the years went by.

One day in February 1673 Louis, desperately seeking to relieve the monotony of the long winter and waiting only for the day when he could resume the campaign against the Dutch, decided to visit his son Louis-Auguste, and the baby, Louis-César. Françoise had kept him informed by letter of his sons' progress, and the move to Vaugirard. Athenais, resenting the amount of time the King was spending with Madame – though she had, of course, no fears in that direction – decided to go with him, though she had not forgiven Louis-Auguste the trouble he had caused her on her last visit.

The visitors arrived at two o'clock when the servants were taking their dinner in the kitchen. Jacques, the old concierge from the rue Birague, recognized them and showed them up to the nursery on the first floor where Françoise was reading a story to the children.

Even Louis, who since the deaths of Minette and of so many of his children had become somewhat world-weary and cynical, could not but be moved by the scene that met his eyes as they entered the room. Louis-Auguste sat in his accustomed place on Françoise's lap, which under no circumstances would he surrender to his brother – so that the baby, now twelve months old, sat in the old rocking-chair in front of her. At the other side of Françoise stood Yvette, Agnès' little girl, and with one arm round the child, Françoise turned the pages of the picture book with the other. The black and white cat lay curled up at her feet.

Louis-Auguste ran to meet his father with a joyful cry. Louis was surprised at the lump that came into his throat in his pleasure at the child's recognition. He and Athenais spent some time chatting with the little boy, who answered them clearly and without any prompting from Françoise. Louis could not help but admire this small son of his, so bright and precocious, so different from the Dauphin who, dull and stolid, took after his mother.

Then the King took little Louis-César on his lap and admired his white doe-skin shoes and the brightly-coloured crocheted woollen ball clutched in his hand which Françoise had made for him.

'Does he walk already?' he asked Françoise in surprise, seeing the leading-strings attached to the shoulders of his frock. Françoise explained that as yet he could only stand by holding on to a table or a chair, but that any day she expected him to take his first steps.

To her utter astonishment, the King then sat down on the floor, his legs outstretched, holding the surprised child upright by his feet. Then, letting go of the child's hands, he held out his arms – explaining to Françoise that he remembered that was how he had taught the Dauphin to take his first steps. Little Louis-César did indeed take a step, but in the wrong direction. Suddenly becoming frightened of the gentleman with the long hair and the sword and the loud voice, he turned abruptly and took two little steps towards Françoise, burying his face in her lap.

Louis-Auguste, his jealousy immediately aroused, rushed to Françoise and neither would be content until she took them both on her lap.

Agnès returned from her dinner to take her little girl away, and curtsied low to the elegantly dressed lady and gentleman. The King's hair, no longer as plentiful as it had been, was now covered by a periwig, Françoise noticed.

'Do you know whose children these are?' the King asked Agnès.

'Indeed, no, monsieur,' she replied, 'but judging by the very great care that is taken of them, and all the servants required for them, they must be the children of someone very important –

perhaps even a High Court Judge.'

This remark sent the King and Athenais into gales of laughter, and Françoise too could not resist a wry smile. Louis-Auguste joined in the general merriment with enthusiasm.

The King found himself taking his leave of Mme Scarron and his two little sons with reluctance. In the coach Athenais chattered gaily, knowing his impatience during these long winter days as he waited to resume the Dutch war. An attempt to move the French troops forward over the frozen waters of Holland had failed when there was a sudden thaw. The King was counting the days until the spring when he could advance and take Amsterdam.

'Mme Scarron is looking a little older, is she not, Sire?' she said at last, when all other subjects of conversation had failed. 'I consider she is looking quite lined.' She was beginning to resent Louis-Auguste's obvious attachment to Françoise.

The King considered her remarks for a few moments. Then she was jolted out of the complacency she was beginning to enjoy after four years as the King's *maîtresse en titre*.

'She knows how to love,' he answered at last. Then, to her indescribable horror: 'It might be quite pleasant to be loved by her.'

Athenais was silent for the remainder of the journey back to the Louvre.

Slowly the dreary winter days passed. Louis occupied himself with rides out to Versailles, to see how the work was progressing there, where thousands of workmen were engaged in creating the palace and gardens soon to be the talk of Europe. His new sister-in-law, Madame, often accompanied him on these excursions, and on hunting trips. Athenais, now that she was four months pregnant, preferred to remain in her rooms, resting, in order to save her energy for the evening. Choosing her gown and jewels and hair-style for the evening entertainments was far more to her taste than getting dirty and muddy on horseback. She thanked her lucky stars that there was no danger of Louis becoming attracted to his new sister-in-law. It was common knowledge that Monsieur's courage had almost failed him at the thought of bedding her, and that only thoughts of the future of France had spurred him on.

However, when it was announced in March that Madame was *enceinte* no one was more surprised than Monsieur. Madame was no longer able to go stag-hunting at Versailles with the King. Louis was disappointed at losing his riding companion. Like Athenais, none of the other Court ladies cared to expose their complexions to the cold air, or make themselves muddy and sweaty with a day's riding.

As the altered palace of Versailles neared completion, the King began to hold the evening entertainments there, the supper parties, the gambling, the balls; and since these went on until the small hours, those who did not possess the King's boundless energy were forced to remain abed in the mornings to summon up their strength for the next onslaught. In these short winter days many did not see the light of day for weeks on end. And because the alterations were as yet incomplete, there was accommodation only for the King and Queen, Monsieur and Madame, and a few of the more favoured courtiers in the redesigned palace – so that the remaining revellers had perforce either to travel back to Paris late at night or to sleep wherever they could manage, in the inns and taverns of the village of Versailles, or even in the back of a coach.

For some time Athenais had been trying to persuade the King to take her with him when he left France for the summer campaigns and the second assault on the Dutch. Louis, however, insisted that she remain at the Louvre to have her baby, or at St Germain, if the Court had already moved there for the summer by the time the baby arrived.

'Won't you let me travel with you?' she pleaded late one afternoon, stroking his forehead and running her fingers caressingly through his dark hair. They were in bed in her rooms, where he always visited her on his return from the hunt or a day at Versailles.

As always when faced with a proposition he did not care for, Louis tried to avoid the subject under discussion. He disliked refusing requests, but did not give in to them for that reason. He swung himself off the bed and began to dress.

'Must you leave already?' pleaded Athenais. 'It is scarcely six o'clock.'

Louis made no answer as he smoothed down his hair in front of the mirror, tucked his shirt into his breeches and carelessly knotted his cravat.

Athenais jumped off the bed, and wrapping herself in a thin silk dressing-gown, came to throw her arms around him. She knew from experience that the closer she was to him the better her requests were likely to be received. Though she normally liked to flaunt herself naked in front of him, her figure, now visibly pregnant, did not warrant display on this occasion.

'*Je vous prie, Sire*,' she begged. 'I can't bear to be parted from you for so long. It may be September before you return.' Knowing how much he adored his children, she decided to appeal to his paternal instincts. She looked helplessly down at her distended stomach. 'Now, of all times, when I need you so much.' She lived in fear of losing him when she was pregnant. She knew perfectly well that several of the prettier maids and ladies-in-waiting at Court had lost their virginity to the King. If Lison had not possessed a face like an old boot she would have sent her packing long ago. But it was not these momentary strayings from her bed that she feared, but the possibility of losing him permanently. She dreaded the time when she would lose her hold over him, though she knew it must surely come. Yet, as time passed, she was beginning to fear even that less and less; she had her luxurious house at Clagny, worth many thousands of livres, and enough jewels and money to keep her well endowed for the rest of her life. In fact, she had achieved everything that she had set out to do.

But how she would hate to leave the Court – the vortex, the centre of the whirlpool, and she at its spinning heart. How she would miss the excitement of the gaming-rooms, the competition amongst the women, constantly vying with each other for their share of the limelight by spending ever-increasing fortunes on their gowns and jewels, their lace and furs. The envious glances of the women as she swept into a room, and the appraising looks of the men – they were the very breath of life to her.

There was no reason why she should leave Court if Louis took a new mistress. But she was not going to become a second Louise de la Vallière, and allow people to patronize her to her face and snigger at her behind her back. Athenais well knew that, amongst the hundreds of people at Court, she did not possess one genuine friend. There was, she knew, not one who would not glory in her discomfiture.

If only she could keep herself from falling pregnant! One day, she knew, that would be when she would lose him for good. None of the powders or potions that old witch Mme Voisin gave her, and which she swallowed by the score, seemed to be any help in that direction. She was beginning to find herself *enceinte* with monotonous regularity. Armand had strongly

240

recommended a Mme Filastre for such problems. She resolved to consult with her next time.

'It's impossible,' said Louis, 'as you well know.' He intended taking the Queen with him, and the whole of the royal suite, in order to create the maximum impression for the rest of Europe to observe when he made his entry into Amsterdam and Utrecht – which, God willing, would not be long now. The whole world was going to see the splendour of the Court of Louis XIV. 'You know perfectly well that the Queen and her suite will travel with me.' He put her gently at arms' length, and picked up his coat and sword.

'But what does that signify?' she pouted. 'You know how discreet I can be.' She looked at him through her long, sweeping eyelashes in the mocking, provocative way he found so hard to resist. 'And after all, once the baby is born, and I'm myself again – won't you want me as much as I'll want you?'

Louis smiled and smacked her rump playfully. 'You little devil,' he said. 'If you weren't in the condition you're in, I'd take you twice again before supper.'

He sometimes wondered, as did the entire Court, what the real secret of her hold over him was. She was lovely, yes, but there were other lovely girls, many of them younger than she was, at Court. Sometimes, when it took his fancy, he would take one or other of them to bed – the Queen had recently dismissed her entire staff of maids because Louis had shown an interest in two of them – but these were momentary lapses. By and large, he had remained faithful to Athenais now for almost five years; a long time when a woman was over thirty. He knew that she took pleasure in humiliating the Queen and Louise de la Vallière, her former friend; that she was vicious to her maids, and cared nothing for her children; but he had a physical need of her that other women seemed unable to satisfy. She was always able to arouse him to fever pitch with her abundant vitality and zest for love-making. There was something feline about her caresses, her behaviour in bed, that never failed to stimulate him, even if he were feeling jaded before he came to her. She was never tired, and never allowed herself the luxury of a headache or a day unwell in bed, as most of the ladies did from time to time. She was always cheerful and in good spirits when he came to visit her, beautifully dressed or provocatively undressed as the case might be. On the darkest, dreariest winter day he could be sure she would be sparkling with fun and have a limitless fund of anecdotes and gay chatter with which to banish the ennui to which occasionally, even in the midst of the brilliant Court with which he had surrounded himself, he was prone.

'*Je verrai*,' said Louis, 'I will see.' It was the invariable answer he gave to all requests, whatever they might be, never committing himself to a straightforward answer. He ruffled the curls of her disarranged coiffure with an affectionate gesture, and left her rooms to change his clothes for the concert that evening.

Overjoyed, Athenais rang the bell for Lison to come and help her dress. At least he had not actually refused her. Somehow, she would find a way to make him take her with him.

Chapter Twenty-three

At long last that interminable winter was over. Louis, straining at the leash, gave the order to leave St Germain, where the Court had spent Easter, for what he hoped would be the conclusive expedition to the stubborn United Provinces of Holland.

The royal party was preceded by a cavalcade of baggage wagons and pack mules, carrying tents, food supplies, furniture, cooking utensils, cutlery and linen for the use of the King and his retinue. In spite of the outriders who rode along the line urging on the horses, it was slow progress as the long winding procession straggled its way along the road down to Le Pecq. More than a hundred servants were also of the party. The King never travelled without his musicians and, of course, his personal physicians, apothecary, valets and barber.

Inside the splendid gilt velvet-lined coach drawn by eight greys sat the quartet referred to by Mme de Sévigné in her letters to her daughter as the Fire and the Snow, the Dew and the Torrent. In short, the King and Queen, Athenais de Montespan and Louise, Duchess of Vaujours. Amongst the Queen's personal entourage were her confessor, her tumbling dwarfs and pet dogs – from whom she was never parted – the faithful Duchess d'Elbeo and Doña Molina. Athenais' attendants, in addition to Lison and the little blackamoor boy the King had given her as an Easter gift, included M. Chais, a Parisian gynaecologist, and the midwife Mme Robinet. Louis had allowed Athenais to travel only on condition that these two accompanied her, though she herself was quite ready to risk having the baby without qualified medical attendants. Swaddling bands, baby-linen and a crib were amongst her baggage.

'Had not Mme Scarron also better accompany us?' the King had asked Athenais jokingly before they left.

Athenais pretended to be amused. Actually she was beginning to dislike the King's frequent references to Françoise, whose regular letters reporting on the progress of the two little boys in her care apparently amused him. He told her that he appreciated Mme Scarron's dry sense of humour, and the way she described the children's escapades made him laugh out loud. Athenais had taken good care to convince him that Françoise could not possibly abandon her charges in order to make the journey.

Louis gazed out of the window, impatient and frustrated at the slowness of their interminable progress. The Queen, as always in public, said little, afraid that Athenais' wicked tongue would make fun of her poor French. Louise kept her eyes steadfastly on her prayer book. It was left to Athenais to entertain them with her never-failing supply of anecdotes and banter, which she did with unflagging energy.

Madre de Dios! Maria Theresa thought sourly, as she looked at the woman she loathed so much, laughing and sparkling with her usual *joie de vivre*. That slut would flirt with the very grooms themselves if the King were not present, for lack of other male company!

And indeed, Athenais, lovely as ever in a loose, flowing gown of flowered taffety, worn the new shorter length with the muslin frills of her petticoat poking daringly out above her embroidered velvet shoes, was powdered and painted within an inch of her life, her patches applied as painstakingly as ever. The draughts and dust from the open windows – the King, lately prone to suffer from headaches, insisted on fresh air – seemed to have no effect on her coiffure, which was bouncy and curly as always; whereas, before they had travelled ten leagues, Maria Theresa's hair was itchy and lank.

The Duchess of Vaujours spoke hardly at all, save to ask the Queen occasionally if she was feeling quite well – to which the Queen responded with a grateful smile. The procession halted only for meals to be taken; other needs were of no interest to the King, so impatient was he to reach the frontier. If his companions felt sick or ill, or merely in desperate need of a close-stool, they must conceal it as best they might. Maria Theresa prayed that the lurching and jolting of the coach might precipitate la Montespan's confinement, or at the very least force her to satisfy the needs of nature. Then, hastily taking out her rosary, she prayed for forgiveness for the wickedness of her thoughts.

After several days' travel, as they drew slowly nearer to Rocroi and the lines of the French army, the King's mood became more cheerful. In the villages they passed through, the peasants stopped work to cheer their King, going to war for the glory of France, and talked to one another in wonder of the 'three Queens' they had seen.

At Tournai, where they stopped for the night, and to take on further supplies, Athenais, bored with the endless hampers of cold food they had consumed on the journey so far, dined not wisely but too well on roast partridge, a tasty *potage*, and fish cooked in a rich cream sauce with plenty of garlic, to which she was particularly partial. Everyone also drank copious amounts of the local hearty wine, which was extremely welcome after the dusty journey. Then, as Louise de la Vallière asked the maids to bring warm water for her to wash in, Athenais threw herself on the creaky bed they were to share and was soon asleep. Lison and the blackamoor boy slept at opposite ends of the truckle bed. The King and Queen were being entertained to dinner by the local civic dignitaries.

During the night Athenais awoke with a sharp pain in her side. She shifted her position – she took up most of the bed already in her cumbersome state – and tried to sleep; but the pain became worse. After a little while she got out of bed and kicked Lison awake.

'Bring me some water, you slut!'

The girl, half asleep, staggered out of the room and returned with a bowl of water. Athenais pushed her with fury and it soaked the girl's nightdress.

'To drink, *stupide*! Can't you see I'm in pain?'

She lurched back to the bed and half fell on it. Louise, woken by the noise, sat up and rubbed her eyes.

'Is it morning?' she asked. 'It's still dark.'

Athenais groaned. Louise realized what was happening. 'Athenais! Is it the baby?'

Athenais began to curse profanely; Louise put her hands to her ears. Lison came in with a drink of water. Athenais gulped down the entire mug and fell back on the bed. The blackamoor boy, terrified, hid himself behind the curtains.

Louise wrapped a dressing-gown round herself and took Athenais' hands. 'Shall I send for Mme Robinet?' she asked. 'Is it time?'

Athenais was violently sick. 'Of course not,' she spat, as Lison rushed to mop her up. 'Another two full moons.'

But another violent pain gripped her, and she knew that the time had indeed come. She lay back on the bed, cursing and swearing. Louise tried to cover her, and turned to Lison. 'Quick! Summon M. Chais and Mme Robinet. Her time is near.'

'Where are they housed, my lady?'

Louise did not know. On their arrival at Tournai the King had ordered the best houses in the town to be vacated for his use, and she and Athenais had been given a house fairly near to where the King and Queen were lodged. But there were only Lison, the black boy and the serving-women downstairs. She had no idea where the midwife and doctor would be.

'Go and see if you can find out where they are lodged. But hurry, hurry!'

She found a bottle of the heavy perfume Athenais always used and, dabbing some of it on a handkerchief, applied it to Athenais' brow. Athenais struggled with her and knocked over the bottle, spilling the entire contents. The smell was so overpowering that Louise tried to open the windows, but they were made of parchment and would not move.

Lison, meanwhile, ran out into the cold night with only a blanket over her nightdress. She knocked up the servants in the neighbouring house, but they could not help her.

'It's three in the morning,' one woman cursed her. 'Can't you leave folk to lie in their beds?' She spat at her. Lison wandered along the dark street in terror, not knowing what to do. A soldier, patrolling the street where the King lodged, came up to her.

'Out a bit late aren't you, *ma petite*?' He was disappointed when he put his arm round her waist and looked at her face. Her face was ugly and she stank of the vomit she had just been cleaning up. But she was not much more than twenty and he had not had a woman in a long time. His arms tightened round her waist. He expected her to kick and put up a fight, but he was wrong. Lison, knowing she would get short shrift from Athenais if she returned too soon from her search, decided that there were worse ways of spending a cold night. As he drew her into a doorway she held out her hand. 'An écu, *s'il vous plaît*.' He was a well set-up young fellow, but why sell oneself for nothing? Athenais' days of glory, she felt sure, were numbered.

He looked at her in horror. 'On a soldier's pay? I'll give fifty sous.'

'A livre.' He hesitated. It was more than three months since he had left his village in the Auvergne. There were camp followers, of course, but the youngest, prettiest ones sold themselves for the highest prices, the oldest and ugliest being left for the youngest recruits. He sighed. '*D'accord*.'

She drew him down on top of her as he took out the money. Afterwards she handed him back the coin. He was a clean young

246

lad, and though her life with Athenais de Montespan was not without its tribulations, she was well housed and well fed. 'Keep it,' she told him. 'Send it to your mother.' The lad kissed her hand in joy.

It was five o'clock when Lison wandered back to the house where Athenais had just given birth to a little girl. The blackamoor clung, terrified, to the curtain, not knowing whether to stay or run away. Louise, wet with sweat, overcome by fear and terror, sat on the bed holding the tiny baby on her lap. She had wrapped it in the sheet, but was afraid to cut the cord or do anything else until the midwife came. Where could Lison be? She had been gone for hours.

Lison wandered in. 'I couldn't find them, madame,' she told Louise. Louise looked at her in despair. Athenais was asleep.

'Then go again, girl. Find the Captain of the Guard and tell him he must find them right away. Do you hear me? *Dépêche-toi!*'

Lison threw on her clothes this time, and again departed. Louise looked down at the tiny baby. Thank God the child was alive. If only the midwife would come soon! She fell on her knees, clasping the baby to her, and prayed for help.

In a few minutes Lison returned. 'I found a sergeant, madame, and he's gone to find the Captain of the Guard and bring them. I told him it was urgent.'

Urgent! The urgency was almost over, Louise thought. She pushed back her blonde hair from her brow and looked down at the blood-stained sheets, and at her clothes, in disgust. 'Bring water immediately, Lison, and clean up this mess. Quickly!' She looked down anxiously at Athenais. Was it all right for her to sleep like this? Might she not fall into a coma – or was it simply sheer exhaustion after her short but agonizing labour? She wondered whether she should baptize the baby herself, in case it should die before help came. But there were footsteps clattering up the stairs. It was Mme Robinet; M. Chais was still dressing at his lodging.

Louise heaved a sigh of relief as the midwife took charge of the baby and issued commands to Lison. Mme Robinet agreed with her that the baby, having arrived before her time, was so small and frail she must be baptized without delay, and Louise sent the blackamoor to find a priest immediately.

Looking down at Athenais' sleeping face, Louise thought how strange it was that she, who hated her so much, should have had to be the one to help her in her hour of need. Yet there had been no hate in her heart as she helped to deliver the baby, only the primeval instinct to help another suffering human being. Perhaps that was God's way of showing us there must be no hate in this world. She looked at the innocent, miniature face of the little baby where Mme Robinet, having cut the cord and arranged the swaddling bands, had laid her on the truckle bed until the crib could be brought; she thought of her own children, Marie-Anne de Blois and Louis, Comte de Vermandois, who had remained behind at St Germain. Would they suffer if the King finally allowed her to retire to a convent? Surely after this Athenais would take her part with the King, so that she might be allowed to leave Court?

She knelt by the bed where Athenais still slept, and covering her face with her hands, prayed for the souls of her two babies who had died, and for all suffering people, whoever they might be.

Louis was delighted with his baby daughter. He cut short the midwife – who, while Louise de la Vallière gazed tranquilly out of the window, was breathlessly recounting for the hundredth time how she had delivered the baby with great difficulty and expert skill, and saved the life of Athenais and the baby for certain – gave her twenty louis d'or and dismissed her. The little one was to be named Louise-Françoise, he decided, a skilful blend of her parents' names, for Athenais' baptismal name had been Françoise. She herself had changed it to Athenais, thinking it more exotic.

The baby was to be taken back to Paris immediately, in the care of Mme Robinet, there to be handed over to Mme Scarron. Louise asked if she might also return with them, and take charge of the child until she was safely with Mme Scarron, and the King thanked her and agreed to her request.

The Queen, meanwhile, was racked with self-hatred, brooding with grief over the fact that la Montespan could give birth to healthy children, even premature and in the midst of a journey, whilst she herself had given Louis only one son. Louis, although he pitied her, was beginning to resent being embroiled in all these domestic arrangements. His one desire was to press on towards Holland.

'*Qu'elle est mignonne*,' he said tenderly, looking down at the tiny face of his newest daughter. Like all men sure of themselves in their sexual role, he doted on little girls. He thought of the dull twelve-year-old Dauphin, his only legitimate son, and the ghosts of the children he had lost – the discarded toys in the empty royal nursery. 'It would be nice to have the children come to live at Court,' he said to Athenais, who was lying propped up on her pillows, trying to look as if she had just emerged from a great ordeal. In fact she was rapidly becoming bored to death with the subject of the baby, and longed only for a good square meal.

Louis was thinking of the two adorable little boys at Vaugirard, with their governess, Mme Scarron. 'Perhaps when I come back from Holland,' he said, as he carefully replaced the little baby in the crib, 'I'll find a way to bring the children to Court.''

Athenais stared at him, open-mouthed, a sudden cold fear gripping at her vitals. Legitimize the children and bring them to Court? That was just what he had done when he had made la Vallière into a duchess, before abandoning her for Athenais. Was it possible that he had her own successor in mind? She resolved under no circumstances to let la Vallière go into the convent, though she had promised Louise her help in the matter that very morning. She knew that while Louise was still near to the King, giving him reproachful looks, Louis still had some pangs of conscience over the way he had treated her. With Louise gone, he might have no compunction over subjecting her, Athenais, to the same fate.

Louis kissed her goodbye affectionately, and bade her take good care of herself. On no account was she to leave her bed before the fourteen days' lying-in prescribed by M. Chais were up. He and his entourage would leave Tournai that same day, the requisite supplies having been made immediately available by the simple expedient of issuing orders to the citizens to give up their stocks of grain and other foodstuffs to the royal party. The grumbling townspeople were to solace themselves with the thought that their hardships until the next harvest were to be for *la gloire de la France*.

As soon as the King had gone Athenais leaped out of bed and looked at herself, aghast, in the mirror. Her stomach, after her fifth confinement, hung loose and flabby, her waistline was thick and her breasts heavy, swollen and pendulous with milk. Even her legs were fatter, she noticed with dismay—she had enjoyed such excellent health during her pregnancy that she had given full rein to her hearty appetite.

Mme Robinet, who came in to tend the baby, assured her

that she would soon regain her former shape, but Athenais, looking at the gross, corpulent figure of the midwife, was not reassured. On Mme Robinet's instructions, she had Lison fasten her so tightly into her stays that she could scarcely breathe. The midwife told her to drink nothing for several days so that the milk would dry up and her breasts shrink back.

Athenais stared at herself anxiously in the mirror once she was dressed. In her corset and her clothes the effect was certainly better, but she knew only too well the distended shape of her figure underneath the gown. She swore at them all, at Lison, the midwife, the wet-nurse and the baby. Then she told all the women to get out of her room. Next door Louise de la Vallière, anxious to return to her children, was preparing to leave.

Athenais began to pace up and down like an angry tiger, trying to decide what to do. Although she took good care to conceal it from the King, she was sick to death of the rigours of travelling and the attendant discomforts. There would be no balls or other entertainments at the military front, no opportunities to make everyone in the ballroom gasp as she made one of her dramatic entrances in a flamboyant gown, loaded with jewels, furs and baubles. And when the King finally entered Amsterdam, it would be with the Queen at his side. She knew that this was one of the few occasions when she would have to take a back seat. On the other hand, how dull it would be at St Germain with all the men between the ages of sixteen and sixty away at the war.

She made up her mind there and then that she would travel straight to Vichy, to take the cure there for a month or two, and improve her figure in readiness for the King's victorious return from Holland.

She went to the door and threw one of her shoes at Lison in the room downstairs, shouting to her to come up and help her pack.

Chapter Twenty-four

Françoise was standing by the door of the house at Vaugirard, calling the children in from the garden. She was to spend the day at Versailles, as the guest of the Duc and Duchesse de Richelieu. Her coach had already been sent to pick up Mlle de Scudéry, who was also invited. Ready dressed, save for her tippet and mittens, which together with her parasol lay on the chair beside her, she waited for the coach to return.

When Mlle de Scudéry arrived, she was shown at once into the room where Françoise sat with the children. Louis-Auguste and Louis-César were playing ball, and the baby sat watching them, propped up in a miniature chair the carpenter had made for her. Agnès, keeping an eye on the children, was winding wool with her little girl, Yvette.

Although it was by now an open secret amongst her friends that Françoise Scarron was caring for the King's illegitimate children in her new large house at Vaugirard, none of them as yet had seen the children, for on the rare occasions when Françoise gave a supper party it was in the evening when the children were in bed.

The secret had not been a difficult one to guess, for although Françoise continued to dress quietly and with restraint in the darker colours she preferred to wear, there was now an unmistakable air of opulence about her clothes, which were now made of the finest materials, and trimmed with gold braids or, in the winter, furs. Her friends, knowing that no men figured in her life, had not taken very long to come to the conclusion that Françoise Scarron had been chosen to care for the royal bastards. Everyone knew that Athenais de Montespan had given birth to at least three children, but no one until now had known where they were. They must be with Françoise; how else was it possible for her to live in a large house, drive a coach-and-six, and employ so many servants, including a coachman and lackeys?

Mlle de Scudéry laughed as little Louis-César came running to Françoise and leaped up into her arms. 'How he surveys the world seated on your arm, for all the world like a general re-

251

viewing his troops!' she said, as Louis-César waved triumphantly to his brother from his perch.

Françoise laughed and kissed him as she gently put him down. As she watched the little boy toddle away after his older brother, the love and adoration she felt for these children was fully revealed in her expression. Mlle de Scudéry, who had never married, also watched him with a slightly wistful expression. He was a sturdy little boy with rosy cheeks and a mop of dark curly hair, who bore a strong resemblance to his father.

'Come, Françoise,' she said, turning to her friend, 'we'll be very late arriving at Versailles.'

Françoise put on her tippet over her gown of dark blue corded silk, and collected her parasol and mittens. She could not be persuaded to leave, however, without a great many last-minute instructions to Agnès, and firm injunctions to the children to be on their best behaviour in her absence and not to pull their sister's hair. At last, however, Mlle de Scudéry succeeded in leading her out to where the coach stood waiting. Françoise was a little upset when Louis-Auguste, who had been pleading with her not to leave him behind, began to cry. As they drove away Agnès came out to wave goodbye, holding Louis-Auguste in her arms, still crying, Louis-César and Yvette pulling at her skirts.

Once they arrived at Versailles, however, the children were temporarily forgotten. The Duc de Richelieu was one of the very few courtiers as yet fortunate enough to have lodgings in the palace. So far, only the State apartments for the King and Queen, Monsieur and Madame, and some other rooms for the use of the King's ministers were ready, he explained to the ladies as they strolled in the gardens. It was a warm, late August day, and the heavy scent from the profusion of tuberoses and jasmine was almost overpowering, reminding Françoise of the suffocatingly strong perfumes Athenais de Montespan always used.

'What changes there have been since my last visit!' Françoise said, marvelling at the seemingly endless vistas of shrubberies, terraces and rose-gardens stretching away into the distance, and admiring the formal elegance of the Italian-style parterres, the fountains and ornamental pools where nymphs carved in stone and naked cherubs with chubby rounded limbs supported the water jets or reclined amongst the water-lilies.

The Duc de Richelieu took her arm as they strolled along the *allées* of clipped yew trees radiating from the Bassin d'Apollon which lay on the western side of the palace. Graceful life-like statues of Greek gods and goddesses and figures of antiquity lined the groves and shady paths. As they walked on they came to a flight of marble steps which led up to a Chinese pavilion of blue and white *faïence*, and the Duke led Françoise to see a small grotto near-by where he pointed out to her the emblazoned emblem of the Sun King, with his motto engraved below – *Nec Pluribus Impar* – not unequal to many.

They were now looking up at the palace, where the workmen were building a new reception gallery which was to be more than a kilometre in length when completed, and lined not only with marble pillars, but with mirrors to reflect the light, a novel Italian idea.

'How much has been accomplished here in such a short time,' Françoise marvelled again as they watched a veritable army of masons, marble-workers, joiners and glaziers at work on the new gallery. A battalion of wagons carrying tools and building materials was lined up, and the whole of the back of the building was covered with scaffolding. It was not difficult to imagine the problem of transportation presented by all those heavy statues and great slabs of marble.

'Are there not many accidents,' she asked, 'amongst such numbers of workmen?'

'Certainly,' the Duke replied. 'Why, only the other day a young man fell from the scaffolding and broke his back.' Françoise drew in her breath sharply. 'There have been dozens of such cases,' he told her as she looked at him with horror. 'But the majority of fatalities here,' he went on, 'have been caused by fever.' He took her arm and began to lead her towards the entrance to the palace. The Duchesse de Richelieu and Mlle de Scudéry were strolling a little way behind them.

'Fever? In the height of summer – ?'

'It wasn't summer when all this work began, my dear, more than three years ago. But in fact summer is the most dangerous time – the heat, the flies, the foul smells caused by the drainage. Think of all the ground that has had to be excavated to create all these pools, and the enlargement of the canal. Why, the digging of that lake alone took several regiments of the Swiss Guard about three months! I believe it is to be known as the Swiss Lake, the King's personal tribute to their industry.'

Françoise looked in the direction of the lake, remembering the magical night of the *divertissement*, five years before, when they had sailed in gondolas in the moonlit dusk to the strains of Lully's music.

'Was there not a small covert over there, near the canal?' she asked.

The Duke nodded. 'Yes, I believe there was a small wood there formerly, but the King had it uprooted, tree by tree, because it marred the view of the lake. The bodies of many hundreds of workmen have been taken away from here,' he told her, as they waited for the Duchess and Mlle de Scudéry to catch them up, 'chiefly at dead of night, so as not to cause unnecessary talk.'

Françoise shuddered. Was the creation of such beauty as she had seen today really worthwhile, if it meant such distress and anguish for those who had lost their husbands and sons in its construction? All for the aesthetic enjoyment of the privileged few?

'Is the King aware of all this?' she asked. Surely, the man she had often seen playing with his children and dandling them on his lap like any loving father could not be the same man who compelled men to work like animals for a pittance, risking their very lives – and not in the construction of essential defences, but in rebuilding houses and gardens.

'Of course,' said the Duke. 'Many men, I believe, have simply collapsed from cold, exhaustion and hunger during the winter days. Their rations, I believe, were quite inadequate.'

'And the King insists on continuing the work?'

'Certainly. I believe he wants it finished before the autumn, when he will make a triumphal return to Paris after decisively routing the Dutch. You know that his troops have already taken Maastricht. It can be only a matter of days now before Amsterdam falls.'

Françoise was silent as the Duchesse de Richelieu and Mlle de Scudéry rejoined them and they all went inside to see the interior of the palace. Here they were shown the splendours of the marble staircases, the ornate silver-gilt wall-sconces and the crystal chandeliers in the new gallery – which, the Duke explained, required a galaxy of no less than four thousand wax candles to light it. He showed them the superb views the King had created of the park and the forest of Versailles from the windows of the first floor, and enthusiastically informed them that there were now three hundred and seventy-five windows on the front of the chateau alone.

They were entertained to an excellent dinner in the Duc de Richelieu's rooms, and then, after another stroll in the gardens, Françoise, looking at the watch which hung from the silver chatelaine about her waist, said that she must be thinking of getting back. She was not concerned about the children, knowing them to be quite safe with Agnès, who was thoroughly reliable; but she was beginning to miss Louis-Auguste.

They said goodbye to the Richelieus, with many thanks, explaining that they were due at the Hôtel de Coulanges at seven that evening, where the Coulanges, together with Mme de Sévigné, were jointly giving a wedding-feast for a young niece of theirs who had recently married in Brittany. The festivities were for Parisian friends and relatives who had been unable to travel to the wedding ceremony. Françoise was hoping to reach home in time to see the children before they were put to bed.

After Mlle de Scudéry had been taken home, Françoise arrived just as the church clock in the village of Vaugirard was striking six for evensong. In the nursery, the two boys were sitting at the table in their high-chairs, and Agnès and the young maid were giving them their supper. In the corner the wet-nurse was feeding the baby, sitting on the low stool. Françoise kissed the children joyfully and showed them the flowers she had brought for them from the gardens of Versailles.

Louis-César was overjoyed at her return, but Louis-Auguste turned his face away as she kissed him.

'He's still sulking because you did not take him with you,' Agnès told her. 'He wouldn't eat a thing all day.'

Françoise looked at Louis-Auguste's porringer, his food hardly touched. 'Come, now, *mignon*,' she said softly to him, taking him on her lap. 'Shall Tata give you your supper?' Tata was his childish abbreviation for *tante*, aunt. She did not allow them to call her *maman*.

Louis-Auguste's face was red with temper as he turned his face away and refused to eat. No persuasion on Françoise's part could induce him to take a mouthful. She put her hand to his forehead. It was rather hot.

'Has he been running about in the sun all afternoon?' she said in some exasperation to Agnès. She had told her a dozen times before she left not to let the children get over-heated. It had been a hot day.

Agnès looked at her in surprise. 'No, madame. They were outside all morning, but then I put the little one to rest after his dinner. Louis-Auguste wouldn't eat his dinner, or sleep, so he just played here with his soldiers until four o'clock, when we went down to the garden for a little while to play with the cat.'

Françoise did not believe her. The child was obviously overheated. Probably Agnès had fallen asleep in the garden, and slept all afternoon. Well, she knew that it was pointless to try to force the child to eat if he was disinclined. That was a certain way to make him sick.

'Prepare a drink of sugar-water for him, then,' she said, 'and we'll put him to bed.' Agnès took him away, and the wet-nurse, who had finished feeding the baby, gave her to the young maid to change into her nightgown, and took Louis-César on her lap for him to suckle.

Françoise went to change her clothes, and before going downstairs slipped into the nursery to say goodnight to the children. Louis-César and the baby were already asleep, angelic in their lace-trimmed nightclothes and lace caps. But Louis-Auguste tossed and turned restlessly, his nightgown awry and his cap askew; his face, normally quite pale, was flushed and rosy.

Françoise looked at him anxiously, and again felt his forehead, which was burning hot. 'Don't you think he has a touch of the ague, Agnès?' she said.

Agnès came over to look at him. 'Perhaps, madame.'

'Did he drink the sugar-water?'

'*Oui, madame.*'

As she spoke, Louis-Auguste brought up the drink she had given him all over his nightgown. Agnès hurried to fetch a clean one.

'What's the matter, *mignon*?' Françoise asked. 'Does something hurt you?' Perhaps he was cutting a back tooth, she thought desperately – though he was now over three.

'My arm hurts,' sobbed Louis-Auguste, bursting into tears, 'and my leg – '

'They were fighting in the garden this morning,' said Agnès, 'the two boys. Probably Louis-César hurt him a little – he's quite strong for his age.'

Françoise prayed that this was the answer. She tried to conquer the cold fear which was beginning to grow in her heart. Louis-Auguste had always been a more delicate child than his sturdy younger brother. Agnès changed his clothes and Françoise kissed him goodnight. He turned his face away and seemed to fall asleep, his thumb in his mouth. The little maid drew the curtains so that it was dark.

'Stay in the room with him,' Françoise told Agnès on the landing outside. 'I'll be home at about half past ten. If you should need me' – God forbid, she thought – 'I am at the Hôtel de Coulanges in the Place Royale. If anything is wrong, be sure to send Gabriel immediately to fetch me home.'

Agnès promised. With a heavy heart, Françoise went off in the coach to call for Mlle de Scudéry *en route* for the Hôtel de Coulanges.

Chapter Twenty-five

At the Hôtel de Coulanges the wedding reception was in full swing. Everyone in Parisian society was there, for the Coulanges were popular and had a wide circle of friends. Although they liked to entertain, it was many years since they had given such a lavish party. Footmen were strolling through the crowds, carrying trays of glasses of champagne, and through the open doors of the salon Françoise could see the long tables laid out with a magnificent supper. A crowd had begun to gather outside in the street, to listen to the music of the violins and scramble for the coins the aristocrats tossed to them. The windows were all open to the street for it was warm, very warm.

The processional dance, the *branle*, was led by the bride and her new husband, the Marquis de Crespigny. Françoise thought she looked so sweet and pretty in her wedding lace, her brown hair wreathed and twisted with the pearls given to her by her parents on her wedding day. The fiddlers then struck up the latest popular tunes, and everyone joined in the dancing. Françoise looked at her watch. It was only just turned eight. Supper would probably not be served until ten. She was more anxious than she cared to admit over Louis-Auguste.

'We must greet our hostesses,' said Mlle de Scudéry, and they went over to where Mme de Coulanges and Mme de Sévigné were greeting their guests as best they could in the crush. Mme de Sévigné was looking extremely fashionable in her dress of green and gold brocade covered by an overskirt of black point lace, her hair dressed and powdered *à la mode* and wearing her emeralds, family heirlooms, brought out only for auspicious occasions such as this.

'You remember my darling Marguerite, don't you, Françoise?' she said, drawing forward with pride her daughter, the Comtesse de Grignan. Françoise curtsied to the Comtesse who, dressed in pink silk in the new style known as the *sac*, extended a delicate white hand for her to kiss. Mme de Sévigné was just about to introduce to Françoise her great friend the Comtesse de la Fayette, the writer, when Baron d'Heudicourt came up and, complimenting Françoise on her appearance, claimed her for a dance. Mlle de Scudéry moved on to pay her respects to the Coulanges. As the music stopped and the Baron mopped his perspiring forehead with his handkerchief, a lottery was announced. Françoise bit her lip. It would be the height of rudeness to leave now.

Tickets were distributed, and all the guests claimed their presents, some of considerable value, others more in the nature of token gifts. Françoise won a hand-painted fan with filigree ivory sticks, and Mlle de Scudéry was delighted with an exquisite cut-glass scent bottle, no more than an inch high, with a silver stopper and a ring to hang from a chatelaine. At long last, supper was served. It was a delightful meal, but Françoise hardly touched her food. Mlle de Scudéry was concerned.

'Are you feeling unwell, Françoise?'

Françoise brushed her question aside. 'Only the long day, and all the travelling. It's very warm in here – '

Mlle de Scudéry offered her the use of her vinaigrette, but Françoise declined. At last one or two people began to bid their hostesses goodnight. Françoise, by now in a fever of impatience to return to Louis-Auguste, asked Mlle de Scudéry if she was ready to go.

'Indeed I am not, my dear. Too many handsome gentlemen here tonight. Come, in the next room there's a game of *brelan*.'

'I'm sorry, I really must go. I have a headache.'

'*Quel dommage!* Don't concern yourself about me, Françoise, if you really wish to go home. The Duchesse de Coislin will convey me in her carriage, be assured.'

Françoise said goodnight to the Coulanges, who pleaded with her to stay longer, protesting that the entertainment was only just beginning. Fortunately, in the crush she became separated from them, and she took the opportunity to slip out of the salon unnoticed, and asked the steward to bring her wrap.

On the way home she told herself that she was being foolish. What was a touch of fever in a child of three? If he was still flushed and hot when she reached home, she decided, she would give him a drink of quinine tea, and call in a physician if he were not better in the morning. She gazed unseeingly out of the windows of her coach at the streets of Paris, where people were sitting by their doors and windows in the warmth of the evening, and walking by the river to take a little air.

Why, why, she thought, should Louis-Auguste be the one to

be afflicted with the ague, when he was such a delicate child? Little Louis-César, a year younger, was so much stronger. He had a hearty appetite and ran about the garden with chunks of bread clutched in his fist like a peasant; whereas Louis-Auguste, at three, still ate his bread soaked in milk like an infant, and had a finicky digestion.

At last the coach rattled through the gate of the house at Vaugirard. Françoise said goodnight to the coachman and opened the door with her key. The coachman led the horses to the stable to settle them for the night. There was a little room in the rafters of the stable where he slept, save for the coldest nights in winter, when Françoise allowed him and the two lackeys to sleep in the house.

The house was dark and silent when she went in, but for a light in the kitchen. Jacques the concierge was sleeping on his pallet bed in the hallway. She stole past him and went straight up to the nursery.

She found that Agnès, sitting dutifully in the corner, had fallen asleep and was gently snoring, her head lolling against the side of the baby's cradle. Hastily she struck a light on the tinder and lit a taper.

Louis-Auguste was lying with his head in the corner of the room, against the wall, with his legs dangling from the edge of the bed. His nightcap had fallen off, his nightgown was soaked with sweat and his face was very flushed. He had thrown off his covers in his restlessness, and she noticed, as she bent over him, that his teeth were chattering, and he appeared to be shivering, though the room was very warm.

She found the cup of sugar-water that was always left by his bed, and offered it to him; but she noticed with fear that his eyes seemed glazed, and he did not appear to see either her or the cup she held in her hand. She quickly pulled the covers up over him, straightening him in the bed, and roused Agnès.

'Agnès! Look at Louis-Auguste! He's feverish! Shall we give him some quinine tea?'

Agnès came to stand beside her, rubbing the sleep from her eyes as she looked down at the child. She shook her head glumly. 'It's the quartan ague, there's no doubt of it, madame.'

Only a four-day fever! Then why was she getting into such a panic? Françoise took a firm grip on herself. 'Sit on the bed, here, Agnès, and keep him covered while I fetch the quinine. He mustn't get chilled.'

Hurrying to her own room, she took the key from her chatelaine and opened the little medicine chest she kept there. When she returned to the nursery, Agnès was looking at Louis-Auguste with a strange expression on her face.

'What is it, Agnès?' Suddenly she was gripped by an inexplicable cold fear.

'I don't know, madame. I once saw a child ill like this . . .'

'And what was the cause, Agnès? Could it – could it be measles?' She could not bring herself to voice the word, smallpox.

Agnès said nothing. She stood up and took the packet of quinine Françoise handed to her.

'Hurry and make the tea, Agnès. Only one spoonful, mind. The sooner he drinks it, the sooner the fever will abate.'

Agnès went out. At the door she turned, hesitated as if to say something, and then disappeared. Françoise stroked the child's burning forehead with her hand and wondered whether to put extra blankets on the bed. She wished Agnès would hurry, so that she could change his nightgown, which was saturated with sweat. Better not change it until he had had the drink, in case he either spilt it or brought it up.

Several minutes went by. Louis-Auguste tried to throw off the covers, but she held them tightly down. Alternately he shivered and sweated, but his moans were quiet, and Françoise was thankful that he would not wake the other two children. When Agnès returned, perhaps they had better move his bed into her own room.

When Agnès still did not come back, Françoise became worried. Perhaps she had fallen on the stairs, for she was still quite sleepy when she left the nursery. Seeing that Louis-Auguste seemed to have fallen into a doze, Françoise went swiftly down the stairs.

Nanon was in the kitchen, sorting out the bottles she intended to use the next day for bottling the raspberries from the garden. Françoise was irritated; sometimes she wished Nanon would take a little more interest in the children. Then she inwardly reproached herself; Nanon was such an efficient and hard-working housekeeper.

'Where's Agnès, Nanon? She came down ages ago.'

'Agnès? I haven't seen her since supper. Isn't she with the children? She told me Louis-Auguste wasn't well.'

Françoise stared at her. Agnès had not been in the kitchen? Then where was she? She turned and went up the stairs to

Agnès' bedroom. Opening the door, she blinked in surprise. The light from the candle in her hand showed her that the beds were empty, both the large bed Agnès slept in and the small pallet bed by its side for Yvette. Where could she have gone at this time of night?

Suddenly a suspicion struck her. She went over to the dresser and pulled open a drawer, and then another. They were completely empty. Agnès had taken everything she possessed, and gone. The crucifix over her bed had gone, but the mirror was still on the wall and the pewter candlesticks on the dresser. Agnès was scrupulously honest.

For a moment Françoise stood stock-still, taking in the enormity of her discovery. For Agnès to wake up her little girl and leave with her in the middle of the night – leave a house where, Françoise knew, she had been comfortable and well provided for – could mean only one thing. It meant that there was something wrong with Louis-Auguste – something terribly wrong, her brain told her relentlessly, though she tried to put the suspicion to the back of her mind – some ailment that made Agnès fear so much for Yvette that she had felt she must take her away, out of the house, immediately.

She sat down heavily on the bed. Was it measles? That she would know in a day or two, if his face showed the unmistakable red blotches. But the pox? She did not know the symptoms of that dreaded illness, having been fortunate enough never to suffer from it. She had never felt so helpless. Her thoughts flew to the King. If only he were in Paris, instead of at war in the Netherlands.

She heard Nanon's footsteps coming up the stairs, and tried to rouse herself, to go back to Louis-Auguste. Nanon saw her sitting there, the candle in her hand, and came into Agnès' room looking puzzled.

'What's afoot, mistress? Where's Agnès?'

'She's run away, Nanon. She must be afraid of catching the fever – '

'Run away? In the middle of the night?'

'Yes. She must have been afraid that Yvette . . .' Enough of Agnès and Yvette. She must concentrate on Louis-Auguste. 'Nanon,' she said, 'come with me and look at him.'

The two women went to the nursery, and Françoise held the candle over the sleeping child. His face was flushed, he was sweating copiously, and his cheeks, normally full and round, seemed sunken. There was no doubt that he was very ill. Françoise told herself to keep calm. The physician she had called once or twice for the children lived right on the other side of the city, in the rue de Belleville. Mme d'Albret had recommended him. He would not thank her for calling him all the way out here in the middle of the night. The church clock in the village of Vaugirard was striking twelve.

'Have you ever seen a child look like this before, Nanon?'

Nanon looked down at the sleeping child, pursing her lips together. 'He's very ill, madame,' was all she said.

Françoise went over to the window and flung back the curtain, desperate for some air, and then, remembering the danger of Louis-Auguste becoming chilled, closed it again and went down into her own room. Nanon followed her. Françoise paced up and down, frantically trying to collect her thoughts. Nanon sat down and folded her hands, and remained silent.

It was stiflingly warm and oppressively stuffy in the room, for the sun had been on it all day. Françoise went to the window and pushed open the shutters. The cool night air felt like a restorative balm on her hot forehead. A picture of the black-robed priest and the silent cradle in the nursery at the rue d'Alexandre appeared relentlessly in her mind. She buried her head on her arms.

Nanon came to stand by her side. 'Don't distress yourself, madame, I beg you. He may recover.'

Françoise found some relief from her tension by bursting into a flood of tears. 'I can't bear it, Nanon, if he should be taken,' she sobbed brokenly. 'You know that, don't you, Nanon? I can't live if he dies.'

To her amazement, Nanon gripped her roughly by the shoulders. Through her tears Françoise looked at her in surprise at this familiarity.

'Oh yes, you can, madame,' she hissed in a voice that bore no resemblance to her normal tones. Françoise stared at her.

'Oh yes you will! You'll live, and you'll suffer, just as any other woman does who loses her child! Because you're an *aristo*, and you ride about in a coach, dress in fancy clothes, and never soil your hands, don't you think that God will spare you!'

Suddenly she began to laugh, a shrill high-pitched laugh such as Françoise had never heard before. 'That won't protect you! You'll weep, and you'll tear your hair and beat your breast and pray for God to take you also, just as any other woman does who sees her child die before her eyes!'

Was this the person Françoise had lived with for the past ten years – ranting like a preacher on the Pont Neuf, her eyes hard and glittering, her bosom heaving with emotion and the knuckles of her clenched hands showing white?

Françoise was bitterly wounded that Nanon should think her to be above the slings of misfortune.

'I'm going to tell you something that I've never told anyone else before, Nanon. I was born in a prison – my father married while he was in prison for debt and I was born within the prison walls. I'm no *aristocrate*! Whatever my position in life is now, I've achieved it through my own efforts!'

But Nanon wasn't listening, she was crying and shouting. Françoise tried to calm the woman, realizing that she was hysterical. 'Hush, Nanon,' she said. 'You'll disturb the children.'

'The children – always the children! What life have you made for yourself, madame? Buried alive here with the children?'

'What are you talking about, Nanon? You know I love them. I'm here with them of my own free will, I assure you. There's nowhere else I want to be.' If that had not been the case in the beginning, she thought, it was certainly true now.

'And if Louis-Auguste should die, madame? What then?'

'He won't – he can't, Nanon! I just told you – I can't bear it if he dies. We must pray, Nanon.'

Nanon laughed, a dry, cackling laugh that brought fear to Françoise's heart. 'It's no use praying to God, my lady. He won't help you. As God is my witness, I know! I saw my children die before my eyes.'

Françoise stared at her, momentarily distracted from her fears. 'You've had children, Nanon? I never thought . . .'

'You never thought! Like all the quality, you never thought that the poor could have children, or have feelings like you do!'

Françoise faced her angrily. 'That's not true, Nanon! It's just that you've never told me before.'

'I had two little ones, my lady.'

'You were married, Nanon?'

'My husband told me that he was never married to me by law, when he took himself a new wife. He tried to throw me out, but then when he found that I was carrying he let me stay, in case it was a boy.'

'And it was?'

'It was a boy, madame, and they treated us worse than dogs, my husband and his fancy woman. Then, when he was four years old she sent him to gather sticks in the covert belonging to the estate, knowing that he would be caught.'

'What happened, Nanon?'

Nanon's face was hard and impassive. 'The seigneur's men chased him – there were other children there, too, but my poor little one's legs were bowed for lack of proper food and he couldn't run so fast. They beat him within an inch of his life. He died that very night.' She threw her apron up over her face.

Françoise sat down on her bed and covered her face with her hands. Louis-Auguste would be four next February, if . . .

'I ran away that night,' Nanon was saying, 'and I walked for many days. Then, when I could go no farther, I came to a farm where I asked for work.'

'Were they kind to you, Nanon?'

'The farmer saw that I was tall and strong, and he let me sleep in the barn and work in the fields. At night he came sometimes and took his will of me. That year I had a little girl, madame.'

'And she . . . ?'

'The winter when she was two, the famine was so bad that the children all took long sticks and were rooting about in the ground for beans that had just been planted, or roots or acorns, for anything that would fill their bellies, for all the world just like pigs. My girl must have eaten something poisonous, for she died in my arms, in terrible pain. She was not quite two, I remember.' Nanon's voice was dry and distant, her expression remote, as if she were talking about someone else. 'I called her Félicité, and truly, she was the only happiness I ever had.'

'Haven't you been happy with me, Nanon?'

'Oh, yes, madame. I have. You are the kindest person I have ever known. But my children, madame!' She fell on her knees and buried her head in Françoise's lap, crying like a child. 'My little ones! Shall I ever see them again?'

Françoise patted the woman's gaunt shoulders, afraid to speak. Though Nanon had become an accomplished cook under her tuition, and ate very well, she was scarcely less haggard than the day she had first come to the convent – the result, Françoise now realized, of her years of privation.

Recovering herself, Nanon dried her eyes and went over to the window, and stood staring out into the night, as if trying to remember the faces of her children. Françoise remembered that the Queen had had a waxen likeness made of one of her little girls who died in infancy, so that she might always be able to recall the child's features.

'There's such a pain, such an emptiness inside me,' Nanon said. 'Shall I ever see my little ones again, mistress, do you think?'

'You will meet them again in heaven,' Françoise said, taking the woman's gnarled bony hand in her own two.

'Do you really think so, madame? If I thought that, I would die happy. Somehow, as the years pass, it seems harder to bear. I have Masses said for my girl on February 23rd each year. That was her birthday.'

Françoise remembered when they had first met each other, in the convent in the Place Royale. That must have been just after the little girl died. She would always remember how ill and emaciated Nanon had looked then. She had always wondered at Nanon's reticence about her early life. Now she could understand it.

'Nanon,' she said, gripping the woman's arms tightly, 'there is nothing to be gained by thinking of the past. We must try to save Louis-Auguste. Will you help me?'

'Yes, madame.' The bitter, resentful expression had left her face and she looked her normal self again.

'Will you take a message to the doctor in the rue de Belleville? If you leave now, you'll be there at first light.'

'Don't call any doctor to attend him, madame, whatever you do! They'll bleed the child to death, and kill him even if the illness doesn't.'

'That's nonsense, Nanon. They must know more than we do. Will you go?'

'Not now, madame. Wait and see how he is in the morning. He may overcome the fever of his own accord. Go to bed now, mistress, save your energy to care for him tomorrow.'

Françoise recognized the wisdom of this, but consented to go to bed only on condition that Louis-Auguste slept in her room. Nanon and the young maid carried his bed in and placed it next to her own. Then, seeing that he was asleep, though his breathing was hoarse and he was still sweating profusely, she managed to change his nightgown without waking him. Leaving the curtains of her bed open, so that she should hear him if he woke, she lay down. Nanon, on her instructions, closed the shutters, windows and curtains so that there was no breath of air in the room to give him a chill. It was unbearably hot and stuffy. As Nanon tip-toed from the room, Françoise fell into a fitful sleep.

In her own room, Nanon sat on her bed and wondered what she should do. She knew perfectly well whose children Louis-Auguste and the others were, for had she not once seen the King out in his coach in the rue St Honoré, waving and cheering to the crowd as he passed, and been amazed to recognize him as the visitor to the rue Birague? So that was Louis-Auguste's father! No wonder the children received such cosseting and such attention. She often wondered who the mother was. That red-haired bitch Montespan or whatever her name was, who sometimes came with him, did not seem very interested in them. If she had not lived with Mme Scarron in such close proximity all these years, she would have sworn that they were Mme Scarron's own children, for she knew that they meant as much to her mistress as if they had been her own, in particular, Louis-Auguste.

The King was not, as Mme Scarron thought, in Flanders at this moment, but on his way home to Paris, a disappointed man. Nanon had heard the talk on the Pont Neuf that morning. The summer campaigns had not turned out as he had hoped, even though the capture of Maastricht had seemed a sure key to the towns of Amsterdam and Utrecht. It was being said that the King was seething with rage because the French troops had been prevented from taking the Dutch capital by the sudden entry of Spain, Denmark and Lorraine into the war; recognizing the growing threat of French power, they had decided to ally themselves against their common enemy. The return of the King to Paris was being kept at low key. Gloomy and frustrated at the collapse of all his plans, Louis knew that he would have to sit out another winter before the attack on Holland could be resumed. He was due to arrive at Vincennes that very day.

'That red-haired whore will have to clear out all her fancy men tonight,' the fishwives at les Halles had joked. 'The men are all the same when they can't get their own way – take out their bad temper on the women, King or no King.'

'La Montespan had better watch out,' the street-sweeper called, 'or he'll have her in the family way again.'

'Who'd like to be a fly on the wall tonight?' called out another of the market women, and they had all roared with laughter.

Nanon looked down at her feet. At least she now had good strong shoes for walking, and a thick cloak, though she would scarcely need it, the night being so warm. The castle of Vincennes lay on the eastern outskirts of Paris, and the way to it lay along the Faubourg St Antoine, not far from the rue des Tournelles. She knew the road well. She took only a shawl and a few sous in her pocket. She decided that on the way she would slip in to St Eustache to pray for Louis-Auguste. There was a child who had suffered from this illness, she felt sure, in the rue St Denis, whom she and Françoise had once helped to nurse, the son of a labourer. He had recovered from the fever, but he had never walked again.

It was not yet light when she slipped out of the house and made her way along the Faubourg St Germain towards the Pont Neuf. There was silence save for the rustling of the leaves in the light breeze, for where they now lived, more than a league from the centre of Paris, it was almost the country. Not a soul was to be seen at this hour. Now and then a dog barked. It was too early for the sound of birdsong. The church clock at Vaugirard struck four as she hastened along the road for Vincennes.

Chapter Twenty-six

By the morning Louis-Auguste's condition had worsened considerably. His eyes were unnaturally bright and feverish, his head and hands burning, and he sweated and shivered alternately. His lips were dry and cracked and he complained constantly that his head and his legs ached.

Françoise decided to keep him in her own room, away from the other children. She told the young maid that she must take Agnès' place, and care for the two little ones that day as best she could. There were also the wet-nurse and Marie-Jeanne, the girl employed to rock the cradle. Surely three women could take care of two small children between them.

When she went back to her own room it was so hot, with the sun shining full on the polished floor, that she closed the shutters and windows firmly. She tied a large apron round her waist and, taking a bowl of water, tried to sponge Louis-Auguste's hands and face – no easy task, for he tossed and turned and tried to push her away, finally knocking the bowl over. She called a maid to wipe it up, and changed his saturated nightgown, tying his nightcap firmly in place. It was important to keep his head warm, she knew.

She gave Louis-Auguste a drink of sugar-water, and this time he drank it thirstily and then fell into a doze. Françoise's head ached, and she could feel the neuralgia she sometimes suffered on one side of her face – brought on by tension – beginning to throb. She asked the maid to bring her a drink of linseed tea, and she sipped it sitting by the side of Louis-Auguste. Outside she could hear the two little ones in the garden. It was going to be another hot day. She wondered where Nanon was. Probably she had gone into the village of Vaugirard to buy fresh vegetables.

By noon, when the younger children came up to the nursery to have their dinner and take a nap, Nanon had still not returned. Françoise wished she would hurry, for she had decided that if Louis-Auguste did not show some sign of improvement by the afternoon she would have to call the physician, and Nanon was the only one who knew the way to that distant district of Paris. Yet she hesitated, thinking of what Nanon had said: 'Don't let the doctors bleed him.' It was true, she knew, that bleeding seemed to achieve little save the weakening of the patient. She had seen that many times, when she had cared for Mme d'Albret's children when they were small, and the children of Mme de Montchevreuil, one of whose little ones had died as a result of the doctors' intervention. Mme de Montchevreuil had wept afterwards that she should never have allowed the physicians anywhere near him with their cures.

She tried to administer quinine tea to the child by feeding it to him on a small spoon, for he refused to drink the dark-coloured liquid. But she succeeded only in getting one or two spoonfuls into him. However, it seemed to have some effect, for he slept fitfully for half an hour or so. But she could see that there was no improvement in his condition, in fact quite the opposite; for his eyes, which that morning had been bright and feverish, were now clouded and lustreless, their normal blue-grey faded; and what frightened her most was that he did not seem to see her, though now and then he called her name and moaned.

At four o'clock she decided that a physician must be called. After all, she was not the parent of the child. She had to consider her responsibility, should the worst happen – she pushed back the hair from her forehead, and tried to think clearly. She would send the coachman for the doctor, she would write down the address, and though he could not read, surely he could find out where the house was.

As she sat down at her desk to write, she suddenly thought of Athenais. She must inform her of the child's illness. Athenais, who had gone to Vichy to take the cure after the birth of Louise-Françoise, had returned a few weeks ago. The Court had dispersed that summer, all the able-bodied men being away at the war. The Dauphin and his suite were at St Germain but Athenais, who loathed the country, had been at the Louvre awaiting the King's return from Holland. She would send a message to Athenais. Why had she not thought of that before?

She wrote two notes, one to Athenais and one to the doctor, and told the maid to send the coachman to her. But hearing a rattle of coach wheels outside, she went to the front of the house to look out, for her own windows overlooked the garden. There in the small courtyard stood a coach with the royal crest and

Nanon and two men she did not know were climbing out of it.

Nanon had had some difficulty in gaining admittance to Louis, for she could not write her name, and the sentries laughed and joked at the servant in her shawl and sabots who was asking for the King. But then the Maréchal d'Albret, passing on his way to a meeting of the Council, recognized her and asked her in surprise what she was doing at Vincennes. She told him that she had a message from Mme Scarron for the King. The Marshal looked surprised, but said nothing. He wrote the name of Mme Scarron on a piece of paper for her, and she handed it to the guard. He told her that he must not be late for his meeting, and he hoped she would be successful. He was deep in thought as he walked away. What business could Mme Scarron have to transact with the King?

Nanon's interview with the King was brief. She told him that Louis-Auguste was desperately ill, and he immediately summoned his personal physicians, told them to accompany her to this child, a relative of his, and do all that was possible to save him. They were to report to him personally that evening at the Louvre where he would be staying. They were Dr d'Aquin, the King's personal physician, and Dr Fagon, his assistant.

Françoise could scarcely believe that the King was actually in Paris and had sent his own doctors to care for Louis-Auguste. She took an immediate liking to d'Aquin, a fresh-faced middle-aged man with a genial manner. Fagon, however, impressed her as being a strange person. He was tall and painfully thin, his complexion was yellowish and unhealthy, and he hardly spoke. D'Aquin chatted away, immediately putting Françoise, who was under severe tension, at her ease. Everyone, including Nanon and Françoise, was asked to leave while they examined the child. Françoise and Nanon waited on the landing. Françoise sent all the servants, who had gathered in little groups, back to their business.

At last the doctors opened the door and called her in. Françoise gripped Nanon's arm tightly and they went into the room together. The doctors had spent some time pummelling Louis-Auguste about, and he was crying; Françoise bent to take him in her arms and tried to gather her courage to look up at the physicians.

'Is it smallpox, *monsieur le docteur*?'

271

Dr d'Aquin's expression was grave. Fagon, standing behind him, looked like some giant bird of prey, his scrawny black-robed limbs gaunt, his yellow face downcast and gloomy.

'It is not the pox, madame, but I fear it's a serious complaint,' Dr d'Aquin told Françoise. 'It's a debilitating fever which can have serious results.'

'Will he live, doctor?'

D'Aquin hesitated. Knowing the after-effect of this fever, he had often wondered if the survival of the patient were for the best.

'Oh, I'm optimistic, madame, knowing the excellent care you will take of him. We must remain hopeful – he will have the best nursing, and after that we must put our faith in God.'

Françoise nodded and crossed herself. 'What is his treatment to be, *monsieur le docteur*?'

The two men put their heads together and conversed seriously for a few moments. Louis-Auguste, silent now, lay with his head in Françoise's lap.

'He must be bled not less than twelve times in the next twenty-four hours, madame. After that, three times daily for a week.'

Françoise opened her mouth to protest, remembering Nanon's warnings against such treatment, but said nothing. What was the use of having the best doctors in France at the child's bedside if one did not obey their instructions?

D'Aquin continued his injunctions. 'A soothing balsam must be made up – I will give you the recipe – it should be rubbed on the affected parts, the aching limbs, and then blotting-paper applied firmly to them to take out the heat. You must administer antimony, as an emetic, twice a day, and the patient should also be given a purge.' Out of the corner of her eye, Françoise could see Nanon shaking her head vehemently.

'*C'est tout, monsieur?*' Françoise hoped she would be able to remember all these instructions.

Again the two doctors consulted. 'If he is in pain, you may relieve his sufferings with black drops, taken sparingly in liquid.'

Françoise's face was horror-stricken. What could that mean? D'Aquin patted her hand reassuringly. 'It's a mild opiate, madame, mixed with vinegar and sugar, which will alleviate his pain. He can take it in a drink, but with caution, remember. Not more than six drops in twenty-four hours, at the most.'

Dr Fagon took her arm and gently led her to the door. 'Send a maid to us, madame, with towels and a basin. It would be better if you were not present when we bleed him. I would not wish to cause you distress.' D'Aquin was already opening the black case he carried, and rummaging amongst his instruments. Françoise, with a backward glance at Louis-Auguste, who seemed to have lapsed into semi-consciousness, hurried from the room.

Louis-Auguste was ill for more than a month. After the first ten days of fever, when bouts of delirium alternated with periods of semi-consciousness, he seemed to relapse into a state of pathetic inertia, lying quite still in his bed, his face of an almost ghostly pallor. Françoise, who scarcely left his side, lost almost as much weight as her patient. Watching him one day as he slept, she noticed how thin he had become, his little face waxen and gaunt. But he had overcome the fever, that was the main thing, d'Aquin told her on his third visit.

'He will live, madame,' he told her, after a thorough examination. Fagon had not accompanied him on this visit. 'The fever has subsided, and now he needs only rest, good care and nourishment.'

Françoise felt ready to faint with the relief that swept over her. He was going to live. She held tightly to the corner-post of her bed. That afternoon, as she gently stroked his forehead, noticing how the skin was stretched tautly over his brow, showing the blue veins, he opened his eyes and recognized her.

'How are you, my darling?'

He stared up at her. His eyes still looked washed-out and grey. Outside, the sound of the children playing could be heard. He licked his dry lips.

'Would you like a drink, *mignon*?'

He nodded. She held the drink to his lips. He drank thirstily and looked at her with a piteous expression in his eyes.

'Does anything hurt you, my darling?'

'My head hurts, Tata, and my legs ache so – '

'My poor darling. But you're so much better now. The doctors say that soon you'll be playing outside again with Louis-César.'

'Can I watch him play, Tata?'

She hesitated. It was a warm day, the room was bathed in late September sunlight. On an impulse she drew back the covers, lifted him in her arms and carried him to the window. How light and thin he was! She could have sworn that he weighed less than little Louise-Françoise.

He looked out of the window, watching Louis-César running about with the ball and the cat, stumbling frequently over his long frock, and the baby kicking furiously, lying on a blanket in the shade of the apple tree at Nanon's side while Nanon industriously shelled peas into a basin. A vestige of a smile passed over his face as he watched the cat run in front of Louis-César and trip him up. Françoise carried him back to bed and covered him warmly.

It was impossible to make him take any nourishing food, however. Nanon made the most tempting soups for him, but he shook his head and turned his face away. Françoise attempted to feed him with the spoon, but she was reluctant to force him, and what he took he usually brought up again. Some days, he took a little bread soaked in milk, as he liked it; other days he would take nothing at all.

On the first day of October, Françoise was lying on her bed. Louis-Auguste was asleep. It was noon, and she could hear Nanon calling the children to come inside for dinner. Her head ached, and down one side of her face her neuralgia was throbbing, so that she was sorely tempted to take one of the black drops the doctors had prescribed for Louis-Auguste. But she knew that they were a sedative, in addition to being pain-relievers, and she did not want to sleep lest he should wake up and call her.

She was thinking about Athenais, and how strange it was that she should never have come to see her son during his illness. The King had called twice, and she knew that the doctors, who now came every other day, were instructed to give him full reports of the child's condition.

Louis-Auguste turned in his bed. He sat up, and she noted with joy that his pallor had lessened somewhat. After all, his complexion was normally pale; and his eyes were a little brighter than they had been since the first attack of fever had left him.

'What is it, my darling?' She lay with one hand pressed to her aching forehead.

'Can I look out of the window, Tata?' He was trying to climb out of bed. There was a chair standing by the window.

'Can you walk, darling?'

'Yes, I think so.' He started to limp, with painful slowness, across the floor to the window, which was slightly open.

'Don't lean out, *mignon*,' she called to him. 'Just kneel on the chair to watch your brother.' She sat up, suddenly alarmed as he limped across the room, and covered her mouth with her hand to suppress a gasp of horror. No, she had not been mistaken. One of his legs was about two inches shorter than the other.

Chapter Twenty-seven

In her rooms at the palace of the Louvre, Athenaïs de Montespan was twisting this way and that, admiring herself in front of the mirror.

The time at Vichy had certainly been well spent, she thought, gazing happily at her beautifully curved silhouette in her Court dress. *Mon Dieu!* What agonies women must endure for the sake of their looks! All that vile-tasting water to drink, which had made her feel ready to vomit – and at the unearthly hour of six in the morning, when the spring water was thought to be at its most beneficial. The sheer horror of standing in a muddy pool, naked as the day you were born, shielded from the onlookers only by screens, while a hose-pipe full of that nauseous water, boiling hot this time, was played by an attendant on the tenderest parts of your body. The only pleasure was that of retiring to the inn to spend the remainder of the day in bed, sweating copiously. And then, the so-called evening entertainment, the high spot of the day. She laughed contemptuously at the memory of a bunch of dirty gypsies dancing the *bourrée* with their cater-wauling flutes. She shuddered at the remembrance of it all. *Nom de Dieu!* What a relief it had been to return to the civilized pleasures of Paris!

But it had all been well worth while, she knew, admiring her reflection in the mirror. She was dressed in a stunning gown of crimson velvet, the bodice embroidered in silver and decorated with bows of silver braid, the low-cut neckline edged in silver lace. Monsieur Picaire, the *couturier*, had certainly excelled himself with this gown. Her shoes were of red velvet, embroidered in silver, and there was a matching cloak of red velvet lined with wolf-skin.

Her skin was fresh and creamy as ever, her blue eyes bright and glowing, and certainly she had never felt so well, so blooming with health and vigour. She would never regain the trim waistline of a year or two ago, but no matter; by dint of an iron corset it could be pulled into shape. Far more important that her legs and her behind were slim again, her belly as flat and smooth as it had ever been. She knew that she could certainly pass for twenty-six or so instead of thirty-four.

If only she could prevent herself from conceiving! Without informing Mme Voisin, whose potions she continued to take, she had also consulted a certain M. Galet, whose admirable powders, Armand swore to her, were taken by all the well-known ladies in Paris as a contraceptive.

'Why do you need to admire yourself so?' the young man lying across the bed called out to her. 'You know full well that you are the most beautiful woman at Court.'

Athenais laughed, and began to fasten a diamond necklace round her throat. 'Do you include your wife in that statement, monsieur?'

The young man blushed as he jumped off the bed and came to help her fasten the necklace.

'Here, let me do that,' he said. He buried his face in the softness of her neck and began to kiss her bosom. Athenais pushed him away.

'Not now, Charles. You'll disturb my dress.'

'A pox on your dress,' he murmured, taking her in his arms and kissing her passionately. She pushed him firmly off.

'No, Charles, not now. Aren't you ever satisfied?'

'Not with you, you little vixen,' he murmured, sitting disconsolately on the edge of the bed as she began to fix the tiny black patches on her face. She stood back to admire her handiwork. It only needed Lison to put the finishing touches to her hair, and she was ready.

'I liked better the patches you wore last night,' the young man said, and they both laughed. The notion had taken her to fix the little patches to the most intimate parts of her body, and they had both thoroughly enjoyed his search for them.

The door burst open, and Lison ran in, her face red and agitated. Athenais, quick as lightning, gave her a vicious cuff.

'How dare you burst in like that, you little . . .' Lison cowered back, her hand to her face.

'Madame – the King.'

'The King!' The young man leapt to his feet and stood stockstill with horror. Athenais looked frantically around the room.

'Make the bed, Lison!' The girl ran to the bed and hurriedly started to arrange it.

Athenais thought quickly, staring at Charles de Crespigny. She could not pass him off as her hairdresser or dressmaker, for he carried a sword and hat, and had too obvious an air of gentle birth about him. He was looking at her with an expression of such abject fear on his face that if she had not been in this predicament, she would have found it very funny.

'Say you're my cousin, Charles! Remember, my cousin!'

The King walked in, standing still in surprise as he saw the elegantly dressed young man lounging nonchalantly in a chair. Cold with fear, de Crespigny rose to his feet and bowed. Athenais turned from her mirror as if in surprise.

'Your Majesty!' She sank to her feet in a curtsy, and rose gracefully. 'May I present my cousin, Charles, Comte de Crespigny?'

The King's eyes took in the good-looking young man at a glance – no more than twenty, broad-shouldered, but with the handsome, finely drawn features which spoke unmistakably of nobility; and in the background Lison, assiduously making the bed at five o'clock in the afternoon. He gave a slight inclination of his head.

'Your Majesty.' The young man performed a graceful bow.

'Crespigny, you said?' The young man nodded. The King's memory for names and faces never failed him. So this was the young man Mme de Sévigné's niece had recently married. The one of whom she had remarked that even the best lands needed manuring from time to time, excusing the fact that his pedigree was less impressive than his father's wealth. 'Were you not recently married?' The wedding had taken place during the King's absence, but he made it his business to miss nothing that took place at Court or amongst Paris society.

The young man reddened guiltily. 'Yes, Sire.'

'And how is your charming wife?'

'Very well, Sire. She is already *enceinte*.'

So that explains it, thought Louis. So many women regarded pregnancy as an excellent excuse to keep a man from their bed. That was one accusation that could certainly never be levelled at Athenais. Watching her out of the corner of his eye, he could scarcely wonder that a woman of her mature years could nevertheless draw a young man away from a wife of only sixteen. She had never looked more lovely in all the years he had known her.

He sat down in the chair just vacated by de Crespigny and drew off his gloves, casting a meaningful glance at Lison who, recognizing his look, drew back the covers of the bed and left the room with a curtsy.

'Pray tell me, Crespigny, why did you not see service with the army this summer?'

The young man, embarrassed, fiddled with the hilt of his sword. He did not look at Athenais. 'I was – too young, Sire.' Athenais had the grace to blush.

'I see. What is your age, monsieur?' Louis decided to let him off lightly this time.

De Crespigny looked at the floor. 'Seventeen, Sire. But I was not yet seventeen when the regiment I am due to enter left Paris for the front.'

The King laughed. 'And are you now ready to join it, monsieur?'

The lad looked up eagerly. 'Oh yes, Sire.'

'Then I give you permission to do so, without waiting for the return of your commanding officer. You may leave for the front tomorrow.' That will teach her to play about with youngsters, he thought. Athenais' face was expressionless.

Crespigny was overjoyed. 'My humble thanks, Sire.' Then, conscious of the sudden silence: 'May I withdraw?'

Louis nodded his assent. The young man, with a bow to Athenais, hastily backed out of the royal presence, scarcely able to believe his good fortune.

As the door closed behind him, Louis and Athenais stared at each other in silence. Then Louis laughed uproariously, slapping his knee. 'Come over here, you baggage! Deflowering boys scarcely out of the cradle!'

She swayed provocatively over towards him, thanking her lucky stars that his mood was jovial. He stared at her, wondering what it was that was different about her. He realized that he had never seen her wear that colour before. How well it suited her. Suddenly he saw that her hair was different.

'You dyed your hair?' Formerly a glowing Titian colour, it was now a golden blonde, not silver-blonde like the Queen. It reminded him a little of the way Louise de la Vallière used to look, so fair, so lovely, all those years ago. But her hair was ash-blonde; this was a darker shade.

'Do you like it, Sire?' She looked at him anxiously.

He needed no time to consider. 'It's charming, and it suits you admirably.' All women with fair skins should have blonde hair, he thought. His own skin being dark and swarthy, there was nothing he admired more than a fine porcelain-like complexion in a woman. Athenais' skin was exquisitely fair, like that of all natural red-heads.

'I did it to please you, Sire,' she lied. After the birth of Louise-Françoise and the rigours of Vichy, she had been shocked to find her magnificent red hair showing streaks of grey. By the time she returned to Paris, it had lightened imperceptibly until very little of the former glorious red remained. Horrified, she had gone straight to Mme Voisin for advice, but no amount of powders or washing it in boiled lime-water until her head was sore had been able to restore its former glory. Armand the coiffeur, however, had made little of her despair.

'*C'est rien, Madame la Marquise*. Do not distress yourself! *C'est plus jolie qu'avant!*'

'Do you really think so, Armand?' she asked, doubtfully, trying to believe him.

'*Mais certainement, madame*. A little application of camomile is all it needs, to bring up the blonde lights! You will see, madame.' He took out a little phial of camomile powder, moistened it with spit and proceeded to brush it through her hair. 'And you know,' he added roguishly, looking at her slyly out of the corner of his little black eyes, '*que les hommes préfèrent les blondes – Voilà, madame!*'

Once she had become used to the new colour, she realized that not only did it in fact suit her admirably, but for the first time in her life she could successfully wear colours like scarlet, pink and lilac, which she had previously avoided. She had ordered dozens of dresses and negligées in these new colours, and was toying with the idea of having sheets for her bed dyed red, on which to achieve the maximum effect in displaying her rejuvenated figure. Armand had promised to procure some gold-dust and gold spangles with which he proposed to dress her hair. She could hardly wait to see the Queen's discomfiture when she appeared before her, looking lovelier and younger than ever. Maria Theresa, she well knew, had been including in her devotions for years a prayer that Athenais would begin to lose her attraction for the King.

Athenais, an inveterate snuff-taker, opened the tiny gold snuffbox Louis had given her, with a miniature of himself set in diamonds in the lid, and offered it to him. Louis hesitated. Fagon, his doctor, had forbidden him to take snuff on account of the severe headaches he suffered. However, after a summer spent away at the front he was feeling exceptionally fit; he had occasionally slept under canvas in a display of loyalty to his troops, and it had been a time of remarkable sexual abstinence, for he had been parted from Athenais now for more than five months. He took a pinch of the fine grey powder.

Athenais put her arms round his neck and, gently removing his wig, ran her fingers caressingly through his hair. The familiar smell of her perfume began to excite him. He had not realized how much he needed her physically. Slowly, deliberately, he ran his hand along the smooth curve of her leg. Under her gown she wore only red silk stockings, held up by lacy garters. He began to fumble at the fastenings of her dress. 'Damn these clothes,' he muttered. 'No man would ever have invented such things.' He began to kiss her passionately, searingly, tasting the cool moistness of her lips like a thirsty man staggering out of a desert.

As he buried his head in the smooth valley of her bosom, he tried to push aside the slight pang of conscience he felt, thinking of Maria Theresa and how gentle and loving she had been to him during the past few months, so ecstatic at having him to herself while Athenais was recovering from the birth of the baby and taking the cure at Vichy. Never once had she reproached him for subjecting her to the indignity of travelling with his pregnant mistress, nor for all the sorrow he had caused her since her marriage. All she had done was to weep broken-heartedly with him when the news was brought that five other countries, joined in their fear of the threat of the colossal and efficiently trained French army, and the growing might of Louis XIV, had joined against him on the side of Holland. There would be no triumphant entry into Amsterdam this year, nor perhaps for many a summer to come. She had sorrowed almost as much as he when the news came – solely on his account, he knew, for she cared nothing for the glory or the spoils of war.

Later, when he had lain in her arms, she had tried in her pathetic way to console him with her love, speaking tentatively in her appalling French. And all she had asked of him was that he should not allow Athenais de Montespan or other women to flaunt themselves in front of her – not for her own sake, but for that of their son, the Dauphin who, as she reminded him, was now twelve years old and at an impressionable age. Louis, in a highly emotional state, had broken down and wept himself, and had promised her that he was almost ready to settle down and become a faithful husband. He assured her that he had always loved her and revered her, despite his mistresses. She had taken the opportunity to put in a word for Louise, Duchesse de

Vaujours, that good sweet person whom he had made so unhappy; and he had delighted her by promising that on his return to Paris he would give his consent to her retirement from Court. Then, his head on her breast, he had slept like a child whilst she stroked his hair and murmured to him the comforting words of Spanish that reminded him of his mother.

'Shall Lison light the tapers?' Athenais asked him mockingly, knowing that he was becoming more and more aroused. The fire was low, and the candles had burned down, so that there was only the faintest glow of firelight and the candlelight reflected in the mirror.

She stood up and pretended to hold the unfastened dress modestly against her, carefully allowing the top to fall well below the full roundness of her breasts, thrusting up above the tightness of her stays to reveal the pink-tipped nipples. Her hair, disarranged by his caresses, tumbled down on to her shoulders in ripples of molten gold, and her lips were parted, still moist from his kisses.

She looked at him in the dim firelight, her lovely eyes glowing with inviting promise, a promise that he knew well would be more than fulfilled. She wanted him almost as much as he needed her – she had been merely amusing herself with young Crespigny – but she knew how to play the game of love.

For answer, he rose and threw the dress to the floor as he pressed her down upon the bed, his body, hard and lean, demanding what she knew well how to give. The familiar heavy perfume she always used rose like a cloud to envelop him in its embrace as her arms went round him and drew him down. The crimson dress lay like a pool upon the floor as the candles burned down in the silent room.

She knew just how much excitement to demand from him, and just when to capitulate, so that when he finally took her it seemed as if it was for the first time.

Afterwards, as they lay in each other's arms, spent from the ecstasy of love, they talked in low voices of their long separation. Athenais told Louis that her husband, the Marquis de Montespan, had been bothering her again, appearing at Court and berating her as an unfaithful wife, threatening to bring her eight-year-old son, d'Antin, to witness his mother's degradation. Louis frowned. The man was a thorough nuisance. It was time he accepted the fact that his wife was lost to him. He decided to banish him to the West Indies.

Lison tapped tentatively at the door.

'Let her light the candles,' Louis said. 'It must be nearly seven.' He rose and pulled on his breeches and shirt. Athenais wrapped herself in her pink satin dressing-gown trimmed with ermine, and called to the girl to enter.

The girl scurried round lighting the tapers and making up the fire. After she left, Athenais sat down before the mirror and began to inspect her face and hair. She gave a faint sigh. All the powder, paint and patches would have to be renewed. No matter – Louis had sorely missed her, she knew that. Gilles Légaré, the Court jeweller, had told her a few days ago that Louis had asked him to re-cut the famous Hope diamond, a magnificent blue diamond recently discovered in India and weighing more than one hundred carats, into a heart-shaped stone suitable for a lady to wear. She felt confident that it would be Louis' New Year gift to her. She smiled into the mirror, well pleased with herself.

'By the way,' Louis said to her, as he pulled on his stockings and shoes. 'Did you know that little Louis-Auguste was ill?'

She shrugged, carefully applying her powder with a hare's foot. 'I believe Madame Scarron wrote to me about it.'

Louis looked at her incredulously. Any maternal feeling had been completely left out of her make-up, he thought. He remembered Françoise Scarron's face when he had told her, a day or two ago, what he was about to tell Athenais now.

'I have decided to legitimize the children,' he said, 'and bring them to live at Court. I do not wish my children to remain hidden any longer.' Since Louis-Auguste's illness he had definitely decided on this course of action, which he had been considering for some time.

Athenais did not turn away from the mirror. Once his mention of this idea had frightened her. Now, secure in his passion for her, it did not even interest her. Carefully she applied small pieces of red Spanish paper to colour her cheeks. He waited a moment, but she was not sufficiently interested to ask him anything further. He thought of Françoise Scarron, who had all but fainted when he told her, on his visit to Louis-Auguste two days before, that he intended to take the children away from Vaugirard. He had seen the effort she made to prevent herself from collapsing, the tears that came into her eyes, the ashen pallor of her face.

'All the children, Sire?' she had asked tremulously, clenching her hands in the material of her skirt.

'All of them. But you will suffer no financial loss, madame.

Your salary will continue to be paid.'

She seemed not to hear him. She made an effort to speak.

'Shall – shall I be allowed to visit Louis-Auguste?' she asked. 'I think – that he may wish to see me.' Will he remember me? she was asking herself. He was only three years old. In a year's time, she thought, he will have forgotten me completely.

Louis took pity on her. 'You will accompany them, of course, madame.' He thought he had never seen anything more lovely than the light in those black eyes of hers.

'I, monsieur?' In her agitation she forgot to address him as Sire.

'Of course. You are their governess, are you not? You will continue to care for them as you have always done, at Court instead of in this house.'

He would never forget the luminous beauty of her face as she thanked him.

The house was to be closed down and the servants dismissed at the end of the year, and they would move into the Louvre immediately after the decree of legitimization, which would become legal some time in December. She had asked him only if she might bring Nanon, to which he had agreed.

'She will soon find another post,' said Athenais, who had been listening with only half an ear. She stood up and let her dressing-gown fall to the floor. Louis looked at that lovely naked body, the dancing firelight casting shadows on the shape she was no longer afraid to reveal before him, and held out his arms to her. She came to stand in front of him, and he snuggled his face in the softness of her belly, his hands going round her to caress the smooth contours of her bottom. The faint aroma of the aftermath of his love and the sweat exuded from their two bodies rose in his nostrils, and he pushed her away.

'Get away from me, you whore,' he swore at her, and slapped her rump as he picked up his coat and sword, and put on his wig in front of the mirror. She laughed as she rang the bell for a lackey to light the King back to his own apartments.

PART IV

THE SUN
IN SPLENDOUR

1674-1683

Chapter Twenty-eight

On New Year's Day, 1674, following the King's decree of legitimization, Louis-Auguste, Duc du Maine, Louis-César, Comte de Vexin, and Louise-Françoise, Mademoiselle de Nantes, went to live at the Court of France together with their governess, Mme Scarron.

When Athenais found out that Louis intended bringing Françoise to Court she was at first furious. She was rapidly becoming sick to death of his constant references to Françoise, and the way she frequently figured in his conversation. But after a while she decided to bury her annoyance. After all, it was better that he amused himself harmlessly in the nursery with the children and their governess, than that he took an interest in other women.

Fortunately, however high his opinion of Françoise Scarron and her skill in looking after children, there was no danger of his developing an attachment for *that* virginal figure – always dressed in mourning for the cripple she had been pleased to call her husband. Françoise was three years older than Louis, almost as pious as the Queen and la Vallière, and never seen wearing a gown cut any lower than her collar-bone. And because she did not approve of the reckless gambling that took place, and the licentious and dissolute atmosphere of the Court entertainments, Françoise rarely attended the *Appartements*, save for the occasions when a play was to be presented.

Louis, on his occasional visits to the nursery, began to look forward to discussing Molière's and Racine's newest plays with Mme Scarron. Not since poor Minette died had there been anyone with whom he could discuss the theatre. Shy at first in his presence, Françoise soon proved herself to be an intelligent and entertaining conversationalist. Louis, who always preferred an amusing remark or a wry comment to an outright joke, particularly enjoyed her sense of humour, so similar to his own.

With the approach of Lent a slightly more solemn atmosphere began to pervade the Court. Louise de la Vallière came to Louis one day after Mass and, throwing herself at his feet, begged his leave to retire from Court and enter the Carmelite convent, to expiate there her sins of adultery and the procreation of illegitimate children.

Louis looked at her lovely face, now so pale and joyless, those innocent blue eyes that once had held him in their thrall, now sunken and cold. There was no life, no spirit, in her movements. She was like a living statue. Strange that this woman, with whom he had once, long ago, known such joy, meant nothing to him any longer. Deeply moved at the reality of her vocation, he gave her his consent. In April of that year, Louise de la Vallière, Duchesse de Vaujours, cut off her still beautiful ash-blonde hair, said farewell to her children and to all who knew her and, as Soeur Louise de la Miséricorde, passed through the gates of the convent in the rue St Jacques to take the veil of the enclosed order of the Carmelites. She was to remain there, in strict seclusion and performing continual mortification of the flesh, for the remaining thirty-six years of her life.

At the *Appartements* that evening, all the talk was of the beautiful Duchess now turned nun; but by Easter, when the Court moved to St Germain for the summer, she was completely forgotten.

Here, Françoise and Nanon had been given two large rooms in the suite of Athenais de Montespan, on the ground floor of the chateau, overlooking the southern terrace. The children were deliriously happy – though it grieved Françoise deeply to see Louis-Auguste struggling, with his poor shortened leg, to keep up with his younger brother. Little Louise toddled after him as fast as her fat little legs would carry her.

'Is there no treatment possible to restore his leg to normal?' Françoise asked Dr d'Aquin when he called in at the nursery one day to see Louis-Auguste.

D'Aquin shook his head gravely. 'I fear not, madame. I am afraid you ask for too much. We are fortunate to have saved him from the terrible illness which he suffered.'

That was true, as Françoise knew, but nevertheless she was not convinced that nothing further could be done for the child of the most powerful man in Europe. She spent some time reading the medical books in the vast library of the chateau, but was able to glean little information from them that could help her.

Dr Fagon, who also took an interest in the subject, and had more modern ideas on the practice of medicine than d'Aquin, suggested one day to Françoise that it might be possible to try to elongate the weakened leg by pulling on it with a rack. At first Françoise was not happy about the idea, but the more she watched poor Louis-Auguste limping, unable to run and play, the more she began to favour the plan. She mentioned it to the King one day.

Louis looked at her anxiously. 'Will this be painful for the child, madame? I should not like him to undergo more suffering than he has already.'

Françoise swallowed. Fagon had already told her that it would indeed be painful. It was the first question she had asked him.

'I believe that it will not be without discomfort for him, Your Majesty,' she replied.

'And do you think that he should be subjected to such an ordeal?'

'I am as reluctant as yourself, Sire, to see him suffer, but I am of the opinion that the child's future must be our prime consideration. To see him walk properly as an adult, and as a credit to Your Majesty, is my only desire.'

Louis followed the direction of her gaze. Outside in the gardens Louis-Auguste sat disconsolately on the stone steps leading down to the terrace, watching Louis-César and his little sister chasing the doves and throwing stones at the cat they had brought with them from Vaugirard.

'We may give it a trial,' said Louis. 'If the child suffers too much, the treatment must be discontinued.'

Françoise could not bear to stay in the room with him while the leg was being treated. Nanon remained to hold his hand and listen to his screams, while Françoise waited outside, covering her ears to blot out his cries. After a month, she could bear it no longer. Dr Fagon was told to abandon the treatment.

Louis, who was leaving for the Netherlands frontier for the summer campaigns, came to the nursery unexpectedly one morning to say goodbye to the children, and, though he would never have admitted it, to Françoise Scarron. Louis-Auguste pleaded with his father to take him with him to the wars. Louis, holding the child in his arms, explained to him smilingly that as yet he was a little too young to fight for France.

'Thank you for all you have done for him, madame,' he said,

taking Françoise's hand as he rose to leave. 'When I return from the war, I shall see about making you a suitable reward.'

Françoise, blushing deeply, shook her head. 'You owe me nothing, Sire.' Her dark eyes were earnestly sincere as she looked up at him. 'Whatever I have done,' she insisted, 'has been solely out of love for Louis-Auguste, and from no other motive, I assure you.'

The King's eyes also revealed his emotion as he murmured: 'You have no need to convince me of that, madame.' She watched, deeply moved, as he kissed the three children goodbye. They were as parents, so deeply involved with these children.

Athenais rarely visited the nursery. 'Who is that lovely lady?' Louis-César had demanded of Françoise one day in the gardens of the castle, as they watched a group of courtiers pass by, including Athenais, holding court amongst her admirers. Françoise and Nanon had looked at each other, not knowing what to say. They had hurried the children indoors, declaring that it was time for their rest. Since his illness Louis-Auguste also took a rest each day after dinner.

The King, remembering something, turned back from the door where the Captain of the Guard awaited him.

'You will not fail to write to me, keeping me acquainted with the children's doings?' he reminded her. Her letters were a pleasant diversion from the problems of war. Françoise gave her promise.

After the royal party had departed for Flanders – only Athenais and the Queen sharing the King's coach this time, since the Duchess of Vaujours had departed – there seemed to be an emptiness and dullness at St Germain. Françoise realized that the emotional strain and stress of the past two years, particularly Louis-Auguste's illness, had left her utterly exhausted, both mentally and physically. But she had had another idea for the improvement of Louis-Auguste's health. She wrote to the King asking him what he thought of Louis-Auguste making the journey to a spa or watering-place, such as Vichy or Bourbon, for the sake of his health. Louis wrote back that he considered it an excellent plan, but that he thought this year the child was a little too young to make such a journey. *Perhaps next year, or the year after*, he wrote, *we can make such an arrangement. In the meantime, I commend him to your care, for I know that your love for him is not less than mine.*

In the autumn of that year, when the King and his party

returned from the frontier, Athenais de Montespan became pregnant once more.

A year later, resting in her apartments at the Louvre, Athenais was wondering how she could rid herself of Françoise Scarron.

She was beginning to find the presence of Françoise at Court a positive thorn in her side. The woman irritated her beyond endurance with her constant fussing over the children's health. She seemed determined to make an invalid out of Louis-Auguste, pampering and cosseting him until he imagined himself frail and delicate, just because he had been ill last winter. No doubt his leg would heal fully, all in good time. She herself had always enjoyed excellent health, as had the King. What reason was there to suppose that their children should be any different? And Louis was beginning to fall into the habit of spending the hour between two and three, when the Council met, in the nursery, playing with the children and chatting to Françoise Scarron. This was the hour which in former years he had spent with *her*, so that she now had him to herself only between six and seven, and at night, after he had taken supper with the Queen and before he retired to Maria Theresa's bed, as was his invariable custom.

She frowned with concentration, wondering how she could dismiss Françoise without antagonizing the King. It would be futile summarily to dismiss her; that brat Louis-Auguste would immediately set up a howl if she took such a step. Françoise Scarron had taken good care to see that she was indispensable to the child by pandering to his every whim – and Louis would refuse his favourite child nothing. The King now spent some time every day in the company of Louis-Auguste, thoroughly enjoying his bright, precocious chatter, while he visited the dull and stolid Dauphin scarcely once a week.

No, there must be a more subtle way of ridding herself of the woman. How she cursed herself for ever having been instrumental in bringing her to the King's notice. She had nothing to fear, she knew, from Françoise's physical attractions, or rather, she thought, the lack of them. Louis was beginning to tire of the pretty young virgins he had often bedded, maids and recent arrivals at Court. She had good reason to know that the physical satisfactions he demanded could only be provided by an experienced courtesan. She smiled contentedly, thinking of his ardour the previous night, when he had not returned to the

Queen's apartments until three in the morning, four hours after the official ceremony of the King's *coucher*. No, there was little reason to suppose that he would ever be attracted by an old maid like Françoise Scarron, married woman though she pretended to be. Everyone knew that her marriage had existed only on a piece of paper.

She moved slightly, causing Lison, sitting by the bedside manicuring her nails, to dig the emery board slightly into her hand. She gave the girl a cuff that sent her flying across the room.

'And how is the lovely Marquise today?' asked a male voice from the doorway. She started up in terror – surely it could not be the King at this hour? Her hair was thick with the camomile powder Armand the hairdresser had given her – he was coming soon to rinse and style her hair – and her face was liberally plastered with a grey balsam which he had sworn would erase the fine lines beginning to appear near her eyes. She sighed with relief as the tall rangy figure of her brother appeared round the door.

'Oh, it's you, Vivonne. I thought it was His Majesty.'

'A thousand pardons for your disappointment. However, you look scarcely fit to receive the King.'

'The King is in Council,' Athenais said with some asperity. 'What business have you here, Vivonne? If you have come here merely to plague me . . .'

'Oho! The King's mistress is now too high and mighty to exchange a few civil words with her brother. Don't forget who helped to put you where you now are, *ma petite soeur.*'

'Oh, nonsense, Vivonne. I required your assistance only to borrow money, which, as you well know, has been more than repaid.'

Vivonne smiled. He had to admit the truth of that statement. He was the Commander-General of the French Navy and their father was now Governor of Paris. Their sister, the Abbesse de Thianges, had been given the wealthy abbey of Fontevrault. Yes, Athenais had certainly not neglected the welfare of her family.

'How is my nephew d'Antin?' he asked, thinking of her little boy whom he had been fond of as an infant. 'I have not seen him for an age.'

Athenais shrugged. 'Oh, well enough, I suppose.' She had not seen him for six years, ever since she had first seduced the King. His grandmother was paid a handsome pension for his upkeep.

She walked over to the mirror and looked with dismay at the slight bulge of her stomach under her velvet dressing-gown. What could be keeping the masseuse? She threw a hairbrush at Lison in a temper. 'Where's that masseuse?' she roared at her. The masseuse was coming to give her her daily friction rub with perfumed spirits, to persuade her stomach back into shape, flabby again after the birth of the little girl in June. If these measures failed, she would have to expose herself to the rigours of Vichy or Bourbon once more. She shuddered at the thought.

'Make up the fire, you slut!' she screamed at Lison. It was freezing cold in the room. The chill gusts of October wind swept relentlessly along the stone corridors, and draughts blew through the cracks in the windows. The Louvre was hundreds of years old, but Louis was not interested in spending money on its upkeep while that accursed place out in the country was costing him a fortune – Athenais knew it was his intention that the Court should one day reside permanently at Versailles. Not me! she thought; I'll be retired and living in luxury at Clagny by then; no one's going to bury me alive in the country! She had been the King's mistress for more than six years now, and had borne him five children. How long could it be before he was attracted by a younger woman? She was nothing if not realistic. She knew that the time must soon come when Louis would tire of her. If she were to fall pregnant yet again, and he began to weary of his cosy chats with Françoise Scarron . . . There were so many beautiful women here at Court, scheming to attract the King as once she had done. But she consoled herself with the thought that she had enough money and jewels salted away to keep her in luxury for the rest of her life, not to mention the numerous church benefices and other sources of income she had managed to wheedle out of the King in his good moods.

Vivonne was stretched out in the chair warming his feet by the fire. 'Did you hear what I said to you, sister?'

'No, I did not. You'll have to go in a moment. The masseuse must arrive soon. The King will be here at five o'clock today. Get out and go and look for her.' She pushed Lison out of the door.

'I told you I was getting married, Athenais.'

She stared at him. Vivonne married? It was unbelievable. He was almost as fond of variety in his women as the King himself. She had seen Louis glancing often at one of her women, Mlle des Oeillets, and knew that he was quite capable of bedding her in the antechamber if she kept him waiting. That was why she was so anxious to be ready for him.

'Yes, at Christmas. Didn't think I had it in me, did you?'

She certainly did not. The girl must have a fortune. 'Who is she?'

'Oh, a pretty young thing, the daughter of the Baron Lamoignon.' The Lamoignons were the owners of the neighbouring estates of the Mortemarts.

'How old is she?'

'Fifteen. She will be sixteen by the time the wedding takes place.'

Athenais sniffed. 'What has this to do with me? I congratulate you and I'll give you fifty thousand livres as a wedding present.' In addition to the huge sums of money she received from the King from time to time, she was a reckless gambler, with a lucky streak. She often won large sums at the card tables, to the despair of those whose need was greater than hers.

There was a tap at the door. It must be the masseuse. 'Now will you please leave?'

'Shall you attend the wedding, my dear sister?'

She looked at him incredulously. Travel to the Auvergne in the depths of winter, a journey of some six weeks, there and back? Was he insane? 'I'm afraid the King would not like me to be so long away from his side.'

Vivonne laughed. 'Don't you mean you are afraid to leave him for so long? I don't blame you. Your time must be nearly up.' He ducked to avoid the candlestick she hurled at him. 'Well, if you change your mind my bride will be happy to make your acquaintance – your son d'Antin also, no doubt.' He went out and she threw off her dressing-gown and lay down on the bed, shivering, as the masseuse made her preparations. Then she quickly pulled up the sheet to cover herself as Vivonne put his head round the door once more.

'And how is your friend the virtuous widow Scarron? I hear that the King is constantly in her company. Perhaps a King may be able to obtain what a mere viscount could not?'

Athenais' expression was thoughtful as the masseuse began her work.

Louis did not return to the Louvre that night. He had gone out hunting with Madame, and they had covered such a distance that he decided to spend the night at St Cloud, Monsieur's country seat, and ride over from there to see how the work was progressing at Versailles the next morning. He sent word to Athenais that she should join him at Versailles in the afternoon, in order to inspect the rooms which were newly completed, for he appreciated her excellent taste in choosing furnishing materials and hangings.

Athenais groaned at the prospect of a journey out to the country on a cold day, but there was no help for it. However she took advantage of Louis' absence that evening to avenge herself on poor Maria Theresa, who had recently cold-shouldered her in public. She swept across the gaming-room that night directly in front of her, without so much as a glance, much less a curtsy, in the Queen's direction. Maria Theresa hurried to her oratory, where she spent some time in floods of tears at her rival's blatant public humiliation of her.

Without the King's restraining presence at her shoulder, Athenais remained in the card room gambling until the early hours of the morning, leaving the card tables the richer by thirty thousand livres. The next morning, returning from Mass, Françoise found her still asleep when she brought her a cup of hot chocolate.

'Athenais!' She shook her to wake her. 'You must be at Versailles at two o'clock. Hurry!'

Athenais rolled over and it took Françoise nearly five minutes to wake her thoroughly. At last she sat up and grumpily drank her chocolate, blinking at the bright sunlight that streamed into the room. Little Louis-César came bounding in and jumped up to kiss her, spilling the cup with its remaining contents on to her nightdress. She pushed him away with a curse, and he ran to Françoise and buried his head in her lap.

At last she got up and shouted to Lison to come and dress her. Françoise sat in the room chatting to her, while the children took their dinner in the nursery.

'My brother Vivonne asked to be remembered to you,' Athenais said. 'He is to be married soon.'

Françoise was delighted. She would never forget Vivonne's help and kindness to her at Chantilly. 'Really? I am happy to hear it. Who is the bride to be?'

'The daughter of the Baron whose estate adjoins my father's.'

'And shall you attend the festivities?'

'I might.' Athenais sat down at her dressing-table to apply her make-up. Concentrating on the powder and rouge, she was not listening attentively to Françoise. She glared at the bright sunlight reflecting on the mirror. It would be a sunny day; Louis would no doubt insist on walking her round and round the gardens of Versailles. How she loathed those gardens with their endless walks, the gravel paths that hurt her feet through the soles of her dainty shoes! Bright sunshine made her eyes ache. In any case, she never felt at her best before five in the afternoon. The dim candlelit evening atmosphere was much more her *ambiance*. She rose and allowed Lison to fasten her sable bracelets. Thank goodness for her new sable cloak, trimmed with ermine; if only her shoes were as warm.

'How long shall you be away?' asked Françoise, idly making conversation.

Athenais looked at her sharply. Was there anything in what Vivonne had said?

'Perhaps I shall take Louis-Auguste with me,' she said, out of sheer desire to shake Françoise out of her complacency. She was not disappointed by the look of consternation that appeared on Françoise's face.

'Surely you would not take him on such a long journey in the wintertime,' she said, aghast. 'You know how delicate he is.'

'Stuff and nonsense!' Until this moment she had had no intention of even going herself. Now, seeing Françoise's outrage, she decided to put her in her place once and for all. Whose children were they, after all? 'The child's in perfect health,' she said. 'You mollycoddle him, that's all.'

'You know that's not true,' Françoise protested. 'He catches colds at the slightest thing, you know that, and sore throats. And he walks with such difficulty . . . You can't be serious.'

Athenais brushed aside her protests. Suddenly the idea of making her appearance at the wedding, weighed down by furs and diamonds, completely outshining the young bride, and holding the hand of the King's son, greatly appealed to her. She would persuade the King to lend her the Sancy diamond for the occasion. It was an almond-shaped stone, which was part of the Crown Jewels, worth more than 600,000 livres.

She put on her cloak and told Lison to have her coach brought to the entrance. 'You forget my relatives have not yet seen the child,' she remarked.

Nor you your son d'Antin, for the past six years, thought Françoise, but she knew that there was nothing to be gained by antagonizing Athenais. 'If you must take one of the children,' she pleaded, 'why not Louis-César? He's so much stronger than his brother. Perhaps next year you could take Louis-Auguste.'

The two women stared at each other in uneasy silence. Both knew that next year, when Louis-Auguste would probably be short-clothed and in breeches, his limp would be far more pronounced than at the moment, disguised as it was by petticoats.

'I've made up my mind,' said Athenais; and as she swept out in a cloud of perfumed furs, Françoise's heart sank. Once Athenais made up her mind about anything there would be some difficulty in persuading her to change it. But for the sake of Louis-Auguste's health, Françoise was determined to prevent her taking him on this winter journey. In addition to the impediment of his shortened leg, he was extremely delicate, prone not only to colds, but also to skin blemishes and abscesses in extremes of hot or cold weather. To be imprisoned in a draughty coach for days on end would be the worst possible thing for him.

She said as much to the King on his visit to the nursery the next day. Louis looked acutely uncomfortable. He knew what Françoise said was true, but Athenais had already told him that Françoise was becoming shrewish, spinsterish, and jealous of the children's affection for their real mother, and that she resented her taking away her own son to see his relatives for a short visit. When Louis had tried to point out the dangers of a winter journey for a delicate child, she was able to play her trump card: 'Who can take care of him better than his own mother?'

There was no answer to that. Louis was forced to overcome his better judgement. Besides, he was becoming involved in an affair with the Comtesse de Soubise, a charming red-head with a white skin and green eyes who had taken to wearing emerald ear-rings to advise him when her husband was out of Paris. He was not at all averse to Athenais' being away from Court for a few weeks.

Athenais left the Louvre for the Auvergne on November 20th. Françoise shed bitter tears on being parted from Louis-Auguste. It was the first time they had ever been separated for more than a few hours since he was born. She had spent the last month knitting and crocheting him warm woollen stockings to wear on the journey under his flannel frocks, and woolly caps and mufflers. Wrapped in blankets so that he could scarcely move, he sat in the coach next to his mother, trying to blink back his tears. Everyone told him that the lovely lady in diamonds and furs was his mother. Why then did he cry at being parted from his

297

beloved Tata and Nanon? Manfully he clenched his lips together, said goodbye dutifully to them all, Louis-César, Louise-Françoise and the baby. Then the coach clattered out of the cobbled court-yard of the Louvre. Louis had said goodbye to him in the nursery early that morning, before he left for a meeting. He had bid him be obedient to his mother so that she would be able to give a good report of him on their return, and he had promised.

'But, Your Majesty,' he had said to Louis, his pale face looking up at his father in wonderment. 'If you the King are my father, why is the Queen not my mother?'

There was no easy answer to that one. Louis, clasping this dear little son to his chest as he kissed him goodbye, resolved to lead a more orderly life in future, for the sake of his children.

Chapter Twenty-nine

With the departure of Athenais for the Auvergne, however, and her return not expected before January, Louis soon found that his good resolutions were short-lived. The Comtesse de Soubise, Mlle de Ludres and many others were constantly vying for his attention. A man would have to be made of stone to resist their wiles, thought Louis that evening at the *Appartements* as he gazed round at the women – like tropical humming-birds in their brightly-coloured dresses. There was one particularly lovely young girl, Mlle de Fontanges, who had a face like an angel. More than once his attention strayed to her and she, aware of it, hid her face shyly behind her fan. She was only eighteen.

'Why do you not attend the *Appartements* this evening, madame?' he asked Françoise Scarron the next afternoon when he visited the nursery before going out hunting.

Françoise did not know what to say. She loathed gambling, excessive drinking, idle chatter and unkind gossip. Conversation between close friends who knew each other well was one thing, but the vicious slanders that passed for conversation at Court were another matter altogether. She decided to be perfectly honest.

'Do you not find, Sire, the chit-chat and gossip of the Court somewhat inconsequential?'

Louis looked at her in amazement. She really was an astonishing woman, he thought. Her deep attachment to the children had long surprised him; for some time he had been under the impression that her care for them was purely for the sake of obeying his wishes, and for the handsome salary she received. Ever since Louis-Auguste's serious illness, however, he had known that it was nothing of the kind; that she loved Louis-Auguste to distraction, more than his mother ever would. Not for the first time, he found himself wondering what it would be like to be loved with such devotion. Athenais' affections, he well knew, would disappear overnight, like snow in sunshine, if he were suddenly to become an ordinary mortal and not the Sun King.

'I find it excessively boring, on occasion,' he confessed, 'but I am the host here. I cannot withdraw at my pleasure.'

Françoise wished he would go. She was longing to write a letter to Louis-Auguste. To change the subject she began to tell him of a shoemaker she had found, who thought he could construct a special shoe with a built-up sole which would make walking easier for the child. Louis listened with interest, and told her to spare no expense in bringing the shoemaker to Court immediately. 'What a pity the child has already left,' he said. 'We could have measured him before he went.

'Tell me, madame,' he asked her. 'You neither hunt nor gamble, nor care for gossip. Then how do you pass your time?'

'I read, I write letters, I listen to music, Sire. I enjoy the gardens in summer and I am fond of the play, as you know. I like to knit and crochet, embroider, and work at tapestry. But most of all, I am happy to chat and play with Louis-Auguste. He is a very intelligent child, Sire. He must be well educated, for I am sure he could achieve great things.'

Louis was delighted with her assessment of his son. 'Tell me, madame, has he no faults?'

Françoise considered. 'He is a little too quick in discernment, perhaps, for a child, but that will stand him in good stead as he grows older. He does not like to be thwarted in his desires.' In that, he takes after his father, she thought.

Louis laughed, slapping his knee. 'Let us hope that he will not have to be.'

Time slipped by imperceptibly when he was talking to Françoise Scarron. It was four o'clock by the time he left her room, too late to go out to hunt.

When Athenais and Louis-Auguste returned to Court early in the New Year, Françoise was bitterly grieved at the child's appearance. He had apparently been ill almost the whole time they were away, and Athenais, with no idea of how to deal with a sick child, had left him to his own devices. His hair needed washing and trimming, his lips were chapped and sore, he seemed to have a permanently runny nose and his limp was more pronounced than ever. In addition, he had lost weight.

Françoise wondered how Athenais still managed to keep her firm hold on the King's affections. Not having seen her for some weeks, and looking at her now with fresh eyes, she noticed that despite the efforts of her *corsetière* Athenais' figure was rapidly thickening, her enviably fine complexion beginning to coarsen and line. There were dark shadows under her eyes, and tiny brown spots had begun to appear on the backs of her hands – though Lison had rubbed and scrubbed them with every kind of cream and powder Mme Voisin and M. Galet could prescribe. She ate and drank to excess, gambled and danced away the night until the early hours – and Louis always glanced to see that she was in her place in chapel the next morning. The hour she tried to snatch for a rest after lunch was usually the time when Louis paid his visit to her apartment, before the Council meeting. Even her once glorious hair was now dyed to conceal its patchiness, the faded colour streaked with grey.

There were so many pretty young girls at Court whose one prayer was that the gaze of the Sun King might fall upon them; Françoise was at a loss to understand his insatiable appetite for the charms of Athenais. Yet she was glad of it, for the thought had more than once crossed her mind that, if it were not so, his sexual needs might have been focused on herself. This was not to say he did not dabble in other waters. But for conversation and friendship he continued to depend upon his visits to Françoise's apartments, and for the rest, to those of Athenais.

Athenais had left Lison behind at Court for the sole purpose of repeating to her when she returned everything that had taken place in her absence. Accordingly, Lison reported that the King and Françoise Scarron were as thick as thieves, though the back-stairs gossip was that his nocturnal and private visits had been paid to the Comtesse de Soubise and Mlle de Ludres.

Athenais paid no attention to these last two. Soubise was in her late thirties, with ten children, and Mlle de Ludres was a fool. She was much more concerned at the amount of time Louis was beginning to spend with Françoise Scarron, on the pretext of visiting his children. *Her* children! she thought, with a sense of outrage. And Françoise's calm serenity irritated Athenais beyond endurance. It seemed to matter to her not one jot that people deliberately snubbed her, patronized her or made sneering remarks in her hearing about her lack of a husband or protector, that she had no jewellery worth speaking of, that her clothes were so simple. Françoise, when she attended the *Appartements*, would simply sit in her usual place in the least draughty corner of the gallery, well away from the doorways where the crowds strolled and promenaded to and fro all evening to see and be seen, and there watch the passing parade with only a polite show of interest. The women who had spent hours dressing themselves in their most expensive and uncomfortable finery were driven nearly to distraction when, as he did almost every evening when she was there, Louis made a point of passing near to where Françoise sat in her plain black dress and, turning, made one of his courtliest bows in her direction.

Was it possible to find a husband for her? Athenais thought in desperation. But she was over forty now, without a fortune, and an old spinster if ever there was one. Who on earth would want her, unless they were paid well enough? She decided on another plan.

'Madame Scarron is devoted to the children, isn't she?' she said to Louis one afternoon as they were lying on her bed. It was five o'clock – there had been no Council meeting that day and the King had come straight to her from the nursery.

'Indeed she is,' Louis said. 'We have ample cause to be grateful to her.'

It was just what she had hoped he would say. She sat up, drawing a wrap round her naked shoulders. 'Do you not consider she should receive some reward, Sire, for all she has done?'

Louis considered. 'She has been well paid, but if you feel . . .'

'I was thinking, Sire, of something a little more tangible. She has no home or parents, as you may know.'

'A house, or estate, for Mme Scarron?'

'Do you not think she has deserved it?'

'Indeed I do. I am delighted that you brought it to my notice. She must be provided with an estate for her eventual retirement.'

Athenais was in seventh heaven when Louis made Françoise a gift of 200,000 livres with which to purchase the chateau and estate of Maintenon. It could only be a matter of time now before Françoise asked leave to retire there. Françoise had never made any secret of the fact that she disliked Court life intensely; and there were servants galore to take care of the children, now that their legitimization had made it unnecessary to hide them away. Soon Athenais would be rid of her and the old battle-axe, Nanon, for good. Mme de Maintenon she had begun to call herself now instead of Mme Scarron! What airs the woman gave herself!

Françoise's happiness, when the purchase of the estate was concluded, knew no bounds. She did indeed, as Athenais had hoped, begin to consider her retirement. But that would mean leaving Louis-Auguste. Besides, the other children were growing up and were strongly attached to her. She knew that, on her departure, they would be well cared for, but there would be no one whatsoever to take a real interest in them. Strangely enough, poor Maria Theresa, pining for her own lost little ones, sometimes visited the nursery, and admired the children growing up there so fine and sturdy – with the exception of the wraith-like Louis-Auguste.

Françoise worried terribly about him. With the approach of spring, she asked Louis if he would consent to let her take the child to a spa for a cure. The King agreed. It was heart-rending to compare the frail and limping Louis-Auguste, now six years old, with his chubby younger brother, and little sisters. And so, to Athenais' fury, Françoise, instead of retiring to her estate at Maintenon as Athenais had planned, announced her intention of taking Louis-Auguste away with her. At least, Athenais consoled herself, she would be rid of her for a while, if not permanently. Françoise made plans to leave on April 1st for Barèges, a watering-place in the south of France. With some trepidation, she asked the Queen if she would keep an eye on the welfare of the little ones in her absence, knowing that she could not depend on Athenais. The King would be departing for the front, to inspect the fortifications, this time leaving the Queen behind. Fortunately Maria Theresa agreed.

When Françoise and Nanon returned with Louis-Auguste from the south of France in August, he had never looked so well. He had gained weight, he had a brighter colour, his pinched cheeks had filled out, and best of all, his limp had considerably improved; with the aid of the special shoe Françoise had had made for him, it was barely perceptible. She had taken great care to teach him to carry himself well, his shoulders square, and had impressed on him that his bearing must show that he was the King's son. Also she had pointed out to him that the better his deportment, the less his limp would show. Soon he would be dressing in breeches like a man. But although this last thought gave Françoise a great deal of pleasure, it was mixed with sadness, for when the boy was breeched it meant that he would be taken away from the care of the women and given a tutor.

Louis, when he arrived at St Germain in September, was thrilled when he saw the improvement in his son's condition. Even Maria Theresa commented on it. Louis began to think of selecting his tutor. He was determined that, though the boy must be well educated, he should not be tutored as sternly as the Dauphin had been. The severity of the Dauphin's upbringing had made him dour, silent and withdrawn, reluctant to speak in company, too mindful of the beatings he had had in the school-room for saying the wrong thing.

One day in November the King came into the nursery at St Germain. The Court was preparing to make the winter move to the Louvre, but Louis, enjoying the wolf-hunting, had postponed it as long as possible – much to the annoyance of Athenais.

'Your Majesty.' Françoise sank into a deep curtsy. She wondered what had brought him here before Mass.

The children ran to him and climbed on his lap, but he pushed them firmly away. 'Not now, *mes enfants*.' Françoise made a signal to Nanon, who took them into the next room. She wondered what the King had to say to her.

'Madame de Maintenon!' It was the first time he had referred to her by that name. From that moment, Mme Scarron existed no more. 'Here is a trifle, in recognition of your services to my son.'

Françoise stared in amazement as Louis brought from his pocket a crucifix made of large, evenly-matched pearls, hanging on a chain of diamonds. It was worth a fortune. Françoise, who disliked ostentatious jewellery, and wore only her wedding pearls and sometimes a cameo brooch, was so embarrassed she did not know what to say.

'I know that your taste is restrained,' Louis was saying. Impossible to imagine Françoise decked out in the showy *parures* of diamonds and emeralds Athenais loved so much. For that reason he had chosen this piece with care, imagining that it would appeal to her. He eyed her high-collared black dress with irritation. Why did she still dress in widow's weeds? She had a good figure, and he guessed her to be only in her early thirties. In fact, she had now turned forty.

'Why does Madame de Maintenon wear mourning?' he said. She knew what he meant. Since Mme Scarron no longer existed, there was no longer a necessity to wear the dark colours of widowhood. She blushed with embarrassment. How could she possibly decline such a generous gift, made with such kindness? Yet she knew that she would never wear it. She gave an inward sigh at the thought of what it must have cost. Enough to feed the starving families of Paris for several winters.

'Your Majesty is more than generous,' she said; she looked down apologetically at her black dress. 'I have always dressed in dark colours.' Many years ago, before her marriage, her dresses

304

had been made over from the discarded habits of the nuns who, feeling sorry for the beautiful and pious young girl in their care, had made clothes for her.

'There is no longer any need,' he said, slipping the jewel over her head. The large pearls, glowing and lustrous against the black bodice of her dress, were exquisite, it could not be denied. 'You are young and beautiful, madame.'

She blushed furiously as his eyes took in her figure. She was slimmer than Athenais, he noted. He thought that he would like to see her in a low-necked dress. She bent to kiss his extended hand, and he saw how the dark curls clustered on the back of her neck. He could smell the freshness of her scent, Hungary water, light and fragrant, not the sickly, cloying perfumes Athenais so liked. There was something about this woman, he thought, which invigorated him; the stimulation of her conversation, the positive work she had done for his son, her pleasant but not overpowering aura of femininity. Athenais exhausted him completely. The sexual excesses in which he indulged with her were giving him blinding headaches, and he was suffering uncharacteristic attacks of lassitude and dizziness. Hunting, an activity he loved, was becoming something of an effort.

'Let us see you in Court dress this evening, at the concert,' he said. She knew that he meant her to abandon her high-necked dresses. She could not resist a smile at the thought of the draughts she would have to suffer, for alone amongst the women at Court she put her comfort before the fashionable effect of her clothes.

A gasp went up when Françoise appeared at the concert in the Galerie du Bal that evening. There had been no time to have a new dress made, so she and Nanon had been forced to spend the afternoon remodelling a gown she had worn last winter, of a soft green velvet. It had, as had all her dresses, a high neck; Nanon had cut it away, and then, having nothing else to trim it with at such short notice, they had unpicked the white ermine trimming from her new winter cloak and used it to edge the gown's neck and sleeves. Pleased with her appearance when the magnificent pearl crucifix was fastened, Françoise had asked Lison to modernize her hair-style, and the girl had skilfully parted her long dark hair in the middle, brushing it firmly away from her forehead but softening the whole effect by coiling clusters of ringlets to hang down at each side of her face.

There were murmurs amongst the men, furious prattlings and speculation amongst the ladies at Mme de Maintenon's changed appearance – and most of all at the priceless jewel she wore, which could be a gift from only one person. Maria Theresa smiled and complimented Françoise on her appearance. She thoroughly liked Françoise de Maintenon, knowing her to be a kind, gentle person, devoted to children who were not her own. On the other side of the King Athenais glowered and brooded behind her fan.

As the courtiers were taking their places for the start of the concert the King went over to Mme de Maintenon and, taking her hand, drew her forward to a better seat just below where he sat with the Queen and Athenais. Amongst the audience, bets were being rapidly made on how soon Mme de Maintenon would replace the Marquise de Montespan as the King's mistress.

Chapter Thirty

That summer of 1677 Françoise had been hoping to gain the King's permission to take Louis-Auguste to the south of France once more. The King, however, who was not journeying to the Flemish front that year, declined, saying that he wished the child to remain at Court with him. Perhaps next summer they might be allowed to make the journey.

Françoise was disappointed, for now that Louis-Auguste was short-clothed, in breeches, and given over to the care of his tutor, she saw much less of him than she would have liked, though she went to his room every day to bid him good morning. Fortunately the King had selected for his tutor M. de Montchevreuil, an old friend of hers, so her mind was at ease – for the child, though so much improved in health, tired easily. M. de Montchevreuil understood the need not to overtire him, and allowed him to rest each day after dinner. In one way she was glad that he was no longer in her care, for he was beginning to understand his ambiguous position at Court and ask why the sentries did not salute him as they did his half-brother, the Dauphin.

With the approach of Lent, Athenaïs de Montespan had gone to make her Easter confession. To her fury, however, the priest refused to give her absolution.

'What, the Madame de Montespan who is scandalizing the whole of France, openly living with a married man, having abandoned her own husband and son; and who has given birth to several children without God's holy ordinance? Go, madame, and truly repent. Resolve to abandon your evil way of life. Then, and only then, can I give you God's forgiveness for your sins.'

Seething with rage, Athenaïs went straight to Louis who, she felt sure, would have the priest not only unfrocked but banished for such insolence. But Louis, who had also been constantly reproached by his confessor for his sins of blatant adultery, was in penitent mood. His mother, Anne of Austria, had been a devout and pious Catholic, as was his wife. Louis himself paid only lip-service to his faith, but however much he might scoff at the devotions of the pious, he could not totally dismiss from his mind visions of hell-fire and eternal damnation. He told Athenaïs that they would have to separate – only temporarily, he assured her. He sent her to her estate at Clagny, and both accordingly made their Easter confessions, vowed to abstain henceforth from sins of the flesh, and were duly absolved.

By the end of May, however, Louis decided that he could manage no longer without the presence of his sensual mistress, though in her absence his frequent attacks of migraine and dizzy spells had seemed to improve. Nevertheless, to the despair of his confessor he invited Athenais to visit Versailles for the day.

The meeting between the two erstwhile lovers was to take place in public, so that the proprieties could be observed. The King and Athenais greeted each other warmly, but with restraint, before a crowd of approving onlookers in the Grande Galerie, the older ladies beaming with approval as Athenais, with a charming show of modesty, curtsied demurely and respectfully kissed the King's hand.

The former lovers drew close to a window-seat where they chatted amicably for some few minutes, still in full view of the Court. Then, to the utter consternation of the assembly, they both bowed politely to the company and withdrew to a near-by anteroom, a pair of Swiss Guards being immediately summoned to stand before the doors. There the pair remained closeted for something like half an hour. Nine months later, exactly to the day, Louis-Alexandre, the future Comte de Toulouse, was born. Those who had thought the long rule of la Montespan over, had perforce to accept Athenais' spectacular return, flamboyantly dressed and bejewelled as always, and, with Lent behind him for another year, the King more in love with her than ever.

Françoise in particular was grieved at the triumphant return of Athenais, for her heart bled for the poor Queen, whose happiness when Athenais was sent away from Court had been transparently obvious. It was a severe blow to her when la Montespan wormed her way back. Though she was at a loss to explain it even to herself, Françoise also felt a sense of outrage at this latest pregnancy.

When the new baby was born, however, Françoise positively refused to take charge of the child.

'How dare you speak to me like this!' raged Athenais, when informed of her refusal. 'Who brought you to Court and placed you in high favour with the King? Would you have your chateau and your estate of Maintenon if it were not for me?'

Françoise thought longingly of her beloved chateau of

Maintenon; since it first became hers, she had scarcely managed to spend more than a few days at a time there. One or other of the children always seemed to have a cold or a sore throat, and besides, she took their schooling very seriously. Louis-César was not as bright a pupil as Louis-Auguste had been. At the age of six he hardly knew his letters. Little Louise-Françoise, at four, was brighter than he was.

'I'm sorry,' she said. 'I can no longer be a party to the sufferings of the Queen. She has had to endure too much on your account, and I refuse to be instrumental in these affairs once more.'

'What business is it of yours, may I ask?' Athenais demanded. 'Perhaps you would like the King for yourself? Jealousy is a hard taskmaster.'

Françoise knew it was useless to have a rational discussion with Athenais. She left the room, merely remarking as she did so that under no circumstances would she be prepared to care for the new baby.

Louis, whom Athenais had thought would be enraged by Françoise's refusal to comply with his wishes, merely bit his lip when she reported it, and after a moment's consideration replied that no doubt Mme de Louvois could be persuaded to care for the baby. He added, however, that Françoise's refusal disappointed him, for he had great confidence in her abilities and good sense.

Louis was beginning to detect a certain coolness in Françoise's conversations with him. In order to talk to her quietly, without the children or Nanon in the background, and certainly without Athenais, he sent for her to come to his apartment one morning. Athenais sulked and glowered when the message came. Never in all her years as Louis' mistress had she ever visited his private apartment, since that first night at the Louvre.

Françoise, wondering what business the King could have with her, stood obediently as Louis first discussed the weather, then his migraine, then the children's health. Then he invited her to rest herself on a folding stool, a *tabouret*, and looking at her earnestly, said without preamble: 'How is it that you have never remarried, madame?'

Françoise was astonished. What on earth could have brought him to ask such a question? Nervously, she fingered the pearl crucifix he had given her while she considered the question. At last she said simply: 'The occasion seems never to have arisen, Your Majesty.'

'How was that, madame?'

'The years have passed so quickly, Sire. I seem to have been always occupied, and have never given it much thought.'

Always caring for others, thought Louis. The Queen had told him of the work Françoise had done for the nuns when she was living in the rue des Tournelles. Before that she had been tied to a crippled husband when only in her twenties.

'But you are a lovely young woman. There must have been many men who took an interest in you?'

Françoise burst out laughing. She was thinking of the courtier to whom Athenais had promised a fortune last year if he would marry Françoise Scarron and take her away from Court. 'I did have an offer last year,' she told him.

The King was immediately interested. 'And you refused? May I enquire who the – ?'

When she said the Duc de Villars Brancas, he joined in her laughter. The Duke had been married three times, was nearly seventy and had only one leg. However, Louis was not to be diverted from his theme. 'But it is not too late for you to marry,' he reminded her. 'You are still on the right side of forty' – Françoise did not correct him – 'still able to have children of your own.' He looked at her piercingly but she showed no sign of emotion. 'Would you not like to have a child of your own?' he asked her.

'May I speak freely, Sire?'

'Of course, madame.'

'Ever since Louis-Auguste was born, he has been as my own child. I have never needed any other. The other children, too, I love dearly.'

'But there is still the matter of your future to consider. You have no family, I believe. When you wish to retire from Court ... The children are growing and the day may come ...'

Was this an indirect request for her to retire to her estate? 'You have provided for me handsomely, Sire. The estate of Maintenon brings me in eleven thousand livres yearly.' She decided to broach to him a matter which had been in her thoughts for some time. 'Sire, there is something on which I should be glad of your opinion.'

'And what is that?'

'There is an old disused barn on my estate at Maintenon. With your permission, Sire, I should like to have it made habitable at my own expense.'

'For what purpose, madame?'

'To organize a small school, Sire, for the village children, that they may learn to read and write.'

Louis looked at her in blank amazement. This woman never ceased to astonish him! Athenais' only interest in life was gambling the fortune she extracted from him in order to win more money.

'And who would instruct the pupils?' he asked her in amusement.

'Myself, Sire. As you have just said, I must begin to think about my retirement from Court.'

Louis was not pleased at the turn the conversation had taken. He realized that he had no wish to lose her. 'You may stay on at Court for as long as you wish. In any case, I am speaking of the future – another five years, perhaps.'

'With respect, Sire, I should not wish to remain at Court for the rest of my life.'

'And why is that?'

'Because, Sire, with the exception of Your Majesty, of course, your ministers, and a few others, the people here are whiling away their lives, fulfilling no useful purpose. For myself, I despise an indolent existence; living only for pleasure is in no way rewarding. My wish would be to make use of the brains and abilities, if any, which God has given me, in the service of others. One finds true reward in this life only by helping others.'

Although these had been her feelings for some time now, Françoise found herself realizing for the first time how much she would miss her conversations with the King. Fond of Nanon though she was, the woman was uneducated, and no real companion. Now that Louis-Auguste had left the nursery, she was deprived of the greater part of his company. Would it be lonely, she wondered with a slight feeling of unease, living alone in the beautiful chateau of Maintenon?

Louis walked over to the window and looked out. Louis-Auguste and his tutor, M. de Montchevreuil, were strolling in the courtyard below. His son wore a green and gold brocade coat over his green velvet breeches, his light brown curls, under his hat of green velvet, tied with ribbons. Wearing the shoes Françoise had had made for him, his limp was scarcely noticeable. He carried himself well, as she had always impressed upon him, and his deportment was as regal as that of a King's son should be.

'Do you remember my mother?' he asked Françoise, suddenly turning to face her.

'I remember her well by sight, Sire, for I saw her drive through Paris; but I never had the honour of conversing with her.'

How much this woman reminded him of his mother – in her calm good sense, her acceptance of the inevitable, her devotion to the welfare of others. Was she not born a Huguenot? Although she did not attend Mass every day, in her way of life she was a truly pious woman. Athenais could give him release from his insatiable physical desires – but only in the company of this woman did he feel at peace.

'When her lying-in is ended,' he said, 'I think Madame la Marquise de Montespan may retire to Clagny.'

She looked at him, startled. Why was he telling her this? It was news to Athenais, that she knew.

He took her hands in his. 'Françoise,' he said. 'I think I am beginning to fall in love with you.' It was the first time he had called her by her name.

She took a step back and looked at her feet, blushing to the roots of her hair with embarrassment. He came forward and took her in his arms. She tried to step backwards and free herself – the only woman in his entire life, he thought with amusement, who had ever tried to release herself from his embrace.

'Françoise,' he murmured, his lips seeking hers. 'Don't turn your head away.' He saw that her eyes were full of tears. 'Kiss me, little one,' he said. 'I love you so much.'

'You must not speak to me so, Sire.'

'I love you, Françoise.'

'You have no right to speak so!'

He looked at her in amazement, surprised at the sharpness of her tone. 'Have I not just told you I intend to part from Athenais?'

'It is not that, Sire.'

Again he took her hands. 'From now on,' he told her, 'I wish you to call me by my name, in private, of course.'

Françoise looked at him in silence. She had no intention of either doing that or of ever being alone with him again, if she could help it. She certainly did not intend to become one of the many women with whom he passed an odd night when the inclination took him.

'Then what worries you, my dear? Please tell me – I want to make you happy.'

She hesitated. 'What is it?' he urged her. 'Will you not allow

312

me to love you?' he added smilingly. There had never been a woman yet who had been able to resist him.

'No, Sire, I cannot allow it.'

'I have told you that Athenais and I will soon part. You may take her place, and live in even greater luxury than she has done.' He knew, however, that Athenais' way of life, her jewels, her furs, her extravagances and her gambling, had no appeal for Françoise. 'How can I make you love me?' he said. 'Have you no affection for me at all?'

'Indeed I have, Sire.'

'Then what is it that holds you back?' He was genuinely puzzled.

He was like a naughty child, Françoise thought, unable to understand what he had done wrong. Hesitantly she said: 'The Queen, Sire. The Queen is very unhappy.'

Maria Theresa had been unhappy since the days of la Vallière, at Fontainebleau so long ago, thought Louis. It was too late to change that now. He said as much to Françoise.

'But it isn't too late, even now, Sire. She loves you desperately, and suffers much on your account. Can't you try to make her happy?'

Could it be possible? thought Louis. The first woman to whom he had ever professed his love since his childhood sweetheart, Marie Mancini – and she not only spurned his protestations but sent him back to his wife!

'It isn't possible,' Louis said, 'for me to love my wife wholeheartedly. I am fond of her, as I would be of my daughter, but Athenais has been my wife for several years now. Only recently have I discovered that my true affections belong to someone else.' He looked at her meaningfully.

'She loves you so, Sire. And she has been so unfortunate, losing so many babies – you both have. But a woman feels these things more. She has nothing else here in France if you do not love her.'

'I do love her, with a sincere affection. But not in the way I love you. Because her command of French is so limited I cannot have a genuine conversation with her, for one thing.'

'Sire, I know that for a man of your nature it isn't possible to refrain from loving other women – but could you not keep these affairs secret from the Queen? These women' – she did not name Athenais – 'flaunt themselves in front of her and cause her untold distress. Surely you would not wish her to suffer so.'

313

'Indeed, I don't,' he said. 'But I can't pretend to love her in the way that you would like.'

'Why not, Sire? Why can't you pretend, and make her a truly happy woman?'

He took her hands again and regarded her with a mocking smile. He longed to kiss her, but would not subject himself to the indignity of being refused.

'If I endeavour to make the Queen a happy woman, will you render me the same service?'

Françoise lowered her eyes. Never had she felt so uncomfortable and embarrassed. How was it possible to have a conversation on such a subject with the King, whose word was law? She decided not to beat about the bush, but to be straightforward with him.

'I cannot – return your affections, Sire, conscious though I am of the honour you have paid me, while the Queen is alive.'

Louis could not help laughing ruefully. Why was this woman different from every other woman alive? No other woman would have lost the chance of accepting his love – on condition that Athenais left Court. But all Françoise could talk about was the Queen!

Françoise backed nervously towards the door. 'May I withdraw, Sire?'

After she had gone Louis sat for some time staring into the fire, deep in thought.

Françoise, once in her own room, sat down on her bed and covered her face with her hands. How much of an effort it had cost her to reject Louis' declaration of love and send him back to his wife, he would never know. Once, long ago, she had thought that she would never be able to return a man's love. Now that she knew there was a man to whom she longed to give herself freely, her ingrained sense of decency and honour would not allow her to follow her heart.

Was it her fate always to be on the wrong side of the wall, watching other people's happiness through a window? Or would the day ever come when she, Françoise, would be able to grasp at happiness with both hands?

Nanon, coming to the door with a cup of hot chocolate, hesitated for a moment, and then stole quietly away, leaving her mistress sobbing as if her heart would break.

Chapter Thirty-one

Christmas and New Year passed in a frenzy of entertainments at the redesigned chateau of Versailles, which Louis intended shortly to make the permanent residence of the Court.

Everyone at Court was talking about the renewed attention that the King was paying to the Queen. There was speculation that la Montespan's downfall was imminent – and would be permanent this time, for soon Lent would be approaching again. Instead of Mme de Maintenon, however, who at one time had looked all set to take the place of la Montespan in the King's affections, Louis seemed to have rediscovered his wife.

Maria Theresa was happier than she had been since the earliest days of her marriage. Louis had told her how much he appreciated all that she had suffered on account of Athenais, and that in future he would not allow the Marquise de Montespan to flaunt herself before his wife. The Queen was to have an apartment next to his own at the palace of Versailles, which the whole of Europe was talking about – all gilt and marble, and facing south so that the sunshine constantly filled the rooms and reminded her of the Spanish sun. She even began to hope that she might carry another child.

Françoise, delighted at the effect her words had had, began actively planning her retirement. The school had been built at Maintenon, and the pupils selected. She intended to leave Court in the summer, after her return from Barèges. Louis had given her permission to take Louis-Auguste there for six weeks. She had not dared tell him yet, however, of her intention of leaving Court.

The journey to Barèges took nearly two months, jolting in the sun over roads of rutted mud, and – much to Louis-Auguste's delight – a week's travelling by river, when the coach was driven on board a barge, fixed in place and the horses taken off. They ate from a plank thrust through the windows of the coach. Louis-Auguste was in seventh heaven.

At last they arrived at the little watering-place near the Pyrenees. The two local inns had been taken for the King's son and his suite, his governess, his doctor and a dozen servants. Françoise looked forward to spending a couple of days in bed recovering from the journey. Louis-Auguste, on the other hand, had never looked better. She thought with delight that they would not need to make this trip again. His limp was improving with every year that passed, and he was becoming an excellent rider.

Immediately on their arrival Françoise ordered a copper bath to be sent up to her room. This caused great consternation, for no such luxury was to be found in the whole of the village of Barèges. At last, however, a large wooden bath was obtained and Françoise, who had had the forethought to bring her own supplies of soap with her, was able to bathe away the dust and grime of the journey.

Louis-Auguste, freshly bathed and in his nightclothes, lay in bed in the room they shared, excitedly chattering about how he and Dr Fagon were going to take a walk along the seashore the next day. Françoise was hardly listening; she was writing a note to Nanon to let her know that they had arrived safely. Two Swiss Guards who had accompanied them were waiting to start the long return journey with the message.

In the morning Dr Fagon, as agreed, took his young charge for the promised walk. Françoise lay in bed, dozing fitfully, looking forward to the weeks they were to spend here in this quiet place. How good it was to leave the scurry and bustle of Court behind, with all its frenzied entertainments and constant changes of clothes. She had brought only two or three plain cotton gowns with her, a large shady hat and a parasol, and was resolved to dress in nothing finer for the whole of her stay. She intended to spend her time catching up on the many books and plays she had had no time to read in the last year or two, and to write long letters to the friends whom she had so sorely neglected of late – Ninon de l'Enclos, Mme de Sévigné and Mme d'Albret. About twelve months ago she had invited Mme de Sévigné and Mme de Coulanges, together with Mme d'Heudicourt, to visit her at Court but, seeing the luxury of her new surroundings, and the respect with which she was treated by the King and Queen, her friends had not felt free to laugh and joke as they had done in the old days. The conversation was forced and stilted, and she had not been sorry when they left.

'Tata!' Louis-Auguste burst in through the door. His face was flushed with the fresh air and the exertion of the walk. 'Look what we found!' His hands were full of seashells. 'Look, I brought these pretty ones for you. Can we make them into a necklace, do you think? Do get up, Tata,' the child pleaded. 'It's wonderful to see the sea! Do come and look! Please, Tata.'

She could not resist his pleas. 'All right,' she agreed. 'Run along while I dress. See if dinner is ready. Then afterwards I'll come along and see your sea.'

Just as they were ready to leave the inn, a little after two o'clock, the inn-keeper handed two letters to Dr Fagon. He turned to Françoise with a bow. 'This one is for you, Madame de Maintenon. The King has written to us both.' He also had a letter.

Françoise took the letter he handed to her and looked at it in some surprise – seeing that it was not from the King, but written in Nanon's poor, mis-spelt, blotchy handwriting. Françoise knew that writing well; she had spent long hours teaching Nanon to read and write, but she had been forced to admit that Nanon made a better cook and needlewoman than she would ever make a scholar.

She opened the letter, mystified. Surely one of the children could not be ill already? But she remembered that the journey had taken almost two months. Anything could have happened in that time.

Return at once, Nanon had written in her shaky, scarcely legible hand. *The King needs you*. Nothing else.

Françoise could not understand it. If one of the children were ill, why had Nanon not said so? And if it were not one of the children, what other possible reason could there be for her return to Court?

Much to the disappointment of Louis-Auguste, she gave the orders to leave Barèges the next day. Throughout the long, wearisome journey back to Paris she puzzled endlessly over Nanon's letter. Could the King himself be ill? But then why did Nanon not say so?

It was the end of July when they arrived back at Court, Françoise so wearied from the interminable journey that all she longed for was to sleep in her own bed. It was there, in the privacy of her room, that Nanon told her that while she had been away a certain Mme Voisin had been arrested, a low fortune-teller and abortionist, on charges of administering and selling poisons. This same lady was also charged with other unspeakable practices, namely conducting Black Masses over the bodies of abducted, murdered newborn babies. And one of la Voisin's most prominent clients was said to be Athenais de Montespan.

The children in the nursery were overjoyed to see their dear Tata back again. Françoise asked M. de Montchevreuil to take Louis-Auguste on outings in the carriage to make up for his disappointment in leaving the seaside so abruptly. Louis-César was also ready, at the age of seven, to go into breeches like his brother and leave his long frocks and the nursery behind. Françoise could not help shedding some tears on parting with him. She promised him that she would come to the rooms he was to share with his brother, the Duc du Maine, every day, and warned him that he must get used to being referred to by his title, Comte de Vexin.

After the two boys had gone out with their tutor, Françoise and Nanon sat talking in low voices while the little ones played at their feet. Louise-Françoise, now five, wanted to know why she could not also go on a ride with the boys. 'Because I need you to help look after the little ones,' Nanon told her. These were Françoise-Marie, now toddling about, and the baby, Louis-Alexandre, whom Mme Louvois had brought to see his sister.

Françoise asked Nanon to tell her all she knew about the horrific scandal which had blown up whilst she was away. But Nanon could say very little.

'This la Voisin woman's a crony of that witch Brinvilliers,' she told her mistress. Mme Brinvilliers had been burned at the stake in the Place de Grève the year before, accused of poisoning several of her relatives. The Brinvilliers affair had been the talk of Paris for months, for it was rumoured that she had not only dealt in poisons and other unsavoury medicines, but had assisted a great many ladies well known in society to rid themselves of unwanted husbands or abort their babies. But there had been many sighs of relief when no names of aristocrats were brought into the open. 'This affair, however, promises to be different. La Voisin's threatening that if she goes to the stake, a great many well-known names will go with her,' Nanon reported.

'What names does she mention?' Françoise asked.

'Why, it's not only la Voisin, but her daughter. She's threatening to name' – Nanon looked round cautiously, but there were only themselves and the children in the room – 'not only Mme de Montespan, but Mme de Polignac, the Comtesse de Soissons and even the Duchesse de Vivonne – '

Athenais' little sister-in-law, not yet twenty, involved in such unsavoury business? Surely not?

'There's reputed to have been a wonderful trade in poisons and other medicines, madame, which make sure a patient will not recover.'

Françoise was thinking about the sudden death of poor little Minette, Monsieur's first wife, the angelically beautiful Mlle de Fontanges, and one or two other people, less well known, who had died suddenly in the past year or two without apparent cause.

'And what part is Mme de Montespan supposed to have played in all this?'

Again Nanon looked round, and lowered her voice.

'She's known to have given the King various love-philtres, madame.' So that explained the King's suffering from migraine and dizzy spells over the past few years, which mysteriously improved whenever he was away from her!

'But that's not all, madame,' Nanon continued. 'She's said to have had a Black Mass said on several occasions, sacrificing a newborn baby; and to have taken part in pagan rites.'

Why? Why? Why should Athenais de Montespan, young, beautiful, rich, with a magnificent house, jewels and furs such as most women could only dream of, and the love of the handsome Louis XIV – why should she do such things?

'She's said to have importuned the Devil to let the Queen die, or the King put her away from him, and take her as his wife.'

Françoise put her hand to her head. She felt ill. Poor little Maria Theresa! If all this scandal had not come out now, probably she also would have died mysteriously within the next few months.

'I don't want to hear any more, Nanon. Oh – but only this – where is Mme de Montespan now?'

'No one knows, madame. She took everything and left here the same day that la Voisin was arrested, a week after you left for the south.'

Françoise went to lie down, instructing Nanon to let no one disturb her. She tossed and turned on her bed, unable to sleep, thoughts of Athenais and the vile practices in which she must have indulged haunting her mind. As Nanon tip-toed in and placed a drink of sage tea by her bed, Françoise said to her: 'Where's Lison, Nanon? Did she go with Mme de Montespan?'

'No, madame. She ran away the night before la Voisin was arrested. She must have got wind of it. Do you remember Mlle des Oeillets?'

Françoise tried to think. 'Wasn't that the pretty maid of Athenais' – she had red hair also, I think?'

'*Oui, madame*. She's had a child by the King, madame, and she poisoned it the week it was born. She's been arrested, too.'

Françoise stayed in bed for the rest of the day. Nanon, who brought her some supper that evening which she would not eat, told her of the talk that was going on. 'There's great speculation, mistress, as to where Mme de Montespan's gone. Some say she's gone to Clagny, others say she'll have left the country if she knows what's good for her. There's bets being placed, madame, on whether the King will see the mother of his children burnt at the stake.'

'Go away, Nanon! I don't want to hear any more.'

She could not sleep that night. In the morning she had a raging headache and her neuralgia was troubling her, but she took an opium drop in a drink of tea, and after bathing her head with scented water told Nanon that she was going to the boys' room to say good morning to them, as she had promised Louis-César she would.

When she returned to her own room Nanon was dressing the younger children to take them outside to play. She wondered whether the King would come to see them. M. de Montchevreuil had told her that the King had not appeared in public for several days now.

'Not even in chapel?'

'I believe he is hearing Mass in his own apartments, madame. He and the Queen are deeply shocked by this business, as you can guess.'

Françoise wondered whether she should ask to see the King. Although she had resolved never to be alone with him again, she knew how bitterly shocked and upset he must be at this terrible business; the Queen also. As she was wondering what to do, a message arrived from Louis, asking her to come to him. Wearily she put her hand to her head. Her migraine was positively throbbing. All she longed to do was lie down and sleep.

Quickly she tidied her hair and accompanied the messenger to the King's apartments. Louis was sitting in a chair by the window, moodily staring at the designs for the gardens of Versailles he had taken such pleasure in creating. The footman bowed and closed the door. Louis motioned to Françoise to come forward. He signalled to her to be seated on the *tabouret*, which she obediently did

'Have you heard of this terrible business, madame?' he said, turning to look at her.

She was shocked at the change in him since she had left. Now turned forty himself, he looked more like a man in his fifties; his face, normally swarthy and ruddy from the open-air exercise of which he was so fond, was pale and haggard, his features tired and drawn. He looked as if he had not left his room for days – which indeed he had not. He had not donned his wig this morning, and his own hair, once so dark and luxuriant, was now thin and streaked with grey. He seemed to have lost weight, and his whole attitude – not erect and tense as usual, but his body slumped in the chair with an air of hopeless lassitude – spoke of a man who has received a severe shock.

'I have heard something of it,' Françoise admitted. 'Are you quite well, Sire?'

'I am well enough. But this business has revolted me. I cannot stomach it.' He turned his face away. She suspected that tears had come into his eyes.

'Is it – is it true, Sire, about Athenais?'

'I don't know yet. I think so. There are many witnesses, apparently, who can swear – ' He covered his face with his hands. After a moment he recovered himself. 'How is the boy, madame?'

'He is in excellent health, Sire. You'll be delighted with him. Will you not see him? He will cheer you.'

Louis shook his head. 'No. I do not wish him to see me like this. Perhaps in a day or two.'

'How is the Queen, Sire?'

'She is as deeply shocked as I am. But she has begged me to show clemency towards la Marquise de Montespan and to remember that she has given birth to my children. I don't know what to think.'

Françoise did not know what to say. After a few minutes, he reached out and took her hand.

'How are you, my dear? How good it is to see you! I am in a pitiable state without you, as you can see!'

'You must try to pull yourself together, Sire,' Françoise said. 'This is indeed a sorry business. But the law must take its course, and if Athenais is indeed guilty you will have the authority to mitigate her sentence. But who knows if it will all prove to be true in a court of law? You know, Sire, how such wild rumours spread – there may be nothing in it.'

'No,' Louis said. He rose and stood looking out of the window.

'Those perfumes that she always used – the snuff she gave me – they were all aphrodisiacs. You know how I have suffered from migraine, and felt unwell from time to time. There is no question but that she has dabbled in this business. She was known to be a regular client of la Voisin.'

'Perhaps only to buy perfumes, Sire?'

He could not help smiling at her innocence. 'She hated her pregnancies and confinements. God knows how many others she and la Voisin have aborted.'

Françoise was thoughtful. Now everyone knew the methods Athenais had used to keep Louis at her side for ten years in the face of competition from younger women.

She came to stand by his side. 'Is there any help I can give you, Sire?'

He put his arms on her shoulders and considered. 'Yes,' he said at length. 'You can tell me that you are as glad to be back at Court as I am to have you here.'

He put his arms round her and drew her slowly towards him, seeking her lips, and this time, she found herself wholeheartedly returning his kiss.

Chapter Thirty-two

One fine spring day, early in the year 1680, a royal procession set forth from Versailles to Vitry to welcome to France the Dauphin's bride-to-be, a German princess, Marie-Anne, daughter of the Elector of Bavaria. The King accompanied his eighteen-year-old son to this first meeting with his future bride, and with them travelled the ladies who had been appointed to be the future Dauphine's ladies-in-waiting, the Duchesse de Richelieu, Mme de Rochefort and Mme de Maintenon, formerly Françoise Scarron.

When the party finally returned to Versailles and drove into the huge Cour Royale, the young princess was immediately invited to meet the Queen. As they mounted the magnificent Escalier des Ambassadeurs, the marble staircase which led up to the State apartments, the young bride-to-be noticed a very beautiful lady, quietly dressed, her hair prematurely streaked with white, pass them on the staircase. It was Athenais de Montespan.

'Going down, Madame la Marquise?' Françoise could not resist saying to her as they passed each other on the staircase, remembering all the unkindnesses and jibes she had received at the hands of Athenais when their positions were reversed. 'I am going up.' At the time, the Dauphine paid no attention to this exchange.

Athenais had got off lightly. No one had ever expected to see her at Court again after the poisons scandal which had rocked all of Paris the previous year. But the King had set up a special tribunal to investigate the affairs of the people named by Mme Voisin before she was burned at the stake. Athenais de Montespan, her sister-in-law the Duchesse de Vivonne, and many other well-known ladies at Court were amongst those mentioned. Some of them, it seemed, were guilty of nothing more than purchasing from Mme Voisin various creams with which to enlarge their breasts; some had made use of la Voisin's love-philtres, guaranteed to make the desired person fall in love with them. Others had administered various aphrodisiacs or poisons to their husbands or lovers. Scores of newborn babies had, it seemed, been either done away with at birth or sacrificed at a Black Mass. For these services la Voisin had been handsomely rewarded. Every day, more shocking revelations came out.

In all, 147 people were finally named in the investigations. Some went to the stake, some to the galleys, others were banished or fined, depending on the severity of their crimes. The remaining 81 were incarcerated in prisons throughout France for the rest of their lives – in solitary confinement, for Louis did not wish the name of his children's mother bandied about the prisons of his realm.

Athenais, after a period of enforced retirement at Clagny, was finally allowed to return to Court, where for some time the King allowed her to retain her apartment next to that of the Queen. He appointed her Mistress of the Queen's Household, created her a duchess, and made her a gift of 50,000 livres. This generosity, it was whispered, was meant to prove to the world that the stories circulating throughout France were without foundation. The King allowed her children to visit her, and occasionally did so himself, to enquire after her health; but he took care never to remain alone with her, no matter how she schemed to arrange a *tête à tête*.

'Tell me, cousin,' the new Dauphine enquired of her cousin Liselotte, shortly after her marriage, 'why does everyone at Court show such respect to Mme de Maintenon? She is, after all, only my second *dame d'atour*, yet everyone bows and scrapes before her as if she were the Queen.'

Madame, not only the Dauphine's cousin but also, since she was the wife of Monsieur, her aunt by marriage, looked round cautiously before she answered. The two German princesses were sitting in the gaming-room, where several people were seated at the velvet-covered tables playing *brelan*. Madame and the Dauphine disliked cards and often sat gossiping together in their native tongue. The King and Monsieur were playing billiards in the next room.

'Surely you know that the woman is the King's mistress?' Liselotte said. She had never forgiven Françoise for robbing her of her riding companion. The King still rode and hunted, but no longer spent whole days stag-hunting with Madame as he had done in the past. After Mass, and his dinner which he took with the Queen, he would make his way to the nursery for a while

324

before going to hunt. Of latter years Madame had been forced to spend her days wolf-hunting with her nephew the Dauphin; between them they had killed practically every wolf in the Ile de France – the species was now almost extinct.

The King's mistress! The Dauphine drew in her breath sharply. So that was the reason why Françoise was treated with such deference. Could it be possible? But even the Queen, she knew, was fond of Mme de Maintenon.

'But how – '

'Does she not invariably pay a visit to those – those mouse-droppings of la Montespan's every day?' Madame, with her strict German upbringing and pride in her impeccable ancestry, was implacable on the subject of illegitimate birth. 'They meet in the nursery, she and the King,' she explained to the bewildered Dauphine, 'and there conduct their adulterous liaison whilst the poor Queen imagines them to be innocently visiting the royal bastards. Could anything be more scandalous?'

'But I thought that after Mme de Montespan – '

'That he would never take another mistress? That, I think, was indeed the King's intention. But this woman Maintenon, by making the bastards take her side, has been able to command his attention. She tended them when they were little, and has frightened them into paying her duty. Have you not seen how they treat their real mother?'

The Dauphine knew this to be true. The Duc du Maine and the Comte de Vexin, when they passed by Athenais de Montespan in the Galerie des Glaces, stood stiffly to attention and bowed to 'Belle Madame', as they called her. But she had seen them run to Mme de Maintenon, throw their arms around her and address her by some loving childish nickname.

The young Dauphine, with her strict Lutheran background, decided that such goings-on as an illicit affair between the King and her own lady-in-waiting were not to be tolerated at the Court where she was second lady after the Queen, and where one day she would reign herself. Accordingly, the next day after dinner when Françoise asked her routine permission to withdraw from the Dauphine's apartments, the Dauphine stared her coldly in the face.

'I had thought that we might go through my winter clothing,' she said, 'to select which gowns I shall be needing this winter, and which are to be given away.'

Françoise hesitated, but said nothing. She went to the sedan-chair which was waiting outside the door of the Dauphine's suite – the distances between apartments in the vast palace of Versailles necessitated such long walks that sedans plied for hire – and sent the lackey away. The afternoon was spent sorting out clothes.

It was not difficult for the King to guess why Françoise did not come to the nursery that afternoon. That same evening, at the *Appartements*, he humiliated the Dauphine in public by addressing Madame and the Duchesse de Richelieu, and ignoring the Dauphine completely. After sobbing her heart out in her own apartment, she was forced to come to the conclusion that it did not pay to antagonize Mme de Maintenon. The Dauphin, she knew, was a weak character, not for one moment capable of standing up to his father, the all-powerful Sun King.

The conclusion reached by the entire Court – namely that Françoise de Maintenon was the King's secret mistress, and that since the spectacular downfall of Athenais de Montespan the King had decided to keep this secret – could not have been farther from the truth. Françoise never had been, and never would be, the mistress of Louis XIV, as she had made clear to him time and time again.

The meetings between Françoise and the King, in the privacy of the children's nursery, were conducted purely on the basis of friendship. Louis was beginning to find that in the company of Françoise de Maintenon he could abandon the mask he had to assume for his public appearances, and be himself. With her he felt relaxed and able to talk freely of his problems; he appreciated her quick grasp of affairs and sound common sense, and found that she was very rarely wrong in the advice she gave him, approaching everything with her own curious blend of practicality and caution. But over and above all this he discovered too that he could talk to her of music, poetry and plays, as he had never been able to talk to anybody since the deaths of Minette and his mother. After the sexual excesses of Athenais' long reign, and the sterility of his conversations with the Queen, with her limited intelligence and poor command of French, it was a pleasure to be able to talk in this happy, easy way with a trusted friend. Remembering the words of Mazarin in his youth, Louis had never allowed any of the men at Court to become friends. The first steps to power lay that way, he well knew. If he did not feel like talking, he simply relaxed in Françoise's presence while she knitted or sewed, and allowed the children to climb on to his lap and rumple his wig. Françoise had given strict instructions to Nanon never to leave them alone together, unless, of course, the King gave his express command.

One day Louis said to her, looking at Nanon who was hovering in the background, pretending to fold some linen: 'Don't you trust me to be alone with you?' – Or don't you trust yourself? he would have said to any other woman but her.

Françoise blushed furiously. He loved to see her blush and often teased her about it – a woman in her forties blushing like a young girl! – for he knew now that she was three years older than he was.

'Send her away,' he said, taking Françoise's hands in his. 'Trust me, my dear.' Seeing the expression of sincerity in his eyes, she motioned to Nanon to leave them.

'Françoise,' he said when she had left the room. 'You know that the whole Court is talking about us, don't you?' Françoise, embarrassed, looked down. 'You know that we are regarded by all as being lovers, don't you?' Still she was silent.

'Why won't you make it the truth?'

At last, she lifted her head. The time had come, she decided, to tell him of her plans.

'Because, Sire, as we both know, you are married, and to a pure woman who has never violated her marriage vows.' Louis had the grace to blush at this. She decided to take advantage of it to make her request.

'Sire,' she began, 'with your permission, I should like to retire from Court to live at Maintenon this year. The school is already opened – I have employed a teacher, but I should like to supervise it myself. The little ones here can be well cared for by Nanon – whom I shall leave here for some time yet, if you should wish it – and the two boys no longer need me. But – if you will allow Louis-Auguste to ride over to see me sometimes – ' Maintenon was only four leagues from Versailles.

Louis looked at her with pain in his dark eyes. 'Françoise!' he said. 'Surely you can't be serious?'

She looked at him in surprise. 'Indeed, Sire, I have never been more serious in my life. As I've told you, the children no longer have need of me – '

'But what of me, Françoise! I need you more than ever as time goes by. I love you, as I've told you many times.' He stood up and his face was dark with anger. 'I love you, Françoise, whether you believe me or not. I can't take you for my mistress against your will, because of my love for you, but you're never going to leave me; at least, not with my permission. I'll never let you retire from Court!'

Françoise had no choice but to reconcile herself to living the rest of her life at Court, in a position that was the envy of every woman in the land, yet in which she herself was not happy.

Now that the la Voisin scandal had died down, the King had asked Athenais to leave her magnificent State apartments and had made over to her some rooms on the ground floor of the palace, the former Appartement des Bains. Françoise, now relieved of the sham of her position of *dame d'atour* to the Dauphine, was given rooms on the same floor as the King and Queen where, to the utter astonishment of the Court, both Louis and Maria Theresa frequently called upon the humble Mme de Maintenon – though not, it was admitted, both at the same time. There was no longer any doubt in anyone's mind that Françoise was the mistress of the King.

Françoise resigned herself to the fact that she was fated never to live at Maintenon, her beloved country chateau, her own home. Patiently, night after night, she sat through the evening *Appartements*, bored and restive, watching the women flirting and stooping to all manner of low tricks to attract each other's husbands, scandalizing about their best friends behind their backs. She had no interest in card games, loathed gambling, and was too shy to dance, though she did enjoy concerts and plays when they were held. Most of all, she resented not being completely occupied. It irked her to while away her life in boredom, yearning for some kind of fulfilment, a sense of achievement.

'I sometimes wonder what on earth it is I want,' she said to Nanon reflectively one day. 'Here I am surrounded by luxury, with rooms, clothes and furniture the like of which I could only have dreamed of in the old days, my own coach outside the door, the respect and kindness of the King and Queen. Yet I am discontented. What's the matter with me, Nanon?'

Nanon looked at her mistress perceptively. She did not understand for one moment why Françoise had not allowed the King to become her lover. But she did know that her mistress was fretting for the freedom and independence they had enjoyed in the shabby little house in the rue des Tournelles. Here, in the palace of Versailles, one had to eat at a certain time, dress at a certain time, always appear smiling and pleasant, and yet, after one had observed all these rules of behaviour, there seemed little else to do. Nanon was finding that more and more, as the children grew up, her own place in the nursery was taken over by the maids.

'I reckon we're not needed here any longer, madame,' she said to Françoise. 'Perhaps one day soon we'll go to live at Maintenon, as you always said we would.' She went on sewing, happy in the thought of leaving this place and settling down in the country, for she was a country-woman born and bred; Court life was not for her.

Françoise, not wishing to shatter Nanon's dreams of keeping hens and bees and growing her own vegetables once more, judged it best to tell her nothing of the King's flat refusal to allow her ever to retire from Versailles.

Realizing how much her inner frustration was growing, however, Louis had allowed Françoise to move the little school she had started at Maintenon nearer to Versailles at a village named Rueil, and once it had been established there she drove over almost every day, if possible, to see how it was progressing and to supervise the supplies. She took great pleasure in selecting the pupils for the school herself, and organizing them into classes. Louis teased her by saying that if she would organize the country for him as efficiently as she ran her school, there would be no more problems for him.

Though she could not leave Versailles, Françoise was happier when she was fully involved with the affairs of the school. She was much more like her old self, and often told Louis-Auguste jokingly on his visits to her apartments that she was putting into practice in the school all that she had learned from him of children and their misbehaviour.

But to her sorrow Françoise was unpopular at Court. Athenais spread vicious stories about how she had lured the King away from her by cunningly getting the children to take her side against their own mother. The aristocrats of the Court, descended from the oldest French families, bitterly resented the fact that she, a Parisian bourgeoise, a humble nobody in spite of the *de* she had put in front of her name, should be allowed to take precedence over them. She was cold-shouldered, for the women were bitterly jealous of her and the men feared that a wrong word or mistaken meaning might endanger them with the King. In public, people mistook her shyness for snobbishness. So

Françoise was lonely, in her beautiful apartment overlooking the gardens of Versailles.

Nanon had remained in the nursery to care for the little ones, but Françoise had promised her that when they were older she should become her own personal maid once more. Meanwhile the children all visited her, in particular Louis-Auguste, Duc du Maine, who never missed a day without enquiring after the health of his beloved Tata.

In July of that year the King announced a fête to be held in the gardens of Versailles. Soon after the announcement, Françoise called on the Queen in her apartments to enquire if she had fully recovered from a dizzy attack of the previous week – and Maria Theresa told her how much she was looking forward to the entertainment.

'You see, *chère madama*' – she had never learnt to speak French properly – 'at the previous fêtes which were given by the King, there has always been some cause for grief, not for rejoicing.'

Françoise thought of the Fête du Carrousel Louis had given on the birth of the Dauphin in 1661, soon after falling in love with the beautiful Louise de la Vallière, and of the Fête du Plaisir des Iles Enchantées when, by now passionately in love with Louise, he had scarcely left her side; and of the many other entertainments he had given for the pleasure of Athenais de Montespan during her long reign.

'But this entertainment,' the Queen continued with delight, her feet, which did not touch the floor, swinging to and fro as she sat in her armchair, 'the King has said that he wishes to be for me, to pay me respect as the mother of the Dauphin, and for the happiness I have given him since our marriage.' The Dauphine had recently given birth to a son, another heir for France.

How happy Maria Theresa looked today, thought Françoise with a pang, so plump and contented; her women had laced her so tightly into her dress that she could hardly move. With her hair dressed high on her head, topped by the fashionable *fontanges*, a head-dress made of pure Alençon lace, she looked like nothing so much as the dolls that dressmakers sent to their customers to demonstrate the current styles.

'Won't you rest, now, Your Majesty?' said Doña Molina, with a slight curtsy to Françoise. 'You must look your best for the fête tomorrow . . .'

Maria Theresa shook her head vehemently. '*Vamos*, Molina!

Can't you see that I am talking to Madame Maintenon – '

'I will leave you to rest, Your Majesty.' Françoise curtsied. 'It's very warm today. I myself feel a headache coming on – '

'No, madame, stay with me a minute, I beg you. I wish to talk to you.' She waited until Doña Molina, tutting disapprovingly, had left the room, and then pointed to a *tabouret*. 'Be seated, madame.'

Françoise stared in astonishment. Sit, in the presence of the Queen?

Maria Theresa gestured authoritatively. 'Sit down, *por favor*.'

This time she obeyed, wondering what was coming. Maria Theresa played with her lap-dog and did not seem to know what to say. At last she began.

'Madame,' she said, 'I know that I have a great deal for which to thank you.'

Françoise blushed and stared at the soft colours of the Savonnerie carpet in embarrassment. Maria Theresa tapped her fingers with the fan she held. 'Do not avoid my look!' she commanded. 'The King has told me of your concern for me.'

Françoise shook her head. 'Your Majesty – '

'He has told me that you asked him to show me more respect, which he was happy to do, though there was a time – ' The little Queen's face clouded at the memory of the days when Athenais de Montespan held sway.

'All that is in the past now,' Françoise intervened, seeing the direction of her thoughts. 'The King loves you, as he has always done – '

'No, madame.' The Queen's face was serious. 'It is you he loves.'

'Your Majesty – '

Maria Theresa held up her hand in warning. 'Don't be like everyone else here at Versailles, I beg you, madame. Because I speak poor French, everyone takes me for a fool. I assure you I am not.' Her eyes flashed and her face was red. 'I know that he loves you,' she continued, 'but that for reasons best known to yourself, you have rejected his love. Well, you will have to wait a long time for him – I will never agree to a divorce. And I am only forty-four, younger than you, madame, if I am not mistaken – '

'Your Majesty,' Françoise insisted, 'such thoughts have never entered my mind. Several times I have importuned the King to allow me to retire from Court. I have no wish to live in these surroundings, matchless in luxury though they may be. I came here only for the children's sake. I long to lead a simpler life – '

'I too,' replied Maria Theresa. 'How the King enjoys his continual pomp and ceremony!' Her eyes were sad, remembering her childhood in Madrid. 'Oh, there was ceremony enough at the Court of Spain, I assure you. But somehow, as a child, one was not conscious of it. Do you remember the old days?' she said, turning to Doña Molina, who had re-entered the room.

'Indeed I do, Majesty. It is time to dine, Your Majesty. The King will soon be here.' Françoise rose to go.

'In a moment, *madremita*,' said Maria Theresa, unconsciously using her old childish name for the woman who had been her nurse. She turned to Françoise. 'Madame,' she said, 'I have wished to give you something as a token of my friendship.'

With a shy smile she presented Françoise with a miniature of herself, painted on ivory and framed in diamonds. Françoise did not know what to say.

'Your Majesty is most gracious, but I seek nothing from you – '

'I know it,' said Maria Theresa. 'That is why I make you this gift. Keep it, in token of my affection for you.' She held out her hand. Françoise kissed it and with a curtsy retired to her own rooms.

In her own apartments, she stood looking at the tiny miniature of Maria Theresa, and thinking of the bride she had seen arriving in Paris one hot August day a lifetime ago. Poor little Queen, she thought. She has everything in the world – everything except the love of her husband. That, as she well knew, belonged to someone else.

Chapter Thirty-three

'*Au revoir, madame! A bientôt!*'
'*Adieu, madame!*'
'Goodbye, goodbye! Until tomorrow!'

Françoise sank back in her seat, exhausted, and fanned herself vigorously as the coach-and-six drove out of the gates of Rueil. She looked back through the window at the girls and their teachers clustered on the steps of the school, so pretty in their summer uniform of cotton gowns, snowy white fichus and straw hats, all of them waving to her, and almost all of them happily clutching a book. Thank goodness the prize-giving ceremony was over. She felt worn out, but delighted that everything had gone off so well. A great believer in encouraging children, she had seen to it that almost every pupil received a prize, for good behaviour if not for brilliance. She took a silver scent bottle from her reticule and vainly tried to cool her forehead and wrists. It was the hottest and most uncomfortable time of the day to be travelling, but she had perforce to leave Rueil at dinnertime, for the King often came to see her in the afternoon before the Council met, on the pretext of enquiring after the children.

Her only disappointment was that he had not been able to attend the prize-giving. He had taken great interest in every detail, and had helped to suggest suitable prize-books for each child. But she had been too busy inscribing names in them to attend last night's glittering reception in the Galerie des Glaces, and of course Versailles had been deserted when she drove out through the gates at six this morning as usual. She liked to arrive early at the school, for there were always so many things to do: discussions with the teachers, lists to make out, problems to settle and papers to check; and her time was limited. Yet she loved every minute of it, for it gave her a sense of purpose in life. There she came alive, as she never did in the stultifying atmosphere of Versailles, where the endless round of banquets, balls and State occasions bored her to distraction.

She had no energy left even to fan herself, though her clothes were sticking to her. When she arrived at Versailles she would have a bath sent up to her rooms.

But as the palace came into sight, she saw to her astonishment the King's magnificent coach-and-eight leaving for Paris at full speed along the Avenue de Versailles, disappearing amidst a cloud of dust.

Françoise's expression was puzzled as she alighted from her coach in the Cour Royale and took a sedan to carry her across the great expanse of cobbled courtyard, across the inner Cour du Marbre, the marble-paved courtyard of Louis XIII's old hunting lodge, and along the corridors and staircases to her rooms. It was unusual for the King to leave for Paris at this time of the day.

The Galerie des Glaces positively swarmed with courtiers rushing this way and that, sedan-chairs pushing and jostling each other. Everyone seemed to be in a flurry, but when she called to one or two people she knew, they shouted unintelligible remarks and disappeared in the crowd.

In her own apartments, she found Nanon and the two boys waiting for her. Louis-Auguste rushed to meet her.

'Tata,' he said, 'the King my father sent for me before he left and told me to tell you to come to him when it is over. What did he mean by that?'

Françoise looked at Nanon in utter astonishment, as Nanon shooed the two boys out of the room. 'Whatever does it mean, Nanon? What's happening?'

'The Queen is dying, my lady.'

'The Queen? Impossible!' Maria Theresa had been complaining for a day or two of an abscess under her arm. 'She isn't ill, Nanon. It's only an abscess – '

'The doctors lanced it an hour ago, my lady, and now the poison has entered her bloodstream. She's dying, madame. Those doctors! They kill more people than they cure, madame, as I've often told you.'

Françoise could not believe it. 'But she's a young woman! Is there nothing that the doctors can do?'

'They've done it already, madame. They've killed her. She's been given the last rites. The King himself held the viaticum.'

Françoise went to the window and looked out. So that was why the King had left at such speed. It was a tradition strictly observed that Kings of France must not look upon the face of death. The Cour Royale was now a positive *mêlée* of people scurrying hither and thither, trying frantically to obtain a coach to follow the King to Fontainebleau, where the Court was to move.

Nanon was weeping quietly. 'The Queen was a good lady, madame.'

'I know,' Françoise said slowly. Only the week before, the Queen had expressed interest in her school, and offered to donate a sum of money to enable Françoise to extend the premises and take in more pupils. Kneeling at her prie-dieu, she crossed herself and prayed fervently for the immortal soul of Maria Theresa, Queen of France.

At three o'clock that afternoon, Nanon came to tell Françoise that the Queen was dead. Versailles was now almost entirely deserted. The two boys had already gone on to Fontainebleau with their tutor. Nanon reported that the maids were still busy packing the younger children's clothes and toys, but would be ready to leave within the hour.

'To think, madame,' Nanon said through her tears, 'how happy the Queen was only last week, at the fête the King gave for her.'

The fête! What a glorious day that had been, a hot July day when the gardens were at the peak of their perfection, the air filled with the fragrance of thousands of rose trees, orange trees and the King's favourite jasmine; strawberries, crushed ice, champagne in tall glasses, and the white doves strutting and cooing on the Tapis Vert. And how happy Maria Theresa had been, with the King sitting beside her and paying her every attention . . . Not for many years had there been such a happy and peaceful atmosphere at Court as on that lovely summer day at Versailles – a week ago? a year? a lifetime? Françoise felt a pang go through her. She looked down at her yellow-and-white striped cotton dress.

'Lay out my mourning clothes, Nanon,' she said. 'Then go to the children.'

'Will you follow us to Fontainebleau, madame? You can't stay here – ' Nanon always worried about her mistress when she was silent and withdrawn. It was unnatural, she thought, not to give way to tears and grief.

'Do as I tell you, Nanon!'

After Nanon had gone, she walked over to the bed where the clothes were laid out, a black dress and wrap, black shoes and stockings, and a black bonnet trimmed with purple ribbons. She knew how the King loathed mourning clothes, and that the very sight of all that black was enough to give him the vapours – he who so loved bright colours, music, food, and the scents and flowers of his gardens, everything in life that was gay and vital. Her heart was heavy as she changed her clothes.

With a last look back at her sumptuous apartments she walked slowly towards the door, knowing that she would never return to these rooms. Louis would marry again in due course and, until then, she could not continue to live here in such close proximity to a widowed King. The late afternoon sun streamed in through the windows, dappling the parquet floors and the Savonnerie carpets with pools of light. On the commode stood the miniature of Maria Theresa, framed in diamonds, which the Queen had given her only the week before. She put it in the velvet bag she carried, and with a last look round, went downstairs to the waiting coach.

The huge courtyard was silent and deserted save for a group of black-clothed figures carrying the Queen's bier, draped in black, into the chapel. She shuddered. Only a few days ago Maria Theresa had been so happy and contented; her husband beside her, the world at her feet. Now everything was over. The little Spanish princess who had arrived in Paris in a golden coach, to the cheers of the crowd, while Françoise, Louise and Athenais watched from the balcony of the Hôtel d'Aumont so long, long ago, had found peace at last.

At least she had this much before she died, Françoise thought: she had told herself that the King loved her – though she had known it wasn't true. Isn't that the best thing to do with our lives, simply to pretend that they are what we want them to be?

– Tell her to come to me when it is over, Louis had said. She stood, irresolute, like an autumn leaf blown this way and that by the wind. Now was the time, she knew, to retire to her home at Maintenon, to involve herself completely in the running of the school at Rueil, and to forget that she was ever loved by Louis XIV, King of France.

But something held her back. The knowledge that not only was she loved by Louis, but that she loved him in return. Whatever the consequences might be, she must go to him now, to be at his side when he needed her.

Except for a few remaining servants, and the ostlers who stayed to care for the horses, she was one of the last to leave Versailles.

Chapter Thirty-four

It was nine o'clock that evening when Françoise's coach drew into the Cour du Cheval Blanc at Fontainebleau. At the top of the horseshoe-shaped staircase was the steward, checking names on a list in his hand. The King had given orders that she was to have rooms across the corridor from his own State apartments. Françoise hesitated. She would have liked to be accommodated nearer to the children. However, the King's orders could not be contravened.

Nanon came to help her to settle into her suite and prepare for bed. Françoise was exhausted, for she had risen very early that morning. Her head ached intolerably after the long bumpy journey and all she longed for was sleep. She asked Nanon how the younger children were settling in.

'Oh, they think it's a wonderful adventure,' Nanon told her. 'They're as happy as kings – '

Françoise turned her face to the wall. Just before her eyes closed she heard herself asking: 'And the two boys?' But she did not hear Nanon's answer, for she was asleep as soon as her head touched the pillow.

In the morning she felt rested and refreshed, but she was somewhat alarmed at the pallor of her face above the plain un-relieved black of her mourning dress.

During the morning a messenger arrived to say that the King requested a conversation with her after he had heard Mass. Special prayers were to be recited for the soul of the dead Queen, so that the service would take slightly longer than usual. The King would walk with her in the gardens at one o'clock.

Françoise sent Nanon back to the children. 'Shall I bring them to you?' she asked.

'No, Nanon, not today.' Today I must think of myself, and my future, she thought. 'Tell them that I'll come and see them in the morning – or perhaps this evening I'll come to say good-night.'

When Nanon had gone, she studied her reflection in the mirror. How thin she had become! The affairs of the school had begun to tire her out lately. There was the constant journeying to and fro from Rueil, and there had been the prize-giving ceremony to arrange. But it was all well worthwhile, she knew, for children who might never in their lives have become literate were now able to read and write. Since launching the venture of the school, she had at last achieved that sense of inner fulfilment and self-achievement which she had sought all her life.

Arranging her hair as best she could, and fastening round her neck the pearl and diamond crucifix the King had given her, she pinched her cheeks and bit her lips to bring them a little colour, put some scent on a handkerchief and dabbed it on her forehead and wrists. The King had sent for her to say goodbye to her. She intended to look her best.

With a last glance at her reflection, she went slowly down the staircase which led from the State apartments to the old court-yard where Louis had danced with Louise de la Vallière on a summer night twenty years before. As she made her way through the Petits Appartements and emerged into the Jardin de Diane, the royal party, the King, the Dauphin and Dauphine followed by Madame and throngs of courtiers, were just emerging from the chapel. Monsieur had been sent for at his Paris residence, the Palais Royal, but had not yet arrived.

Everyone was dressed in black or violet, with either a long train or bands of violet crêpe falling from the shoulders, men as well as women. As Françoise stood there, not knowing what to do, the King, seeing her immediately, came forward. She made a deep curtsy.

'Your Majesty.'

He gave a slight inclination of his head. 'Madame.' His face was grave and unsmiling, but he extended his hand for her to kiss. He wore violet mourning clothes, buttoned up almost to the neck and scarcely revealing his shirt, and black shoes and stockings. He had discarded his sword, and carried a black hat trimmed with purple ribbons in his hand. Behind him the Dauphine and Madame exchanged meaningful glances.

The King made a graceful gesture in the direction of the lily pool farther away at the other end of the garden. 'Will you walk a little way, madame?'

As she joined him and they began to walk slowly towards the pool, the two German princesses, the Dauphine and Madame, giggled and whispered together. 'She is about to receive her *lettre de cachet*,' whispered Liselotte to her niece. 'Watch carefully, *meine Liebe*, for you are about to witness the downfall of the great Mme de Maintenon.' She had never realized that her bitter resentment of Françoise was because she herself was in love with Louis.

'Do you really think he will dismiss her from Court?' whispered the Dauphine.

'Of course. How can she remain? He must marry again, he is only forty-five. And a new Queen, if she is possessed of any common sense, will soon give her short shrift. Who would be as gullible as Maria Theresa – who obviously believed that Mme de Maintenon's interest was only ever in the children! A commoner, a mere nobody, to be given precedence as she was over duchesses and countesses of ancient French lineage!' Not to mention princesses of pure Hanoverian blood, she thought sourly.

Amongst the black-clothed throng of courtiers strolling along some little distance behind the King and Françoise, Athenais de Montespan could hardly keep herself from laughing. Now was the moment she had awaited so long! The moment when Louis would say goodbye to that viper Françoise Scarron, or whatever she might call herself now – whom she, Athenais, had been foolish enough to nurture in her bosom.

Louis and Françoise were walking slowly through the Jardin de Diane in the direction of the pool with its fountain and statue of the huntress Diana.

'How did it happen so quickly?' Françoise was asking the King, after expressing her condolences on the death of Maria Theresa.

'I can't tell,' Louis replied. He was drawn and haggard, and looked very tired, she thought. 'The Queen had had this abscess for some days, and the doctors were called in. The next thing I knew, they came to tell me that they had lanced it – and she was dying. It seems the poison was driven inwards into her bloodstream, and although they bled her several times they could not save her.'

Françoise did not know what to say. 'Poor creature,' he said, looking at the carp darting to and fro in the pond. 'She was never happy in France.'

'But she told me recently that you had indeed made her happy, Sire.'

'Yes,' he said. 'At least I have the pleasure of knowing that she was happy when she died. Do you know,' he said slowly, remembering with pain all the sorrow he had caused her in the days of Louise de la Vallière and Athenais de Montespan, 'do you know that in all the twenty-three years that we were man and wife she never once caused me any grief? Until now,' he added.

She stole a glance at him. How pale and weary he looked, and there were traces of beard on his usually clean-shaven face. Noticing her look, he rubbed his chin ruefully. 'I had no patience for the valet this morning,' he explained apologetically. 'I shall attend to it after dinner.' Again he stared absently into the depths of the pool, remembering Louise de la Vallière, that lovely face from the past; poor little Minette; and Maria Theresa. Athenais, though she was here at Court, never crossed his mind. For some time now he had been unable to look at her without shuddering, remembering the fearful practices in which she had been involved.

In the background, the courtiers murmured and gossiped amongst themselves.

'How soon do you think she will leave?' the Duchesse de la Vrillière asked her husband.

'As soon as possible, if she knows what's good for her,' said someone else. Bets began to be laid on the chances of an Austrian princess, reputedly very beautiful, versus the Infanta of Portugal, for the honour of becoming the next Queen of France.

Meanwhile, as they stood watching the fish in the Fontaine de Diane, Françoise was trying to summon her courage to say goodbye to Louis, to turn her back on him for ever. Yet she found herself dreading the idea of leaving him. With all his faults, which were many, she knew that she loved him, and realized that he loved her – in a way in which he had never loved any of the other women in his life.

Suddenly he drew something from his pocket. She fought back the tears. He was going to give her a keepsake, something to remind her of him always. As if she would not carry a picture of his face for ever in her heart!

'Françoise,' he said, with a tremor in his voice, 'I want you to have this.' She looked at what he held in his hand, and gave a gasp. It was Maria Theresa's wedding ring. Surely he had not removed it from her finger –

He saw her look of horror and gave a grave smile. 'The Queen gave this to me yesterday, some time before she died,' he explained. 'Before she commended the Dauphin, the Dauphine, and their son to my care, she also said a prayer for the other

340

children. Then, drawing this ring from her own finger, she asked me to keep you by my side, for she knew that you were the only woman who could make me truly happy. She herself asked me to give you this.'

With a glance round at the people following them, he drew her into a secluded arbour some few yards from the pool, where they could not be overheard or seen. There, with a smile, he slipped the ring on to her wedding finger. She looked at him incredulously. What could he mean – wasn't he going to send her away?

'Françoise,' he said to her quietly. 'Will you be my wife?'

There was a long moment's pause while Françoise tried to understand the significance of his words. 'It isn't possible, Sire,' she protested. She felt her face reddening with embarrassment. What kind of jest was this?

'It is no jest,' he said to her, easily divining her thoughts. 'In all seriousness, I am asking you to become my wife.' He took her hand and kissed it.

'But how – ?'

'You would never become Queen of France, for reasons of birth. But there is such a thing as morganatic marriage.'

Morganatic? She struggled to collect her thoughts. For once her composure had deserted her, Louis thought with secret amusement.

'It would mean that you were my legal wife,' he explained, 'with the ceremony solemnized according to the rites of the Holy Church. But it would also mean that neither you nor your children could succeed to the throne in the event of my death – in other words, that you had no rights other than those of a wife.' He took her hand and kissed it solemnly. 'You will never be crowned Queen of France, *ma chérie*, but in all other respects you will be my dearest wife.

'I've no desire to marry another Spanish princess hardly out of the schoolroom, my love,' he said. 'But marry I must. The people expect it of me. No legal complications will arise, for I have given my country heirs; and the Dauphin already has a son. And we need no family, you and I, for we already have our children.' On the far side of the garden, they could see the Duc du Maine and the Comte de Vexin going towards the chapel with their tutor.

Françoise nodded. For some time now there had been good reason for her to know that she would never bear a child of her own. But it was of no consequence – there were five children to whom she was a mother, the only mother they had ever known.

'How strange,' Louis said, watching his sons as they passed, 'that Athenais should have borne children for you and me to rear.'

'I could have sent for you, to talk of this,' he admitted, 'but I thought that to see you in private, today of all days, might compromise your reputation which, if it is not already lost, I know is dear to you.' Françoise could not help but laugh. 'That is why I asked you to meet me here, in the open, for everyone to see, though admittedly I have been unable to resist this arbour!'

She looked at him with love and gratitude. Could it be that his vast experience with women had taught him at long last how to treat them with respect and appreciation? If so, then she was to be doubly fortunate, not only in winning the love of *le Roi Soleil*, but in being his last love.

'Will you be my wife, Françoise?' he asked her. 'Don't speak to me of your school! We'll move it nearer to Versailles if that is what you wish, for above all I want you to be happy. I need you so much, my dear. You already know how much I love you and admire you. You are the only person I have ever known to be completely without self-interest, caring only for the happiness of others. Will you allow me to take second place in your heart, my dear, after Louis-Auguste? For I believe that you love my own son more than I do myself.'

For a few moments they sat there, their hearts too full to speak. In the sheer joy of knowing that she was not to be parted from the man she loved, Françoise had forgotten how much she had once longed to leave Versailles. Now, she knew, her place would always be beside him, wherever he might be.

'Will you be my wife, Françoise?' he repeated. She nodded, twisting on her finger the ring he had given her, not trusting herself to speak.

'There must be twelve months of mourning,' Louis reminded her. 'What is the date today?'

'The second of August, Sire.' He put his finger to his lips. 'Louis,' she added, as he smiled. It was the first time she had ever called him by his name.

'Then on August 1st, in a year's time, we shall be married, you and I, in the chapel of Versailles. Let us hope that the workmen can be persuaded to complete the chapel for the occasion.' They rose, and looked each other full in the face. 'Maria Theresa would not begrudge us one extra day,' he said. 'Françoise,' he murmured, in a low voice, taking her hands in his, and looking pleadingly into her gentle dark eyes. 'I have waited so long for you, my love. When will you be mine?'

In the background there was a discreet cough. The King's chaplain and two other priests stood waiting to be given the King's instructions for the funeral.

The look of fond love on the King's face immediately changed back to its normal expression of grave severity. 'There are – arrangements to be made,' he said, offering Françoise his arm. Together, they walked slowly back to the chateau, the chaplain and the priests following behind. In the distance the Court stood watching, gossiping, bursting with curiosity.

At the steps of the chateau he made his bow, which she acknowledged with her curtsy. He turned to look back at her as she stood there, glowing and beautiful, her black dress stark against the background of the roses in the sunshine, her face alive with happiness, a woman of over forty in love for the first time in her life.

Almost imperceptibly, his lips framed the words: '*A ce soir?*'

Oblivious of the people standing near, she joyfully nodded her acceptance. Tonight, in the ancient palace of Fontainebleau, twelve months before their marriage would take place, they both knew that she would finally become his wife.

Background Reading

Madame de Maintenon by Charlotte Haldane. Constable, 1970
Madame de Maintenon by M. Cruttwell. Dent, 1930
Madame de Maintenon by C. Dyson. Bodley Head, 1910
Madame de Maintenon by Taillandier. Heinemann, 1922
Louis XIV by Vincent Cronin. Collins, 1964
Louis XIV by J. B. Wolf. Gollancz, 1968
Louis XIV by P. Erlanger. Weidenfeld & Nicolson, 1970
Historical Memoirs of the Duc de St Simon. Hamish Hamilton, 1967
Louis XIV and His World by Ragnhild Hatton. Thames & Hudson, 1972
Louis XIV by Joanna Richardson. Weidenfeld & Nicolson, 1974
Life and Times of Louis XIV. Paul Hamlyn, 1968
Life in France under Louis XIV by J. L. Carr. Batsford, 1966
The Bourbon Kings of France by Desmond Seward. Constable, 1976
The Ancien Régime by Goubert. Weidenfeld & Nicolson, 1973
The Sunset of the Splendid Century by W. H. Lewis. Eyre & Spottiswoode, 1955
The Age of Louis XIV by Voltaire. Dent, 1961
The Sun King by Nancy Mitford. Hamish Hamilton, 1966
Versailles by Ian Dunlop. Hamish Hamilton, 1970
The Court of Versailles by Gilette Ziegler. Allen & Unwin, 1966
The Royal Chateaux of the Ile de France by Jacques Levron. Allen & Unwin, 1965
Great Days of Versailles by Bradby. Smith, Elder, 1906
Letters of Madame de Sévigné. Dent, 1960.
Letters from Liselotte translated and edited by Maria Kroll. Gollancz, 1970
The Affair of the Poisons by Frances Mossiker. Gollancz, 1970

Victoria Holt

The supreme writer of the 'gothic' romance, a compulsive storyteller whose gripping novels of the darker face of love have thrilled millions all over the world.

Pride of the Peacock

Lord of the Far Island

Bride of Pendorric

The Curse of the Kings

The House of a Thousand Lanterns

King of the Castle

Kirkland Revels

The Legend of the Seventh Virgin

Menfreya

Mistress of Mellyn

On the Night of the Seventh Moon

The Secret Woman

The Shadow of the Lynx

The Shivering Sands

The Queen's Confession

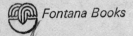 *Fontana Books*

Victoria Holt *also writes as*

Philippa Carr

Lament for a Lost Lover
Saraband for Two Sisters
The Witch from the Sea
The Miracle at St. Bruno's
The Lion Triumphant
The first five novels in a series that will follow the fortunes of one English family from Tudor times to the present day.

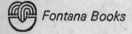 *Fontana Books*

and as

Jean Plaidy

'One of England's foremost historical novelists.' *Birmingham Mail*

Murder Most Royal
A Health Unto His Majesty
The Haunted Sisters
St. Thomas's Eve
Gay Lord Robert
The Captive Queen of Scots
Here Lies Our Sovereign Lord
The Prince and the Quakeress
The Wandering Prince

The Third George
The Princess of Celle
Queen in Waiting
The Thistle and the Rose
The Sixth Wife
The Three Crowns
The Queen's Favourites
The Spanish Bridegroom
Royal Road to Fotheringay
The Murder in the Tower
Caroline the Queen

All available in Pan Books

Catherine Gaskin

'Catherine Gaskin is one of the few big talents now engaged in writing historical romance.' *Daily Express*

'A born story-teller.' *Sunday Mirror*

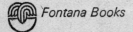 *Fontana Books*

Winston Graham

'One of the best half-dozen novelists in this country.' *Books and Bookmen*. 'Winston Graham excels in making his characters come vividly alive.' *Daily Mirror*. 'A born novelist.' *Sunday Times*

The Poldark Saga, his famous story of eighteenth-century Cornwall:

Ross Poldark
Demelza
Jeremy Poldark
Warleggan
The Black Moon
The Four Swans

He is also the author of historical novels including:

Cordelia
The Grove of Eagles

His immensely popular suspense novels include:

Woman in the Mirror
Take My Life
Marnie
Greek Fire
The Little Walls
Night Without Stars
The Tumbled House
Night Journey
The Walking Stick

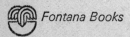 *Fontana Books*

Taylor Caldwell

One of today's best-selling authors, Taylor Caldwell has created a host of unforgettable characters in her novels of love, hate, drama and intrigue, set against rich period backgrounds.

'Taylor Caldwell is a born storyteller.' *Chicago Tribune*

Ceremony of the Innocent
Captains and the Kings
Testimony of Two Men
Glory and the Lightning
A Prologue to Love
The Romance of Atlantis
The Arm and the Darkness
Tender Victory
This Side of Innocence
Let Love Come Last
The Beautiful is Vanished
Dear and Glorious Physician
Great Lion of God
Never Victorious, Never Defeated
There Was a Time
The Wide House
Dynasty of Death
The Eagles Gather
The Final Hour

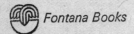 Fontana Books

Morris West

'A great writer.' *Daily Mirror*. 'An able novelist . . . skilled in characterization and in generating an atmosphere of emotional tension.' *New York Times*. 'A first-class, professional writer.' *BBC*. 'A craftsman.' *Time*

The Navigator

The Big Story

Children of the Sun

Daughter of Silence

The Devil's Advocate

Harlequin

The Second Victory

The Shoes of the Fisherman

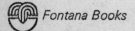 *Fontana Books*

Fontana Paperbacks

Fontana is a leading paperback publisher of fiction and non-fiction, with authors ranging from Alistair MacLean, Agatha Christie and Desmond Bagley to Solzhenitsyn and Pasternak, from Gerald Durrell and Joy Adamson to the famous Modern Masters series.

In addition to a wide-ranging collection of internationally popular writers of fiction, Fontana also has an outstanding reputation for history, natural history, military history, psychology, psychiatry, politics, economics, religion and the social sciences.

All Fontana books are available at your bookshop or newsagent; or can be ordered direct. Just fill in the form and list the titles you want.

_____

FONTANA BOOKS, Cash Sales Department, G.P.O. Box 29, Douglas, Isle of Man, British Isles. Please send purchase price, plus 8p per book. Customers outside the U.K. send purchase price, plus 10p per book. Cheque, postal or money order. No currency.

NAME (Block letters) _____

ADDRESS _____

_____

_____

While every effort is made to keep prices low, it is sometimes necessary to increase prices on short notice. Fontana Books reserve the right to show new retail prices on covers which may differ from those previously advertised in the text or elsewhere.